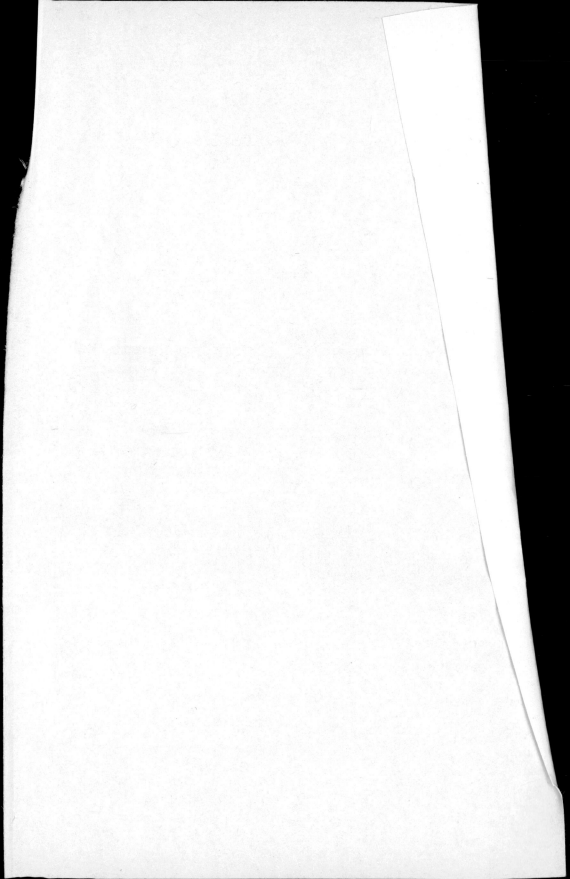

THE SPLIT

Also by Sharon Bolton

Sacrifice

Awakening

Blood Harvest

Now You See Me

Dead Scared

Lost

A Dark and Twisted Tide

Little Black Lies

Daisy in Chains

Dead Woman Walking

The Craftsman

THE SPLIT

SHARON BOLTON

MINOTAUR
BOOKS
NEW YORK

First published in the United States by Minotaur Books, an imprint of St. Martin's Publishing Group

THE SPLIT. Copyright © 2020 by Sharon Bolton. All rights reserved. Printed in the United States of America. For information, address St. Martin's Publishing Group, 120 Broadway, New York, NY 10271.

www.minotaurbooks.com

Library of Congress Cataloging-in-Publication Data

Names: Bolton, S. J., author.
Title: The split / Sharon Bolton.
Description: First U.S. edition. | New York : Minotaur Books, 2020.
Identifiers: LCCN 2019049526 | ISBN 9781250300058 (hardcover) | ISBN 9781250300065 (ebook)
Subjects: GSAFD: Suspense fiction.
Classification: LCC PR6102.O49 S68 2020 | DDC 823/.92—dc23
LC record available at https://lccn.loc.gov/2019049526

Our books may be purchased in bulk for promotional, educational, or business use. Please contact your local bookseller or the Macmillan Corporate and Premium Sales Department at 1-800-221-7945, extension 5442, or by email at MacmillanSpecialMarkets@macmillan.com.

Originally published in Great Britain by Trapeze, an imprint of The Orion Publishing Group Ltd, an Hachette UK company

First U.S. Edition: April 2020

10 9 8 7 6 5 4 3 2 1

For Lupe, who makes me laugh and keeps me fit.

Part One

SOUTH GEORGIA

Present Day

'Lands doomed by nature to perpetual frigidness: never to feel
the warmth of the sun's rays; whose horrible and savage aspect
I have not words to describe.'

Captain James Cook, 1775

1

It's not a ship. It's an iceberg. Oh, thank Christ. She drops her binoculars and feels a thudding in her chest that might be her heart starting to beat again. There is no smoking allowed on the island, but she pulls out her cigarettes all the same, because if she can subdue the shaking in her hands for long enough to light one then she might feel like she's in control again. The wind, though, won't let the flame catch.

She checks the horizon again. The speck in the distance is still ice, floating east into the vast, cold emptiness that surrounds the Antarctic.

The ocean is troubled today, steel-grey as the sky and broken like shattered glass. Storms come so fast here, and sunshine turns black in the blink of an eye. The bad weather will be working in her favour, slowing the ship, but not for ever.

The last ship of the season. One more and she's safe.

She thinks of the fear inside her like a cancer, eating away at muscles, organs, bone, growing all the time, until there is nothing left of her but a rotten, stinking mass in skin stretched like an overfilled balloon. How will the terror burst out, she wonders, when it inevitably does. A scream? A petrified whimper?

An alarm sounds on her phone, letting her know that life doesn't stop, even when it's on the brink of ending. She turns to walk back, knowing that she's running out of places to hide.

The ends of the Earth. That's how far she ran this time.

Not far enough.

2

Felicity

On a morning in late March, the end of the summer in the southern hemisphere, a woman stands high on the Konig Glacier on the island of South Georgia. She is as tall as an Amazon, with the long silver hair of a Nordic princess and a delicate prettiness that is quintessentially English, but none of that is visible for now. The thermal diving suit she wears renders her sexless and featureless, indistinguishable from the man crouched nearby on the ice. As he goes about his business, checking air tanks, valves and weights, Felicity stares into the depths of a glacial blue lake.

Beneath her feet, the packed snow groans as she moves to the water's edge. The ice around her is so white, so bright, it burns her eyes, but the lake is the iridescent blue of liquid sapphires. Its depth is immeasurable, compelling and terrifying at once. It is like looking into eternity.

Her eyes drop to the letter she is holding.

My dearest Felicity,
    Finally, I've found you. South Georgia? Wow! Know, my
darling, that there is nowhere you can go that I won't follow—

A hand lands on her shoulder and she leaps around in fright.

'Sorry, sorry.' Jack takes a startled step back. 'Only me.' He lowers his voice. 'Are you all right?'

There is a lump in her throat that won't seem to swallow away. 'I'm fine,' she croaks. 'Just nervous.'

Jack's eyes narrow before he bends to the ice. 'You dropped something. You know this is going to get wet, don't you?'

He's got the letter.

'It's fine, I've got it. Please?' Felicity grabs it back and bends to tuck it into her kit bag.

'Flick, what's up?'

She has to get a grip. She has time. She's prepared, even if the worst happens. She just has to get through today.

As she straightens up, Jack's voice is still pitched low, so that only she can hear him. 'Flick, seriously. I can do this myself. You can talk me through it from here. You don't have to—'

Normally, it isn't hard to smile at Jack. His face is so open, so kind, so entirely dependable. Today, though, she can't even force it.

'I'm fine,' she says. 'Let's do it.'

She takes her comms equipment and a few seconds later the sound of wind on snow becomes that of radio static. Jack hands over her mask and she waits a moment before fixing it in place, as though this might be the last time she sees the horseshoe of snow-capped mountains, the pale turquoise sky, and the shadow of albatross wings over silver ice.

'Can you hear me, Flick?'

The voice in her ear-piece is that of their team mate, Alan, twenty yards back from the lake edge. He will direct the dive from the surface.

'Loud and clear.' Felicity allows Jack to lift the oxygen tanks onto her shoulders.

'Konig Glacier team to King Edward Point,' she hears. '22 March, 0915 hours. Flick and Jack are going down now. Thirty-minute dive to position depth sensor and underwater camera. Conditions good.'

'Take it easy,' comes the reply from base. 'No unnecessary risks.'

'You ready, Flick?'

At her signal, Jack steps out and a blue wave swallows him up. Felicity follows and falls into a world of pain. Cold-water shock. She forces her breath in and out and waits for it to pass. When she is calm enough to open her eyes, she sees Jack taking hold of the underwater camera. She looks up, sees the depth sensor being lowered, and grasps it.

'Time to get moving.' Jack's voice, rasping over the comms system, is unrecognizable.

They leave the surface and are consumed by a world of blue and white, in which the only sound is that of heavy, laboured breathing. Felicity and Jack follow the ice wall down, their headlights picking out fantastical shapes. Faces peer at them, animals from legend spring and coil in the ice crevasses.

The blue lake, which forms every spring from meltwater, has been steadily accumulating for five months now. Sometime in the next few weeks, possibly even today, the ice of the lake's bed will fracture. The lake will drain, sending a hundred thousand cubic metres of meltwater through an intricate, hidden drainage system until it reaches bedrock. From there, it will flow out into the southern Atlantic ocean. The release of so much water might be the trigger that forces the ice to break apart, to send another massive iceberg tumbling into the sea. Blue lakes, it is believed, play a crucial part in the movement of glaciers and the creation of bergs.

The alarm sounds on Felicity's depth gauge. She and Jack have reached the flat shelf of ice that will hold both the camera and depth sensor to measure movement in the lake over the next week. She hovers in the water, and takes her time fixing the instruments in position.

'I'm switching on, Alan,' she says.

'Hold on. Yeah, we've got it. Looking good, Flick. What's it like down there?'

Jack, she sees, is some way below, his suit ghostly pale against the blue depths.

'Not sure I've the words,' she tells Alan.

Jack is coming back. He swims fast, as much at home in the water as the millions of seals that live around South Georgia.

'What do you think?' he says, as he draws level. 'You up for it?'

It is her idea. *It*, though, seems a very different proposition now that she is in the heart of the lake. *It* could be very dangerous.

On the other hand, there are worse places to die.

'What's up, guys?' Alan's voice crackles at them from the surface.

'We're thinking of having a quick look for the plug hole.' Jack holds eye contact, waiting for her answer.

The plug hole is a theory, completely unproven, that, at the deepest part of the lake's bed, a weak spot of ice lies directly above a central drain.

There is a hiss of static in her ear and Alan says, 'I don't know, Jack. It's clouding over up here.'

Weather changes so quickly in South Georgia, even in summer.

'Your call, Flick,' says Jack.

If she dies today, it's over. No more running. No more hiding.

Felicity puts a finger to her lips. She feels, rather than sees Jack's smile and then she flips.

'Guys, what's going on?' Alan's voice is breaking up.

Directly below, Felicity sees the ice forming a conical shape.

'Reckon that's it?' Jack asks.

'Guys, we've got movement on the surface. Air bubbles that aren't coming from you two.'

Felicity and Jack stop swimming and look at each other. Other bubbles could be caused by movement on the lakebed. Were it to fracture now, draining the water, the two of them would be sucked into the glacier. They would die in an icy grave or be swept out into the Atlantic.

They hear Alan's voice again. 'Doc says I've to pull you up. Ten seconds, then we're winding you in.'

Felicity reaches behind and unhooks her safety line. She feels Jack's hand brush her ankle as he tries to catch her and misses. Her head begins to throb as she swims lower and it might be her imagination, but breathing seems to be getting harder. She focuses only on the dark blue cone at the lake's inner core, hears crackling on the radio and thinks she can make out Jack asking for a few more minutes.

When she is only a few feet above the blue circle she pulls a small plastic bottle from the pouch around her waist. As she loosens the top, a crimson liquid bursts out like a fleeing genie. It hangs in the water for several seconds and then blooms like an alien flower, spreading slowly in the almost non-existent current.

Then, it begins to spiral, like water draining from a wash basin. It goes slowly, little more than a trickle, but there is definitely centripetal movement.

'Flick, we need to get out of here.' Jack has swum down to join her. 'My airways might be icing up.'

Felicity can't breathe easily any more but that seems less important than what she's learned. This is definitely the plug, and the water is draining already. It isn't apparent on the surface because enough meltwater is replenishing the levels but when the plug disintegrates, the lake will empty rapidly.

Jack clips her safety line back on.

'We're done, Al,' he says. 'We're coming up.'

★

When they are ready to leave the glacier, Felicity stands on the edge of the lake once more, with Jack, who is holding the video camera. Over one shoulder she has a bag filled with nearly a hundred small orange plastic balls.

'Sometime in the next few weeks,' she says to camera, 'the lake will drain. The equipment we've just installed will alert us to it happening, and there's a chance we can get over in time to film it. These balls might allow us to trace where the water meets the ocean.'

She lets them fall into the lake and they spread out over the surface of the water like sweets on a child's party cake.

'Are we done?' Jack asks, as she bends to gather her equipment. 'I've some stuff arriving on the boat.'

Felicity stops moving. 'What boat?'

'Last boat of the summer. The *Snow Queen*, I think. Why, what's up?'

'That's not today.'

'It is, if today's the twenty-second. Seriously, are you OK?'

Felicity resumes packing, faster now, and not nearly so carefully. 'Yeah, just cold,' she manages.

She's got it wrong. The boat is coming. The boat is coming today.

3

Freddie

'Good morning, sir. Have a seat.'

The ship's doctor is young, a thin, sandy-haired man who probably can't grow a full beard. Unlike the other ship's officers, he isn't wearing uniform but has opted instead for chinos and a sweater. He holds out a hand for Freddie to shake.

'We passed our first berg this morning? Did you see it? There was a whole gang of us on deck at first light. I didn't notice you there but, as I say, there were a lot of us.'

Freddie sits.

'Massive thing.' The doctor is still on his feet. 'Must have been fifty metres high. I've done this trip twice now and I'm not sure I'll ever get used to them.'

'I was in my cabin,' Freddie says.

'It's the colours I can't get over. People talk about bergs being white but, I tell you, there was a blue near the water's edge that was pure copper sulphate. And the noise they make – how can a lump of ice make so much noise?'

'Mainly, you'll be hearing millions of trapped air bubbles being released as the ice melts,' Freddie tells him. 'A sort of fizzing and crackling, was that it?'

'Exactly. And a groaning. It was actually a bit unearthly.'

'The ice will be breaking apart and moving within the berg.'

The doctor makes a puzzled face. 'You're very well informed.'

'I'm a geologist. Ice isn't really my thing, though.' Freddie looks at his watch.

'What can I do for you this morning?' the doctor asks.

Freddie unbuttons his shirt. 'I have a recurring, low-grade abscess that might have flared up again. Lower back, right-hand side.'

Without being asked, he stands and pulls off his shirt. The air in the medical centre is cool, but everywhere on the ship has chilled down since they left the Falkland Islands three days ago to travel south. The heating does its best, but every time a door opens, a blast of cold air races in.

Freddie feels cold fingers pushing into his skin a few inches to the right of his spine. 'Is that painful?' the doctor asks.

'Yep.'

Freddie feels the other man's breath on his skin.

'How are you feeling otherwise? Sweating more than usual? Dizzy spells?'

'Like I'm coming down with flu. Alternating hot and cold, aching, sweating a lot at night.'

The doctor doesn't reply.

'I've kept to my cabin for three days,' Freddie adds. 'Just in case. But I have an infection. I'm not infectious.'

Cold fingers touch him again. 'This is a nasty wound.'

Freddie says nothing.

'How old is this scar?'

'Three years, pretty much to the day. My last doctor thought some foreign body had been left behind. Not metal, that would show up on X-rays. More likely wood, or a scrap of clothing. Every now and again it flares up, but they didn't want to operate because of the proximity of the kidney.'

He should have worked it out by now. A badly healed scar, no access to decent surgery. Freddie will despise him for a fool if he hasn't.

The doctor is no fool. Lightly, he touches Freddie's right arm.

'May I?' he asks, as he raises and straightens it.

Freddie waits while the doctor examines the tattoo. A spider's web, encircling his elbow and reaching several inches along both upper and lower arms. An elaborate design, because time hadn't been an issue, drawn entirely in black, because colours weren't available.

'It symbolises boredom,' Freddie says. 'Sitting around for days on end with nothing to do. Spiders make webs on limbs that don't move.'

'I know,' the doctor replies. 'I've seen them before. You were stabbed, weren't you?'

'In the prison library. Most of the blood spatter went over the crime-fiction shelf, but they threw thirty books out all the same. Shame really. We never had enough to read.'

The doctor thrusts a thermometer towards his mouth, as though to shut him up.

'Can you help?' Freddie says, when his temperature has been taken. Slightly raised, nothing to get excited about. 'With the abscess, I mean. I realise the tattoo is permanent.'

'Lie on the couch, please,' The doctor says. 'Face down.'

Freddie does what he is told. It's a habit he'll probably never shake off now.

'I can drain, clean and dress the abscess and give you a course of antibiotics,' the doctor says, to the accompaniment of rattling instruments. 'When you're home, you might want to consider some exploratory surgery, see if you can fix the problem once and for all. It should be easier now that—'

'Now that I'm out,' Freddie finishes for him.

The doctor works in silence. Freddie closes his eyes, feeling nothing once the anaesthetic has kicked in.

'I'll be OK to go ashore tomorrow?' he asks, when he's been told he can get dressed.

'As long as you're feeling well enough.' Sitting at his desk, the doctor starts typing. 'What brings you to South Georgia?'

'There was a book in the library,' Freddie tells him. 'Written by a couple who'd sailed there in the 1990s in an engineless sailing ship.'

'Fair play.' The doctor makes an impressed face.

'Exactly. I thought they were mental. And brave. So, when I had the chance to do a trip, I thought I'd come here. Honour their journey, if you like.'

'It's certainly a beautiful and unique place. Did you come via South America?'

The doctor will know this already. All the passengers on board are on a three-week package tour that will take them, ultimately, to the Antarctic. He has been helpful, though, and the last thing Freddie needs now is to become the target of official attention.

'Flight from London to Santiago, then on to Stanley,' he says. 'Coming here independently was beyond my means.'

The doctor hands over a slip of paper. 'Give this to the pharmacy. They open in half an hour.'

Freddie takes the prescription.

'How long did you serve?' the doctor asks.

'A long time,' Freddie tells him. As he turns back to smile at the doctor, the other man takes a small start. 'I deserved it,' he says.

4

Felicity

A low mist hangs over the ring of mountains as the Rigid Inflatable Boat, the RIB, turns around Larsen Point. In Cumberland East Bay three private yachts swing at anchor close to the shore and a large cruise ship is parked up a little further out. With trembling hands, Felicity lifts her binoculars and sees the *Southern Star* on its port bow. Relief seems to suck the air clean out of her body. This ship has been in harbour for three days and is due to leave today. Its replacement, the last of the season, hasn't arrived. She has time.

The RIB that has brought the team back from the glacier nudges the jetty and she jumps to her feet.

'Whoa, steady on there, missy,' Ralph, the head boatman, grumbles.

'I'm fine, really. I've got it.' Already out of the RIB, Felicity wraps the rope around the cleat to secure it. She runs along the jetty, across the stretch of land between the administrative buildings and the sea, and into the harbour master's office. The wind takes the door from her hands and slams it open. Papers flurry, blinds rattle, and cigarette ash puffs into the air.

Nigel, one of three government officers who lives and works on the island on a rotational basis, isn't alone. There are eight other people in the room, none of whom she recognises.

She does not need this right now.

'I'm not sure how else I can explain it to you,' Nigel is saying. 'The nearest police are on the Falkland Islands, nine hundred miles away, and the only way they can get here is via a three-day boat journey. Four days if the weather's bad. It's a matter for your ship's captain.'

Acknowledging Nigel's nod of greeting, Felicity slips inside and glances around the desktops. There is a pile of paper on Nigel's desk but she is too far away to see it properly.

'And I'm telling you, the woman who took a knife to my husband is not from the ship.' Someone at the front of the group steps forward. 'She was from here.'

'Impossible,' Nigel replies, as his desk phone begins to ring. Taking advantage of his distraction, Felicity moves closer to his desk but she'll have to push him out of the way to reach it. She glances at the nearest screen but can see nothing on the radar.

'Why is it impossible?' The speaker is in her mid-forties, a tall, well-built woman with a long face and short hair.

The horizon is clear. It takes about an hour, once ships can be seen with the naked eye, for them to dock. An hour isn't enough.

'It's impossible because the only people who live on the island, other than Sandra and Ted at the museum, and myself, are employees of the British Antarctic Survey.' The ringing of Nigel's unanswered phone seems to get louder. 'They are highly trained scientists and technical personnel—'

'And we don't go around knifing visitors,' another voice chips in. As Nigel answers the phone, Felicity sees Jack in the doorway.

'What's going on?' Jack asks.

'Bit of argy-bargy last night,' a man in his sixties tells Jack. 'The captain gave some people permission to have a party on shore. Things got a bit out of hand.'

Felicity reaches Nigel's desk. It's a mess, as usual. She spots something, but it's half hidden under a book of tide charts and she can hardly help herself.

'I want to see the man in charge,' the agitated woman demands.

Nigel puts the phone down with a heavy sigh. 'That would be me.'

'Of these scientists, I mean.'

The horizon is still clear. Still nothing on the radar, but Felicity has never learned to use it properly.

From the back of the group, another woman speaks. 'We need an identity parade. Get all the women lined up and your Andrew can pick her out.'

'Is someone actually injured?' Jack asks. 'We have a doctor at the base if your ship's medical officer needs help.'

This lot will be here forever. And Jack is hardly helping.

'It's just a cut,' someone mutters. 'We're not even sure there was a knife.'

'I heard he fell over,' someone else says.

'Ladies and gentlemen,' Nigel raises his voice. 'I don't wish to be alarmist, but your ship will sail in an hour and the first mate wants you back. That was him on the phone. We don't have the supplies to feed extra mouths and anyone choosing to stay will be relying on reindeer meat and krill to survive the winter.'

They'll leave now, thank God. They won't risk being left behind.

'What did she look like?' Jack asks and Felicity wants to kick him.

'Young? Middle-aged? Blonde? Dark?' he prompts. 'There are five women in the team and none of them carry knives to my knowledge.'

They all carry knives, and Jack knows it. Working in this environment, knives are essential.

'Did anyone actually see her?' Jack asks.

Around the room, eyes drop to the floor.

'Anyone?' he repeats.

'It was dark,' someone offers. 'Couldn't see more than five feet in any direction.'

'She was called Bambi,' someone adds. 'At least that's what I heard.'

A shudder runs through Felicity's body. Will they never leave?

Jack turns to the man who's spoken. 'Bambi? You sure?'

'Bamber, I thought,' someone else says.

'Know anyone called Bamber, Nige?' Jack asks.

Nigel shakes his head. 'Last call down at the harbour,' he says.

Grumbling, frustrated at finding themselves in a place where the usual support systems simply do not exist, the group finally leaves Nigel's office. Looking troubled, Jack follows them.

'When's the ship due?' Felicity demands as soon as she and Nigel are alone.

'And a very good morning to you too, Felicity.' Nigel pulls out his chair and collapses into it. 'I hear it went well up at the lake.'

'Sorry. I can see you're having a bad day. It's important, though. Do you have an ETA?'

Nigel sighs. 'Tomorrow morning, reasonably early. Bit later if the wind gets up even more. There's some heavy seas out there.'

'Not today? Jack said it was today.'

'It could have been, but they hit some bad weather and had to slow down.'

Not today. She will kill Jack. She sinks into the nearest chair and feels sweat break out between her shoulder blades.

'You'll be wanting this.' Nigel hands over the document she's already spotted on his desk. The ship's passenger manifest. The ship is called the *Snow Queen*.

'Thanks.' She spins the chair around so that Nigel won't see her hands shaking and runs a finger down the first page. Mostly European sounding names, some South American. Nothing. Second page, nothing, nothing. Two more to go. Her fingers run ahead too fast and she has to start the third page again. It's clear. Hope is building as she reaches the fourth and last page. She's halfway down. He isn't on the ship. It's going to be OK after all. Then—

'There's a page missing,' she says.

Nigel is typing, a slow, two-fingered operation. 'I hear you're off to Bird Island in the morning,' he says.

'I said I'd give Jan and Frank a hand with the fledging. Nigel, why is there a page missing?'

She holds the last page out to him. 'Page four of five.' She shows him the numbering system in the bottom right hand corner. 'There should be a page five.'

Infuriatingly slowly, Nigel takes the sheets and checks each one. 'I suppose so. I think this is all that came through. I can request it again, but it may take a while.'

This is too cruel. 'Can you? Please?'

Nigel is frowning at her. 'What's up, love?'

She can't stay here. She gets up and turns for the door. 'Thanks Nigel,' she says. 'Wow, is that the time. I have to pack.'

Back in her room, Felicity locks the door. From the top shelf of her wardrobe she takes the kit bag she's had ready for days and starts to lay things out on her bed. Water flagon, two torches, one hand-held, one headtorch. The bag slides off the bed, spilling its contents noisily over the floor and she has to fight back the urge to burst into tears.

Deep breath. Start again.

Cooking pot, tin opener, sleeping bag, change of clothes. Everything is here. She's ready. Groundsheet and sleeping mat, first aid kit, matches, toilet paper and insect repellent. She's ready. She needs to go today, not hours from now when Nigel finally gets the missing page.

She closes her eyes, takes a moment, and carries on. In a

waterproof bag she has charts and a compass. A separate bag holds the food she's either bought or stolen – she thinks she'll need nine meals, twelve at the most – and water purification tablets. Finally, in the inner pocket of her kitbag are the knives that Jack has just denied she carries.

A knock sounds on her door. She starts, and then freezes.

'Only me,' a voice calls. Jack.

Felicity looks in panic around the room, at her all-too-obvious preparations for flight.

'Hang on a sec.' She pushes the knives out of sight and hides the charts before unlocking and opening the door. He stands in the corridor, smiling and expectant. 'I've come for my briefing.'

She asked him to come. How could she have forgotten?

Jack's head lifts, his eyes focusing over her shoulder. He's seen her kit on the bed. 'So, what am I in for?' he asks.

She has no choice but to let him in. Ignoring the pile of stuff on the bed, praying he won't ask her about it, because she will have no idea what to say, she steps over to the cage on her desk. Its two occupants start up again when they see her.

'You weigh them every morning,' she tells Jack. 'They have ten per cent of their body weight, five times a day.'

Nervously, Jack lowers his finger into the cage. Elsa reaches up and wraps her beak around it. 'Half their body weight every day?' he queries. 'Bloody hell, this one's got a nip on it.'

'King penguins grow quickly.' Felicity opens her wardrobe to show him the feed timetable on the inside of the door.

'I've made up enough formula to last till I'm back. Kitchen fridge, labelled *Elsa and Anna*.' She is talking too fast. She needs to slow down. Jack is already suspicious. 'You need to heat it to thirty-five degrees,' she continues. 'And you feed them with this.' She lifts the syringe that she keeps next to the cage.

'Formula?' he asks.

'Mixture of cod, krill, saline and vitamins. They wolf it down. It's really not hard. And I've left the recipe in case I'm delayed.' She takes a step towards the door. 'Thanks, Jack, I really appreciate it.'

Bolder now, Jack runs his hand over the soft brown feathers of Anna's head. He doesn't see her glance at the wall clock.

'You are nuts,' he says.

He means her, not the penguin baby. His eyes move, once again, to the stuff on the bed.

'How long will you be up at Bird?' he asks.

'Couple of days,' she tells him. 'Maybe three.'

Three days and the ship will sail away again, taking with it all its passengers. Three days and this will be over. She might not have to go at all. If the passenger list shows up in the next few hours, if the name she's looking for isn't on it, that's it. She can get drunk tonight and wake up tomorrow with a raging hangover, knowing she's safe.

Jack asks, 'What if the lake drains?'

'I'll keep an eye on the levels. I doubt it will be in the next week.'

As she reaches for the door handle to speed his departure, she can see that Jack is about to argue with her, tell her there is every chance the lake will drain in the next few days. He's right. The event she's waited for the whole of her seven months here could happen in the next day or so and she might miss it.

She might miss more than the lake draining.

'Once they can fend for themselves, these two need to go back to their colony at Right Whale Bay.' She steps away from the door and back towards him as she speaks. 'Will you do it? If I can't be here, will you make sure they're OK?'

Jack is silent for several seconds. 'What's going on?' he asks at last.

Felicity tries to turn away but he catches hold of her arm.

'You've been jumpy for weeks,' he says. 'Especially when a cruise ship is due. This stuff' – he gestures at the bed – 'there's no way you'll need that on Bird Island. And now you're talking as though you won't come back. Seriously, Flick, what the fuck?'

And now she must lie to her best friend.

'Of course, I'll come back,' she says. 'But you know what the weather's like. If I get delayed, I need to know someone will be watching out for these guys.'

Jack doesn't reply immediately and she walks to the door again. Still, he doesn't follow.

'What did you make of that lot from the *Southern Star* today?' he asks. 'That story about the knife-wielding madwoman?'

For a moment, she can't think what he's talking about. Then she remembers, the group of tourists in Nigel's office.

'I figured they'd all had a lot to drink.' She is thinking out loud, the visitors' complaint had barely registered in her over-anxious brain. 'The husband had been enjoying a bit of extra-maritals and when he was almost discovered, he invented a story about being attacked to deflect his wife's wrath.'

Jack's smile fades. 'The trouble is, someone has been seen wandering around the whaling station at night. Before the *Southern Star* came into dock.'

Felicity hasn't heard this before. 'Who'd do that?' she says. 'It's not safe.'

'Even so, three people I know have seen movement down there.'

'It'll be a seal. A large bird.'

'Seals tend not to light fires.'

In spite of everything, Felicity is intrigued. 'You're talking about someone living here alone, finding shelter, keeping themselves warm, catching enough food to survive. It simply isn't possible.'

'You wouldn't think so, would you?'

5

Bamber

During the day, Grytviken is a ghost town; at night, the ghosts rise up and walk its streets again. At its commercial height, over a thousand men lived and worked here and each one left something of himself behind. Now, their footsteps echo along the dirt tracks and they call to each other across the water. They bang flensing tools against the rusting towers of the oil tanks and swear at the wind as it hurries them along the abandoned streets.

They are still here, the whalers, and Bamber is getting to know each of them.

They are black from the smoke of coal fires, these men of the sea, their clothes gore-stained, hands greasy with animal fat. They are tough, cruel, unforgiving in life, and death has not improved them. They avoid the church and the cemetery; both are reminders of the fate they've not escaped. They linger instead where life and death mingled on a daily basis. They've shed blood, these men. They ripped apart flesh, turned a deaf ear to the pain and cries of the innocent. They killed and killed until their souls bled from them, drifting away in the crimson, congealing mass of fat that the ocean became. They'll never be able to leave.

Bamber loves the ghosts. She walks with them, eavesdropping, watches with a breathless excitement their card games and their gambling. Sometimes she lies down beside them in their rotting bunks and rises with them in the misty dawn. The ghosts are her constant friends, the only ones she needs.

On the night after the *Southern Star* sailed south, she approaches the settlement along the coast road. From the adjacent beach comes the sound of a dozen angry skirmishes as the seal colony fights to maintain its pecking order. Yards away, the heavy mass of a bull seal thunders over the rocks whilst the cows and the young wail in fright. The noise from the seal colonies is constant. Those who can't get used to it leave or buy ear plugs.

The moon is nearing full by this time and the night is clear. As she turns the last bend before the settlement she sees the body in the middle of the road. Human in size, but not human. The corpse of a fur seal is being fought over by a gaggle of huge birds. Like vultures they swoop down on to what is already a ragged and bloody mess. Bamber presses close to the rocks at the side of the road. The birds are giant petrels. With their six-foot wingspan, strong legs and huge hooked bills, they are some of the most aggressive and successful scavengers on the island. The whalers called them *stinkers*, or *gluttons*, because of their voracious appetites. Bamber rather likes them. But not enough to become a meal herself.

As she passes, slowly and a little nervously – she isn't a fool – she sees their heads and beaks are stained dark silver. Knowing that blood turns silver in the moonlight, Bamber smiles. She finds the sight of blood calming.

Once past the feeding frenzy, it is a few strides to the settlement. She avoids the big white house with its red roof. The former manager's villa is the museum and general store now and still the province of the living. For the same reason, she never goes to the church. Keeping close to the sea, she walks past the remains of the blubber factory, hears the keening of the wind in the steam pipes. Corrugated-iron flaps beat out a rhythm and a glass bottle comes scurrying up the street towards her. She kicks it away, and it rattles along the stones until the wind, or perhaps a ghostly boot kick, catches it and sends it back.

The cold bites into her exposed flesh but she likes the pain and never dresses for the climate here. As she nears the flensing platform she can see the old accommodation block behind it. The remaining glass in the windows gleams pale in the moonlight, casting back a light of its own and, for a second, the passing clouds give the illusion of smoke rising from its chimneys. The building where the men once lived is one of her favourite places. There are still remnants of the life they had here, empty cans of the food they ate, a discarded packet of cigarettes, a photograph of a loved one. The place she likes best, though, is the flensing platform.

The steps leading up to it are rotting but she is careful, and she isn't heavy. Twenty yards long by ten wide, made of wood and concrete, the platform is where the whales were brought to die. Exhausted, fatally wounded, they were hoisted by cranes from the sides of the boat and laid out on the platform before the flensers, skilled men armed with long sharp knives, cut the blubber away using a spiralling technique. Once separated from the meat, the blubber was rendered down into the prized and commercially valuable whale oil.

In the old days, the stink of boiling flesh and rotting meat fought with that of coal fires and the ocean. Now, a hundred or more different scents come from the land and the sea, but for Bamber, there is something missing.

She needs the blood.

She has to be more careful. Last night was a close one. She shouldn't have cut the man from the ship, even though she barely scratched him. If it happens again, they'll look for her and this isn't the easiest of places to hide. For now, though, she has a more pressing problem to deal with.

From the inside pocket of her jacket she takes the stolen photograph. Taken a little under a year ago it shows Felicity leaving a house in an English city. It is early evening, and Felicity has no idea that she is being watched or photographed. She is glancing at her phone, striding off along the busy street to where she left her car. The image is entirely unremarkable, but the handwriting on the reverse is quite the opposite. It reads:

I will kill you.

Tucking the photograph away, Bamber shuts her eyes and thinks of the old days. The men gathered round a huge catch on the flensing platform. The animal's big black eyes already starting to dull. The fires in the factory stoking high, ready to begin the rendering process. Huge blades being sharpened against stone. One last cry of pain from the whale and the knives begin cutting deep into its sides.

Blood pours from the fresh wounds, over the platform's edge, into the ocean. Bamber opens her eyes and sighs happily. That's better.

6

Freddie

South Georgia is more beautiful than he could have imagined. Ribbon-thin streams pour over mountains that shine gold in the early sun. The water of Cumberland Bay is aquamarine, still as glass. Even the derelict whaling station is picturesque at a distance, a scattering of rust-red buildings along the curve of the coast. Across the bay from the station lies King Edward Point, home of the British Antarctic Survey.

The mountains are astonishing, circling the bay, towering above the tiny buildings, sweeping almost down to the sea edge. A single dirt track links the two settlements of Grytviken and King Edward Point, but elsewhere roads don't exist. Human life can barely survive here.

And yet this is where he's found her.

'Morning, sir. Nice to have you join us.'

A hand brushes Freddie's shoulder as the man in an officer's uniform squeezes his way past. Several of the other passengers, most wearing the ship-issue orange anorak, follow him along the deck.

'South Georgia is truly a wildlife paradise,' the steward tells the group. 'All the seals, birds and penguins that inhabit the seas around Antarctica need to come ashore to breed and South Georgia is one of the few places in this part of the world that isn't permanently covered in ice and snow. Most of them come here.'

'The grass is so green.' One of the women is looking at the shore through binoculars. 'Is that because of all the rain?'

'Grass as you know it doesn't exist here,' the steward tells her. 'What you can see above the coastline is actually emerald moss. You should also be able to make out the spire of the Norwegian church. Built in 1913, it's been the venue of sixteen weddings.' He grins at a couple in their thirties who are holding hands. 'Until tomorrow,' he adds.

Freddie fixes his binoculars on the buildings of King Edward Point. Felicity will be in one of them, maybe still in bed, maybe eating breakfast. Porridge. With blueberries. That was her favourite.

'Over two million fur seals, some ninety-five per cent of the world's population, live here in summer,' the steward continues. 'As well as over half the world's population of elephant seals and four types of albatross.'

She probably can't get blueberries. It doesn't look as though anything can grow here.

'I thought there'd be more snow,' one of the passengers says.

Frozen blueberries, maybe.

'Snow usually starts to fall in April,' the steward says. 'You will see snow and ice while you're here, though, as roughly half the island is covered in it permanently. And there are some one hundred and fifty glaciers.'

At the word *glacier*, Freddie turns back to the group. Glaciers are Felicity's thing.

'We'll be anchoring in the bay directly ahead,' the steward explains. 'King Edward—'

'How soon can we go ashore?' Freddie interrupts.

The steward's eyebrows flick a fraction closer together. 'First trip is at 10.30.' He turns his attention back to the group. 'That gives you two hours to enjoy breakfast and get wrapped up. As

I was saying, King Edward Point has an interesting history. For some time after the Falklands War, it was the military base here on the island . . .'

Freddie leaves the deck.

Two hours. He should eat. He has no idea when he'll have the chance again and he really isn't sure when he last ate. The communal dining room on board is intolerable with the mindless chattering of the other passengers, and since boarding the ship he's taken every meal he can in his cabin. Managing to stay calm for most of the trip, he's found his hands trembling uncontrollably as they near South Georgia. Nicotine isn't helping any more, nor is the whisky he's been pouring in his cabin each night. His head is dull and his mouth tastes tight and sour. Drinking will have to stop now that he's arrived. He'll need all his wits about him.

On the plus side, the antibiotics are kicking in and he's feeling much better.

Time to pack. He pulls his rucksack down from the top shelf and then, one by one, the other things he'll need. The single shell, one-man tent won't be much of a match for a South Georgian gale but it folds up small. So does the sleeping bag, the thermal blanket and the groundsheet. The largest, bulkiest item is one he spent months researching – an inflatable, one-man kayak with foot pump.

He checks that his torches, his Swiss Army knife, his compass and his matches are where they should be. He counts the protein bars that will keep him alive the next few days. Everything else he'll need, including his life jacket, he will wear.

He checks that his recently purchased satellite phone and back-up battery are fully charged.

The orange anorak can stay in the cupboard. He pulls his own dark-khaki jacket off its hanger and checks that his gloves are in the pockets. Finally, he unfolds the best chart of South Georgia that he's been able to get hold of.

The main island is a little over a hundred miles long and twenty wide. Much of its internal landmass is covered with glaciers or mountain ranges that will be challenging, if not impossible, to cross. There are no roads, other than a few dirt tracks around the main settlements. The tiny population lives at either King Edward Point or Grytviken. Other places where people stay temporarily are few in number and are mainly ad hoc bases of the British Antarctic Survey. There is a small station on Bird Island and a former manager's villa at the abandoned whaling station of Husvik. Nothing else that he's been able to find. There are no airstrips, no regular ferry crossings. The only way to arrive is by sea voyage and once here, no other way off.

Freddie turns on his swivel stool to the newspaper cutting tacked to the headboard of his narrow bunk. A photograph and accompanying story, the only online trace he's found in months of searching.

Glaciologist Seeks Antarctic Challenge

World expert glaciologist Felicity Lloyd, 28, is about to set sail on the trip of a lifetime to the remote island of South Georgia in the Antarctic Circle where she will spend two years studying the formation and movement of some of the planet's lesser-known glaciers. Dr Lloyd, who has worked for the British Antarctic Survey (BAS) for five years, described the opportunity as 'unique' and says she isn't remotely concerned about the harsh conditions so far south, or about the lack of human contact.

Fewer than fifteen people live on South Georgia in the winter months when temperatures rarely rise above freezing and snow covers most of the land. 'I'm hoping to improve my skiing,' Dr Lloyd adds.

South Georgia is a British Overseas Territory that was once one of the world's most commercially successful whaling stations. During the

Falklands Conflict of 1982, it was temporarily occupied by Argentina and was later retaken by British forces in a daredevil helicopter mission. Today, its income derives largely from the sale of fisheries licences and tourism.

The accompanying photograph is amateurish, the subject sitting straight on to the camera, poor lighting creating shadows behind her head. Her long blonde hair has been tied back and her large, deep-set eyes wear no makeup. She isn't smiling. She hadn't wanted her photograph taken, had probably been bullied into it by her employers.

It doesn't do her justice, gives no hint of her height, the slender grace of her limbs, the way her hair shines silver in some lights. Not that Freddie needs a photograph. In his head, he knows every inch of her. There hasn't been a day that he can remember when he hasn't longed to run his hands over the silken skin, feel her hair tickling the underside of his chin, press his face against her to find that unique smell.

And now, at last, he's found her.

7

Felicity

'Morning, love,' Ralph says, as Felicity joins him at the jetty. He is in the RIB she's requisitioned for the next few days. 'Nice day for it.'

The first forecast of the day is good. Cold and clear for most of the morning, clouding over towards mid-afternoon, snow on the upper peaks. Light winds.

'You're fuelled up, spare tank in the locker. Comms working fine. Keep her below thirty knots unless the sea's like a mill-pond, which it won't be, and the kill-cord doesn't leave your wrist.'

Felicity nods to the horizon, where the black speck isn't yet distinguishable to the naked eye as a ship. 'What time do you think it will dock?'

Ralph licks a finger and holds it up into the wind. 'Another hour. Maybe more. You wanting to get away before it arrives?'

Joining him on the RIB, Felicity tucks her food bag into the far corner of the stern locker. 'No, I'll wait till its anchored,' she says. 'No rush.'

'Sure, you don't want me to come with you?' Ralph says.

'I'll be there for three days, maybe more. You're needed here.'

Ralph nods but looks troubled. Every member of the BAS South Georgia team has boat-handling skills, but the boatmen are supposed to do the long and difficult journeys. Bird Island is at the very north-west tip, over seventy miles distant. It is a long way, even in the powerful RIB.

Of course, she isn't planning to go anywhere near Bird Island. Bird Island isn't nearly safe enough. On Bird Island she can be found.

He says, 'Well, you let me know when you get there safe.'

'No problem.'

It could be a problem. She can hardly announce her arrival at Bird on an open radio frequency when Jen and Frank who are actually there will almost certainly hear it and contradict her. Maybe a brief transmission will work, round about the time she would be expected to arrive. She can say she's pulling into the bay and that everything is fine. Jen and Frank aren't actually expecting her today, just sometime in the next week or so.

The speck on the horizon is bigger.

'How long before it gets here?' she asks.

'Still an hour. Less the five minutes since you last asked me.'

Ralph takes her through safety procedures one last time and then she runs up to the admin office. Nigel looks up as she enters.

'Manifest?' he asks.

'It's arrived?'

He hands over the list. All five pages this time and she turns straight to the last. The name leaps out at her and she feels every ounce of strength draining away.

'Not spotted the one you're waiting for?' Nigel asks.

She can't lose it now. 'You got me,' she says. 'My boyfriend said he was hoping to make it out here. I guess he didn't.'

Nigel's eyebrows lift. She has never mentioned a boyfriend before. 'There are no phones where he lives?' he asks.

'He wanted to surprise me. What time will they anchor?'

'An hour or so. You still planning that trip today?'

'Yes. I'm off anytime.' She makes for the door, on legs that feel unsteady. 'Now I know there's no one on the boat I need to see.'

'Because the latest weather report isn't so good. Winds getting up later. If you have to go, why don't you take Jack with you?'

'Actually, that's not a bad idea. I'll ask him if he's free. Thanks, Nigel.'

'Mind yourself.'

She curses as she leaves Nigel's office. Now, on top of everything else, she has to avoid Jack for the next hour.

8

Bamber

Bamber has a special place. A place she goes to when the rage builds to the point where she thinks it might tear her head apart. The *Petrel*, the beached whaling ship in Grytviken harbour is never visited by tourists. It simply isn't safe.

The entire structure of the *Petrel* is unstable. Constantly buffeted by gale-force winds and storm seas, it seems to hold together on nothing more than the memories of the power it once had. Even in moderate seas, waves come crashing over its decks. At any moment the masts, the cranes, even the harpoon gun at the bow could plummet, crushing anything beneath. Guano covers the structure, turning the decks into a slippery, foul-smelling sponge. Much of the iron has corroded, rendering its decks treacherous. One unlucky footstep could send her plummeting into the black prison filled with icy water that the ship's hold has become. If she falls in there, there will be no way out.

Bamber never makes the dangerous journey along the rotten jetty without knowing it could be her last trip. She doesn't care because the *Petrel* hosts a thriving colony of sea birds and the racket they make is constant. When she is on board the *Petrel*, no one can hear her scream.

No one sees her slip aboard. The colony of sea birds that use the wrecked ship as a daytime perch watch her curiously, but they aren't afraid of people.

No one but the gulls hear her pick up the long flensing knife and hurl it against the wall of the main cabin. It strikes with a deep resonant boom and then clangs to the rivetted floor as the air becomes alive with the beating of a hundred or more strong wings. From above the ship they yell down their annoyance and she yells back at them. She kicks a wooden casket and sees it shatter with satisfaction.

The *Petrel*'s crew ate and slept in this cabin and some remnants of their furniture remain. Bamber finds an iron club hammer and batters it down on to a chair. When the chair retains no memory of the shape it once held, she turns her attention to the bunks. Only when she's exhausted herself does she put down the hammer. Her hands are sore and she is gasping for breath.

Pulling herself onto the bridge she risks looking out at the cruise ship. He will be making preparations to come ashore.

She is running out of time.

Bamber never takes her rages out on the bridge. She needs to keep this space intact and weatherproof. It is where she keeps her secret things. She opens the locker at the rear of the cabin and at the very bottom of a waterproof bag she finds what she's come for, double wrapped in waterproof cloth. A Sig Sauer P238 handgun.

Bought in South America, recommended by the shop owner as the best self-defence handgun for use at short range by women, she hoped she'd never have to use it.

She's always known that she would.

9

Freddie

The ship has been anchored for nearly an hour. The harbour master from King Edward Point has been on board to check the paperwork and explain the rules.

Footwear has to be spotlessly clean and disinfected to avoid contaminating the local soil. No food of any description is to be taken ashore due to the same biosecurity protocols. Fishing and hunting on the island are prohibited. There is no accommodation for tourists and overnight camping requires an expensive permit, so all visitors are expected to report back to the ship by nightfall. Visitors have to stay with their guided group at all times.

Freddie has signed his agreement to rules he has no intention of keeping, and for nearly twenty minutes he's been waiting in the hull of the ship to be on the first boat going ashore. So far he's been alone – the rest of the three hundred or so passengers have been taking their time, but now he hears the metal stairs clanging and two pairs of footsteps.

'Steady on. Hold the handrail.' A young man's voice.

'Thank Christ we've arrived.' The second voice belongs to a woman. 'I had no idea waves could get that big. Did you know waves could get that big?'

A stout pair of legs in hiking trousers appears. The man says, 'I'm not sure anyone else is here yet.'

'I don't care. I just need to get off this godforsaken ship.'

'You have no idea how many times you nearly did,' the male sounds amused. And also, a little tired. Freddie does not recognise either of the voices.

'Why we couldn't have flown.'

'You could have flown. I don't have a broomstick license.'

The pair have made it to the bottom of the stairs. The woman is in her early fifties, blonde and a little overweight. The man is younger, tall and dark-haired. Neither wear the orange ship-issue jacket.

Freddie has seen neither of them before.

The blonde woman's skin looks like uncooked pastry and there are mascara smudges under both eyes. She looks Freddie up and down in a way that, had they been in a bar, would feel predatory. 'I see you haven't been tangoed either,' she says.

'Excuse me?'

'You're not wearing orange.'

She is talking about jackets. 'They didn't have one to fit,' Freddie lies.

These two must have joined the boat in Stanley. He feels sure he would have spotted them if they'd been on the trip since London. The woman in particular, seems incapable of not making an impact upon her surroundings.

She gulps and takes a deep breath. 'We didn't want to frighten the wildlife.'

Freddie gives a tight-lipped smile.

'You know, not everyone thinks you're hilarious.' The younger man holds out his hand. 'Joe Grant. Don't think I've seen you in the dining room.'

'You didn't see me in the dining room either,' the woman says. 'Don't remember you complaining about that.' She turns to Freddie. 'Were you sea sick?'

'Wasn't everyone?' Freddie replies, although he hadn't been.

'I'm Delilah,' the woman offers. 'As in the Tom Jones song.' She begins to sing the unforgettable lyrics.

'I beg her not to,' the man called Grant says. 'She will insist.'

'There you are!' A voice with a hint of the West Country sounds from above as a pair of dusty black boots appears. 'Sorry to keep you. I tripped in my cabin and knocked myself out. I had to sit down for a few minutes.'

The newcomer is a police officer. Freddie doesn't recognise the badge on her hat but has a feeling it indicates a senior rank. She is in her late-forties, with curly red hair cut just under her chin. Her skin is fair, and finely lined, her hands seem huge and she wears a gold wedding ring. She too has avoided the orange jacket. Over what is presumably her uniform, she wears a police issue high-vis coat.

'I'm Skye.' She beams at Freddie. 'Five times I've done this trip. It never gets easier.'

Her uniform says she is on official business. The frequency with which she makes the visit means she is probably the police superintendent from the Falkland Islands and the fact that she knows the odd couple, might even be travelling with them, suggests they too could be police.

'Not a problem, I hope?' he says.

The boat rocks at anchor and the blonde woman gives a low moan.

'No, no. Just routine,' Skye says. 'I always come out at the end of the summer. If I can't get anyone to volunteer to take my place that is. And funnily enough, I never can.'

'You travelling alone?' the blonde woman asks Freddie. 'Don't mind me, I'm nosy.'

'As you see.' Freddie gives a tight smile and half turns away. Thank God others are coming down the stairs now.

'Lot of equipment you got there,' the blonde woman says, her eyes fixed on the rucksack at his feet.

'I'm a photographer,' he tells her.

'Me too,' says a man who's just arrived. 'What shutter speed are you planning for the birds in flight?'

The boat rocks again and Freddie fakes a stagger to avoid the question.

'Oh my God.' The blonde woman, Delilah, is clutching her stomach. 'I'm going to chuck. I'm actually going to chuck.'

'Everyone get back,' the man with her calls.

It is too late. With a sound like that of a cistern emptying, the blonde woman vomits over the policewoman's shoes. In the ensuing chaos, when the three of them return to their cabins to get cleaned up, Freddie quietly stakes his claim to the front of the queue.

10

Felicity

Trembling, fighting back the urge to leap into the RIB and speed out of the bay, Felicity watches the first launch getting ready to leave the ship. She has to be sure. It's a common enough name. There is still a small chance that all will be well.

For a moment, she lets herself imagine the day she might yet have. Breakfast watching the ocean, checking the levels on the blue lake, relieving Jack of penguin duty. It could still happen.

The passengers to go ashore have all taken their seats. The lines are released and the skipper steers them across the bay towards Grytviken. It will take them less than five minutes to reach shore. Unloading will take some time, the jetty is narrow and unstable. Even so, every half-hour the launch will unload more passengers until everyone has left the ship. They'll spend the morning looking around the museum and those parts of the old whaling station that are safe to visit. They'll walk up to the church and to Shackleton's grave. Some of the fitter ones might climb up to the hydro dam. After lunch – sandwiches supplied by the ship – they'll be taken around the bay to the penguin and seal colonies. If the weather holds, some might hike into the interior.

Knowing that he could easily be on the first boat ashore, Felicity checks each passenger in turn. At the front of the launch are a youngish couple. Most of the other passengers look older, people in their late forties, fifties, even early sixties. Visiting the

Antarctic is expensive, out of reach for most young people.

Only one is not wearing the regulation orange jacket. He sits at the back of the launch with his face turned away. He looks tall, though, and about the right build.

Her mouth has turned dry as bone.

Telling herself that she has to hold it together, Felicity looks back towards the ship. The boat has turned with the tide and its bow is facing out to sea. The passengers who aren't below waiting for the launch to return are all at the stern, lining the rail and staring out at the mountains, the whirling sea birds, the derelict whaling station. Felicity gives herself time to be sure, but he isn't among them.

Her eyes are drawn back to the man in the dark jacket at the rear of the launch. He seems to have no interest in Grytviken or the seals that play in the shallower waters. Instead, he is looking at the collection of low white buildings that make up the research station at King Edward Point. He too holds binoculars to his eyes.

Fighting the sudden panic, the almost overwhelming temptation to duck and hide, Felicity lifts her own binoculars. She sees a large, oval face topped with thick fair hair streaked with silver. She knows those deep-set eyes are the cold blue of hard-packed ice. His binoculars are moving slowly along the coastline. They freeze. It is impossible to be sure, but they seem to be fixed directly on her.

Felicity and the man on the launch look at each other across the bay. As one, they both lower the magnifying instruments. Neither need them any more. Both know who they are looking at.

It's Freddie. He's found her. And he's minutes away.

11

Freddie

He's found her. She's actually here. He hadn't quite believed it until this moment. Freddie watches Felicity turn and run to the water's edge, then vanish inside a boat house. He has to restrain himself, physically, from standing up in the launch and yelling at her across the bay. Vaguely, he registers someone asking him if he's all right and he flicks up a hand to ward off the unwanted attention.

For the ten minutes it takes to get to shore, he sits in silence, knowing that every passing second takes her further away. He hears the distant roar of a RIB and knows she has speed on her side.

He can hardly restrain himself from pushing everyone out of the way to leave the launch first but after what seems an age they are all on dry land. Immediately, the ship's tourism officer starts fighting with the wind to tell them about the settlement they've just reached.

'So, when the whaling industry of the southern ocean discovered the riches of the seas around South Georgia, they needed sites to build on,' he yells. 'Grytviken's sheltered harbour, its large area of flat land, and plenty of fresh water made it the obvious choice. At its height, over a thousand men lived and worked here.'

Faces creased against the wind, the visitors look around at the ramshackle collection of rust-red iron, faded ochre paint and dull grey-white wood that lines the head of the coast. They see abandoned factories, lodging houses and oil tanks. Behind them a steam whaling boat, the *Petrel*, lies abandoned at the oiling jetty, firmly embedded in the mud of the bay.

Freddie has no interest in Grytviken but he tells himself to be calm. He cannot draw attention to himself by leaving the group too soon.

'By the 1960s, though, dwindling whale populations made continued activity uneconomic and Grytviken closed in 1966.' The officer waves his hands around at the derelict buildings. 'The infrastructure of the whaling station – its oil tanks, blubber factory, chimneys, machinery, accommodation and stores – was kept intact for the day the whales returned. They never did.'

'Ghost town,' a man at the back mutters.

Following the rest of the group, Freddie makes for the museum. As they wander around the exhibits, he goes into the shop and approaches the woman behind the counter.

'Has Felicity been in today?' he asks.

She gives him a quizzical look. 'Felicity Lloyd, you mean?'

'That's right. She's an old friend. We arranged to meet up.'

The woman plants her feet apart. 'You've come a long way to see an old friend.'

Like it's any of her business. 'That's right,' he says.

The woman frowns. 'Does she know you're coming today?'

Jeez, he's knifed men in the showers for less. 'I think so,' he says. 'Why? Is there a problem?'

She turns to the man with her. 'You were here when Flick came in yesterday, weren't you?'

Flick? She is known as Flick now? That shouldn't bother him. It does.

'Aye,' the man says and then he too looks Freddie up and down. 'She said something about going up the coast for a couple of days.'

44

The woman nods. 'That's right. She was stocking up on provisions.'

Another customer approaches the counter, standing far too close to Freddie. 'To Bird Island, wasn't it?' the man says.

'I thought that's what she said. Thanks, love. That'll be nine pounds fifty.'

'And is that far?' Freddie asks. There are tiny islands dotted all around South Georgia. Without the chart he can't remember them all.

''Bout as far as you can get,' the woman tells him. 'Why don't you ask up at the base?'

'I'll do that,' he says. 'Thanks.'

At the rear of the museum, out of reach of the wind, Freddie unrolls his chart. Bird Island is at the most north-westerly tip of South Georgia, a good sixty, maybe seventy miles away. He cannot possibly reach her there. Panic churns inside him. He cannot have travelled so far to have it all slip away.

He wants to talk, that's all. To explain. And maybe hold her again, just once. Just the tips of her fingertips will do.

He can't give up now.

Jogging back down to the beach, he catches the skipper of the launch before it sets off back to the *Snow Queen*.

'I'm going up to the scientific base.' He points to the buildings across the bay. 'I know someone who works up there. I'll get them to bring me back to the ship, probably after dinner, so don't worry about collecting me.'

The boatman frowns, but it is early in the day and he has a lot of other passengers to ferry to shore.

Freddie sets off walking towards King Edward Point.

12

Felicity

If Grytviken is a grim place, Husvik is worse. Bigger than its sister settlement, long since forbidden to visitors, it lies in the southern arm of Stromness Bay like a malodorous corpse. Grytviken might be dreadful, but Husvik is dangerous. Riddled with asbestos and dripping with broken glass, Husvik is entirely unstable. More than half the settlement's buildings – the catcher's store, guano factory and carpenter's workshop – have caved in on themselves and the frequent gales send their roof tiles scurrying around the bay like missiles. The few buildings still intact seem to be holding together just long enough to collapse on an unwary intruder.

Oil tanks, pipework, factory chimneys and vast sheets of corrugated iron lie strewn around the settlement in disordered heaps while the skulls of long-dead animals grin up from the shale. When the winds blow down from the mountains the whole unruly mess jumps and sings and dances like a ghostly percussion band.

Felicity's heart sinks as she steers into the bay. She hates Husvik and is already regretting her decision to come here. She is hardly any distance from King Edward Point by boat and Freddie has seen her. He might persuade people to come looking. He might get hold of a boat somehow. He could be here within hours.

Scattered along Husvik's foreshore is a graveyard of ship's propellers, and a huge old whaling ship is beached near the water's edge. The colour of dried blood, it lies on its side, beaten and exhausted, denied even the watery grave of other shipwrecks.

For a moment, Felicity is tempted to turn the RIB, head out to sea again, but there is nowhere else to go. Apart from King Edward Point and Bird Island, the only place on South Georgia where people can stay in anything close to comfort is the BAS station at Husvik. And since she left base, the weather has turned. A storm is getting up. She has no choice.

She avoids the crumbling jetty. Seals risk it, and most of them weigh more than she, but they'll survive a plummet into icy water when the rotting planks give way. She might not. Instead, once she reaches the shallows, she cuts the engine and paddles into the shell of an old boat house. Only when the RIB is securely tied does she unload her stuff. The rucksack goes onto her shoulders. The rest of the kit she carries in two holdalls.

The BAS station is housed in the villa that once belonged to the manager of the whaling station. It is only half a mile along the waterfront, but the rail locomotives that would have made the journey easy in the old days lie rusting beneath scattered stones. Nor can the coast path be attempted. Since she was here last, the buildings that were the meat freezers and the blubber cookery have become unrecognizable. Wood, tiles, bricks and pipework are strewn down to the shore and beyond. She will have to make her way through the settlement.

She sets off, walking inland, careful where she puts her feet, because machinery parts in the tussock grass have become treacherous as mantraps. A penguin chick, separated from its parent, stares at her curiously as she reaches the first corner and for a second, she wants to pick it up, because its soft brown feathers and mild gaze offer a crumb of comfort in this horrible place. She's almost stooped to touch it when a clatter of falling tiles a few yards away sends it scurrying into the tussock.

Reluctantly leaving the chick to its own devices, she makes her way between the barrack blocks and the boilers. The wind, rarely still on South Georgia, seems to revel in the old whaling settlements. It bounces off sheets of corrugated iron and whistles through felled chimneys and broken pipework. On the wrecked ships, it echoes the moans of dying whales. In Grytviken, it is easy to remember the years of slaughter. In Husvik, one need only close one's eyes and hear it happening still.

Halfway along the remains of the street, when she is surrounded by the creaking, groaning buildings, Felicity hears someone call her name.

13

Freddie

Freddie has already spotted the accommodation block from the deck of the ship, and he makes his way over to it as soon as he reaches King Edward Point. A one-storey, white-painted, red-roofed building, it lies in the centre of the linear settlement. He keeps his hood up as he approaches. Tourists do visit King Edward Point, mainly to have their postcards franked in the harbour master's office, but they typically arrive in groups. A lone traveller will raise questions. In particular, he doesn't want to be spotted by the policewoman from the ship or either of her two companions. Something about that trio didn't feel right.

He leaves the track as he draws near, crossing mossy ground to cut the corner. Up to thirty people work for the British Antarctic Survey in summer but two thirds, he reckons, will be away from the base at any one time on field trips. Some will be in the boatsheds, others in the lab. He steals a glance through the lab window as he passes but the white-coated bloke rinsing glass tubes at a sink doesn't look up.

The accommodation block lies like the rest of the buildings a few yards from the shoreline. He walks along its rear and the rooms he glances into seem identical. Small, single-occupancy, simply furnished. The fourth window along has a pair of enormous hiking boots drying on the ledge. The fifth has its curtains closed. The next room, the sixth, is neater than the rest, the only visible sign of an occupant a white dressing gown hanging on the back of the door. It looks small, a woman's size.

There is no one around, so he steps closer and presses his face against the glass. On top of the bedside cabinet is a trinket box that, with a start, he recognises, and a wooden framed photograph of a young blonde woman, dressed all in black, standing amid blue, white and grey columns of glacial ice. On the desk is what looks like an incubator, but he cannot see what, if anything, is inside.

Counting windows, he walks quickly to the corner of the block. There is a side door and he isn't surprised to find it open. There is no need for security here. He hears voices, the blare of a radio and the rattling of crockery as he walks down the corridor. A credit card slid into the gap between door and frame makes short work of the simple Yale lock.

The room beyond is neat, with the functional simplicity of a college student's room. The watercolour prints of seabirds look mass produced, and the colour scheme is the bland cream and blue of a budget hotel. The narrow bed is as neatly made as one in a hospital, there are no clothes lying over the armchair nor shoes behind the door.

A high-pitched chirruping catches his attention. He had forgotten the incubator on the desk. He steps over and peers inside to see two fat, brown feathered creatures with long, thin beaks looking back at him. Penguins, he thinks, although he has no clue which species.

The faint smell of something floral is released as he opens the wardrobe. A row of shelves holds her sweaters, T-shirts and underwear. Trousers, a spare coat and a single dress are hanging up. He steps closer, pressing his face against fabric, breathing in her scent. The clothes are simple and functional, designed for comfort and warmth. And yet, if the photograph is recent, she is still the lovely young woman he dreamed of, night after night in his prison cell.

The trinket box is made of white bone china, oval in shape, with a circle of violets on the lid and, for a moment, Freddie is lost. Once, he saw that box every morning when he woke. The lid feels cool and delicate under his fingers. Inside are hair grips, a couple of pairs of stud earrings, a silver lily on a chain and a wedding ring.

He feels tears rising, his throat tightening. He bought this ring himself, when he couldn't imagine not being in love, not looking forward to the future with anything other than joy. He'd thought that man was dead and buried, and now he finds he was here all the time, just waiting to be woken.

Unable to help himself, he slips the ring into his jacket pocket. He bought the silver lily too, a birthday gift, but she can keep that. The wedding ring he needs.

A little unsteady, he sits on the narrow bed. Outside in the corridor a door opens and footsteps walk away. He is wasting time. She's gone to Bird Island and if he wants to find her, he has to go there too.

He gets up. On the desk beside the incubator is an open chart, weighed down with a stapler, a calculator and a reference book. It shows the entire island of South Georgia, a circle drawn in red ink around Bird Island in the top corner. To one edge of the chart are stuck several Post-it notes. The first seems to be a crude calculation of the journey time in a RIB. Six hours, at an average of twenty knots. The next is a list of items she needs to take for people called Jan and Frank. The final one contains radio frequencies and a weather forecast for that day.

Is it odd, he wonders, that she has taken none of this with her?

The noticeboard above the desk holds a computer print-out of a work timetable. She's outlined that day and the following two in red ink and written: *Bird Island, fledgling tagging.* Her plans really couldn't be clearer.

So, she is six hours distant, and the only way to follow her will be by boat. Somehow, though, he doesn't think stealing a RIB will be quite as straightforward as picking a lock. If she's gone to Bird Island, she's successfully put herself beyond his reach and he's travelled across the entire world for nothing.

He wanted to talk, that's all. To fucking well talk.

Freddie is overcome by a sudden urge to wreck, to destroy. He turns to the penguin chicks and imagines hurling their cage against the far wall, taking his knife to her clothes, smashing the glass of the photograph into fragments. He steps towards it.

Except . . . in one of the neatest rooms he's ever seen, she's left a chart open on the desk, left behind weather reports she'll probably need.

Freddie takes a moment, breathing deeply, until the rage subsides. Then he reaches beneath the desk to pull out the wastepaper basket and upends it. Crumpled tissues, a can of diet Coke, and an empty box of – he holds the label up to face the light – water purification tablets.

Why will she need water purification tablets at a BAS base? Why circle Bird Island on a chart that she'll need again? And according to the woman in the shop, she's been stocking up on supplies when she'll surely be able to get everything she needs from the base. A smile breaks Freddie's face. He's done here.

The door of Felicity's room closes softly behind him and he turns for the main entrance.

'Help you, mate?'

Freddie spins back to face the slim man in jeans and a sweater. He is in his mid- to late thirties and something about his stance, if not necessarily his build or his stubbled beard, suggests the military.

'I'm looking for Felicity,' Freddie says. 'Have you seen her?'

The man's blue eyes narrow as he glances towards Felicity's closed door. 'You were in her room?' His voice is pitched low, with a trace of a northern English accent.

'No, I just knocked. No answer.'

'How did you know which room is hers?'

'She told me.' The lie comes easily. 'Number six. She's expecting me.'

'You came on the ship this morning?'

'How else? So, do you know where she is?'

The man speaks reluctantly, unhappy, but constrained by politeness. 'She's planning to head out to one of the other bases. Up on the north-west coast. Hours from here. Did she know you were coming?'

'Bird Island? Is that the place?'

'Jack, have you got a sec?'

A woman in her forties, heavily built, with dark curly hair and thick glasses, has appeared at the far end of the corridor.

The bloke, Jack, half turns. 'Hi, Susan, what's up?'

'Nigel wants to talk to us both. You haven't seen Felicity this morning, have you? Ralph thinks she's off to Bird Island but I've just spoken to Jen and she says the arrangements were all very vague. Only that she'd come up if she could and let them know. They've heard nothing today.'

Catching sight of Freddie, the woman's eyes widen. 'Good morning,' she says. 'I'm Susan Brindle, station chief.' She takes a step towards them. 'And you are?'

'Also looking for Felicity,' Freddie says. 'And frankly getting worried about her. Is she actually missing?'

Susan's eyes dart from one man to the other. 'Well, that's what we need to find out. Maybe you should come with us.'

'I need to let the ship know where I am. I'll come back. Where do I report to, the harbour master's office?'

'Well . . .'

'Thanks for your help.' Freddie turns on his heels and walks back to the side door, knowing the man called Jack wants to follow him, but will probably prioritise finding Felicity. Getting outside unhindered proves him right. Not wasting any time, he sets off, crossing the rough ground to where he's left his stuff. He is no longer the only one looking for Felicity and the chances of stealing a boat, slim to begin with, have dwindled to zero. Luckily, those idiots don't know her half as well as he does. They'll chase her to Bird Island. They won't find her.

14

Felicity

Felisssitee . . . Is that his voice? She turns on the spot, peering in doorways, through shattered windows, looking for anything that moves. It might not even be a voice at all. The wind makes all manner of weird and unearthly sounds as it slides in and out of the dereliction here.

Felisssitee . . .

Impossible. He cannot be here. No one could have got here before she did, especially not the man she saw last on the launch heading towards Grytviken.

To Felicity's right are the barrack blocks, where the whalers lived in the old days. There are eight, maybe ten of them, all more or less intact. Doors swing on hinges, broken window glass hangs like icicles. He could be watching from any of them. To her left is the long, thin building that housed the station's boilers. A deep, rhythmic clanging comes from within. Is he in there, tapping a metal rod against the rotting tanks?

No. It is not humanly possible. It's the wind, playing tricks on her overwrought, nervous imagination.

A sheet of iron falls across the path and panic snaps the spell that held her frozen. Dropping both bags, she runs. Directly ahead are the huge tanks where the whale oil was stored before being shipped back to the northern hemisphere. Taller than most of the buildings, more intact than all of them, they are great circular towers and offer no hiding place. On impulse she darts into the provision store.

Instantly, the wind drops.

The building is large and rectangular. Light streams in through a hole in the roof but the walls are solid. She sees a counter stretched across the width of the room in the manner of a shop front and behind it stand row after row of shelving units. Some have fallen, knocking others, like dominoes. There is even some food left behind. The tinned goods have long since gone, and the sugar has been eaten by rats, but packets of flour and salt have solidified where they sit.

Felicity's feet crunch on broken glass as she creeps to a window. A petrel is perched on the guano factory opposite. It watches her, head on one side, before throwing back its head and screeching.

Felisssitee . . .

She spins around. That sounded so close, as though he was directly behind her, and yet she is still alone in the provision store.

Not him then, but voices she is conjuring in her own mind again. A wave of despair sweeps through her. She'd been so sure she'd left the madness behind in Cambridge and yet just the sight of him has brought it all back.

Are those footsteps outside, crunching over gravel? They are heavy, regular and seem to be getting closer, and yet a large bird hopping around could make a similar sound. Outside, the day darkens as storm clouds move in front of the sun. In the provision store, Felicity's breath is visible in the cold air. She backs away, with no idea whether or not there is another way out of the store, only knowing she has to get away from the footsteps that are tracking her down. Her rucksack slams into the counter and she jumps, spinning herself over it and dodging behind one of the few shelving units that are still upright.

The black silhouette that would prove her worst fears doesn't materialise.

Unable to take her eyes away from the door, she backs further into the store, only to hear the sound of something moving in the shadows behind her. Impossible. He cannot be approaching from outside and be in the store with her at the same time. All the same, she is definitely not alone. In the darkness, something slithers. There is a clattering sound. She has no idea which way to turn.

Her foot backs up against a fallen shelf unit and she loses balance. Something strikes her head. She lands hard and dust surrounds her. She hears the sound of something sliding closer and then all light leaves the store.

Ten, nine, eight, I hope you're in a good hiding place, Felicity.

This is a dream. It has to be. It is exactly the same as all the others. She crouches in the darkness, naked and terrified, and somewhere outside the man she dreads plays a grotesque parody of hide and seek.

Seven, six . . .

She presses herself against the rough wall of the cupboard beneath the stairs. No, no, she is in the provision store at Husvik, a dreadful enough place, but not the one that haunts her nightmares. She really has to wake up now.

Five, four, three – oh, my, this is exciting!

She can't scream. Screaming makes him worse. It always hurts more if she screams.

Two, one, coming ready or not. Are you ready, sweetheart, because you can bet your ass I'm coming.

Felicity screams, long and loud and the sound brings her back to herself. Pain in the back of her skull tells her she may have blacked out for a few minutes. Outside the store, a flurry of gulls takes to the air. Spotting a broken stretch of pipework she grabs it and gets to her feet.

She remembers the sounds she heard from inside the store and spins on the spot. The shadows remain still, but is that heavy, laboured breathing she can hear?

Outside, the wind keens its lonely path around the chimneys.

The doorway is empty. The footsteps have gone. She waits for that cruel, teasing voice to call out her name again. Nothing. He isn't here. He can't be here. Everything is fine. She'll make her way to the manager's villa, find somewhere en route to hide her stuff, and then sit it out. When the *Snow Queen* has gone, she'll return to King Edward Point, with a story about how an oncoming storm and problems with the RIB engine forced her to take shelter for several days. She'll apologise for any alarm and then she'll get on with her work. There are no more cruise ships due until spring and private yachts never come in winter.

She'll be safe. Her troubled mind will heal itself again, and no one will know that anything was wrong.

She pulls herself up onto the counter, is about to swing her legs over and down the other side, when a great lumbering beast, nearly four metres long and weighing well over a ton, looms out of the shadows with a great, throaty roar. She feels the elephant seal's huge snout against her thigh a second before it bites.

15

Freddie

In May 1915, at the height of the South Georgia winter, British explorer Ernest Shackleton landed his open boat along with a handful of crew at Haakon Bay on the north-west coast of the island. Exhausted, half-starved and frostbitten, Shackleton and two of his men began the first confirmed land crossing of South Georgia's interior.

Their twenty-mile hike took them into the history books. With no map, they improvised a route across uncharted terrain, hammering nails into the soles of their boots to help them grip the ice. They scaled mountains, stumbled down shale fields and fought their way out of snow drifts. Crossing glaciers riddled with crevasses they knew that each step they took on virgin snow could be their last. They walked and climbed without a break for thirty-six hours before reaching Stromness and safety.

A little over a hundred years later, nothing in that barren landscape has changed. The two advantages Freddie has over Shackleton and his crew are that he is travelling in summer and doesn't have quite so far to go.

Felicity isn't heading for Bird Island, he is sure of that now. She would never have left such an obvious trail. There is only one other place she can be.

He wonders, if she has been planning to hide from him for as long as he has been planning to find her. It was a mistake, sending that letter, warning her of his plans, but how could he have known she'd become so fucking unreasonable?

He leaves Cumberland Bay trekking north-west, up a path that is little more than an indentation in the grass. Weighed down by kit, he nevertheless is over the first rise and out of sight of Grytviken by noon. He pauses on the brink of the hill to train his binoculars on King Edward Point and thinks he can see people at the wharf. As he watches, a launch with several passengers on board pulls away and heads north.

From this point on, he is forced to leave the path behind and hiking over tussock grass slows him further. After another hour he stops to rest and by two o'clock he is descending the steep shale slope into Cumberland West Bay.

This side of the bay differs substantially to its eastern counter-part. Three glaciers finish their journeys here and even in summer, their icy feed has a constantly chilling impact upon the water and its surrounds. Small icebergs, known as *bergy bits*, litter the water.

Freddie has a decision to make. Hiking around the bay will involve climbing and crossing the mouths of three glaciers. There is no way he can do that before nightfall, and he might not survive a night on a glacier. The bay, on the other hand, is only two miles across.

The canoe inflates in fifteen minutes. It takes him five more to assemble the paddle and transfer his life jacket to the outside of his coat. From the waterline along the shale beach, he knows the tide is high and that its pull will be at its weakest. The bergs are moving slowly close to shore, sometimes hardly at all, suggesting little or no current. Only when they reach a mile or so out, do they pick up speed. If he stays close to land, he should be able to avoid being sucked out to sea.

He pushes off. Immediately, the cold seems to wrap itself around him. The bergs radiate frigid air, and the wind sweeping down over the glaciers chills his bones. He paddles hard and seems to make no headway. He hadn't realised, from the shore, how strong the wind is. Keeping an eye out for bergs floating too close, or over-curious seals, he tucks his head down and paddles for his life.

16

Felicity

Felisssitee.

That voice again. And footsteps coming down the stairs. She can hear them, thumping above her head, each one slightly different in tone as though the stairs are a musical instrument and he is playing a scale.

Three, two, one. Coming ready or not.

The last step creaks. From there it is six strides to the cupboard door. She always counts the strides. She can't help herself.

The door opens, she starts awake, and remembers.

She is in Husvik.

She remembers nearly being bitten a second time by the huge seal but managing to slip past it and run until it stopped chasing her. She remembers hiding her stuff and then limping towards the shelter of the manager's villa.

There are two bedrooms in the villa and her sleeping bag is unrolled on a bunk not two feet away from where she is huddled in the corner. It is unzipped, so she must have been in it at some point.

She is shivering and yet her clothes are damp with sweat. The wound on her leg where the elephant seal bit her feels hot and sore in spite of the paracetamol she took earlier. How much earlier? The room is entirely dark. She glances at her watch. Nearly two hours have passed while she's been sleeping. She shouldn't have slept. She has to keep watch. If her decoy hasn't worked, if he's managed to get hold of a boat, he could be here by now.

She pulls herself to her feet and using only the headtorch, rolls up the sleeping bag and tucks it away at the back of a cupboard. Then she checks the bandage on her leg. The bleeding seems to have stopped but an infection is entirely possible. She glances around the bedroom as she leaves it and sees nothing to indicate she's ever been in.

She is hungry. She hasn't eaten since morning but to get to her food she'll have to go outside again. Most of her stuff is in another building, tucked away behind debris. Anyone looking for her in Husvik will come to the manager's villa first so she cannot keep her stuff here. She has to be able to leave quickly, leaving no trace behind.

She checks the small kitchen and bathroom before going out again but neither show any sign of her occupancy. Neither does the office and field lab that takes up the greater part of the building. She'll bring back soup, maybe a tin of ham. She'll eat quickly then wash up. If he comes, she will need to leave without a trace. She opens the door and goes out into the wet and windy night.

17

Bamber

High above Husvik, in the lee of an outcrop of rocks, otherwise oblivious to the cold and the increasing storm, Bamber sits watching. The settlement below her isn't still, the wind won't allow that, but it is in darkness. Not the faintest trace of light can be seen from the manager's villa but it will still be the first place he'll look. Felicity has been smart to store her things elsewhere, but he is smarter. Felicity has never been a match for him and she won't be now.

Freddie will have made plans. Freddie will have learned everything he can about South Georgia before setting out. He will know the places she can go and where she can't. Her attempts to throw him off the trail and send him all the way north to Bird Island can't be relied upon.

Lucky for Felicity that she has Bamber to watch out for her. She feels for the gun in the inside pocket of her jacket, and imagines Freddie's fair-haired, handsome face bursting apart in an explosion of blood and bone.

She looks out to sea, because it isn't impossible that he'll come by boat. Stealing one will be easier after dark and the treacherous journey around the coast from Cumberland Bay at night won't faze Freddie. The insane have an unshakeable belief in their own invincibility. Even in this storm, even with the swell beyond the bay reaching ten metres or more, he might risk it.

It is far more likely though, that he'll come by land, that he'll have found a way to cross the glaciers. So, for every minute she's spent watching the waters of Stromness Bay, Bamber has spent four or five looking south-east towards Grytviken. It is ten miles, as the crow flies, between the two settlements and his ship docked more than twelve hours ago.

Something. Movement on the hillside. A light.

She watches until she is sure. A light, probably a head torch, is making its way down the last stretch of hill towards the station. Bamber presses further into her shelter beneath the rocks and waits. The light descends until it reaches the level ground on the edge of the settlement. The manager's villa, where Felicity plans to sleep, will be the first building he'll come to. Of course he'll look there first.

He's found her.

Bamber gets to her feet. It's time.

18

Freddie

The door to the BAS sub-station, once the home of the whale station manager, is locked, but the four-digit key code is conveniently written on the underside of the mechanism.

The door opens into an office. Two desks face opposite walls, a bookshelf sits atop a cupboard and noticeboards are littered with charts and listings. Computer monitors are protected by plastic dust covers. Through an open door, Freddie's torch picks out the steel cupboards and storage equipment of a field laboratory. There are powerful lights on the ceiling but he doesn't switch them on. Instead he goes through another door into a rear corridor and a small galley kitchen. It is neat, no sign of recent cooking. The sink is dry. He sniffs the air but the smell of guano, rotting kelp and the sea has crept in here too. He is on the brink of leaving the kitchen when he spots a towel hanging from a rail. He touches it and finds it damp.

The next room he comes to is the bathroom. Again, no sign of occupancy. He walks on to the first bedroom. Empty, like the rest of the place. Without much hope of finding anything, he opens the cupboard door. Rolled on the top shelf is a padded blue sleeping bag. He pulls it down and presses his face against the slippery fabric. The faint floral scent he remembers from her room back at King Edward Point. This is hers. She is here.

He feels excitement building. He is close.

He puts his gear in the other bedroom and leaves the station, quickly crossing the few hundred metres to the main settlement and trying not to be unnerved by the great ghostly shipwreck that rears above his head. He tries the foreman's residence first. He isn't surprised to find her gear beneath canvas sheeting but there is no sign of Felicity herself.

Outside again his nerve breaks.

'Felicity!'

His voice echoes back at him. Christ, she could be anywhere. They could spend all night dodging each other around this ghost town.

'Felicity, we need to talk.' The wind takes his voice and whisks it away.

The shipwreck is freaking him out. Leaving it behind, he walks inland. At this end of the settlement, there are several buildings more or less intact.

He takes a detour around the oil tanks, banging on the rusting iron and calling her name again.

'Felicity! For God's sake, where are you?'

Reaching the end of the tanks he thinks he sees the shadow of a woman slipping inside a building directly ahead of him. He follows, running over the rough ground and finds himself inside an old provision store. He shines his torch around. Nothing, but beyond a central counter is a chaos of fallen shelving units.

'Felicity?'

'Felicity isn't coming.'

He jumps round. She's tricked him somehow, slipping outside and doubling back to block the doorway. Except, it isn't Felicity. The height is similar but her posture is all wrong. This woman's voice is entirely different and her walk, as she steps inside the store is nothing like the way he always pictures Felicity's graceful way of moving.

He moves his head, trying to focus the beam of his torch on her face, but she half turns away. Not before he's seen what she is carrying in her right hand. Christ. Whoever she is, she is armed.

'Who the hell are you?' he asks.

His headtorch beam reaches her face a second before she raises her arm. Jesus wept, how is this—

'I'm Bamber,' she says. 'I won't let you hurt Felicity. Never again.'

She fires.

Part Two

CAMBRIDGE, ENGLAND

Nine Months Earlier

'The earth had donned her mantle of brightest green and shed her richest perfumes abroad. It was the prime and vigour of the year; all things were glad and flourishing.'

Charles Dickens, *Oliver Twist*

19

Felicity

It is unseasonably warm in the city of Cambridge. As dawn breaks on the morning after the Trinity May ball, chiffon-clad girls are sleeping on the lawns and river banks, their heads resting on the dinner jackets of boys with whom they may, or may not, have begun the previous evening. The boys lie beside them, still as fallen statues.

Yards from where they sleep, the River Cam winds its way through trailing willow fronds, relishing the silence. Within hours the punts will be out, and punts cannot move through water without an accompaniment of shrieks, cries and general merriment. For now, only the college rowing teams skim across the surface like water-borne insects. Below Jesus Lock, the canal boats, like dusty jewels, begin to rock on their moorings as their occupants wake up.

In the market square, traders greet each other with the news that it's going to be a scorcher. They've said the same thing every day for over a week now and will go on doing so without embarrassment for as long as the heatwave lasts. The early sunshine lifts their spirits, though, and the two carrying crates down the main thoroughfare don't even grumble as the androgynous figure on roller skates speeds past them, almost sending everything tumbling.

Through the claustrophobic heart of this medieval city, a

crocodile of choristers winds its chattering way to choir practice, or maybe back for breakfast. It is impossible to silence pre-teenage boys and the choir master has long since given up trying. The line weaves its way around the woman with pink hair who is walking in the opposite direction, and if one or two of the boys snigger – well, they're young.

On heels that are too high and clothes that she has slept in, the woman barely sees the boys or their smirks. She is no May reveller, her studying days are long over, but her head throbs as intensely as that of any waking student, and for the same reason. Unlike the careless young, though, this woman's heart hurts more than her head. Odd as it may seem, she is a senior police officer and a little over a week ago, a young woman was murdered on her watch.

The rough sleepers, because even a city as enlightened and progressive as Cambridge has them, don't wake to see her staring down at each dirty, sleeping face. They don't notice her counting, ticking them off on a page in her notebook. All present and correct; this morning at least. As she walks past a terrace of houses built by merchants in the seventeenth century, she glances up at a row of three windows on the top floor. Her steps falter, and the line between her brows deepens, before she walks on and passes out of sight.

Staring out of one of those windows, standing in a room full of sunshine, is Felicity. Morning light floods the yellow walls and pale orange carpet. The sofa, empty for the moment, is the salmon pink of a sunrise. From the top floor of the old house, she can see towers and spires, crenellations and turrets, all gleaming gold. It is the most beautiful city in the world, she thinks.

A male voice says, 'Why do you think you're here, Felicity?'

The voice is at odds with the feminine room. Surely no man bought vases the exact shade of apricot as the bon-bon bowl on the coffee table. No man would have chosen armchairs in a warm white, patterned with orange and crimson daisies.

'Felicity?'

The man who almost certainly hasn't decorated the room, because if he had, he wouldn't be wearing frayed jeans, trainers and a Nike sweatshirt, is waiting for an answer. Dr Grant, who has asked her to 'call me Joe', is young, late thirties at most, although his dark brown hair is receding above his temples. Below the stubble of his beard, his neck is thin and pale.

Felicity says, 'I like this room.'

She likes his eyes too, hazel green under dark brows. He smiles readily, but gently, and his voice is soft and low pitched.

'Thank you.' A blush warms his cheeks. 'My wife decorated it. I was away for a week and she said leave it to me, I'll have it all sorted by the time you get back.'

The corners of his mouth turn down as he looks from the swagged curtains to the plump cushions. 'A month later, she asked me for a divorce. I should have seen it coming.'

Felicity is not sure how she is supposed to react, and wonders if perhaps he didn't intend to reveal quite so much about himself. With a sudden insight, she sees that he too is nervous.

He says, 'Why don't we start with how you got those bruises on your face?'

'I fell.' She says it too fast. It comes out slick, rehearsed. Her first mistake. On the surface, Call-Me-Joe's face doesn't change; behind his eyes, though, something has shifted. It's what beaten women always say. *I fell. I walked into a door. I didn't see the drawer was open when I bent—*

'Where was this?' he asks.

'The common. I live next to it. I must have gone out and . . . fallen.'

His face is still open, interested, but she no longer trusts it.

'Must have?' he says. 'You don't remember?'

He will know this already. The police were called to Midsummer Common that night. The people who found her had been scared at the sight of her torn clothes and bleeding limbs. She'd told the police and the hospital staff that she couldn't remember what had happened. They didn't believe her, and now Call-Me-Joe isn't believing her either. She can hardly blame them, and yet she is telling the simple and complete truth. The events of that evening on the common are – absent.

'That was quite some fall,' he says. 'According to your notes, you were bleeding and distressed, with concussion, a badly bruised face and lacerations on your arms and legs. You were kept in hospital overnight.'

Call-Me-Joe is drinking strong black coffee. Every time he sips she catches a whiff of its steam. She regrets, now, turning down his offer of a cup.

'How did your employers get involved?' he asks. 'Did you tell them?'

'No, I wouldn't have made a fuss, but it was too late. The police went to my house while I was in hospital. They couldn't find any information on my next of kin, so they contacted my employers. The head of human resources came to see me in hospital and then it all became official.'

He is still nodding. He knows this too. 'Your employers need your GP to certify you fit to return to work and your GP isn't happy to do that without a psychiatric assessment?'

Felicity's voice lifts, but her cheeriness is forced. 'And that's why I'm here.'

She waits for him to acknowledge that finally she has answered his question. Instead, he says, 'Do you want to go back to work?'

'Very much. Work is all I have.'

Suddenly, his soft hazel eyes are sharpened and he does not

blink as he stares straight back at her. She is unnerved by his stare. This man sees more than he has a right to.

'What about friends?' he says. 'A significant other?'

'An opportunity has come up,' she hurries on. 'It's the chance of a lifetime. If I'm not fit, I won't be considered for it.'

'I see. Let's go back to that night on the common. What do you remember?'

'I remember being at home before it happened. Having some dinner, catching up on admin. After that, nothing.'

'We're talking about a gap in your memory of several hours?'

'Four hours. I sent an email at eight o'clock. I was taken to hospital shortly after midnight.'

He waits, as though he knows she has more to say. After a moment, she drops her eyes. Still he doesn't speak. When she looks up again, Call-Me-Joe has a file on his lap.

'Tell me about your job,' he says. 'What do you do for a living?'

He knows. It will be in her notes. This is not about what she says, it is about how she says it. Or maybe, about what she doesn't say.

'I work for the British Antarctic Survey,' she says. 'I'm a glaciologist.'

'You study glaciers?'

Felicity opens her mouth to give the stock response about how glaciology is an interdisciplinary Earth science that involves geology, physical geography, geophysics, climatology, meteorology, hydro—

'I study ice,' she says. 'It's mainly about ice. And its decline.'

He nods, vaguely, already losing interest. 'The polar bears,' he says politely. 'Very worrying.'

He is humouring her, as so many do, and for a moment she forgets herself.

'Ice isn't just about polar bears.' She leans forward, closing the distance between them. 'The bears are dying because their entire food chain, just about every living thing in the Arctic region, is under threat.'

He smiles and looks down at his notes, already seeking a retreat, but she is only getting started.

'Ice is an insulator, a cushion,' she tells him. 'As ice melts, heat from the ocean escapes into the atmosphere, warming the planet even more and creating a vicious circle. Without ice reflecting back sunlight, the oceans get warmer still. Cold seas produce a huge amount of methane; ice keeps it under the surface. You know that methane is a greenhouse gas, don't you?'

He nods, a little nervously. 'I knew that.'

'Ice stops water evaporating. More water in the atmosphere means more of the big catastrophic storms we've been seeing, with the resulting loss of life and economic devastation. And don't get me started on nearly two hundred Arctic communities that are struggling to maintain their way of life as the ice shrinks.'

'I won't,' he says.

'Ice is everything. Without ice, the planet's finished. We all die.'

Silence. Joe picks up his pen and writes.

'You're writing *crazy person*, aren't you?' she says.

He laughs. 'I'm writing *knowledgeable, caring and passionate*,' he says. 'And thank you. I won't make that mistake again.'

He closes her notes with a decisive snap. 'OK,' he says. 'You're twenty-eight, in good physical health, with no recorded history of mental illness. Your parents died when you were very young, and you were raised by a maternal grandmother and then in local authority care when she passed away. You're single, with no other nuclear family. You've worked for the BAS in Cambridge for a little over five years and even though you're still quite young, you're considered one of Europe's leading experts in your field. Have I missed anything?'

'I suppose not.'

'Just trying to save us some time. Normally, the background can take the entire first session.' He smiles again. 'Tell me what you're feeling right now, Felicity. How do you feel about being here?'

She weighs her words carefully, knowing he will be listening for what she leaves out. 'I'm angry,' she says. 'Because someone I've never met before has what I believe to be an unreasonable power over me. I can't get on with my life without your permission.'

He makes a thinking face and waits for her to continue. She doesn't.

'I'd say that's an extreme interpretation of the situation but I commend your honesty,' he says after a second or two. 'Anything else?'

'I'm scared you'll say no. That I'm not fit to go back to work.'

'Do you think you're ready to go back?'

'I'm fine. It's been over a week.'

He doesn't respond.

'I can't afford to be ill,' she says. 'Who employs a mad woman?'

For the first time, he looks surprised. 'Why on Earth would you describe yourself as "mad"?'

She holds his gaze for a second, and then can't. Her eyes fall to her lap. Silence. She hears rather than sees him get up from his armchair. A second later a box of tissues – white, Man-size – is pushed into her line of vision. She ignores it and blinks away the tears.

'It says in your notes that the doctors at the hospital found evidence of previous injuries,' Joe says. 'You broke your wrist at one time, there's evidence of several cracked ribs, and you have a number of scars on your body.'

Felicity feels a sudden stabbing pain between her shoulder blades and sits up, away from the chair back. 'I explained all that,' she says. 'I spend a lot of time outdoors. I run, I climb, I ski. Glaciers are extreme environments. I have to be fit. Sometimes, I get injured.'

The shrill tune of a mobile phone sounds. Joe picks a phone up from his desk and checks the screen before getting to his feet.

'My ex-wife,' he says. 'It could be about the kids, will you excuse me a sec?'

She nods her permission and he leaves the room. From the hall outside she can hear the low murmur of his voice. She too stands and walks towards the window. A copy of the local newspaper is on his desk, open at page two. The headline reads: *Rough Sleeper Murder – Police Clueless.*

There is a photograph of a department-store doorway in which a couple of indistinct figures lie in sleeping bags. She thinks it must be a stock picture, the scene has a wintry look about it. Next to the photograph is an artist's drawing of a young woman with long fair hair, captioned: *Bella Barnes.* Further down, halfway through the copy, is a small portrait picture of a man.

She looks up to see Joe in the doorway. 'Sorry about that,' he says, before he sees what she is looking at and his expression darkens.

'You're in the paper.' She feels guilty, as though she's been caught snooping, even though a newspaper is the opposite of a confidential document.

'I knew the woman who was killed,' he says.

'A friend?' Felicity says. 'I'm so sorry.'

'No, nothing like that.' He strides across the room and takes the newspaper out of her line of sight. 'I barely knew her, on a personal level I mean.'

He seems on edge, and she wonders if the phone call was bringing bad news. Or that he is cross with her for looking at something on his desk.

'I do some work with the homeless and she was someone I saw regularly,' he says. 'The press came after me for a comment. I told them nothing, so they made it up.'

Uncomfortable, for reasons she can't name, Felicity goes back to her seat. Joe rolls up the newspaper and drops it into a waste bin. His face is still closed, defensive.

'Her name was Bella,' he says, after a moment. 'She was a nice girl who had a lot of bad luck.'

There is a moment of silence, as Felicity waits for Joe to resume his questions. His mood has changed, with the phone call, with finding her snooping.

She wasn't snooping, it was a newspaper for heaven's sake.

'Being homeless is always down to bad luck,' she says in the end. 'Bad luck, leading to bad choices, then a downward spiral.'

'You sound as though you know what you're talking about?'

She lowers her eyes. 'I had a friend,' she says. 'When I was in my late teens. She spent time on the streets.'

'Is she OK now?'

She looks up again, but briefly. 'She's fine, thanks. She got herself sorted out. She even started volunteering. Like you do. It's good that you help them. They need people like you.'

Again, a shadow crosses Joe's face, and for a moment, Felicity is tempted to pursue the conversation about the murdered homeless woman. Before she can speak, though, he takes a deep breath. 'I'm happy for you to go back to work,' he says. 'As soon as you like.'

'Today?'

He lifts both hands in a gesture that says, 'it's up to you'. 'But I'm attaching a condition.'

'What?'

'I want you to agree to continuing therapy with me. Once a week for six weeks. That's the deal.'

Her first instinct is to refuse. Sit in this chair for six more hours, fending off his questions, watching every word she says?

'And will my employers know I'm seeing you?'

'Only if you tell them. Unless I think you're about to harm yourself or others, these sessions will be completely confidential.'

Six weeks, six hours.

'OK,' she agrees.

Joe gets up and walks towards the window. She watches him as he looks outside, wondering whether he is giving himself think-ing time, or her the chance to speak without looking directly at him. Given time, she will learn his tricks, be prepared for them. For now, she has to be careful.

'Felicity,' he says. 'Has anything like this happened before?'

'No,' she says.

He turns to face her again, and with the light behind him, she can no longer see his face. She doesn't have to. He knows she is lying.

20

Joe

Joe's last appointment runs over time but it's only a five-minute walk to the pub. It takes him several seconds to spot the woman at the corner table of the courtyard garden. She has two pints of beer in front of her, one of them half empty. He makes his way over, edging past one of the university football teams, still in training kit. She's changed her hair colour again. On top of the bleached blonde she's added a pink rinse and, in all fairness, it is the exact same colour as her ripped jeans and the round circles on her cheeks.

Delilah stands up, letting him see that she's gaining weight again. 'Darling,' she says as she wraps one arm around his waist. She kisses his cheek and holds on to him for a second longer than he is expecting. Joe wraps his arms around her and lets her hug him.

'Put her down, you dirty bastard, she's old enough to be your mum!'

Joe and Delilah break apart. The goon who is about to wish he'd switched to lime and soda a couple of pints ago is grinning from a crowded table several feet away.

Joe puts his hand on Delilah's shoulder. 'Can't you just—' he says, and decides not to bother. Of course she won't let it go, she never lets it go, already she is reaching into her bag and striding across the courtyard.

'Come on then, love.'

'Fancy a toyboy, do you?'

Joe lifts his pint as Delilah reaches the boys. The table bounces as she slaps her warrant card down hard on its surface. Beer spills. Ignoring their outraged splutters, Delilah leans towards the boy who insulted her.

'I am his mother, Shit-For-Brains,' she says. 'I'm also a very senior local police officer. So, if I hear another word from you, or any of your intellectually challenged mates, I will arrest the lot of you for breach of the peace, being drunk and disorderly in a public place and behaviour that I am interpreting as a racist hate crime. Is that understood?'

Five pairs of eyes stare back at her.

Delilah takes a deep breath and yells. 'Is that understood?'

The courtyard falls silent.

'Yes, ma'am,' one of the smarter – possibly more sober – says.

Everyone in the garden watches the overweight, middle-aged woman with pink hair and jeans walk back to her own table.

'Racist hate crime?' Joe asks, as his mother takes her seat again.

'Welsh is a race,' she tells him. 'Cheers.'

'Actually, I'm not sure it is.'

They chink glasses.

'Good day?' he asks, although he knows what the answer will be. He's read the local papers the last couple of weeks. The serious crime squad are not enjoying their finest hour.

'Pissing awful,' Delilah says. 'First murder in God knows how long and we have squat. The gaffer is talking about getting me some help, meaning take me off the case.'

'Can he do that?'

'He can do what he wants. And I'd agree with him if I thought we'd missed something, or if we'd cocked up somehow.'

Joe says nothing. There is nothing to say. Bella had been a good kid. One he'd thought he might be able to help. He'd taken time with her, developed a rapport, thought he was getting somewhere.

'On the plus side,' Delilah adds, 'my granddaughter phoned me.'

Joe puts his pint down. 'What did she want? Is she OK?'

'Keep your knickers on, she's fine. She wanted to know if she and Jake could stay with me on Saturday night. Sarah's got a last-minute Ann Summers party.'

'They can stay with me. Why the hell didn't she ask me?'

'Might have been Tupperware. Do they still do Tupperware parties? And she said she'd called you once already and you'd bitten her ear off for disturbing you when you're with patients. You come too. If you stay over, I won't have to worry about getting called out if another rough sleeper decides to get himself knifed.'

'That's the spirit.'

His mother grins at him. 'How was your first day back?' she asks.

Joe takes his time. 'It went well, actually. Mainly admin, getting in touch with people to let them know I'm available again. And I've got a new patient.'

'Well, I hope to God it's not another potential student suicide. If I have to scrape another kid off the pavement at the bottom of St John's tower . . . God, I hate exam term.'

'You should talk to someone.'

'I do. I talk to you.'

'I mean someone with whom you can have a professional relationship. Can't the police organise it?'

'And trash my reputation as the most heartless bitch in Cambridge?'

'Well, I don't think suicide is on the cards for this one, although you can never be sure. Very anxious young woman. High achiever, holding down a responsible position, terrified she might lose it if she's diagnosed with a mental illness. I suspect she's been concealing symptoms for some time.'

Joe stops himself. He'd been about to refer to Felicity's adventure on the common but that had involved the police. His mother might know about it.

'You said "young".' Delilah's face has darkened. 'Is she attractive?'

'Didn't notice.'

Delilah breathes out, noisily, through her nose. 'Another young woman, Joe? Is that wise? I mean, so soon after—'

Joe interrupts, before his mother can speak the name he dreads hearing. 'Mum, her youth, and her looks, are irrelevant. I'm not allowed to date patients. Plus, starting a relationship with a woman suffering mental health problems would be—'

'Tediously normal for you?'

Joe slips his hands between the seat and his thighs to stop them shaking. 'That was not a relationship,' he says.

'If only you'd made that clear to her.'

'She wasn't even a patient. And I did make it clear. She refused to accept it.'

Delilah has the grace to look away. 'All I'm saying is you got too close. You mean well, but there are boundaries and you're the one who should be defining them.'

Joe drinks some more, and tells himself his mother knows nothing about the enormous task of getting society's most damaged to learn to trust. Delilah imagines there is a rule book, that actions and reactions are entirely predictable and controllable. She has no idea that every day he is battling chaos. He will finish his pint and go. There are times when he can't be with his mother.

'How's your scar?' Delilah asks, as her eyes fall to Joe's midriff.

'Healing,' he says. 'And no, I'm not going to show you in public.'

Silence.

'So, can you help this girl?' Delilah asks after a moment, and it takes Joe a second to realise she is talking about Felicity again.

It is a good question. He has only given himself six weeks. And something tells him Felicity Lloyd is a very troubled young woman.

'Because if you can't,' she goes on. 'You should refer her to someone else. Before she brings you down with her.'

21

Felicity

Felicity parks her car on the edge of Midsummer Common and walks the short distance to her terraced cottage. She is hot, in spite of the air conditioning in the car and is grateful for the breeze that being closer to the river brings. The scent of evening honeysuckle drifts towards her as she unlocks the door to her courtyard garden. Keen to get inside and unload her shopping, she feels the familiar fear stealing over her. Once again, she is afraid of what she might find in her own home.

The kitchen is as she left it. No empty beer bottles – she doesn't drink beer – in the recycling bin. Dropping the bags on the pale limestone floor, she runs quickly around the house, checking the master bedroom and bathroom on the ground floor, the sitting room and spare bedroom on the first. The bed in the spare room is neatly made, with no sign of the covers being disturbed.

She even goes down to the basement utility room, making sure the pile of ironing is where she left it, and the laundry basket is largely full of whites, which it always is on Tuesdays. She doesn't look at the big cupboard under the basement stairs, because she never looks at that, but everything else is as it should be. Her heartbeat begins to settle, and a sense of calm creeps over her.

Maybe the session with Dr Grant has helped after all.

She likes him, she realises. Such a calm man. She cannot imagine a man like Joe becoming ruffled or losing his temper. And he works with the homeless, something she did herself, as a volunteer, years ago. Maybe she will again.

She has had a good day at work too. The BAS has been approached by a documentary production company about a TV series on icebergs and the whole team is excited about it. She has finished a presentation that she began before the accident. And, as the day has gone on, she's found herself warming to Joe's suggestion that keeping a diary for the next few weeks will give a focus to their discussions. She likes the idea of having a record of what she's done each day. It will be nice to be able to look back and see – completeness. She even nipped into town and bought a beautiful silk-bound notebook.

As though relief has given her permission to feel hungry, she returns to the kitchen. She carries the bag with chilled goods to the tall aluminium fridge and pulls open the door.

It is full.

Every shelf is packed with food. The salad tray is full. There is a chicken, a pack of bacon and two salmon fillets on the meat shelf.

She does not eat meat.

A dozen yoghurts sit neatly beside a block of cheese on the dairy shelf. In the fridge door are two untouched pints of milk, a carton of orange juice and a bottle of sauvignon blanc. Two shelves are filled with fruit. Everything, bar the meat and salmon, that is currently in the supermarket bags. This is her second bulk shop in days.

She tells herself it's no big deal, that she's been distracted and stressed since the incident on the common. She tells herself it's understandable that the shop slipped her mind and knows she isn't listening.

She will have to check the house again.

The kitchen cupboards are in order. One time, maybe last week, she found everything had been taken out of the cupboards and put back in different ones. Today, though, everything is fine. So is her sitting room. There is a fine scattering of ash over her hearth, but even in summer the wind finds its way down the chimney.

She checks outside but this time, at least, there are no cigarette butts in the courtyard. She has never smoked, but someone has been smoking recently, directly outside her back door.

She makes her way upstairs to the second bedroom that doubles as an office. There is nothing in the wastebin other than Post-it notes. All in her handwriting. In her in-tray are several articles that she has found online and printed off, all relating to early-onset dementia. Reading them has brought her no comfort at all. The condition is rare, but not unknown. It is entirely possible.

Her appetite is gone and so she decides to start the diary. Joe suggested that a physical diary, rather than one online, will feel more personal and she agrees. She will record everything: what she wears, what she spends, where she goes. On edge, she is startled by a loud and unexpected sound from directly outside. For a moment, she thinks a vehicle is heading for her cottage, but the noise fades and dies. It is only a kid on a skateboard, or roller skates.

She sits at her desk, pulls open the drawer to find a pen and sees instead an elegant fold of black leather, fastened with a jewel clasp. Trembling again, she opens it to see the words *My Journal* on the inside page.

Someone has beaten her to it.

22

Joe

Joe drinks more than he should. He accepts a third pint because he knows he has no food at home and after three pints of beer his appetite is more or less gone. And then a fourth, because Delilah is matching him pint for pint. If he leaves now he has a feeling she might stay and after four pints, Delilah makes bad decisions.

Not for the first time, he wonders if bad decisions run in the family. Arguably, he's made a few himself of late. And then he wonders if the reason he is so on edge this evening is because it's almost exactly a year since he met the woman he still can't bear to think about.

He isn't cold, but he pulls on his sweater all the same.

'You know these homeless types,' his mother says, brushing crisp crumbs from her blouse. Unlike Joe, Delilah never loses her appetite when she drinks. She'll be heading for the kebab van when they leave, rowing with the taxi driver who won't allow food in his cab. She'll threaten him with a parking violation or some such bollocks and he'll make a complaint against her, which will probably be upheld.

'I know people without homes,' he replies. At the far end of the pub garden, sitting beneath an arch of yellow roses, is a tall young woman with blonde hair that reaches her shoulder blades. He thinks – Felicity – and doesn't know whether he hopes it is her, or that it is not. 'I also know a number of rough sleepers. Is that what you mean?'

He has a sudden flashback to how her face lit up, completely losing its haunted look, when she talked about ice.

'Yeah, yeah.' Delilah crumples the crisp packet. 'Ever hear of anyone called Shane?'

It isn't Felicity. The woman by the rose arch is younger, not unattractive, but with a long face and hooked nose.

He shakes his head. Shane? No. For the most part, the rough sleepers come and go and rarely confide their real names. Many of them are running from something, real or imaginary, and dread being traced. 'Doesn't ring a bell but I have been out of circulation for a while. Why?'

'He's a person of interest.'

'You'll have to give me more than that. Is this about the Bella Barnes murder?'

Delilah sighs and it's as good as an answer. 'We've got nothing, Joe. No suspects, no witnesses, bugger-all physical evidence.'

She has already told him this. Twice.

'It was the car park by the Grand Arcade, wasn't it?' Joe thinks about the huge, central car park. Security around it is normally pretty tight, but Bella had been small and good at hiding.

'And she decided to kip down in a corner where CCTV doesn't reach,' Delilah grumbles.

'They do that for a reason,' Joe says. 'So where does Shane fit in?'

'There's CCTV over the vehicular entrance to the car park and the cameras picked up the figure of a male leaving it around the time we think young Bella was killed. The sweatshirt he's wearing is distinctive and one or two of the other street people we've spoken to think it could be someone called Shane. Trouble is, no one knows anything about him. He appears from time to time, acts a bit creepy. No one likes him. And then he vanishes.'

'Got a picture?'

His mother reaches into her bag and pulls out a slim cardboard file. She opens it to show a poor-quality still shot from CCTV footage. Joe recognises the car park, the entrance lane, and the few yards of street. Walking towards the camera, but with his face down, his hood up and shoulders hunched is the tall, slim figure of an adolescent male. His sweatshirt is dark but there is a white logo and lettering that Joe can't quite make out.

'Estimated height is five ten,' Delilah says, 'and we've had gait experts look at the footage. You know the theory that everyone's way of walking is as distinctive as their fingerprint? Load of bollocks if you ask me, but this guy talked about length of stride, movement of the pelvis, the way the shoulders are carried. The speed of his movement suggests someone young or at least someone very fit.'

'It's not much to go on,' Joe agrees.

'Bella had no enemies,' Delilah says. 'You knew her, you don't need me to tell you she was a nice kid. No one had a bad word to say about her. It wasn't about Bella, it was about the man who killed her. It could happen again, Joe. I really need to find this Shane.'

23

Shane

There is an hour, after the nightclubs have closed and before the first dawn deliveries arrive, when Cambridge falls silent. The clocks chime two thirty and, as if by general agreement, a hush descends. Those already asleep sink a little deeper; those who are not either drift away at last, or fall into a state that is so close to sleep as to be indistinguishable from it. The cats slink guiltily home and the dogs stop barking. Maybe these two are connected. The wind takes a breath and then a breather. Even the river seems to slow its course and at the punt docks, the bumping of wood and creaking of ropes stops.

This is Shane's time.

His trainers make no sound as he slips around Jesus College. The porters are snoozing and they don't hear him pass. The two constables in the patrolling police car don't notice that the shadow in the corner of Magdalene Street Bridge wasn't there the last time they passed, and they will not drive this way again tonight.

Shane makes his way around Cambridge and he counts as he goes. The sixteen-year-old who left home last year because all the money he begged and stole was taken from him by his drug-addict mother. The soldier who served in the Falklands Conflict, and who still does, most nights, in his dreams. The woman from the Middle East and the child she hides from social services, because she knows she will lose him. The woman whom the fairies stole from her mother and father fifty years ago when she was a baby and who has been looking for them ever since. 'Are you my daddy?' she says to Shane, when she wakes and sees him watching her.

He flees when this happens. Shane is a watcher. He does not like to be seen.

Some of the people Shane looks for hide in plain sight, stretched out on park benches or slumped in doorways. Some hover where people buy food, because as they leave the supermarkets, people's wallets and purses are always to hand. Most though, are very good at becoming invisible. The women in particular slip away into the darkest of places where few can find them. The old lady with the green coat and the shopping trolley has become particularly hard to find of late. She's developed a nervous habit of huddling down in corners, even in the daytime. This saddens Shane, because when he first got to know her, the old lady was fearless.

Since the young girl was murdered in the car park, though, the old lady and the rest of the homeless stay on the move, crossing the city during the day to bed down somewhere new each night. Sometimes they vanish for days, even weeks on end. Sometimes they never come back. Those who are seen sleeping rough on the streets of Cambridge are the iceberg's tip. There are so many more.

They are the unseen. They are his people.

24

Felicity

It's not safe, Felicity. It's not safe. He's coming.

Felicity starts awake, fists clenched. Instead of black eyes, staring into her own, she sees the hazy outline of her bedroom ceiling, and yet the sense of being watched feels as real, as immediate, as it did just now in the dream. She lies still, skin tingling, knowing she isn't alone.

And yet the presence is invisible, or has fled, faster than she could open her eyes. A dream then? Or an actual voice, dragging her from sleep?

The room isn't dark. Enough light comes in from outside for her to make out the edge of the double bed, the empty fireplace, the dressing table, the upright chair. There are shadows, of course, and places that she can't see. She breathes in, deeply but silently, like a terrified animal searching for an alien scent. Is she imagining the hint of cigarette smoke hanging in the air?

Her right hand shoots out and finds the switch on the bedside light. Only then does she thoroughly check her room. A glance at the clock tells her it is close to four o'clock in the morning and it will be getting light soon. Beyond the curtains only a small square of garden separates her bedroom from the vast stretch of land that is Midsummer Common. Anyone can walk over the common, at any time of night or day. Anyone can step over the tiny railing that edges her property and walk right up to the bedroom window. The voice she heard could have come from directly outside.

She runs from the room, padding barefoot along the hallway and up the stairs. Her sitting room on the first floor, directly above her bedroom, has two sash windows and she never draws the curtains in summer. She approaches cautiously, conscious of the vast, concealing darkness outside. Streetlights illuminate the first few yards of the common but beyond that, there is nothing but emptiness.

No one stands on the grass, staring up at her house. She steps a little closer and can see the railing that edges her small front garden. The flower beds come into view and then, finally, by pressing her face against the cool glass, she can see the whole of the front of her property. There is no one in her garden, which means the voice she heard could only have come from inside the house.

Heart thumping, she searches the living room and finds a soapstone statue of a polar bear, smooth and very heavy. The bear's head and neck fit perfectly into her right hand and its body becomes a weapon. She makes her way into the only other room on this floor: the spare bedroom that doubles as a study. It too is empty.

Back downstairs again, the front door is locked and bolted. There is no one in her bathroom and the sense of being watched is fading. For some reason, though, she is still reluctant to open the last door into the kitchen. She has a sudden vision of someone crouched on the central island, waiting to spring, or hanging above the door frame like a bat.

With a burst of courage, she pushes open the door, reaches for the light and the room is revealed in all its clean white lines. Exactly as it should be. Except for the muddy footprints leading from the patio doors. Knowing the worst now, she enters the room. She avoids the mud as she steps to the door. Locked and bolted.

The prints are indistinct and incomplete, but she can see traces of a pattern from the underside of a large trainer. She runs to the cupboard by the back door where she keeps her outdoor shoes. Dreading what she will see, she lifts the right foot of her running shoe. It's spotless. So is the left foot. She has not made these prints and she doesn't know whether that is a good thing or the worst possible.

She backs away until her shoulders are pressing up against the cool of her back door, knowing that she cannot stay in this house a moment longer. She does not believe in ghosts, in the supernatural of any kind, but there are things happening to her that she can't begin to explain and she is more afraid than she ever imagined possible. She has to get out.

She has nowhere to go.

From a short distance away a church bell begins to chime the hour. Four o'clock in the morning. She doesn't go back to bed. Instead, she opens the door of the cupboard under the stairs. This is a cupboard she uses frequently, unlike its twin in the basement, at which she never looks and certainly never opens.

She keeps this cupboard neat and there is a square of carpet on the concrete floor. A single duvet is rolled neatly in the corner around an old pillow.

Felicity crawls into the cupboard and wraps the duvet around her as she settles herself into the corner. She balances the pillow against the wall and goes to sleep. And finally, like the last trace of a dream, she remembers what the voice in her ear said to her:

He's coming.

25

Felicity

'So, how have you been, Felicity?'

'Good, thank you. It's good to be back at work.'

It is early evening, a week after her first appointment, and all the windows are open in Joe's consulting room. Felicity can smell the traffic fumes and food cooking in nearby restaurants. Occasionally, though, a waft of summer flowers steals inside.

She has a plan for her second session with Joe. She will be cheerful, upbeat and chatty. She will enthuse about her work, and the fact that she feels fit enough to go running again. She will show him her diary, a week full of recorded activity.

'Your face looks a lot better,' he says.

Her hand goes up to her right cheek, the worst of the grazes. 'I heal fast,' she says.

'Given your line of work, that's probably a good thing.'

'Actually, I spend relatively little time on glaciers. They're expensive trips. Most of the time I'm behind a desk.'

He asks, 'Do you have a trip coming up?'

She thinks, this is going well. She just has to keep the small talk going.

'Actually, there is talk of a trip that would be great. Possibly the best thing I've ever done. I think I mentioned it last week.'

'Oh?'

'We have a base on South Georgia. Mainly it's about studying the wildlife, which is remarkable, but there are over a hundred glaciers there, and we know very little about them.'

'South Georgia? The southern United States?'

She forces a laugh. 'No, sorry. I'm talking about the island in the South Atlantic. Between the Antarctic and the Falkland Islands. It's a British protectorate, and one of the most remote places on Earth. No resident population, just a couple of government officials and our scientists. And tourists in the summer. In the winter, though, practically no one.'

He makes a deeply puzzled face. 'And this is somewhere you want to live? For how long?'

'I'd love it. It would make my career. And it would be a two-year assignment.'

'But to be allowed to go, you have to be fit? They'll expect a medical report and that will include a psychiatric assessment.'

And, with that, she knows he's seen her game. Of course, the Survey will never send her to South Georgia without a clean bill of health. Physically, she's absolutely fine. It all depends on Joe.

'When would you leave?' he asks.

'The last week in August. When the worst of the southern hemisphere winter is over.'

'Just over two months then.'

'Is it enough time? To get me better. To sort me out. If I agree to two whole months of therapy, will you be satisfied?'

His eyebrows bounce.

'I'm sorry,' she says. 'I know you're trying to help.'

'I'll answer your question,' he says. 'Because I think it's fair. Two months may be enough time. But I won't be able to say with any level of confidence until you start to trust me.'

She stares back at him.

'I think there's much you're not telling me,' he says. 'And that's OK. We move at a pace you're comfortable with.'

98

She's been a fool, to imagine she can keep these sessions under control.

'And I think you've been trying to steer the conversation today so that I won't ask you anything difficult.'

'So, ask me something difficult,' she says.

Smiling, he shakes his head. 'That's not how it works. I'm not here to make you uncomfortable. What do your friends think about your South Georgia plans?'

The question throws her. 'My friends?' she repeats, playing for time.

'You've yet to mention friends,' he says. 'But those closest to us can be instrumental to our emotional wellbeing. Is there a significant other in your life? Someone who might, understandably, feel left behind by your plans to move to the other side of the globe?'

'My memory's playing tricks on me,' she says, before she can stop herself.

Joe's eyes narrow.

'The day I first came here, this time last week, I did a big supermarket shop after work. When I got home, I found I'd done exactly the same thing a couple of days earlier and forgotten all about it. And I'd bought things I'd never eat.'

Joe makes a note in his pad. 'You've been under some stress,' he says. 'It's understandable things will slip your mind.'

Can she leave it at that? She should, except she finds she doesn't want to.

'I keep finding things that aren't how I left them,' she says. 'Things in the wrong place. Sometimes it's little things like car keys not being on the right hook, but the other week, someone emptied all my kitchen cupboards and put everything back in different places.'

'Someone?' he prompts.

'Exactly. It can only have been me. I'm doing all these things and I can't remember them happening.'

He is writing again. She should stop now. But she finds she can't. She has opened a flood gate and can no longer hold back the flow.

'I'm finding cigarette butts,' she says. 'I've never smoked. But I find them in the garden near the back door several times a week. This is going to sound mad. I know its mad, but I can't help think-ing that someone is sleeping in my spare bedroom.'

That's it. That's enough. Stop now.

'More than once, I've gone past the door and seen it open, which is not how I keep it. I'm pretty tidy around the house. And when I look inside, the bed is all rumpled, as though someone has just got out and not bothered to make it. And the curtains are drawn too. I hate drawn curtains during the day.'

'This must be very confusing.'

'It is. I'll tell you the worst thing, though.'

'What's that?'

'You know you suggested keeping a diary?'

Joe inclines his head.

'I went to start it that night. I thought it was a good idea. Only I'd already done it. I'd started a diary, but it was full of really hor-rible stuff.'

'What sort of stuff?'

'Abusive, horrible things about me. It was written by someone who really hates me. Except, I wrote it myself.'

She is starting to cry. She cannot believe how quickly this has gone wrong, and how incapable she is of turning it back around.

Joe leans back in his chair. 'Felicity, I don't want to scare you, but is it possible someone has keys to your house? An old lodger, maybe? A cleaner?'

She shakes her head. 'No. I changed the locks when I moved in and had two sets of keys made. One set is in the safe. I checked. I've never had a cleaner.'

Joe seems at a loss.

'I know it's me,' she goes on. 'I know I'm doing these things and not remembering them. But some of them are so out of character. It really is like someone else – someone invisible – is living in my house.'

26

Joe

The punt glides under the bridge at St John's College and cold water trickles down Joe's forearms. At the front of the boat, Torquil relaxes into the padded cushions and sips from his bottle of Becks.

In common with many members of his profession, including those who have their own practice, Joe has a professional supervisor, someone with whom he talks on a regular basis to discuss client care. Not all are as fortunate as Joe has been, because not only is Dr Torquil Bane a wise and insightful man, he has become, over the years, a good friend.

He is, though, a huge man and his end of the punt is several inches lower in the water than the end Joe is standing on.

'Nicely done,' Torquil says as they slip out the other side of the bridge. 'You're getting better.'

'Any time you want to show me how it's done,' Joe offers.

'Once I'm sitting, I can't get up. So, the reluctant patient decides to open up. Must have felt like a big step forward.'

'I thought I'd have to tease it out of her, session by session. Turns out all I had to do was ask about her private life.'

'And these memory lapses presented suddenly and recently?'

'So she says. Within the last few weeks, coinciding with nothing that she can think of.'

'And are they affecting her at work too?'

'She insists not. And given the glowing report her company gave her GP, she's probably telling the truth about that.'

'Acute symptoms that only happen at home?'

'Exactly.'

They are approaching the second of St John's bridges, the Bridge of Sighs. Joe bends low. Torquil reaches up, touches the roof and pushes them on. 'Did you ask about head injuries?' he says.

'I did. She says there's been nothing. She doesn't even get headaches.'

'Sleeping well?'

'So she says.'

'Amnesia often has a physical cause. Alzheimer's isn't unknown in people her age. Are you organising the various tests?'

'All in hand.'

'That's twice now you've said, "so she says". Do you think she's lying to you?'

'I think she's holding a lot back. Tell me something, Torq, does her suspicion that someone else is living in her house sound delusional to you?'

Torquil thinks about it. 'Not sure. It sounds as though she knows this can't be the case, that somehow she's responsible for the fag ends, and the unmade beds and the mysterious diary. That suggests the opposite of delusional to me.'

Joe's arms are aching. Thank God, they are almost back at Magdalene Bridge and the punt dock.

Torquil asks, 'Do you still suspect her of being a self-harmer?'

'Hard to say. Her medical notes weren't specific about where her scars are. Or whether they could have been self-inflicted. I haven't felt there's been the right time to ask.'

Their punt nudges up against the jetty. The boatman takes the pole from Joe and waits for them to climb out.

'So, that's all your patients sorted,' Torquil says, as he wobbles to his feet. 'How are you doing?'

Joe has been waiting for this. 'I'm fine,' he says. 'It's good to be back at work. Good to be busy again. Two months of convalescence was sending me stir-crazy.'

'Any news on our roller-skating friend?'

Joe tries, and fails, to stop the shudder. 'Nothing,' he mumbles, as he climbs onto the bank. 'Mum would tell me right away if she'd been seen.'

She would, wouldn't she? She would tell him? Joe has a sudden flashback to a spring evening, to his mother spreading crime scene photographs over his hospital bed. He'd looked, trying to feel something other than numb, at a picture of the river bank just outside the city, and a rucksack containing a homeless girl's entire belongings, including a pair of roller skates, lying in the mud. There had been no trace of the owner. After several weeks and an extensive police search, the young woman called Ezzy Sheeran had been declared missing, presumed dead.

'Not everyone who goes in the river comes out again,' Joe says. 'The police think she was washed into the Ouse and then out into the North Sea.'

'A body would be good, though,' Torquil says. 'Just to make it official.'

Joe cannot bring himself to agree with this. Not out loud, at any rate.

'This time last year, wasn't it?' Torquil says. 'That she first turned up, I mean.'

'Last Friday in June.'

'I'm probably stating the obvious, but your mum and her mates have considered a link between what happened to Miss Sheeran in April and Bella Barnes' death, haven't they?'

It takes Joe a second or two to catch up. 'You think they could both have been murdered? By the same killer?'

'Is it impossible?'

'Bella was stabbed. The theory is that Ezzy committed suicide after what she did to me.'

'But in the light of new information, I mean Bella's murder, maybe Ezzy suffered a similar fate and her body was thrown in the river.'

Delilah hasn't said a word about any new theories regarding Ezzy Sheeran's disappearance. Joe feels sure she wouldn't keep him in the dark. On the other hand, she knows how difficult it is for him to talk about what happened in April.

Torquil is watching him closely. 'Pint?' he offers.

Joe shakes his head. 'I've got my first session back at St Martin's. It wasn't available on Tuesday. Exam time.'

'Want me to come?'

Joe reaches out a hand and pats Torquil on the shoulder. 'Mate,' he says, 'I'm fine.'

The look his supervisor gives him as Joe turns away is one he's seen many times before. Usually, though, on his mother's face.

'But I only looked at the baby.' A tear zigzags down the elderly woman's cheek. Her face is so wrinkled it can't flow in a vertical line.

'Dora, you took the baby out of its pram while its mother was attending to an older child. You know you can't touch other people's babies.'

'She hit me.'

'The baby hit you?'

'The mother. She snatched it back and hit me. She called me horrible names. She should have been arrested, not me.'

Behind Dora, the woman from the charity who organises the

weekly drop-in is hovering. His next appointment is waiting.

'Mothers are fierce if they think their babies are under threat,' he says.

'I wouldn't hurt a baby.'

Dora's lip is trembling and another tear spills out from the corner of her eye.

'I know,' Joe says, although the truth is, he doesn't, because decades earlier, married to a solicitor and teaching at a local girls' school, Dora lost three infants to cot death. Sympathy at the time was huge, until she was arrested and charged with the murder of her own children. The charges were dropped for lack of evidence, but the resulting depression cost Dora her job and her marriage. Long ago, she began drinking and lost her home. Now she lives on the streets and no one knows whether she is the unluckiest woman alive, or a monster.

'You've been cautioned again, haven't you, Dora?' Joe says. 'An incident in the shopping centre.'

'Those girls were bullying Martin,' Dora says. 'I couldn't do nothing.'

Martin is one of Dora's homeless friends who got into an argument with some school girls. Dora, begging nearby, pitched into the fray, swinging her shopping trolley at one of the girls and giving her a nasty cut on the leg.

'You'll be arrested if you do it again. You could go to prison.'

'You won't let that happen to me.' Dora grips Joe's hand. Her skin is scaled and rough. 'You have a word with that mum of yours. Tell her I wouldn't do any harm.'

Joe sighs. No one is supposed to know his mother is with the police.

'When can I see you again?' Dora asks. She still hasn't released his hand. 'It hasn't been the same without you these last few weeks.'

'I'll be here on Tuesday. How about twenty past eight?'

'Is that your last appointment?'

It isn't, but he's learned from experience never to give Dora the last appointment of the evening. Getting her to leave is always twice as hard.

'Last available. Look, I'll write it down for you.'

He writes *8.20pm, Tuesday* on a business card and she grabs at it, tucking it away in an inside coat pocket. Her sweater is a blue fleece, he sees, with insignia from the film *Frozen*.

'You take care, Dora.' He gets to his feet. *And don't hurt anyone,* he thinks to himself.

'I need some cash,' the man in his forties says before he's even taken a seat. 'I need some money. A loan. I'll pay it back.'

'What do you need money for, Michael?' Joe asks. 'Take a seat.'

Michael sits on the edge of the chair.

'Fifty quid will do it. Twenty. Can you lend us twenty?'

'I can't lend you money, you know that.'

Michael leans forward, letting Joe see his blackened teeth. 'I need to go somewhere safe.'

The evening is warm, but Joe feels a cold breeze sweep through the hall. 'Why do you think here isn't safe?' he asks.

'Well, you know. That Shane fella.'

Joe sits up a little straighter. 'Who's Shane?'

'You know, the fella that's been knifing homeless people. You probably don't know about it, what with you being sick and all for weeks. Stabbed young Bella, he did.'

'Michael, if you know something about what happened to Bella, you really should talk to the police.'

'I'm not talking to no fucking police. I just want to get out of here.'

'Ok, talk to me then. Tell me why you're frightened of Shane.'

Michael glances back, as though someone could be eavesdropping. 'He's not right.'

'In what way.'

'He watches us. While we're asleep.'

'I'm not trying to be clever, but how do you know if you're asleep?'

'We're never really asleep. We can't afford to be. We, like, doze. I saw him, the other night, down at Silver Street. He was staring down at this geezer like he wanted to – you know – eat him.'

'What does he look like?

'It was dark. I wasn't close.'

'How old?'

A shrug.

'White? Black? Asian?'

'White guy, I think. I don't know. I didn't get a good look. Fucking Norah, what is she doing here?'

Joe follows Michael's gaze. His mother is standing in the doorway.

'You'll never find him.' Joe catches Delilah by the shoulder. She'd been about to tear out of the hall in hot pursuit of Michael. 'He'll be on the other side of the city by now.'

Delilah pushes out a heavy sign of exasperation. 'What is wrong with these people?'

'Where do I begin?' Joe has four more people to see and he'll be lucky if any of them stay now that his mother has arrived.

'And he definitely knew this Shane bugger?'

'White guy, possibly, watches the homeless while they sleep. All I could get out of him.'

Delilah pulls out a chair. 'You've got to help me out, Joe. These people of yours know Shane. If they start co-operating, we can find him before he hurts someone else.'

Joe hears the sound of the main door opening. He looks back into the hall to see the last of his evening's appointments disappearing and remembers that Bella Barnes may not have been the first person that Shane hurt.

'Is it possible that Ezzy Sheeran's disappearance and Bella's murder are linked?' he asks.

'Who put that idea in your head?' Delilah snaps.

'Is it?'

Delilah makes an exasperated gesture. 'We can't rule it out,' she says. 'Two young homeless women in the same city, within two months of each other. We really need to find this Shane.'

'I'll do what I can,' he says. 'And for what it's worth, I agree. Shane sounds dangerous.'

Sometime later, Joe sits, on a wooden bench by the path on Midsummer Common, enjoying the cool of the evening. There is a scent in the air that he thinks might be jasmine, and crickets sing in the grass at his feet. Joe closes his eyes, wonders what Sarah and the kids are doing, and feels a wave of loneliness wash over him.

'You're Joe, aren't you?' says a voice in his ear.

Joe opens his eyes to see a girl sitting by his side. She is small, maybe in her late teens, and would be very pretty, except that she has too many piercings for his taste, and green hair doesn't really do it for him.

'That's my name,' he agrees. 'Who are you?'

'Erzebet,' she says. Her voice is low pitched, with an Irish lilt.

He blinks. 'I'm sorry?'

'It means devoted to God.' She smiles at him. It would be a sweet smile, but her teeth are a little crooked, and don't look entirely clean. 'I'm not though,' she says. 'Devoted to God, that is. People call me Ezzy.'

She moves a little closer to him on the bench and he notices that over her trainers she is wearing roller skates. She is very thin, and her skin has a dry, grey look about it. Her pupils, he sees now, are dilated.

'Well, nice to meet you, Ezzy. How do you know my name?'

'I was at St Martin's in town just now. Your people back there were talking about you.'

Joe wonders if the girl, who seems to be edging closer along the bench, has followed him here.

'How old are you, Ezzy?'

'Eighteen.'

She barely looks fifteen.

'If you're under eighteen, I can call social services. There are charities that can help. Do you have somewhere to stay tonight?'

'Can I stay with you?'

Joe gets to his feet. 'That won't be possible, I'm afraid.'

She is upright too, like a child beside him, even with the added height of the skates. 'They said at St Martin's that you look after the pretty girls.' She pushes her bottom lip out. 'They say you take them home and make them nice and comfortable.'

'I don't know who—'

'Are you cheating on me already, Joe? We've only just met and you're cheating on me.'

The girl's face is twisted with rage. She isn't Ezzy, any more, though, she's Felicity, and that is a knife in her hand.

'Serves you right,' she hisses, as she drives the knife into his stomach and his whole body begins to burn with shock and pain. 'Cheating bastard.'

Joe wakes with a start to find that he is in his bedroom at home, and the clock by his bed reads 02.45. He has had the dream again.

It has never featured Felicity before.

He gets up, to let the night air cool his body, and checks the locks on the doors and windows before he gets back into bed. He lies, trying to think about anything but Ezzy and finds himself thinking, instead, about Bella and the mysterious Shane.

Watching people while they sleep? Joe wonders if he will ever sleep soundly again.

27

Shane

Shane is very good at entering property. He doesn't like the term *breaking and entering*. There is no need to *break* if you are good at what you do, and Shane is very good at what he does. Of course, he doesn't usually enter properties when people are inside, but he likes a challenge.

The fire escape makes it easy because people are never as security conscious on their top floors as they are on the ground, and the locked yard around its base gives an odd illusion of safety. Don't they know how easy it is to scale a stone wall that's no more than seven feet high? Child's play.

He ascends the steps slowly, knowing how noisy iron can be, and how close to sleeping people he will be as he climbs to the first floor, the second and then the third and last. On the third floor a doctor lives and works.

A special doctor. A doctor who treats the mind. A doctor called Joe who spends a lot of time with the homeless. Shane isn't sure whether or not he trusts Joe with his people. It is time Shane paid Joe a visit.

When Shane reaches the top, he tries the door handle, because you never know, but it won't budge. His bump keys will not work on this sort of lock. There are two windows to the left of the door, a larger one that he could climb through easily and a much smaller one above it. The smaller one is slightly open to let in the night air.

Shane swings one leg over the side of the fire escape and feels it shift on its clamps. Using his other leg as an anchor, he leans out towards the open window, until he can slip his thin hand in through the two-inch gap. Reaching the lock, he turns it. The small window can now be opened fully and by balancing on the sill, Shane can reach down and unlock the larger window. Getting in now will be easy. He climbs in, onto the worktop surrounding the kitchen sink and drops to the floor.

He waits to check that all is silent. He has made no sound and in his dark clothes it is unlikely that he has been seen. Cautious, though, he unlocks the back door. He closes the lower window and returns the smaller one to the position he found it in. Only now, can he take stock of his surroundings.

He is in the small, functional kitchen of a professional single male. He sees the cheap IKEA crockery and the top-of-the-range coffee maker. There are economy bags of basmati rice and penne pasta on the shelves but the wine on the rack is good quality. To one side of the sink is a knife rack. Shane is never entirely sure how he feels about knives. On the one hand, they feel nice when he's holding them. On the other, they cut through skin and flesh so easily and there have been accidents before now. He chooses the one from the middle of the row. It is a perfect fit in his right hand.

Armed now, he steps out onto a narrow landing and passes a bathroom on his right. The door that will open on to the internal staircase has a Yale lock and bolts at both top and bottom. He draws back the bolts and puts the lock on the latch. A second escape route never hurts.

The room ahead is large and lit by the streetlamps outside. Even in the poor light he can see the warm colours, the good-quality furniture. He spends longer than he should at the window, looking out at his city by night. He cannot see any of the sleepers from this height but he knows where they are. Before the night is over, he will have visited them all.

A clock strikes the quarter-hour and breaks him out of his reverie. He returns to the landing. There are two more rooms in the top-floor flat.

The first is a living room, with sofa, armchairs, bookcases and a TV; smaller, shabbier and more cosy than the room where the doctor sees his patients. Most of the books are about psychology or psychotherapy but there are a few novels. Shane has little interest in books.

His heartbeat is building a little as he opens the last door into the bedroom. It is small, like the living room, and dark because the window overlooks the back of the house. There is a form in the bed, but the duvet is pulled up high.

Shane moves closer. People are so easy to read when they are asleep. Shane feels, sometimes, as though he can see into sleeper's souls, that their stories float around their lifeless bodies like an aura. He can tell the good from the angry from the damaged beyond repair. Sometimes, not often on the streets, but sometimes, he sees the bad.

He needs to see the doctor's soul.

As though sensing the approaching danger, the sleeper stirs. He mutters something and pushes the duvet a little further down the bed. Now his face, damp with sweat, can be seen. He is a youngish man, only a little older than Shane, and his face is handsome in the poor light.

He is talking in his sleep. 'No,' he says. 'No, get away from me.'

The aura around him is deeply troubled. This man seems lost, more in need of help than many of the street sleepers he spends time among.

So worried does the sleeping doctor look, that Shane begins to back away, but a folded newspaper on the bedside cabinet catches his attention. Another story about the murdered girl; Bella, he's learned she was called. Shane has followed the investigation, stealing newspapers whenever he can, picking discarded ones up off the ground when the newsagents are more vigilant.

Pain is building in Shane. Thinking about Bella is so hard. His breathing is getting deeper and faster. His fists clench and the handle of the knife digs deep into the flesh of his palm. Sweat breaks out all over his body. He pictures himself slashing the knife indiscriminately around the room, ripping open everything in its path. He howls his misery but the sound doesn't escape his head. Shane has had years to perfect the art of silent rage.

His head is spinning.

The doctor called Joe is waking up. His breathing is no longer audible. He is lying still; is possibly even conscious. Without making a sound, Shane turns and leaves the bedroom.

He relocks the door to the stairs and leaves the knife on the worktop in the kitchen. He makes sure the windows are as he found them and then steps out through the door, locks it and then takes a moment to throw the key carefully back through the narrow gap in the window. He hears a low thud as it lands on the rug.

The pain is beginning to subside by the time he reaches the bottom of the fire escape. He scales the wall and sets off through the night-time city.

28

Felicity

When the River Cam leaves the city behind, it loses much of its reflected colour and nearly all of its noise. Also, quite a bit of its momentum. The Cam of the countryside is a slow-moving waterway of gentle greens, lit by lightning bolts of silver where the light can reach the water. Once out of the city, the willow trees become bolder, leaning perilously close to the water, as though they might take hold and halt its progress altogether. Nettles, brambles and ferns join the conspiracy from the banks as do the weeds that stretch out in the flow. Both the river, and the surrounding vegetation seem to soak up all sound. The river, once it leaves Cambridge, becomes a slow, silent slither of green.

On this evening in early July, the heat of the day is gone and a breeze lifts the surface of the water. The hedge beyond the tow-path is dense and the trees behind that are high. The rear end of a mother duck bounces around near the bank whilst her babies mill about her, hoping she might disturb something that they can gobble up. In the fields nearby cows will graze until darkness claims the land. It is a scene of perfect English peacefulness, marred only by the fair-haired young woman, staring wildly about her, on the verge of screaming.

Felicity isn't injured this time – she checks quickly – but she's exhausted and her clothes are damp with sweat. Her phone tells her it is 9.15 on Tuesday 2nd July. She has four missed calls and two messages.

Her phone starts ringing and she answers in a low, hesitant voice.

'Felicity? Are you OK? I've been worried about you.'

'I'm OK,' she says, although she knows she is not. She wishes it hadn't been Joe, and yet who else would call? A wave of loneliness sweeps over her. She has no one but a man whom she pays to talk to her.

'You missed our appointment. I've been ringing you for three hours. I'm outside your house right now.'

He is persistent, her only link to humanity. He says, 'I'm sorry if that seems intrusive. I didn't want to cross the line, but I've just finished work and thought I might as well drive round.'

'Is my car there? Is my car outside the house?' She speaks without thinking.

'Felicity, where are you?'

'I don't know.'

His voice drops. 'Felicity, talk to me. Don't hang up. Are you hurt?'

She checks again. She can feel no blood on her face, no fresh tenderness. She doesn't think she is hurt and tells him so.

'I can get the police out to you if you're in danger. I've got contacts.'

'No!' She cannot be involved with the police again.

'Are you alone?'

'Yes,' she says. 'I'm by the river.'

'In the city?' She hears the fear in his voice. Does he imagine she is about to throw herself in?

'Felicity, listen to me. Does your phone have Google Maps?'

It takes her a second or two to process the question, then, 'I think so,' she says.

'If you open that app, it will tell you where you are. Can you do that now?'

She should have thought of that herself. She would have thought of it given time. She puts the call on hold and finds the app.

'I'm between Waterbeach and Upware,' she says, when the GPS has found her.

'OK, bear with me. I'm trying to find you on my phone. All right, I've got it. You're actually on the towpath? Are you closer to Waterbeach or Upware?'

She checks the app again. 'Upware. I'm not far from Upware.'

'Right, I want you to walk upstream. I think I can see a road that runs close to the river. I'll be there as soon as I can.'

It is dark by the time he finds her. She doesn't see him until he shines a torch in her direction. He walks towards her and for a second she thinks he is about to take her in his arms. He lowers the torch and they stare at each other in the moonlight.

'Do I need to take you to a doctor?' he asks.

She shakes her head. 'I'm fine. I'm so sorry.'

He takes her back to his waiting car. There is a blanket on the front seat and she doesn't object when he places it over her.

'Do you have your keys?' he asks, as he sets off along the narrow country road that will take them south.

She feels her shirt pocket and finds the irregular lump. 'I do.'

Only when they are on the edge of the city does Joe speak again. 'Can you tell me what happened.'

She replies, 'I don't know.'

They drive in silence for a little longer then he gives a heavy sigh.

'I should have made it clearer when you came last week that there are physical causes of memory loss,' he says. 'Even if we can rule out a head injury, there are other possible problems.'

She turns to look at his profile. 'I've thought about Alzheimer's, or a tumour.'

He half smiles, but kindly. 'You've leapt to two of the worst possible scenarios and also the most unlikely. Memory loss can be a result of problems with the thyroid gland, or an infection. It's even possible, although unlikely, that you had a mild stroke.'

She finds she is comforted, a little, by the possibility of a physical cause to what is happening. Given the choice between cancer and insanity, who wouldn't choose cancer?

'The sudden onset of your symptoms suggests a physical cause,' he says. 'I can try and speed through the tests tomorrow.'

'Thank you.'

He doesn't need directions to her home and she is relieved to see her car in its usual place. He parks and switches off the engine.

'I'd like to come inside and make sure you're all right,' he says. 'May I?'

She doesn't feel she can refuse him. It is as though the incident has drained her of confidence. She is not fit to be in control of her own life.

'What's the last thing you remember?' he asks, when they are both in her kitchen.

'Leaving work and heading into the city to see you,' she says. 'I don't know if I arrived or not.'

'You didn't,' he says. 'You look cold. Why don't you get changed? If you don't mind me helping myself, I'll put the kettle on and get you something to eat.'

He has taken over and she has no idea how to stop him. She leaves the room and while she is changing into tracksuit bottoms and a sweatshirt, she hears him moving around in the kitchen. He is whistling softly to himself.

Freddie won't like this.

Felicity almost cries out. Someone is in the room with her. And yet no one is. She checks quickly in the wardrobe, beneath the bed. She is alone in the room and yet the sense of an invisible presence is so strong she feels she can almost reach out and touch the person who spoke to her.

'You OK in there?'

This time it is Joe's voice, and she heads back to the kitchen. He's found bread and butter, cheese and olives. She grabs the breadknife and cuts a slice, then cheese. She eats like a savage.

'Sorry,' she says when the trembling in her limbs is slowing. 'I was starving.'

'Ready to talk?' he asks.

29

Joe

'Ready to talk?' Joe asks.

'Of course.'

'I'd like to look round your house. Will you show me?'

'There's not much to see,' she says. 'There's a basement down-stairs, do you want to start there?'

'Please.'

He follows her down the narrow staircase into a small, tiled room. He hears the gurgling of a central-heating boiler and registers the washing machine and tumble dryer, the ironing board tucked behind a tall cupboard. There is a small pile of ironing in a basket on the worktop. A sizable cupboard beneath the stairs is padlocked shut.

'What do you keep in here?'

No answer. Joe turns to find Felicity is heading back up the stairs. When he follows her, she is waiting for him on the ground floor by a narrow hall table.

'Nice polar bear,' he says, spotting the smooth and stylised statue that she is looking at.

'I usually keep it upstairs.' She is frowning, not remembering, or choosing not to acknowledge, their previous conversation about polar bears. 'But I think I moved it myself the other night. Yes, I did. That was definitely me.'

Brightening, she shows him into the bedroom. The room is

simple and neat, with fitted wardrobes. The only furniture apart from the bed are two bedside cabinets. On one is an iPad and a box of tissues. The other is empty.

They climb another set of stairs. As they near the first floor, Joe spots the loft hatch directly above the head of the stairs. She shows him into the living room, striding ahead to rearrange cushions on one of the sofas. He watches as she looks around, as though trying to spot anything out of place, and her eyes rest on the TV set. A red light shines from the bottom right-hand corner. She walks towards it and presses the on/off switch.

'I don't like to leave it on standby,' she says. 'I don't know why I did.'

'Can we see what channel you were watching?'

She doesn't reply. Her attention has been caught by something directly below the TV on its supporting glass table.

Joe says, 'If you don't normally leave it on standby, you could have been watching it when you went into your fugue state. We might be able to pinpoint a particular programme that triggered you.'

Felicity looks up, uncertain.

'Can it do any harm?' he says.

She switches the TV back on. They wait until the picture emerges of a back alley in an American city. A woman runs screaming towards the camera.

'The horror channel,' she says. 'I've never watched that.' She bends to pick something up from the glass table. A pair of spectacles in a brown case. 'And these aren't mine.'

Joe takes them from her as screaming fills the room. Felicity switches off the TV and the screaming stops. He opens the case and peers through the glasses. Distance vision.

'I don't wear glasses,' she says. 'I have perfect vision.'

'Could a friend have left them?'

'No. No one comes here.'

Joe says, 'Are you sure no one else has keys?'

She shakes her head.

'There's something I want to do before I go. Will you indulge me?'

She looks wary.

'I want to look in your loft.'

Her eyes open wide. 'My loft? What on Earth for?'

He doesn't want to answer that. To answer it would be to frighten her.

'It will set my mind at rest. Please?'

She shrugs and he leaves the room. He is tall enough to reach the catch on the trapdoor. The loft ladder glides down sound-lessly. The space revealed by the loft light is low, with barely enough headroom for Joe to stand upright. Along one edge is a neat line of packing cases and holdalls, standing opposite them a row of plastic storage boxes. He can see a pair of skis in a canvas carry bag and a tool kit. At the far end, pushed against one wall and barely visible in the shadows, is a large trunk-shaped object covered in old curtains. Felicity's loft is as neat as her house and were the circumstances different, he would ask her, not entirely in jest, if she dusts up here.

'Joe, why are you in my loft?'

'Give me a minute.' He begins to crawl along the plyboard floor, away from the curtain-wrapped trunk. A cold-water tank ahead of him is lagged to prevent freezing in winter and beyond that is the dividing wall between Felicity's loft and that of the next house along. He has a suspicion, and until it is laid to rest, he won't be easy. He has reached the wall. He uses his phone as a torch and sees that the wall is made of plywood. He pushes it gently and it falls away, landing with a clatter on the floor of the next loft.

'Joe!'

He turns to see Felicity's head appear in the hatch and waits until she has crawled to join him. Together they look to the loft space that stretches the entire length of the terrace. His torch isn't strong enough to reach the end, but he remembers a row of half a dozen or so houses. If the other dividing wall is also plywood, then six sets of neighbours, and people with keys to their houses, can access Felicity's home.

'I had no idea,' she says.

'When cottages like these were built, people didn't need their lofts,' he says. 'They didn't have enough stuff to worry about storage. The roof void is just an empty space at the top of the house that nobody bothered about. It's only in the last few decades that people have started cutting access doors and building dividing walls.'

'Anyone can get into my house,' she says.

'Come on,' he tells her. 'We've got work to do.'

'Were you a boy scout?' she asks, a half-hour later.

He has found several empty cans in her recycling basket and using a screwdriver from the tool kit in his car, punched a hole in each. They hang now, on string, from the loft door like a cut-price Christmas decoration.

'Anyone tries to open that hatch tonight, the racket will wake you up in an instant and scare the crap out of them,' he says. 'You dial 999 and leave via your bedroom window, waiting in your car for the police to arrive. Tomorrow, I'll put a heavy-duty bolt on that door and you need to get on the phone to some local builders. I doubt your insurance policy is valid without solid dividing walls on both sides. You also need to ask some hard questions about whatever survey was done when you bought the place.'

'I can do that. The bolt I mean. You've done enough.'

'When I'm gone, I want you to lock and bolt front and back doors and check all the window locks. Tomorrow, changing the locks would be a very good idea.'

'You really think someone is coming into my house? When I'm out and when I'm asleep?'

He is saddened by the look of hope on her face. 'No, Felicity, I don't. I think you're suffering temporary bouts of amnesia that have either a physical or a psychological cause. Whatever the cause is, though, we'll find it and we'll treat it. All this stuff' – he gestures up at the swaying cans, 'We're just ruling out all other possibilities and making sure you can sleep at night.'

He says good night shortly afterwards and drives home, wondering if he's done the right thing by drawing her attention to the communal loft. He may have fed her anxiety, put ideas into her head about intruders and made her condition worse.

30

Felicity

No sooner than Joe has driven away, Felicity goes back to the loft, letting the cans clatter against the wall as she lowers the hatch. Once inside, she ignores the cord that would turn on the light and turns away from the still-collapsed plyboard wall that Joe discovered. She has no interest in that. She has come for a better look at something else. Something she spotted earlier as she climbed up to join Joe. Something that has appeared, as if by magic, in her loft.

She is carrying a more powerful torch than the one Joe used, but for the moment she doesn't switch it on. There is something about what she is doing that feels shameful, better suited to darkness, and so she crawls carefully along the boarded loft floor towards the opposite wall.

Only when her fingers touch the old curtains does she switch on the torch. She lets her hands rest on the fabric that she can see now is a deep maroon.

The trunk beneath is black, heavy-duty plastic. It has a military look about it, as though it is holding weapons, or explosives, or something that needs a solid casing. There are two locks, neither of which she could force open. The trunk is something she has never seen before, and had no idea was in her house.

She knows that this is impossible and yet the evidence is right before her eyes.

31

Joe

Joe goes back the next evening, as promised, with a drill and two heavy duty bolts.

'How've you been today?' he asks, as he follows her into the downstairs hall.

'Good,' she says. 'The hanging tins were very reassuring.'

He isn't sure he believes her, Felicity doesn't look like someone who has slept well. In her own home, he has noticed, she is less relaxed than when she comes to his consulting room. In her own house, she starts at sounds that he can't hear, and seems constantly on edge.

When the bolts are fixed to the loft hatch, the tin cans retired to the recycling bin, and Felicity has vacuumed the dust, she offers him a glass of wine and with a twinge of discomfort, because he knows it is probably unwise, he accepts. They sit at the island in her kitchen.

'You mentioned a diary,' he says. 'Not the one you brought me last week. The other one.'

'The one written by someone who hates me?' she says. 'It's upstairs. Do you want to see it?'

He tells her that he does and she goes to find it. When she comes back, he notices that her hair is different. Loose before, it's scraped back behind her head and tucked into a scrunchie.

'It's not pleasant,' she says, when the fold of black leather is on the counter in front of him.

'So you said. Can you read it to me?' He pushes it back towards her.

'Do I have to?'

'It will help.'

He waits. She begins to read.

'"Twenty-eighth of March. I can't stand Felicity's hair. I can't stand the time she spends on it, washing, conditioning, combing, plaiting, weaving, twisting it this way and that. It's only fucking hair."'

Joe isn't sure what he expected. Not this.

'"I hate the greasy mat it makes in the shower drain, catching scum and soap and pubes and toenail clippings. I hate finding it on clothes and even food. Felicity's hair is disgusting."'

She glances up and meets his eyes. He motions for her to go on.

'"One morning, I swear, she'll wake up, lift her head off the pillow and – this is the good bit – her hair won't come with her. She'll leave it behind like sheared wool around a sheep."'

Joe is familiar with how Felicity speaks. In the few hours they have spent together, he has absorbed many of the rhythms and inflexions that are peculiar to her. He'd thought that if he heard her read the diary aloud, he would know whether or not she was its author.

'"No, better than that, I'll have taken it all away, and she won't have a clue anything's wrong until she sees the scissors on the bedroom carpet. She'll realise then, maybe feel a draft on her neck and she'll run into the bathroom and – hello, skinhead!"'

Joe has never heard Felicity swear. Her vocabulary is more sophisticated than he is hearing now, but he isn't sure.

'You have absolutely no memory of writing this?' he asks.

She shakes her head.

'Is the handwriting yours?'

'Hard to say.' She meets his eyes and shrugs. 'I'm – not ambi-dextrous exactly – but my left hand is quite agile. I can write with it if I have to. This is a bit like when I do that, but I can't say for certain.'

Joe thinks about this for a second. Handwriting can be ana-lysed. It will be possible to find out for sure if Felicity has written the hostile journal.

'And there's more?' he asks.

'You want me to read it?'

The act of reading is making her both embarrassed and miser-able and he doesn't want to put her through it again. He reaches out and she hands him the journal. The second entry is even angrier.

6 April

Why the fuck does the bitch have to be vegetarian? We have a fridge that's always packed with food and never anything to fucking well eat. I don't buy it, this refusing to eat meat shit. She doesn't give a fuck about animal welfare, it's all about Felicity's non-stop campaign to prove to the world that she's better than the rest of us.

Oh, I'm Flawless Felicity, I don't eat animals.

Oh, I'm Faultless Felicity, I'm passionate about animal welfare.

Hello, I'm Fabulous Felicity, and my body is a temple.

Self-righteous bitch.

A feeling of deep unease is stealing over Joe and he is more glad than he could put into words that he has bolted the loft hatch, that she is getting her locks changed. There is only one more entry in the diary.

19 April

The others have been on at me to say something nice about Felicity so, here goes – she's kind. She found a young bird that couldn't fly the other day and she was worried that the foxes would get it if she left it outside overnight, so she put it in a box with holes in the lid and put the box in her log store overnight. She even drove to the pet store to find some wild bird food so it wouldn't starve. She was planning to let it out the next morning if it had recovered enough to fly away.

I waited till she was asleep and then I crept into the courtyard. I opened the log store, and then the box. The bird looked up at me with big black eyes. I think it was on the verge of hopping out of the box when I grabbed it and broke its neck.

I put the box back. She found the bird the next morning. Sentimental bitch actually cried.

Felicity is kind. I'm not.

'Have you got to the bit about the bird?' she asks him.

He looks up. 'Just finished.'

'It was a young starling. I thought it died of cold or was too weak. But what if it was me? What if I got up in the night and I broke its neck. What the hell is wrong with me?'

Her face creases into an expression of unbearable pain. She needs to cry, he realises. She needs to let out some of the tension she's been holding back, but her fists are clenched and she's biting down hard on her lower lip. And then, with a moan, she drops her face into her hands and begins to sob. After a few moments, he is worried that she will never stop.

He wants nothing more than to cross to her and take her in his arms. No one should have to cry like this and not be comforted. He is even on the point of easing himself off his seat when he has a sudden vision of his mother.

Delilah is standing at the foot of his hospital bed, the morning after he almost died. Her face is drained of colour and there are mascara smudges around her eyes. He knows she has been up all night, hunting down Ezzy Sheeran.

He owes something to his mother, and he knows that Delilah wouldn't want him even to be here. He cannot go anywhere near Felicity in her distress. All he can do is wait. And be practical. In the bathroom he finds a box of tissues.

'I'm actually going bonkers, aren't I?' Felicity says, when he hands it to her.

'That term is losing favour in clinical circles.' He doesn't resume his seat. 'It's late, I should leave you in peace.'

She mutters something he doesn't quite catch.

'What did you say?'

'I hear voices too,' she tells him.

His heart sinks. Even so, he has to go.

'We'll talk about it next week. In the meantime, if anything happens, call me.'

Joe makes himself leave. Before switching on the ignition he turns to wave at Felicity in the window of her spare room and is surprised to find it empty. He could have sworn, for a moment there, that someone was watching him getting into his car.

So convinced is he that he waits for her to reappear. He lowers the car window so that he can hear the late birds, the distant traffic, the laughter of people at a nearby barbecue. The spare room window remains dark and empty.

He gets out of the car and walks away from it. 'Anyone there?' he says, in a low voice.

Silence answers him. Silence, not emptiness.

He is some distance from the park bench where he first met Ezzy Sheeran but his eyes are drawn to it all the same.

'That won't be possible, I'm afraid,' he'd said to her, when she'd asked about coming home with him, and he'd walked swiftly away. She hadn't followed him that time, and he hadn't looked back, but the following Tuesday she'd been waiting in line for him at St Martin's.

In a safer environment, surrounded by other people, he'd felt comfortable enough to spend time with her. He'd liked her bright mind, her independence, even her sense of fun. He'd viewed her interest in him as nothing more than healthy empathy – so often the homeless were entirely self-absorbed – and he'd been convinced he could help her.

His mother talked about boundaries, unfairly in Joe's view. He'd tried so hard to draw them with Ezzy but she'd not so much sidestepped as bulldozed her way straight through them. Over the following weeks and months she'd become his shadow, to the point where he'd forgotten what it felt like to be alone.

He is getting that same feeling now.

More troubled than ever, Joe gets back into his car. He has made Felicity as secure as possible. He can do no more for tonight.

He is almost back in the city when something occurs to him. He should have thought of it before. The third diary entry.

The others have been on at me to say something nice about Felicity . . .

Who the hell are 'the others'?

32

Felicity

'Hello.'

Felicity's voice cuts through the quiet of the darkened room. She is lying on her bed and it is twilight outside. Her mobile phone is in her hand, pressed to her ear. Outside, someone on roller skates glides past the house.

'It's Joe,' the voice on the phone says. 'Hope this isn't a bad time.'

'No, it's fine.' She makes no attempt to move as she flicks through pages in her recent memory. It is Saturday – she hopes to God it is still Saturday – and she remembers shopping and doing chores in the morning. She remembers going for a run at lunchtime, a little earlier than usual, because she had to get back to take a Skype call from South Georgia.

So, did she talk to the woman on South Georgia? Yes, she can picture her face on the computer screen, and behind her a window overlooking a huge and turbulent sea. The two of them talked about a blue lake on one of the glaciers that fills over the course of the summer and then suddenly, and without warning, drains until it leaves behind an empty basin on the ice. Yes, she can remember the Skype interview very clearly, but after that . . .?

Joe is speaking and Felicity forces herself to listen. 'So, the results of the CAT scan are back and the good news is there's no sign of anything out of the ordinary.'

'I don't have cancer,' she says. 'What about dementia?'

'Nothing. And no sign of stroke damage. Your brain is perfectly healthy.'

'Right.'

She hears an exhalation that could be a soft laugh. 'You sound disappointed.'

'Of course not.'

Maybe she is.

'We should get blood results in the next week or so,' Joe is saying. 'In the meantime, I wonder if we can increase the number of sessions? After what happened on Tuesday I feel as though we have a lot to explore.' A short pause. 'If there's a problem with payment, most companies have insurance schemes that can cover it.'

'There's no problem.' She isn't short of money and she really doesn't want her company to know she is still in therapy. Once they know, the people on South Georgia will inevitably find out.

'I've got a slot on Fridays at six,' Joe says. 'What do you think?'

'I can make that.' She gets up off the bed.

'And I'd quite like to try hypnotherapy,' Joe says. 'Would you be OK with that?'

A voice inside her screams, *No, no, don't even think about it!*

Out loud she says, 'You want to hypnotise me?'

'It's a common therapeutic technique,' Joe says. 'It's really just about putting you in a very relaxed state so that you can allow some hidden memories to come to the surface. You'd be conscious and aware at all times.'

No, she cannot be hypnotised.

'Can I give it some thought?' she says.

'Of course. How've you been since I saw you? Anything else happen I should know about?'

Felicity finds that she can remember the Skype call ending.

Susan Brindle, her potential new boss, has offered her the job but stressed the need to think carefully. 'South Georgia is a very long way from just about anywhere,' she'd said. 'And two years is a long time with only a dozen other people for company.'

Still holding the phone to her ear, Felicity goes into her office and activates her laptop. The Skype call finished at two forty-five in the afternoon. It is now after nine and the light outside is starting to fade. Six hours have gone.

Outside the skater is back, performing some sort of manoeuvre directly in front of her door. There is something about the sound that is annoying, even aggressive.

'Felicity?' Joe sounds anxious.

'No,' she says. 'Nothing else. Situation normal.'

The situation is very far from normal. She has lost six hours out of her day.

'No more lost time?' Joe says.

She steps to the window to draw the curtains.

'Felicity?' Joe prompts.

'Oh,' she says. 'I got the job in South Georgia. They've given me a couple of weeks to let them know.'

She is on the point of closing the curtains when she sees the vacant space where she usually parks her car. Her car is missing.

'Congratulations.' He sounds more concerned than pleased.

'Joe, I should go, I'm expecting a Skype call,' she lies. 'Thanks for letting me know about the scan. I'll see you Tuesday.'

She puts the phone down before he can ask her anything else and runs downstairs. There is no sign of her car keys on the hall table and she is about to check the kitchen when she spots a small padded envelope that must have arrived in the post while she was out running.

She has an idea of what's inside, and finds her hands trembling as she rips the seal apart. A pair of small keys fall out, an identical pair fastened together with a thin steel loop. They are the ones she found online and ordered two days ago. She realises, as she balances their flimsy weight in her hand, that she has been hoping they wouldn't arrive.

Pushing thoughts of her missing car to one side, she finds her torch and enters the loft. She crawls along the loft floor thinking, perhaps the keys won't work. She searched the exact make of the trunk and even the model number, but there is no guarantee.

They work. The locks spring apart and she has no choice but to open the lid.

The scent of violets steals out before she can properly see inside, surprising her. Sweetness is not what she expected. She shines the torch inside and sees a large, decorative box covered in roses and with plaited silk handles. Wondering if this is some weird version of Russian dolls, that she might have to open box after box, she pulls the lid up.

And the surprises keep on coming.

She is looking at a wedding dress, carefully folded, the lace bodice lying neatly upon the heavy folds of the skirt. A glimpse of the hemline shows her that it is slightly soiled, and there are flakes of dried confetti scattered around the box.

Opposite the scalloped neckline is a pair of white satin shoes, the soles and thin heel stained green. Size seven. As though moving in a dream, Felicity removes the slipper from her left foot. The satin shoe fits her perfectly. She pulls it off, as though it has burned her foot, and tucks it back into the box.

There is more to discover in the trunk. She spots a leather-bound photograph album that she doesn't quite dare look at yet, and a small jewellery box. This feels safer so she opens it to find two items inside.

The first is a wedding ring, simple, gold, inscribed on the inside. *F & F, for now, for always.* She tries it on the third finger of her hand and feels sick. It slips on as though it knows where it belongs. She rips it off so fast that she hurts her knuckle. The other item in the box is almost worse. A silver lily on a chain that she recognises instantly. It is the emblem of her Cambridge college, and this is a piece of jewellery that is only available to members of the college. Several of her friends were given it on graduation by parents or boyfriends, but she'd had neither and hadn't wanted to buy her own. The chain is fastened around a folded note. She opens it to read: *From Freddie, for now, for always.*

She has no idea who Freddie is, and at the same time, knows the name means something to her. No, it means everything.

She is going to have to look at the album. She lifts it and spots what might be a reprieve. Beneath is what looks like a single photograph, framed and wrapped in a protective black cotton. A single photograph feels easier than an album, and so she unfolds the cotton and shines the torch.

It is a stylish, silver-framed, black and white wedding photograph, taken from the back of the church. The veiled bride and a tall, fair-haired groom are small figures in the distance at the chancel rail. Both are looking back over their shoulders, a little startled, towards the focus of the photograph, a tiny blonde bridesmaid, hardly two years old, who is running for the church door with a look of joy on her face.

It is a charming picture, and yet Felicity can find no pleasure in it. She shines the torch on the face of the groom and knows, with an instinct she can't explain, that this man is Freddie. She knows that she has loved him with all her heart and that he has caused her unbearable pain. She knows, from the trembling in her hands, and the sickness in her stomach that she doesn't feel will ever leave her now, that she is terrified of him.

She almost doesn't need to look at the bride, but she shines the torch all the same. The woman's face is difficult to make out behind the veil, but Felicity can see a hint of blonde hair swept back into a graceful bun, the curve of the cheekbone, the full lips and arched brows. She is looking at a photograph of herself on her wedding day.

She is married. To Freddie. And she has no memory of it at all.

33

Joe

Joe, Jake and Ellie have dinner at his mother's house, as they often do on Sunday evenings. All three of them relax around Delilah. He loves his kids, of course, and needs them in his life, but this once-a-week intensity is tough. When you live with your children, and see them every day, there is natural downtime, when you can co-exist in the same house for hours without paying each other any particular attention. On the other hand, when interaction is restricted to a few hours a week, the pressure to make those hours count becomes enormous.

After dinner, both kids pull out their iPhones and take themselves off to the lounge. Joe's suggestion that they help with the clearing away and then play catch in the garden falls on deaf ears. Including those of his mother.

'You're trying too hard.' Delilah throws him a tea towel.

'They have all week to play on their phones,' he grumbles. 'Jake's too young for an iPhone anyway. I'm surprised he's allowed it at school.'

'He isn't,' Delilah says. 'And Ellie has to keep hers in her locker. Sarah didn't want to buy them, but they kept on at her for months, claiming all their friends had them.'

'Which probably isn't true.'

Delilah bends to close the dishwasher. 'She knows that. But she feels guilty.'

'How do you know all this?'

'She talks to me. I listen.'

Joe hears the rebuke in his mother's voice and wonders whether to acknowledge it. She's right that he keeps conversation with his ex-wife to a minimum. It's too easy to slip into bitterness and blame. For the first time he realises that his relationship with his former partner is mirroring that of his parents. His mother, as far as he knows, hasn't spoken to his dad in over a decade.

From the next room, they can hear the low buzz as one of the kids watches a YouTube video.

'There's something I need to tell you,' his mother says and Joe braces himself for bad news about Sarah, even the kids, and is a little surprised when Delilah continues, 'It's about Bella Barnes.'

The murdered rough sleeper. The immediate relief Joe feels is followed quickly by the guilt that always accompanies any thoughts he has about Bella.

'What about her?' he asks.

'We did an appeal for information, especially any sightings during that last week.'

'And?'

'We got a few. Mostly not significant, but a couple that worried me.'

Joe knows that look on his mother's face. 'Spit it out, Mum.'

'She was seen, by more than one witness, hanging around your flat.'

Inside Joe, something twists. 'Seriously?' he says.

'Joe, did she ever come into your flat?'

He knows she has to ask him this. 'No.' Doesn't mean he has to like it.

'Are you sure?'

'Yes, I'm bloody sure.'

'Did you ever meet her in private?'

His mum is doing her job. 'I saw her on the street, occasionally in one of the parks, mostly at the church hall. That's it.'

'Did you know she was hanging around your flat?'

He hadn't, but he isn't entirely surprised. He'd suspected Bella had a crush on him. Coming after what happened with Ezzy, this could be bad for him.

'You may be asked to come in and say all that officially,' Delilah says.

Bella and Ezzy. Two young, vulnerable women hanging around his home, trying to make the relationship personal? One time, anyone would put down to bad luck, but twice?

'Joe, don't worry about it. We already know you knew each other. I had to ask, you know that.'

He does. Work always comes first with Delilah. They are silent for several minutes and then she says, 'So what's really bothering you?'

He picks up a pan lid and envelopes it with the towel. 'Something happened. It might be nothing, but—'

His mother stops moving. 'What? What happened?'

'Someone may have broken into the flat last Sunday. During the night.'

Instantly, he has his mother's full attention. 'When you were asleep?'

He lets his head nod.

'Was anything taken?'

'Nothing that I can see. The only sign someone had been in at all was the back-door key on the mat by the fire escape rather than in the lock.'

'Could have fallen out,' she says.

'Yeah.'

She knows him too well. 'What else?'

'A knife,' he says. 'Mine. I found it on the kitchen worktop and I know for a fact I put it away the night before. Or I'm going mad.'

'Why the fuck didn't you tell me before?'

Joe has no answer to give her.

'Please tell me you haven't washed the knife.'

'I put rubber gloves on and wrapped it in clingfilm,' he says.

'I'll have a team round tomorrow. For heaven's sake, Joe, what were you thinking? After what happened with—'

'It wasn't Ezzy Sheeran, Mum. It can't have been. One way or another, at her own hand or someone else's, she's dead.'

'We'd better bloody hope so. Get the locks changed tomorrow. And you're sleeping here tonight.'

Joe doesn't argue. He might be pushing forty but – there's no getting away from it – being with his mum makes him feel safe.

34

Felicity

Felicity does not find her car. She combs the nearby streets, checks every town-centre car park and even jumps on a bus out to the west campus to make sure it isn't at work. Her missing car, though, feels like the least of her worries. If anything, it pales into insignificance beside her missing husband.

She tries to look through the wedding album for clues but finds she can't see Freddie's smiling, handsome face without wanting to be sick. After several attempts she gives up. The photograph of the two of them at the altar, along with the dress and the jewellery is proof enough. Before locking the trunk, she searches beneath the wedding-dress box but finds nothing else. Certainly nothing to indicate when the wedding took place or how long she has been married. She finds nothing to suggest where Freddie might be now. Alive or dead, in the UK or on the opposite side of the planet.

Closer than you think, whispers a voice in her head in the early hours of Sunday morning.

Getting up soon afterwards, she brings the wedding photograph and the trinket box downstairs, locking the trunk behind her and tucking the keys at the back of a drawer in the kitchen that she rarely uses. The two retrieved items are in the bedside cabinet now, the one furthest away from where she sleeps. She has yet to bring herself to look at either again, but finds their very presence is staining her thoughts.

She wanders her house, opening cupboard doors, checking everything is in its proper place. As she does so, she knows that lurking at the back of her mind is the dangerous thought that she may not, after all, have been responsible for the disorder in her home. Remembering Joe's advice about changing the locks, she finds the number for local locksmiths and determines to contact them first thing on Monday. She tells herself that it is a sensible precaution, but the question she asked of Joe keeps coming back to haunt her.

You really think someone is coming into my house? When I'm out and when I'm asleep?

By mid-morning, she is unable to stay in the house a moment longer. She goes out running, but the church bells that fill the city on Sunday mornings make her think of weddings. The scent of flowers in the gardens she runs past remind her of a church filled with roses and lilies, but whether the memory is real or imagined, she cannot tell.

The run is a failure. It's far too hot and her heart isn't in it. Exhaustion sweeps over her after only two miles and she turns for home. Limping back across the common she catches sight of a man who looks a little like Joe, and for a moment her heart leaps. But even if it is him, how can she possibly tell him this?

Oh, by the way, I'm married. Sorry, I should have mentioned it before. My bad. No, I don't know where my husband is. I seem to have mislaid him. This won't impact upon your assessment of my mental state, will it?

This is not something she can tell Joe.

She spends the rest of Sunday numb with anxiety and indecision, unable to see any way forward. She has no idea how she can be married and not know it until now. Losing a few hours of the day is one thing; losing months, even years of her life is another altogether. The trick she's developed out of necessity, of flicking back through pages in her memory, has been no help to her with this, because no one can keep a detailed record in their head of every day of their lives. Until recently, she has never thought of keeping a diary of any kind so she cannot go back through the years and say, on this day I was not married, nor on this one, nor this.

She cannot be married, to a perfect stranger, and yet she knows with a certainty she can't explain, that Freddie is no stranger.

As the clocks strike four in the afternoon, she plucks up the courage and pulls the photograph from the cabinet. She wastes no time looking at herself but focuses all her attention on her husband. Freddie's face is faultless, handsome as a dream. He is tall and looks both strong and athletic. She cannot imagine a man more perfect, or any she would sooner choose to spend her life with. And yet merely looking at his image makes her sick with fear.

She loved Freddie once. She knows this as surely as she is afraid of him now.

By Sunday evening, she hasn't come to any decisions about her marriage. She has though, devised a plan for dealing with her car. She will report it missing on Monday morning, claiming she hasn't used it over the weekend and has only just noticed it's gone. It takes her a long time, even after that, to fall asleep.

You think there's any place on Earth he won't find you?

'Stop it. Leave me alone.'

Felicity is dreaming. She is trapped in a cramped, dark space. She is afraid, but not of her immediate surroundings. This is her hiding place. Bad things don't happen to her in here. Bad things happen when he comes to take her out of it.

The voices come at her from the darkness.

He's getting closer.

You think the South Atlantic is far enough? Idiot, you can run to the moon and he'll find you.

'Stop it.'

In her dream she can feel the cold wall against her face. She pulls the duvet up over her head, trying to shut out the voices.

Joe won't let you go. He'll never agree that you're fit enough.

Unless you sleep with him. That might work.

'Shut up. For God's sake, shut up!'

Maybe he's found you already. Have you thought of that? Maybe he's just fucking with you. Any time now, there'll be that knock on the door. Honey, I'm home.

A knocking sound wakes her, to find no difference between sleeping and waking. She is still crouched in a small dark space, huddled in a duvet, damp with sweat. Sometime in the night she has crawled into the under-stairs cupboard again. The knocking from her dream is going on, loudly, insistently, on her front door

Stiff, trembling, she opens the cupboard door and gets to her feet. Through the glass of her front door she can see the silhouette of someone on her doorstep. In her pyjamas, she creeps forward.

'Who is it?'

Her whisper gets an indignant response. 'Harold from next door. Your car's blocking the road. You can't leave it like that.'

Her car is back? How is this possible?

'Look, love, I don't want to be a pain, but if you don't move it, I'm going to have to call the police. You couldn't get an ambulance through at the moment, or a fire engine.'

'I'll move it,' she tells him. 'Give me a minute.'

She finds shoes and a coat and grabs her car keys from the hall table. When she opens the courtyard door, she hears her neighbour doing the same thing next door. He appears at her side.

'Were you drunk?' he asks her.

She can't exactly blame him. Her car bonnet is in the parking slot, the rest of it sticking out into the road at an angle. No normal person leaves a car like that.

Watched by a scowling Harold, she climbs inside. The seat is too far back. The mirror needs adjusting too. She starts the engine and reverses out, before backing the car properly into its space.

'Thank you,' she says to Harold.

As she returns to her house, the thought strikes her that not only did her car mysteriously reappear but her car keys did too. They were not on the hall table when she went to bed, she knows this for a fact.

She sinks to the cold hall floor and thinks: *This, this is what despair feels like.*

35

Felicity

Felicity spends the next two days trying, and failing, to learn more about her newfound marital status. Her phone calls to the registrar have proven fruitless, as she has nothing more than her own name to offer them. She has no idea what her married name is.

Nor can she think of anyone who might be able to help. She had few close friends at university and has lost touch with all of them since. In any event, they weren't really friends. She has never really made friends.

For what feels like the first time, she wonders why.

She has been unable even to put a timescale on her marriage. The silver lily gift would date back to their student days, making it likely she and Freddie met at Cambridge, but without an idea of his second name, or the college he attended, her old university can't help.

She makes an appointment for the locksmith to change her locks later that week and devises, for the next few days, a plan that should keep her home safe. She locks every window and tucks the keys away at the back of a kitchen drawer. She bolts her front door top and bottom and arranges a pyramid of empty cans behind the back door before she leaves, squeezing herself out through the narrowest of gaps. If she doesn't send the cans tumbling when she arrives home, she will know someone has been in before her.

Late on Monday, it occurs to her that she might be divorced, that the marriage failed, maybe in a messy and painful fashion, and that that might be the reason she has blanked it from her mind. The surge of hope is soon gone, when she acknowledges that on some level Freddie is still a presence in her life. She might have divorced him. He hasn't gone away.

As she is driving to Joe's on Tuesday evening, she makes her decision. She will tell him nothing about what she has learned over the weekend, but she will agree to the hypnosis. Something might emerge, that could give her some clue as to how to proceed. Any way forward has to be better than the state of limbo she is currently in.

36

Joe

'When you're ready, Felicity, I want you to tell me what happened last Tuesday evening. I want you to talk me through everything you did, from leaving work, to the moment you heard my call on your mobile.'

For nearly five minutes, Felicity has been in a hypnotic trance. It has taken longer than usual to get her into the deeply relaxed state necessary for hypnotherapy to work, but when Joe lifts her hand from her lap, it falls back in the manner of someone fast asleep.

'You left work at five thirty,' he prompts. 'You were planning to come to me.'

'I stopped at the garage.' Her voice is deeper pitched than usual. 'I needed petrol. And some fags.'

'Do you smoke?' he asks.

'So, shoot me.' She gives a disdainful shrug.

This is not Felicity's normal way of speaking. He wonders if she is putting on an act when she is with him, deliberately trying to seem more refined.

He asks, 'Where did you go after the petrol station?'

'Home. Got changed. Had a fag.'

'You decided not to keep our appointment?'

'Waste of bloody time. No offence.'

'None taken. Where do you smoke at home?'

'In my courtyard. The basement if the weather's bad. I only had one, though. And then I did some handwashing. I'd left one of my shirts to soak, and I checked to see if the blood had come out. I rinsed it through, hung everything up to dry and then checked my home emails.'

'How did you get blood on your shirt?'

'I'm not supposed to talk about that.'

'Why not?'

Her breathing is quickening. Behind closed eyelids, her eyes are flickering.

'That's OK, Felicity. You don't have to tell me anything you're not comfortable with. This is your time. I want you to concentrate on breathing for me.'

For several more minutes, Joe focuses on getting her back into her deep trance. As he does so, he writes on his pad: *Blood on shirt? Not supposed to talk?*

'Can you remember who your emails were from?' he asks.

'My bank, telling me my monthly statement was ready. A delivery company, about something being delivered the next day. Boring. I checked through some news sites. I read a piece about the murder of the homeless woman – I'd say the daft cow asked for it – and then I went out for some food.'

Joe thinks, were he to close his eyes, he would not believe he was still speaking to Felicity.

'You didn't have anything at home?' he asks.

She scoffs. 'Rabbit food. I wanted a burger. I walked. I was almost there when—'

She stops and her calm face takes on a troubled look.

'What happened?'

Felicity's head begins to make small twitching movements. She says, 'Someone was watching me.'

'You saw someone watching you?'

'No. They kept out of sight. But you know, don't you, when you're being watched? It's an instinct. We know when we're in danger.'

He writes *paranoia* and *delusional?*

'Do you know who was watching you?'

Her breathing is quickening again.

'So what did you do?' he asks.

'I knew I couldn't go to the burger bar, never again, because he'd obviously worked out that I go there and will be watching it, waiting for me. And I knew I couldn't go home, because he knows where I live.'

Her eyes open and her head shoots round to face Joe. 'He knows where I live. I'm not safe there. I think he can get in. I'm getting the locks changed but it might be too late.'

She is still in her trance. In spite of her frantic words, her eyes have a vague, unfocused look about them.

'Go on,' Joe says. 'Tell me what you did.'

'I knew he was following me. I just ran. And when I couldn't run any more, I carried on walking. I could feel that he was behind me, so I kept going. I think I would have walked all night. And then you rang.'

Joe notices, although she may not have, that the vague *someone* has become a very specific person. A *he*. The hypnosis has gone better than he could have hoped, and he wants more than anything to push her further on the man she believes was following her. But there is not much of the session left, and he needs to talk to her out of the trance state. Regretfully, he brings her back.

'How do you feel?' he asks.

'I'm not sure.' She looks bewildered and, also, a little ashamed.

'Do you remember everything we talked about?'

She nods her head. 'In a way, it's a relief,' she says, 'to know what I did. And I can remember more now, I think. I remember putting petrol in my car. There was a man at the next pump on his phone while he filled up, and someone else told him off.'

Her eyes drop to the flowers on the coffee table. 'I could smell them, while I was – you know – under,' she says. 'It was nice. Calming.'

The flowers, a huge bunch of tall, columned blooms, have a powerful scent. The first night after they came, Joe had put them in his bedroom. In the small room, the smell had become slightly nauseating.

'Scented stocks,' Felicity says. 'There's something very English about them.'

'From my mother,' Joe tells her, and wonders why he feels the need to point it out. 'She thinks I need cheering up.' Again, the wrong thing to say. 'I don't,' he adds hurriedly. 'She's very protective.'

'I'm sorry about our appointment,' Felicity says. 'I don't know what got into me. And, of course, I don't think they're a waste of time.'

'No apology necessary.'

They hold eye contact for several seconds, then several more, and he thinks she is on the verge of saying something. Then her eyes fall. 'We must be out of time,' she says.

'Would you like to talk about who you think was following you?' he says.

She bends to pick up her handbag but he sees the shudder all the same. 'No. I mean, that has to be nonsense,' she says. 'Who would be following me?'

There are still several minutes of the session left, but Felicity gets to her feet, pays him and leaves.

Joe is straightening his desk when he hears voices on the stairs. Felicity has bumped into his mother. He listens to Delilah panting her way up the last flight and then her heavy footsteps along the landing. She knocks and pushes the door open in one swift movement.

'Met one of your patients on the way up,' she says. 'Pretty girl. Seems nice.'

'You don't know she was one of my patients,' he replies. 'And I have nothing to say on the matter. Tea?'

She looks at her watch.

'You can have a drink if you've finished work for the day and didn't come by car.'

'Tea it is,' she grumbles.

'Heard from the lab,' she tells him, when the tea is made and they are sitting in the white armchairs. The big room in his flat doesn't get the evening sun, but the light on the rooftops of King's is almost better than the sunrise.

'Definitely prints that aren't yours on your knife,' she goes on. 'The same recent fingerprints on your fire escape, back door, window frames and throughout your flat.'

This is not good news.

'No match on the system that we can find.'

This might be good news.

'But Ezzy Sheeran's prints aren't on the system,' she says. 'She was wearing gloves when she came at you. And we found nothing on her belongings.'

'Is she still presumed dead?' Joe asks, because he knows he must.

Delilah's face is grim. 'She is. But I don't need to tell you there's some distance between presumed dead and a body in the mortuary. She was slippery as an eel, that one.'

'Can you tell anything from the prints?' he asks. 'I heard you can identify gender, age, history of drug use, that sort of thing.'

Delilah sighs. 'You're talking about technology that won't be in common use for years yet. I can request advance fingerprint screening but it costs an arm and a leg and I can't see it being approved for a break-in.'

She falls silent for a moment, thinking. 'If I can demonstrate a link between the attack on you in April and the break-in, then I might have more of a chance. It will take a while though.'

'Has Ezzy actually been seen?' Joe asks. 'Any remotely possible sightings?'

Delilah shakes her head.

'It can't be her,' he says.

'No, it's more likely to be one of the other nutters you make your living from. It could even be one of the nutters you spend most evenings of the week with and who don't even pay you for your time. Are you seeing them tonight?'

'Mum, how many times—'

Her mug lands on the table a little too fast and tea spills over the edge. 'I know,' she snaps. 'The homeless need help and there's practically none available from the state. And the mentally ill are far more likely to harm themselves than others. I know all this, Joe. You've told me till I'm sick of hearing it. And I'm sure it's all true. Until they *do* harm others. Until they harm you.'

'Nothing happened, Mum.'

'Somebody broke in here and helped themselves to one of your knives while you were sleeping. I'd call that something. I want to put a camera on the back of the building.'

'OK.'

Joe sees his mother's surprise that he has agreed so quickly. She doesn't know, because he won't tell her, that his ability to sleep for more than a few fitful hours has abandoned him since the incident.

'Nice flowers,' she says, as she picks up her mug again and wrinkles her nose. 'Powerful scent.'

'Sorry, Mum, too much on my mind. Thank you, they're lovely.'

The mug of tea makes its way back down to the table. 'What are you talking about?' Delilah says.

Joe nods down at the flowers he's just learned are called scented stocks. 'Thank you, for the flowers,' he repeats. 'I'm not sure I can make that any clearer.'

Delilah glares at the coffee table as though it has suddenly become a crime scene. In a slow, low-pitched voice she says, 'What on Earth makes you think they're from me? When have I ever sent you flowers?'

'They were waiting by the internal front door when I got home on Monday. You and your lot were here for most of the day. There was no card, so I assumed you'd left them. To cheer me up.'

Delilah's face is hard as stone. 'If I thought you needed cheering up, I'd tell you a joke. And I didn't come here on Monday. I couldn't get out of a meeting.'

Joe wonders if it is possible to feel any more of a fool.

'Are you telling me someone came into the house, while my frigging people were here, and left you flowers?' Delilah gets to her feet. 'Jesus wept, Joe.'

She leans down, as though to lift the flowers and stops herself. 'Did they come wrapped?' she says. 'Have you still got the cellophane?'

'Kitchen bin,' he tells her.

She strides from the room, pulling disposable gloves from her bag. He hears her rummaging around in the kitchen, the sound of the bin lid swinging, then she is back, with the florist's wrapping.

'They're from the flower shop on Chesterton Road.' She pulls the flowers from the vase. 'I'll go round tomorrow myself. And I want a burglar alarm installing in this place.'

'It's against the terms of the lease.'

'Bollocks to that.'

Joe sighs. 'I'll talk to the management company.'

'How did the bugger get in the building?'

'The other tenants aren't that hot on security. It's possible someone in one of the other flats buzzed them in. And if your lot were coming and going most of the day, the front door could have been left open.'

Delilah looks ready to rip the flowers into pieces. 'I can't frigging believe this. I don't know who I'm more livid with, you or the idiots I sent to check the place out.'

'Mum, they're only flowers. I'm fine.'

Delilah takes a deep breath. 'Can you stay away from the homeless for a while?'

'These people depend on me.'

'Your kids depend on you.'

Joe is astonished to see tears in her eyes. He had no idea his mother could cry.

'I depend on you,' she says.

Joe takes the flowers from his mother and pulls her into his arms. They stand together for some time. He isn't entirely sure who is comforting whom. He also knows that the entire time he is in the church hall this evening, talking to Dora, and Michael, and whoever else wanders in, his mother will be in her car, outside, watching over him.

37

Felicity

Felicity returns to work after her appointment with Joe. She has several outstanding projects to close if she is to travel to South Georgia before the summer is out, and she is more productive when the office is empty. She works until nearly ten, when it is almost completely dark outside and when she suddenly becomes aware that the lights in her large, open-plan office make her very visible to anyone outside.

You think there's any place on Earth he won't find you?

She calls down to the front desk to check security are in place, but even though her call is answered immediately, she isn't reassured. She decides to call it a night.

She locks her car doors the second she is inside, but still her heartbeat increases each time she has to stop at lights or pedestrian crossings.

He's getting closer.

Outside her house, she sits in her car for some time, watching the rear door of her property. She sees nothing to cause her alarm and so plucks up courage and leaves her car. It is a beautiful summer evening, rich with scent and bird song and she feels a moment of anger that she is too afraid to enjoy it.

There is no one in her courtyard.

She makes for the large kitchen window, intending to peer inside and see if the triangle of cans is still behind the door but stops, feet away. Someone has been here. Someone has drawn, in black paint, on the glass of her kitchen window. A simple, cartoon-style drawing. Two large upright ovals with a single black dot in each. Cartoon eyes. The paint is on the outside of the glass, which is better she supposes, than being on the inside, but the message is as plain as if it had been written in words. Someone is watching her.

38

Shane

It is the silent hour of the night and Shane is walking. He walks swiftly, because the voices are loud inside his head tonight. They remind him about every mean and shameful thing he has ever done, every dirty thought that's crossed his mind, everyone he's hurt or thought about hurting. They tell him he is useless, that he will always be useless, and that everyone he meets turns away from him like toxic waste.

He strides down Portugal Street and has to curl both hands into fists to stop himself breaking into a run, because when he runs, the panic and the rage build and the voices rise from incessant whispers to screams in his ears.

Normally, the quiet of the city calms the voices. On most nights when he walks, the gentle sleeping noises the city makes – the distant hum of traffic, the musical chimes of the church clocks, the mew of a cat – lull the voices back to sleep. Nothing is working tonight and they keep on at him, voices that have plagued him for all of his life, and others that he hasn't heard before. They tell him to cut. They tell him to stop wasting his time making ever more scars on the flesh of his lower back and make one final sweep across his throat. They tell him to cut the flesh of others. They tell him to kill.

He walks on, because the saner, better part of him knows that only the walking and the silence will keep him grounded.

He turns into New Park Street and makes for the car park where the homeless hang out. Seeing their sleeping faces can help, but tonight he fears it might not. The voices are telling him to hurt and the homeless lie so quietly and so helplessly. He passes the old woman in the green coat dozing on a bench. Beside her is a shopping trolley that probably contains everything she owns.

A sound startles him. A harsh discordant humming. An image leaps into his head: that of a giant insect. He turns, and the insect is there, coming straight at him, low-flying, huge, humanoid in shape. Shane cries out in horror. His mind has finally parted company with sanity.

The insect is a girl on roller skates. She hurtles towards him, the wheels of her skates screaming over the rough tarmac of the road. At the last moment she swerves, avoiding him, hissing in his face. He catches a glimpse of a face, young but twisted with anger, and then she is gone. She skates like a professional. The bumps and holes in the road make no difference to her. She turns a corner and vanishes from sight.

The voices, shocked into silence by the girl, start up again. They are loud, insistent. Shane pulls his knife out and lifts his sweatshirt. He reaches up and back. The blade makes contact with his skin.

A siren sounds loud through the night and in the reflections of a nearby window, he sees the blue flashing lights. The car is almost on top of him.

Shane drops the knife and flees.

39

Felicity

Felicity is being pinned, face down. She cannot see the burning end of the cigarette, but she can smell it.

'No, please don't.'

A searing pain tears into the soft flesh of her left buttock.

'No, please. I'll do anything. Just stop.'

She is turned on the bed, and then the burning is replaced by a different pain, every bit as bad and when she opens her eyes, the face above her in the darkness has handsome, clean lines and golden hair.

She starts awake in the dark of her own bedroom and feels a cold breeze on her face. Her bedroom door is open and she knows she never leaves it like that. She cannot sleep with a bedroom door open.

Switching on the light, she gets up, as a church clock somewhere strikes the quarter-hour. The chill in her house increases as she steps into the hallway, and a door slams shut. She walks towards the kitchen, even though she knows she locked and bolted the back door before she went to bed. No one can have entered her house.

She moves down the hallway in a state of calm that feels beyond despair. She pushes open the kitchen door and is not remotely surprised to see the back door is wide open.

When she has checked her house from top to bottom, even the

loft; when she has locked and bolted the doors and windows, she goes back to her bedroom and turns on every available light. She pulls off the T-shirt she sleeps in and stands naked with her back to the full-length mirror. Using a hand mirror, she angles it until she can see the cluster of burn scars around the creases where her buttocks meet the top of her thighs.

Not a dream then. A memory.

40

Joe

'It'll have to be quick, Mum. I've a patient on the way up.'

'We've made some progress,' Delilah says. 'It might be good news.'

'Always up for that,' Joe replies.

'Well, first up, I went to the Cambridge Flower Shop, where your secret admirer bought your floral tribute. Turns out she, or he, didn't buy them. A bunch was stolen from the buckets outside the shop early on Monday morning. The owner was pretty pissed off about it. I think she thought I'd nicked them myself when I walked in with them.'

'Is this the good news?' Joe asks.

'Just being thorough. So, that was a dead end. But then, last night, a patrol car pursued a white male down New Park Street. They only caught glimpses of him but he seemed to fit the description of this Shane we've been trying to track down. He got away, but he left a knife behind, and the fingerprints on it match those found in your flat.'

'And this is good news?' Joe is teasing. He knows exactly why this is good news. Fucking hell, it's good news.

'Well, all things are relative. If this guy Shane has been stalking you, we know it's not that roller-skating psycho. We can breathe more easily on that one at least.'

'We can.' Joe feels his whole body relax. He starts to laugh. The relief is overwhelming.

'But he's still the prime suspect in a murder, Joe. Really not someone you want in your flat at night. Don't suppose you can account for that?'

Joe waits for the fear to come back. It doesn't. A disturbed homeless man called Shane. Bad enough, of course. But compared to what it could have been . . .

'I get waylaid a lot,' he says. 'Some of these people are very wary of approaching me in anything like an official capacity. Maybe he just wanted to talk.'

He hears his mother let out a long, deliberate breath.

'So did Shane leave me the flowers?' he asks.

'No prints other than yours and the florist's on the cellophane wrapping, but probably. Joe, I'm not kidding. You need to watch yourself until we find him.'

'Understood. Thanks, Mum.'

Joe is smiling, as Felicity walks in through the door.

41

Felicity

This time, Felicity is determined not to be hypnotised. 'There's something I want to tell you,' she says. 'While I'm myself.'

'Whatever you want,' Joe agrees. 'What would you like to talk about?'

She takes a deep breath. She has decided and she will not back out now. 'That time on the common,' she says. 'When I ended up in hospital. It wasn't the first.'

Several seconds of silence and then, 'I'm listening.'

'I lose time,' she says.

His brows contract a little but the half-smile remains. 'Can you explain what you mean by that?'

'When it happens, it's as though I've been lifted out of my life and kept somewhere in suspended animation for hours, then dropped back. Time has moved on, and I have no memory of what I did or of what happened to me during those hours.'

'And are you usually in the same place when you come back to yourself?'

'No. It wouldn't be too bad if I was. I could tell myself I'd fallen asleep or something. I'm always somewhere different, with no idea of how I got there.'

Joe takes up his notebook. 'Felicity, I'd like you to tell me about each of these incidents. Start with the first that you can remember, please.'

'I think the first time was back in March. I was down by the Backs, in the middle of the night. I'd climbed over the wall and was on the lawn at the back of Clare College. It was as though I'd been carried there in my sleep and suddenly woke up.'

'And you have no idea how you got there?'

She shakes her head. 'I'd gone to bed, same as normal.'

'What did you do?'

'I ran home. I was frightened and freezing. It's quite a way from Clare College to where I live.'

'Did you tell anyone?'

'There was no one to tell. I assumed I'd been sleepwalking, although I'd never done it before. It was pretty scary. I started hiding my keys before I went to bed and putting obstacles by the doors so I'd wake myself up.'

'Did it work?'

'No, it happened in the daytime next.'

'Go on.'

'A week or so after that, on a Saturday, I found myself in the shopping centre with no idea how I got there.'

'And was that the last? Before the incident on the common, I mean?'

'No. On the twenty-fifth of April – I made a note of the date that time – I was suddenly in the office at two o'clock in the morning. I'd driven there and let myself in. And then, last Saturday – do you remember you phoned me in the evening? – well, it had happened then as well. I lost about six hours of the day.'

Joe finishes writing. 'Right, to make sure I've understood everything, beginning in March this year, you started experiencing episodes of what we call a fugue-like state, periods of time that slipped out of your memory. There have been six such episodes, is that right?'

'Six that I can remember.'

'And have you ever experienced anything like this before? Before March I mean?'

She cannot tell him about Freddie. Not yet at any rate. One serious mental health problem at a time. 'No, never.'

'Did anything happen in March?' Joe asks. 'Anything out of the ordinary at all?'

'I don't think so.'

'A sudden change to one's mental wellbeing can be sparked by a difficult or traumatic occurrence. Being in a car accident, even witnessing an accident.'

'I can't remember anything like that.'

She can't, but maybe she has forgotten that too. She is starting to wonder if she can rely on her own memories any more.

Joe watches her carefully as he says, 'The death of a loved one, a friend or close relative falling ill, these things can also be a trigger. Maybe a break-up of a long-term relationship?'

She shakes her head. 'Nothing like that.'

'Do you feel able to talk about the voices you hear?' he asks her.

'I thought I was dreaming at first. I still could be. Mostly they happen when I'm half asleep but a couple of times, I've been awake and I hear them clear as day. It's like someone's in the room with me, I can actually feel their presence. It happened when you were in my house.'

'Maybe it was me.'

'No, it was a woman's voice.' She stops. 'I never realised that before. That it was a woman talking to me, I mean.'

'Is it always a woman?'

'I think so.'

'A woman you know?'

She shakes her head. 'No, but a familiar voice for all that. Like someone from the television. Or maybe someone I knew years ago, if that makes any sense.'

'And when you hear her, does she sound as though she's in your head, speaking to you, or in the room?'

'The room. Not in my head. She sounds real. Am I schizophrenic?'

He smiles. 'Let's not get ahead of ourselves. It's a possible diagnosis but there's a lot that doesn't fit. What does this woman say to you?'

'She taunts me. She's trying to frighten me.'

'How does she do that exactly?'

Felicity drops her eyes. 'I can't remember exactly what she says, just that she's mean.'

He's coming, the woman in her head says. *You can't get away from him. He'll always find you.* She cannot tell Joe this without telling him who she suspects the 'he' is, and that she is not ready to do.

Joe waits for her to say more. In the end, he breaks the silence. 'So, we have three groups of symptoms. First, the random occurrence of fugue states, which last several hours. Second, the disorder in your home, and third, the voices. And all this began in mid-March. Have I missed anything?'

'No, I don't think so.'

'Right, what I'd like to do, with your permission, is to continue hypnotherapy to unlock what happened during your various fugue states. That might give us a clue to what's triggering them.'

More hypnotherapy? More opportunities for her to give too much away. Joe will be suspicious, though, if she refuses and so reluctantly, she agrees.

On Joe's doorstep, she stops to collect her thoughts. Schizophrenia sounds bad, but she thinks it might be a relief, in a way, to have a definite diagnosis. Except . . . *There's a lot that doesn't fit,* Joe said. Like Freddie. How does a real Freddie, possibly in town, fit in with her mental health problems?

She is on the point of walking back to her car when, once again, she gets the feeling that she is being watched. Her eyes flit up and down the street. Lots of people about. Lots of tourists milling around King's College opposite. So many windows on her side of the street. She is surrounded by a hundred or more hiding places and she has no idea whether this sudden fear is real, or entirely in her own twisted imagination.

42

Joe

The day of Bella Barnes' funeral dawns bright and clear and Joe is awake to see the sun come up. He pulls the dry-cleaning ticket off his suit and polishes shoes that are already gleaming. At the agreed time he collects his passengers and tries not to show surprise that they are all punctual. He lets Dora hug him and hands her into the front seat like a queen but he breathes through his mouth all the way to the crematorium on the Huntington Road. When Torquil, also with a full car, pulls up beside him, Joe sees that his friend has been less tactful. Torquil has driven over with every window open.

'Well, you can put that down.' Dora glares at the can of cheap lager in Michael's hand. 'It's not respectful.'

Michael drains the can, tossing it into a nearby waste bin. 'Fucking rozzers,' he belches. 'You never said the Old Bill was gonna be here.'

Following his eyeline, Joe sees a couple of police cars and recognises his mother's Toyota. 'Bella was murdered,' he says. 'Of course the police will be here.'

Apart from Dora, who marches to the front and puts her shopping trolley on the seat beside her, the rough sleepers slide into the back row. Joe and Torquil take their seats next to Delilah.

An old photograph of Bella has been found from somewhere.

In it, she looks even younger than Joe remembers her. Her blonde hair waves past her shoulders and her face is full and glowing with health.

'Any progress?' Torquil asks.

Delilah scowls and shakes her head.

She smells a little like the homeless, Joe realises with a jolt. She is sweating inside a suit that is too tight and that needs cleaning, and a haze of stale alcohol hovers around her.

The service begins, but the words wash over Joe. He is thinking of the Bella he knew, whose pretty young face always looked anxious, and whose spindly body shook and flinched, as though in the constant expectation of violence. He thinks of how grateful she always seemed for his attention, and how guilty he felt that he had so little to give. As he sees more than one of his mother's colleagues watching him, he wonders whether the little he gave was actually too much.

It is soon over, and the day is already warming up by the time they leave the chapel. Joe breathes in the scent of midsummer roses and wonders what burning-Bella will smell like. He wants to be well away before there is a chance of finding out.

'Dad called,' he says and sees his mother's face tense. 'Gran fell out of bed and wasn't found for a couple of hours. I'll try to get over there in the next couple of weeks.'

'Long drive on your own,' Delilah says. 'Let me know and I'll come with you. I can sit in the car.'

Joe opens her car door for her and bends to kiss her cheek. As he straightens up, he sees Dora and the others in a huddle near the covered walkway where the flowers are laid for mourners to admire. Kirk, the old soldier, beckons him over.

'What's up, guys?' he says, when he's close enough.

'I didn't see her,' Michael replies. 'No good asking me.'

'OK.' Joe looks from one face to the next.

'I not see her,' the woman from the Middle East with the young baby says.

'See who?'

'Whom,' Dora corrects.

'It could be nothing, Joe.' Even Torquil looks worried. 'It could have been one of the local kids.'

A pulse is starting to tick in Joe's temples. 'Guys, who did you see?'

Torquil sighs. 'They think they saw a girl, young woman, whatever, at the end of the drive as we were all coming out.'

Joe looks down the crematorium drive that stretches nearly a quarter of a mile towards the main road. His mother's car is about to reach the end.

'Too far away to know for sure,' Torquil says. 'It could have been anyone.'

Joe looks from one face to the next. He knows what's coming.

'A young woman in a blue hoody,' Torquil says. 'On roller skates.'

43

Felicity

'Felicity, we've had South Georgia on the phone.'

After a weekend in which each hour stretched interminably, when she had been afraid to leave her home and afraid to stay in it, Felicity arrives at work on Monday morning close to exhausted. She is conscious of a sinking feeling as she looks back at Penny, her boss. 'Is there a problem?'

She'd had no idea, until now, how much she'd been relying on the South Georgia job. One of the most remote, inhospitable places on the planet. Somewhere difficult to visit in summer, impossible in winter. In South Georgia, no one will find her, and to have it pulled away will feel like standing on the deck of the *Titanic* watching the last lifeboat row away.

'The opposite, actually,' Penny says. 'They've secured additional funding for the glacier project. And the BBC are definitely interested in the iceberg series.'

'All sounds good.'

'It is,' Penny agrees.

There's a *but* coming, thinks Felicity.

'But they need a commitment from you more or less straightaway.'

'They said I had a couple of weeks to think it over.'

Joe will never sign her off fit to take up a new job if he learns about Freddie. She's been a fool to be as confiding as she has been.

'That was before,' Penny says. 'And they want you to leave at the end of the month, first few days of August at the latest.'

The end of the month is just over two weeks away. She has five more sessions scheduled with Joe, including the extra Friday slots. Can she convince him, in that time, that she has made sufficient progress? On the other hand, what might she give away?

'Opportunity of a lifetime, Felicity,' Penny says. 'You don't need me to tell you that.'

Joe thinks she'll be in Cambridge until the end of August. She doesn't need to tell him her departure has been brought forward. And she can cancel a session, maybe two, claiming pressure of work.

'It's what we sign up for,' her boss says. 'And it's not as though you have any family ties.'

Apart from her newly found husband.

'Can I tell you tomorrow?' Felicity asks.

Penny nods. 'That should be fine.'

She wakes in darkness, with a sour taste in her mouth, a clamp-like pain in the back of her skull, and the knowledge that she is not alone in the bed. The man beside her is snoring gently. For a split second she thinks Joe, but no sooner has the thought crossed her mind than she knows it cannot be Joe. This man is tall, like Joe, but much bigger built. He seems like a massive presence in the bed. She can feel the length of his naked body pressing against hers. Her face is pressed into the back of his neck and he smells nothing like Joe.

Freddie? Can it possibly be Freddie?

The bed smells of sweat and sex and stale beer. What the actual f—?

She catches herself in time. Felicity does not swear, not even to herself. Swearing is for – others.

She cannot move without disturbing him because they are squeezed into a single bed and she is between him and the wall.

His snoring stops. He grunts, pushes back the duvet and gets up. In the dim light she can see he is as tall and broad as she had pictured him. He doesn't look back as he crosses the room in three strides and pulls open a door. An internal light flicks on and a second later she hears the sound of him urinating.

She springs out of bed, ignoring the pain in her head and her rising nausea. There is barely enough light to see clothes scattered around the floor. She recognises none of them, but sees a pair of ripped jeans and a brightly coloured top that are in her size. There is underwear too and this does look familiar.

She dresses quickly, spotting her handbag on a desk by the window. She has seen enough by now to know that she is in a student's bedroom in one of the more modern residence blocks. In the adjoining bathroom, the lavatory flushes. In the bedroom, she cannot find her shoes.

'Going somewhere?'

She jumps around to see the boy – he cannot be much more than twenty – in the doorway to the bathroom and her first thought is relief. Whatever absurd situation she has got herself into, this dark-haired boy is definitely not Freddie. She drops her eyes – he is still naked – and looks frantically for her shoes. She spots them by the door.

'Sorry,' she mutters. 'I've got to be – I have to go.'

He doesn't move.

'You married?' he says.

She shoots a startled look at his face. 'Why would you say that?'

He looks down, uncomfortable. 'I know Ben Styles,' he says. 'We're on the same course.'

She has no idea who he is talking about.

'Who's Ben Styles?'

He gives her a look that suggests disappointment, and then reaches back into the bathroom for a towel that he wraps around his waist. She is dressed by this stage and wants nothing more than to be out of the room.

'Ben is the dude you were with last week,' he tells her.

'I don't know what you're talking about.'

He presses the light switch and the sudden brightness throws her. He is a good-looking boy, she sees, but so young.

He holds up a hand as though to fend her off. 'Look, don't get any ideas about claiming lack of consent.' She sees now that he is scared too. They are like two frightened wild animals that have encountered each other in the dark.

'All my mates were in the bar tonight,' he says. 'They all saw you coming on to me. Most of them saw you with Ben last week.'

He sits down on the bed and now he looks sad rather than scared.

'I'm not judging,' he says. 'I thought we had a good time. But running off in the middle of the night like you've done something to be ashamed of?' He shakes his head. 'That's not cool.'

There is nothing else she can say to him. She grabs her bag and leaves the room. When she is outside again in the cool night air, she doesn't think. Acting entirely on instinct, she runs through the quads of Emmanuel College, out through the porters' gate and across the city towards Joe's house.

44

Joe

Joe is dreaming of Ezzy again, but although the figure pursuing him through the streets of Cambridge is wearing Ezzy's clothes, has Ezzy's green hair and is demonstrating her unique skill on roller skates, the face in the lamplight has become Bella's. The knife clenched in her hand is the same, though, and it is dripping with red liquid that he feels sure is his own blood. He runs, hot and breathless, through medieval streets but no matter how many corners he turns, the safety of his own front door eludes him.

He wakes in the early hours of Tuesday morning with a painful thudding in his chest and his skin prickling. This is not at all unusual for him and so he lies still, waiting for his heartbeat to calm and his breathing to slow. In a few seconds, the bad dream will seem more ridiculous than real. He will remind himself of all the security features his mother has installed in and around his flat and conclude, again, that he is better guarded than the crown jewels.

He waits, until he feels secure enough to turn over and try to return to sleep – and hears something. Something that makes his already frayed nerves burn. He remembers the huddle of homeless people at the crematorium, Dora's insistence that she'd seen a young woman on roller skates at the drive.

He lies still and hears it again. A creaking of iron, and then a gentle thud repeated several times. Someone is climbing up the outside fire escape.

He does not investigate straight away. He simply does not dare. Instead, he switches on the bedroom light, and then the one in the hall. He knows that to turn on the kitchen light will blind him and turn him into a target at the same time and so he stands in the doorway of the still-dark room, looking for the face at the window, hoping to see the troubled young man who is known as Shane because the alternative is unthinkable.

There is no one there. He hears a clang and a scuffle from several feet below the window and he reaches it in time to see what might – only might – be a dark shadow slipping over the yard wall. He goes back to bed, telling himself that the creaking he heard was nothing more than the wind, rattling the old iron ladder.

He lies awake for a long time, listening for wind. There isn't any.

45

Felicity

Felicity stands in the street outside Joe's front door wondering what the hell she is thinking. She cannot ring the bell at this hour. Even if it weren't completely inappropriate and, let's face it, a bit mental, it would effectively scupper her chances of convincing him that she is emotionally sound.

Oh, hi Joe, sorry to disturb you, but I've just learned that I have a habit of picking up young men in bars for casual sex, only to forget about the encounters entirely afterwards. I'm probably riddled with venereal disease and pregnant. Oh, and there's the small matter of my husband. It won't be a problem for you to sign me fit to leave the country by the end of the month, will it?

She turns to head home. Joe can't help her. But before she has taken half a dozen steps, something small and metallic bounces along the road behind. She spins around in time to see the empty Coke can dance across the street and knows that it has just been kicked. A can dislodged by the wind – there is no wind – would clatter and roll a short distance. It wouldn't spring, with force, keeping its momentum until it almost reaches the opposite pavement.

The can has appeared – been kicked – from a narrow alley, one that probably leads to the back of this terraced row of houses. Someone in that alleyway has kicked it, possibly even to attract her attention. She looks around, but the street is deserted. There is plenty of soft, golden light around the front of King's College but the beautiful old buildings look empty and still.

She remembers the eyes drawn on her kitchen window. The disorder in her home. The missing car. Its unexplained reappearance.

You think there's any place on Earth he won't find you?

Still she waits, frozen with indecision and fear. Joe is close by. Asleep, but close. He will help her if she phones him or presses the bell, but she will have to explain why she is on his doorstep in the early hours of the morning.

Desperation gives Felicity courage and she steps silently back to the alleyway. She takes a deep breath before she steps out of the shelter of the corner but, once committed, she stands at the alley's entrance to face whatever is down there.

And sees a human figure, thirty yards away, wearing dark clothes and with its head covered. It looks tall, but the lights in the alley are creating odd illusions. There are several shadows spiking off from the figure like rays from a dark sun.

The figure – he or she – Felicity cannot tell – moves towards her and its shadow becomes huge, tall and broad as a giant. Felicity starts to back away. The figure keeps coming and as it does so, it raises one arm. It is holding something long and thin that gleams in the dim light. A blade.

Felicity doesn't stop running until she is home. If she is followed, she has no knowledge of it because she never looks back.

Felicity manages only a couple of hours sleep before she has to get up for work. She showers and flicks the kettle for coffee. Strong coffee. She is walking back to her bedroom to get dressed when she spots the small pieces of paper that have been pushed through her letter box sometime in the night.

They are all photographs, taken on a smart phone, and printed using an attachable printer. She catches sight of one that is face up and decides she has no desire to touch them. Using a pen from the hall table she turns them around. There are five in total and she features in all of them.

In the first, she is leaving Joe's house in the early evening. In the second, she is arriving back at her own home, in the dark, by car. The third has been taken through the kitchen window, at night, from someone in the courtyard outside and the fourth is of her standing at the window of her office on the west campus, again at night. The fifth is the worst. The fifth shows her stumbling out of Gonville and Caius College in the early hours, her make-up smudged on her face.

In a strange way, the appearance of the photographs is almost a relief. She might be losing her mind, in fact she almost certainly is, but she cannot have taken these herself. She gathers them up, and places them on the hall table, but one slides off and flutters to the floor. It lands face down, and she sees what she missed before. There is writing on the reverse of the photograph taken of her outside Joe's house. It says:

I will kill you. And I will kill him too.

At eight thirty on the morning of Tuesday 16th July, Felicity formally accepts the job in South Georgia and instructs human resources to arrange her travel documents.

46

Joe

It is golden hour in Cambridge, and the warm rays of the dying sun cast an elusive glamour over the city. The beauty of golden hour is all the more valued for being transient, because the term *hour* is used figuratively and no one knows quite how long the world will appear this perfect.

At golden hour, the Cam below Jesus Green Lock is more rainbow than river. Here we see a blue narrow boat, patterned with diamond shapes and sporting a jaunty yellow canopy. Over there is a yellow-hulled vessel, broad in the beam, its decks awash with scarlet chrysanthemums. Nestling up against its bow is a dainty little craft, bottle green, currently under siege from a family of swans.

'They can break your arm, you know,' says Joe, as a cob swan rises out of the water, wings spread, to take something from his supervisor's outstretched fingers. The swan's mate, more reticent, waits for food to be thrown. Her three cygnets are almost her size now, but still carry the dove-grey feathers of youth.

'Don't be so bloody daft,' Torquil replies.

The pen, the female swan, looks Joe's way, opens her beak and emits a guttural hiss.

'Come aboard,' invites Torquil with an evil smile.

'Call off the dogs first.' Joe will not bet the farm on a swan's ability to break human limbs, but he is pretty damn sure that they can give him a nasty peck. He waits until a handful of avian treats is thrown into the middle of the river and then leaps for it.

The cockpit of the boat is small – ridiculously small given how huge the boat's owner is – and the seats are wooden planks over lockers, but the cold box is full and Torquil has provided bread, cheese, pâté and olives. Joe sits and opens a beer. The evening is perfect; warm and safe, full of colour, food and cold beer and for several long moments, Joe wishes he had nothing more to talk about than the cricket.

'How's it going?'

Joe knows this is no general enquiry. 'Just had my seventh session with Felicity Lloyd. Another couple of weeks and she's no longer my patient.'

He acknowledges, but doesn't quite know what to do with, the wave of sadness. Not every patient can be helped. Over the years Joe has parted company with several, knowing their problems will be ongoing, and that their future is out of his hands.

'How did the hypnotherapy go?'

'It didn't. She cancelled Tuesday's session, citing a last-minute meeting at work.'

The swans are back. The male is by the rudder, looking directly at Joe.

'Today, she arrived late, very apologetic, and declined to be hypnotised. Said she was feeling much better, that she's had no more worrying incidents, and that she didn't see the point in uncovering more episodes of smoking and eating junk food.'

The cob is gone from sight and Joe has the uncomfortable feeling that it is creeping closer, tucked away beneath the hull.

'It's so bloody frustrating, Torq. She was starting to open up, about the voices, the fugue states. Now almost complete withdrawal.'

'It's not uncommon after a big leap forward. Patients get frightened of what they might uncover.'

From the water comes the sound of light splashing and Joe cannot resist looking down. A foot or so below his head, he meets the cob swan's black gaze.

'What's happening with the South Georgia job?'

'She says she's still thinking about it. And at the same time, trying to convince me it will be good for her. Quiet environment. No distractions. Challenging project.'

Torquil takes a long drink of beer. 'Seems fair.'

'You weren't there. You didn't see how shifty she got.'

'You think she's lying to you?'

'I know she is.'

Several minutes go by, and Joe is relieved to see another boat has started feeding the river birds.

His supervisor asks, 'Has she said any more about who she thinks is chasing her?'

'Nothing. She says it was always a very vague idea of a stalker, and that she now knows such a person doesn't exist. She claims everything is much clearer now, and that she's not having any more problems.'

Torquil smiles, but there is no joy behind it. 'She's trying to convince you she's cured.'

'I know.'

Joe helps himself to another beer. 'She's also changed her GP,' he says after a few more seconds. 'She said she'd never felt entirely comfortable with him and prefers the idea of a female GP. I wonder whether she's trying to muddy the trail.'

'I don't follow.'

'Felicity needs to be certified fit to take up her job in the South Atlantic. Her new GP will carry out a physical examination and certify her perfectly fit and well. Unless Felicity specifically tells her that she's been in therapy these last few weeks, the new GP won't know. She'll want Felicity's medical records transferred over, of course, but you know how long that can take. I wonder if she – Felicity, I mean now – is banking on them not arriving in time to stop her going to South Georgia.'

'Blimey, that could work.'

'I know.'

'So, Felicity is afraid that a psychiatric report from you will scupper her chances,' Torquil says.

'Her medical records, when they eventually arrive, will reference her treatment with me,' Joe says. 'And her new GP will refer to that in her report. Knowing she's had treatment, I would expect the BAS to want me to sign her off as mentally fit, wouldn't you?'

'You think she's counting on them not arriving in time, so she can get away with not mentioning that she's been in therapy for several weeks?'

'I think that's exactly what she's doing. And trying to convince me that she's co-operating and improving is her backup plan.'

'Let's say the BAS do find out and want you to certify her fit. Is that something you would be happy doing?'

'To be honest, I'm not close enough to a diagnosis to be able to say she shouldn't take up a new job. And would it be fair of me to stand in her way? She's obviously perfectly capable of fulfilling her current role.'

'This South Georgia post sounds very different to an office job in Cambridge.'

'Yeah, but I'm not sure that's for me to say.'

Torquil gives a deep sigh. 'We can't cure them all, Joe.'

'I know.'

'Still doing the Tuesday pro bono work?'

Joe inclines his head.

'You can be stretched too thin you know.'

'I'm coping.'

'Really?'

Joe opens his mouth to say that he's fine and thinks better of it. 'The break-in knocked me back,' he admits. 'I can't be in my flat without checking Ezzy Sheeran isn't in one of the cupboards or under the table. Forget sleeping. I barricade myself into my bedroom with any number of alarms and booby traps and I still can't manage more than an hour or two.'

'Still having the dreams?'

Joe doesn't need to ask which dreams. 'Not sure they'll ever stop,' he says.

'They might. If your mum and her squad find a dead body. Or apprehend a live one. Any news?'

Joe shakes his head. 'None. The girl you all saw at the crematorium – probably just coincidence.'

'And the police are convinced it was a man called Shane who entered your flat?'

'There's no doubt. Two uniforms saw him drop the knife. The prints match those in my flat. It was definitely Shane.'

'The same Shane who's the prime suspect in the murder of Bella Barnes?'

'That's the one.'

'Why would a homeless man called Shane break into your flat at night?'

'Very good question. The only thing I can think of is he knows about the work I do with the homeless and has a problem he thinks I can help with. Maybe he didn't mean any harm, he just wanted to talk to me.'

Torquil's heavy ginger eyebrows rise. 'And is this what your mother thinks?'

'My mother thinks he's on a mission to rid the city of the scourge of rough sleepers, and is targeting me because I'm known to be someone who helps them. She thinks I narrowly escaped being stabbed in my sleep. Which, to be fair, is what happened to Bella.'

'And they still haven't found him?'

'Every rough sleeper knows him, but no one knows where he comes from, where he beds down, how he can be found.' Joe sighs. 'I tell you, Torq, the man's a ghost.'

47

Felicity

The Rosemary Clinic on the ring road around Cambridge takes extremely good care of its patients. The sofas in the reception area are clean and comfortable and the coffee table has a perfect fan of lifestyle magazines. A side table is stocked with hot coffee, artisan biscuits and eight different kinds of tea, not one of them Tetley.

Felicity has been at the clinic for the past hour and a half. She has peed into a small plastic jar, had her upper arm squeezed by a blood pressure machine and her heart has been monitored. She has been weighed and measured, and an electronic machine has told her the exact proportions of bone, fat and muscle in her body. A nurse has given her a fitness test that she has passed with flying colours and now, for the last twenty minutes, she has been with the doctor. It has all gone exactly to plan.

The only tricky moment came when he questioned the number of scars on her body, but seemed satisfied by her account of missing her footing and sliding down some ice, studded with razor-sharp pieces of scree.

'South Georgia?' he says now. 'Not a place I know anything about.'

'Cold and remote,' she tells him. 'But crucially important to how we learn about the polar regions.'

He smiles, and looks interested, although she suspects he isn't really.

'Well, I can't see a problem,' he says. 'It will take a few days for the tests to come back, but I can have a report to you within a couple of weeks. Copy to your GP, of course.'

'Perfect,' she says. She has not given the name of her new GP to the clinic yet and will not do so until reminded. Every day's delay will help.

After she is done, she drives to Joe's office for her Tuesday evening appointment. The buzzer sounds to indicate the front door has been unlocked. She doesn't hear Joe's voice, but the door latch has opened, and she knows her way up. The stairs are carpeted, and she makes no sound as she climbs. At the top, the internal doors to Joe's flat, and to his consulting room, are open. As she steps into the room she can see him at the window, resting his forehead against the glass. He looks weary and terribly sad, and she knows she has intruded upon something private. For a second, she thinks about retracing her footsteps, but knows she won't get away with it.

'Hi,' she says, instead.

His reaction is instant and terrifying. He leaps around, grabs a paperweight from the desk and raises his arm as though to throw it.

'Jesus, I'm so sorry.' His arm falls to his side.

It would be hard to say which of them is the more startled. Joe is trembling. His face has turned ashen and there are beads of sweat on his forehead.

'Joe, are you OK?' Felicity ventures.

He slumps into a chair. 'I didn't hear you come up.' He can't look at her.

'I think someone else buzzed me in,' she replies. 'I'm really sorry.'

He holds up a hand to stop her apologising. 'Please,' he says. 'Sit down.'

She sits, nervously.

'A couple of months ago,' he says. 'I was attacked by a patient. A very disturbed, very sick young woman.'

She waits, knowing there is more to come.

'When you first came to see me, it was my first day back from convalescence. A lot of people thought I wasn't ready. Maybe they were right.'

He seems to be thinking for a moment and then lifts the flap of his shirt. She sees the ugly raised scar, six inches long, running diagonally across his abdomen.

'Oh my God,' she says.

Joe forces a smile, as though to soften the impact of what she is seeing. It doesn't work. 'Not so long ago, someone broke into my flat at night, while I was asleep,' he says. 'It wasn't her, but it shook me up. When you took me by surprise just now I panicked. I'm sorry, it was very unprofessional of me.'

'Please don't mention it again. But, and I'm sorry if this sounds impertinent, are you getting help?'

This time his smile looks less forced. 'I have a friend who acts as my supervisor for my own caseload and a therapist for more personal stuff. And then there's my mother, who you met last time you came. She can't resist being helpful.'

'The lady with pink hair?'

'That's the one.' Joe reaches back for his notebook. He still looks pale. 'How was your weekend?' he asks.

She has her answer all ready. She has learned that detail reassures Joe so she tells him about the film she saw on Friday evening, her early morning swim in the Jesus Green lido and the pub by the river where she had lunch on Saturday. She talks about the bike ride she took with the local cycling club on Sunday afternoon and the enormous late Sunday lunch she cooked for herself when she got home. Some of what she tells him is true. She really did swim in the lido and cycle to Bury St Edmunds on Sunday. Not with any club, of course, she has never been a joiner. As for the rest, she's picked up enough information on the internet to sound convincing.

'The rest of the time, I was reading about South Georgia,' she says. 'Did you know Ernest Shackleton is buried there?'

She can see from his wary look that he doesn't know who Shackleton is.

'Explorer in the early twentieth century,' she says. 'His ship was stranded in the Antarctic ice so he set off in a tiny boat, with a handful of crew, to cross the Weddle Sea in the middle of winter. He landed on South Georgia's west coast, the really wild bit, and then had to hike across the island to reach help at the whaling stations.'

Joe is smiling now.

'There are no roads on South Georgia.' She is pretty sure she's told him this before. 'No footpaths, not even animal trails, the mammals aren't big enough. They really were crossing virgin land.'

'You seem to be looking forward to it,' he says.

'Very much,' she agrees, and wonders how long she can keep the conversation on South Georgia up. 'It's a unique opportunity.'

He nods, and she can't help feeling he knows exactly what she is doing. 'I haven't heard from your new GP yet,' he says.

'Really? I was told my records would have been sent over by now. I'll chase them up tomorrow.'

Again, a look that lasts a second too long.

'What would you like to talk about today?'

He has never given her the choice before. 'Under hypnosis or normally?' she asks.

'Up to you.'

She wonders if this is a trap.

'I'm curious as to why, in all the time we've been meeting, you've never wanted to talk about your personal life.'

Felicity can feel her body stiffening in the chair and tells herself not to let it show, not to move an inch on the outside. She makes herself keep smiling.

'I've been focusing on my problems,' she says. 'My private life isn't a problem.'

'Have you ever been married?'

Where is this coming from? Can he possibly suspect something?

'Why do you ask?' she says.

'Standard procedure,' Joe tells her. 'We'd have got into it before now but your issues seemed all encompassing.'

'I'm not sure my personal life is relevant.' She knows how defensive she sounds.

'How can your personal life not be relevant to your mental wellbeing?'

She has no answer to give him.

Joe asks, 'When was your last long-term relationship?'

She doesn't know. 'A while,' she says. 'I've been concentrating on work. I'm posted abroad a lot. My lifestyle isn't conducive to relationships.'

'We all need someone,' he says. 'When did you last have sex?'

'Excuse me?'

He holds up a hand. 'Felicity, I'm your therapist. All these questions are relevant and important.'

'I'm sorry, I don't feel comfortable talking about things that are so personal.'

'Tell me about your last relationship.'

'Stop it!'

She drops her head into her hands. Seconds go by, and then more seconds. She hears the sound of Joe getting to his feet.

'I'll give you a moment,' he says.

She hears the door close and then his footsteps on the hard-wood floor of another room. She gets up too and walks to the nearest window, wishing that it was on the ground floor and that she could simply climb out. Some way below, at street level, she can see the elaborate Gothic screen and gatehouse to King's front court. Beyond the screen, mostly hidden by the pale stonework, a pale face stares back at her. At first, she thinks it is a child, then perhaps a young-looking student. The intensity of the other woman's gaze is unnerving, and she makes no move to turn away or look elsewhere.

The sound of the door opening alerts Felicity to Joe's return and she is glad to escape the stare of the student across the street. She turns to face him as he stands in the doorway, almost as though he needs permission to return.

'Would you like to continue?' he asks.

She shakes her head. 'I'm not feeling great,' she says. 'I've had a headache for most of the day. Can we leave it at that?'

He agrees, of course, and she says goodbye. When she steps outside into King's Parade, the intense young woman is still there, still staring at her.

48

Shane

Shane wakes to find himself in a bed. This is unusual. Normally, he wakes in a shop doorway, or a bus shelter. More frequently, though, on a park bench. The other rough sleepers are nervous of him and he has learned to avoid them when they are awake. Asleep, though, that's a different matter. He likes to watch them sleeping.

Confused, he lies in the darkness trying to remember how he got here, what day (or night) it might be, and where here is. He remembers following the tow path from Victoria Bridge towards the colleges and peering under the tarpaulin covering the punts at the Magdalen Street dock. Lately, the city's street dwellers have taken to bedding down in punts, especially as some of the lazier dock hands leave the cushions out overnight.

He remembers finding the old lady in one of them, curled up with her arms around her shopping trolley and her beret pulled down over her eyes like a sleep mask. He'd watched her for a while, until her snoring quietened, and he'd thought she might be waking up. They often woke up as he watched them, as though they could sense him there.

After the dock, he walked across Jesus Green, and then to the common.

He is hot, which isn't surprising because he is still dressed. His black sweatshirt is damp with sweat and his jeans are sticking to him. He pushes back the covers and swings his feet to the hardwood floor. His shoes are by the bed. There is pain between his shoulder blades and when he reaches behind his back he can feel the burning pain of a fresh wound. He has been cutting himself again.

His hands are sore too and he can feel the stickiness of blood. This feels wrong, somehow. He doesn't normally cut himself where the marks will show. He has a flashback to broken glass, squeezing himself through a narrow window and his anxiety builds. He doesn't break windows, he doesn't leave a trail, he comes and goes like a ghost. Except now, it seems, he doesn't. Things are unravelling.

He sniffs the air and can smell a familiar mix of furniture polish, fabric conditioner and coconut shampoo. Of course, he is in Felicity's house, he has been sleeping in her spare bedroom.

Treading carefully – he knows which floorboards creak and which are silent – he crosses to the window. Her car is parked outside. He lets the curtain fall back and returns to the bed. He straightens the quilt and plumps up the pillow. It looks the same as when he got in, but he knows it will smell of the streets now and that she will know he has been here again. She always knows.

He leaves the room and heads for the stairs. Several of them creak, but he has learned to walk at the very edges. As he reaches the ground floor, he hears a church clock striking four in the morning. It will be getting light soon.

The door to Felicity's room is ajar. He pushes it slowly and it inches open.

49

Joe

Joe almost expects Felicity to cancel their Friday appointment. He sits at his desk, waiting for the phone call that will tell him he won't be seeing her again, and wonders, a little curiously, about the impending sense of loss that he feels. He tells himself that she is just a patient, and once again, that not all patients can be helped. Or even understood. The sound of the doorbell startles him, that of her voice over the intercom even more.

It will take her two minutes to climb to the second floor. He crosses to his bathroom and checks his face in the mirror. He looks pale, the creases from the corners of his eyes more pronounced than usual. She is at the top of the stairs when he steps back out onto the landing.

'Hi.' She is flushed, having taken the stairs at a run.

'Good evening,' he replies. 'Come through.'

She follows him into the consulting room and closes the door. She looks different. He'd spotted it immediately but in the better light can properly appreciate quite how much. She is wearing a dress of white lace, cut high at the neck and with sleeves to her elbows. It has an underskirt of bright fondant pink. It should be demure, and it is far from revealing, but it is tight and ends a couple of inches above her knee. Her hair is curled and she is wearing make-up.

'Are you on your way out?' he says, because to ignore such a transformation would feel dishonest.

'We had a drinks reception at work,' she says. 'These heels are killing me.'

He looks down at her high-heeled pink shoes and sees, as he is intended to, that she is barelegged, that her skin is a pale apricot colour and that her ankles are very slim.

'I'm so sorry about Tuesday,' she says.

'Have a seat,' he tells her. 'And please don't be sorry. You became distressed and you let me know about it. That was absolutely the right thing to do.'

She smiles, letting him see her white, even teeth, and sits, crossing her legs. She has great legs. And, just like that, he knows he is being played.

He comes out from behind the desk and walks to his armchair. Pulling it back a few inches he sits.

She does not wait for him to ask her any questions. 'The truth is,' she says, 'I've never had a long-term relationship. I was embarrassed to tell you that.'

'Why would that be embarrassing?'

She half shrugs. 'Because it's weird. I'm twenty-eight. Most women my age are married with babies or planning their weddings.'

'I'm not sure that's true. Lots of young women put their careers first until they're well into their thirties.'

She looks down, then peers back up at him. 'It's kind of you to say so. But I feel weird.'

Conscious of feeling stiff and uncomfortable, Joe tries to relax a little in the armchair. 'Why do you think you've never had a relationship?'

She answers quickly. 'I think it's partly circumstantial. I work overseas a lot, and it's difficult to put down roots when you're never in one country for more than a couple of months. But also, on some level, I think I'm afraid of intimacy. I lost my parents very young. I didn't have the normal opportunities to bond at an early age.'

This is starting to feel like a rehearsed speech.

'Do you remember your parents?' he asks.

'Not really. I remember my grandmother. She didn't die until I was thirteen.'

'Were you close to her?'

She makes a thinking face. 'I'm not sure I'd say close. She took good care of me. But she was quite elderly and also, I think, a bit detached. In any case, it's not the same, is it? Not the same as having an actual mum and dad.'

Joe thinks about his own relationship with his mother, how at times it seems too close, almost claustrophobic.

'Did she talk to you about your parents?' he asks.

'Never.' Felicity frowns. 'I'm not sure I realised that before. That she never mentioned them. I don't even have any photographs.'

'What happened to them?'

For a second, Felicity's face becomes entirely vacant, then she looks bewildered. 'I don't think she told me that either. I've always assumed it was a car accident but I can't actually remember her telling me so.'

He waits, to see if she has more to say. She doesn't. He writes, *Parents. What happened?*

'Do you think your difficulty making connections with people is what draws you to extreme environments?' he asks. 'On glaciers there can't be many people to worry about.'

'That's true. Maybe my career choice does spring from being uncomfortable around people.' She matches his smile. 'Mind you, it's never going to get any better if I keep jetting off to the other side of the planet.'

'Are you having second thoughts about South Georgia?'

'No, I still want to do that. It will be good for me. I think now that these problems I've been having, the memory lapses, the confusion, have been my subconscious trying to tell me something's wrong. South Georgia will give me some breathing space. Some time to think about what I really want. I feel I'm really on the way to getting better. You've helped me so much.'

She smiles again. It becomes a little fixed when she sees that he doesn't return it.

'Why do you think refusing to admit the truth about commitment issues has manifested as a belief that someone is stalking you?'

Her smile fades. 'What do you mean?'

'Under hypnosis, you talked about someone watching you. Someone you called "he".'

She takes her time. 'But I never actually saw anyone, did I? It was just a vague uncomfortable feeling. Maybe it isn't a stalker so much as an unwanted presence in my life.'

Joe wonders how much time she has spent planning this.

'Are you afraid of men?' he asks.

She answers a little too quickly. 'No, of course not.'

'What are you hoping to get out of the session today, Felicity?'

'Well, I thought I'd thank you, for your time. And say that you've helped a lot and that I'm grateful. And I suppose, I wanted to say goodbye.'

He glances at the clock. They are barely halfway through their allotted time. 'You want this to be our last session?' he asks.

Maybe it is a good thing, that this is the last he sees of her.

'Well, we agreed to six, not including the first time we met, and then we added Friday appointments as well. We've covered a lot of ground in that time.'

'Do you think we've got to the bottom of your problems?'

That bright smile is back. 'I honestly do. I've had no more episodes since we started hypnotherapy. I'm sleeping well, I'm doing well at work, looking forward to the new job.'

He says nothing, waiting for her to fill the gap.

'I'm cured,' she says cheerily. 'Well done.'

50

Felicity

Felicity breathes a sigh of relief when she leaves Joe's office. It's done, she's made it through therapy. A few more days and she will be gone. Safe.

Her car is in the Grand Arcade car park but an order she placed last week at Heffers is waiting for collection and the detour won't take long.

The bookshop is busy and she has to stand in a queue at the enquiry desk waiting her turn. She is almost at the front, one more person to go, when she gets a sense of someone standing too close behind her. She looks back, but the Japanese tourists to her rear are keeping a polite distance. As she returns their smiles, she hears a buzzing sound, low and insistent, below the hum of conversation in the shop. She is suddenly breathing heavily.

The noise she can hear is internalised, a humming in her ears, her own body telling her that something is wrong. The damn woman at the front of the queue cannot remember the title of the book she is looking for, nor its author. Her attempts to describe the plot, and the blue and yellow cover, are met with patience by the server but Felicity has to fight back the urge to yell at them both.

Heffers is a huge bookshop, over several floors, but the walls seem to be closing in. She is getting hotter, in spite of the air conditioning, and the rattle of voices around her is becoming ever more shrill. She is scanning faces, but no one will keep still, and there is a heat boring down onto the top of her head. She can feel herself fading, slipping back into herself, as though she might faint. She looks up and sees him.

Freddie is on the gallery that runs around the first floor. He leans on the rail and watches her. When their eyes meet, he does not move. He does not try to hide, but neither does he acknowledge her presence in any way. He is waiting to see what she will do.

There is only one thing she can do. Run.

51

Joe

When most of the pubs are calling last orders, Joe leaves his flat. He checks his mobile phone has a full battery and in his pockets he carries a high-pitched rape alarm and a can of mace. Ashamed of his cowardice, he knows that without a few safeguards he won't get through the night. His rucksack is filled with sandwiches, cakes and tubs of fruit, all donated by the city's sandwich bars, all slightly past their sell-by dates.

He tells himself that the sadness he has been feeling all evening is nothing more than an attack of the glums, a period when he feels down for no apparent reason. He tells himself that it is nothing to do with Felicity's imminent departure and that it will pass.

He starts in the parks. There is a small collection of tents and awnings by the bowling green on Christ's Pieces and he calls out a greeting as he approaches. They all know who he is. He stays a while with the dark-eyed mother and baby and the sixteen-year-old Scottish boy whom she seems to have adopted.

'I'm sorry,' Joe says, when the boy comments upon his absence over the last few weeks. 'I had some personal problems I needed to sort out.'

'It's not about the stuff,' the boy says, looking down at the sandwich wrappers. 'It's – you know – someone to talk to. Knowing someone gives a shit.'

In his absence, the street people have become angry. The failure of the police to find Bella's killer has convinced them that no one cares what happens to the poor and the miserable.

'You remember that hostel I mentioned in Peterborough?' Joe says. 'They've got a space for you. They can help you find work. Even go back to school if you want.'

The boy looks back at the woman and the sleeping child. 'Nah,' he says. 'I'm needed here.'

Talking to the homeless usually makes Joe feel better about his own life. Tonight, every encounter seems to depress him more. Once he leaves the parks and hits the streets, he finds it harder to track down the people he's looking for. Their number seems to have diminished. This should feel like progress but doesn't. There is a nervousness in the city tonight, and even those people who know Joe shrink away at his coming, as though he too has become someone to fear.

In his pocket he has a pack of giant chocolate buttons for Dora, her favourite treat. She isn't by the market. He knows that she sometimes sleeps on deck of an empty boat at Jesus Green Lock but there is no sign of her there tonight.

The vague sense of unease that has dogged his footsteps since he left home assumes a more solid form as he approaches the skatepark on Jesus Green. Taking seriously the possible sighting of Ezzy at Bella's funeral, the police have been on the lookout ever since but there has been nothing further.

'Have you seen Dora?' he asks Kirk, the old soldier.

'Who?'

'Dora. In her sixties. Wears a green coat and a blue hat most days.'

'Daft old bird, pulls a trolley around? I think she's down by the pond.'

'OK, I'll try there. Thanks, Kirk, look after yourself.'

He is glad to leave the skatepark behind. Even in the darkness, the sound of skating seems to haunt the place and he can't quite push away the thought of Ezzy, small and slight but phenomenally strong, hurtling towards him with a blade in her hand.

It's a fair walk from Jesus Green to Silver Street pond, and he thinks he might call it a night soon, whether he finds Dora or not. He leaves Sidney Street to walk past Boots on Petty Cury, because she sometimes sleeps in the doorway, but she isn't there tonight. From there, he passes through one of the quieter, older parts of the city centre. As he walks down Free School Lane, the buildings keep out what little light the moon and stars throw down, and there are no streetlights. He quickens his pace, knowing how quickly a skater would speed along the smooth road surface. Telling himself that it is Shane, not Ezzy, who broke into his flat doesn't help. The dread of her follows him like an ink-black shadow.

And whilst Ezzy might be long gone, Shane haunts the city still. He has seen it in the faces of the homeless tonight. They are living in perpetual fear.

He is halfway along the narrow street now, the furthest point from potential escape and his heartbeat has been picking up for several minutes. The university buildings on his left are empty at night and the street is overlooked by dozens of small black windows, without blinds, curtains or shutters. He has no reason to believe himself in danger on this particular street, but the anxiety he has sensed tonight among the homeless is infecting him too.

Something falls at his feet. Small stones, or maybe a broken tile from a roof. He steps away from the building and looks up in time to see a shadow dart behind a chimney stack. He sets off again, faster this time. There cannot be anyone on the roof. People do not climb the roofs of Cambridge at night. The legendary night climbers are exactly that, legends. The university clamped down hard on the suicidal practice of scaling roofs and peaks at night and even the most idiotic of students doesn't risk it any more. That thing behind the chimney stack, that is watching him even now – he can see the gleam of eyes when he glances back – is a cat, not a stalker.

Still Joe moves quickly, towards the end of the street, scanning the rooftops as he goes. Once, he hears a sound like that of a foot sliding along tiles. His nerve breaks, he turns and runs. He holds his breath as he plunges into the darkness at the corner and turns into Botolph Court. Still he runs. By the time he is out of breath and must stop he is at the corner of Trumpington Street, not far from the river.

He cannot go on like this. Either he gets over this unreasonable fear that Ezzy is alive after all and back in Cambridge, or he stops his night-time patrols.

A glimmer of movement in the distance down Silver Street catches his attention. For a second there, he'd seen a figure in white running across the bridge. Still breathing heavily, he crosses the street and walks until he has passed the apex of the bridge and is heading down to the common land behind Queen's College. There, behind a clump of laurel bushes.

'Felicity!'

The white figure disappears.

She cannot be out on her own at this hour, still wearing that skimpy white dress. Joe pulls out his phone and dials her number. After four rings it goes to answer mode. He tries her home number and by the time he has reached the spot, it has rung seven times.

No sign of the figure in white. Unwilling to give up, he heads across the grass in the direction of the Backs. He can hear movement.

'Felicity?'

He walks quickly towards where he is sure now that he can hear voices and comes across them before he expected to.

'All right, mate?'

The group of youngsters who are camped on the river bank regard him with surprise. Felicity is not among them, but one of the girls is wearing a white T-shirt.

'My mistake.' Joe turns and walks back into the city.

52

Felicity

It is the smell that brings her round. Felicity tries to cough it away but it comes back, stronger than ever. She sits up, gasping, and feels a moment of crippling fear when she realises she has no idea where she is. She can see nothing beyond a brick wall inches from her face.

The air is damp and full of sound. From somewhere nearby the yellow gleam of a streetlamp fights off the darkness. In the distance she can hear a siren. Beneath her is something that feels silky and sticky at the same time. Putting her hand down she touches the smoothness of a sleeping bag. She pulls her knees up and they rustle over carrier bags.

With an effort, she gets to her feet. She is in a rough sleeper's den, between the unused rear doorway of a tall building and a refuse skip. Possessions lie scattered around her. It is urine that she can smell.

The gravel bites into her bare feet as she slides out from behind the skip. Her shoes are nowhere to be seen, neither is her hand-bag, but she is still wearing the white lace dress. She is filthy. The dress has a dark, damp stain on the front. She emerges from the alley into Downing Street and knows, from how few people she can see, that it is late.

It has happened again, except this time, instead of a great gaping hole in her life, flashbacks come thick and fast. She remembers

Freddie staring down at her from the gallery in Heffers.

She reaches the end of Downing Street. She has no idea where her car is. She has no money to pay for a cab, and what cab would pick her up in her current state? She will have to walk home, barefoot.

The flashbacks keep coming. She remembers driving her car too fast and braking hard. She remembers people outside a pub, coming over to speak to her, the concern on their faces turning into alarm. She distinctly remembers, as she ran from them, someone mentioning the police.

She remembers hiding in a doorway, hearing a siren go past. Then she was driving, heading out of the city, with no thought in her head but that she had to get away. No, she's getting confused, that was earlier. She put her shoes on the passenger seat because the heels were too high to drive in safely. She drove away from the city and yet somehow she has found herself back here.

She keeps going, leaving the city centre behind, and reaching Maids Causeway as the church clocks chime two o'clock in the morning. She is nearly home. Her car is not parked outside her house, haphazardly or otherwise. She has to climb over the fence that surrounds her courtyard.

She has never left a spare key outside the house because she has never found a hiding place she trusts. She will have no choice but to break the smallest window and squeeze through into the basement. She finds a stone garden ornament and sees the large recycling bin has been moved to block sight of the basement window. She wheels it back to where it should be and then drops to all fours in front of the tiny window.

It is already broken. Someone is inside.

She follows the intruder in. She has no choice. She has reached a place where no one can help. Her feet crunch on broken glass.

Stepping away from the shards she picks up the sharpest one that she can see. She doesn't look at the under-stairs cupboard in the basement, because she never looks at the under-stairs cupboard in the basement, but if she did, she would see that the padlock is still in place.

Conscious of treading blood through the house, she climbs to the ground floor. The bolts are drawn shut on both front and back doors. Her intruder is still inside.

He's here.

She ignores the voice. The voice isn't real. It is the man she must find. The man who spotted her in Heffers and who somehow knows where she lives.

He's known for weeks. He's been coming here for weeks.

'Stop it.'

The silence in the house seems to shift. She has been heard. The sense of another presence is so strong she can't understand why he isn't in the same room. One by one, she checks the kitchen cupboards that someone could hide in, and those that no fully grown human male could possibly squeeze into. Her cleaning materials are in the cereal and pasta cupboard but that hardly feels like the most urgent problem right now. She takes a second to wrap a towel around her right foot and then makes her way into the bathroom. She searches the bedroom, inside the wardrobe, behind the curtains, even the drawers beneath the divan bed.

She climbs the stairs, and her eyes go to the bolts that Joe fastened on the loft hatch. They are closed. He cannot be in the loft. The glass shard is cutting into her hand as she enters the spare bedroom and her palm is sticky with her own blood. She wipes it against her dress and looks down properly in the light. The stain on her bodice is blood, she is sure of it now.

There is no one crouched under her desk, or in the corner of the room between the filing cabinet and the bookshelf. There is no one beneath the spare bed. She checks her living room last but there are no hiding places in this room. Only when her heartbeat is starting to slow does she remember the under-stairs cupboard on the ground floor.

Well, this is a turn-up. How many times has he come looking for you under there?

'Stop it. It wasn't him. I made a mistake.' As she says this she feels a surge of hope. The man she saw in Heffers wasn't exactly like the man in the photographs. He looked older, for one thing, and not so handsome.

She's fooling herself. It was Freddie.

Eight, nine, ten. Coming ready or not!

'Shut up.'

She reaches the bottom of the stairs, wanting nothing more than to run out of the front door and never return. She jumps back as she opens the cupboard door, knowing he will spring at her. Nothing happens. Her duvet is curled around her pillow as she left it. Her house is empty.

She removes her dress and underwear and switches on the washing machine. The dress is torn as well as badly stained. She will never be able to wear it again. And yet, still, she feels this irresistible urge to wash it and to do so in the dark. She has turned out all the lights in her house.

She cleans the blood from the kitchen floor in the dark.

She is stepping out of the shower, towelling her hair, when the knock sounds on the front door. She dresses quickly, and knows before she opens the door that it is the police.

'Felicity Lloyd?' The male constable holds up his warrant card and after a moment's pause, the female constable with him does the same. 'May we come inside for a second?'

Felicity's heart is beating so violently she has to resist the urge to clamp hands to her chest. She turns without a word and leads the way back to her kitchen. From downstairs she can hear the rhythmic gurgles of the washing machine.

'Can you confirm that you're the registered keeper of a black Audi A3 registration number KL61 RZM?'

'Yes,' she says, 'that's my car.'

The man looks at her dressing gown, at her trembling, grazed hands and says. 'Can you tell us what happened this evening?'

'I'm not sure,' she says. 'A dog ran out in front of me. I thought there was a child chasing it, but I'm not sure about that. I swerved. I think I banged my head.'

She reaches out and takes hold of the worktop. 'I'm sorry, I don't feel too well.'

The police officers steer her to a chair and she can hear the sound of the kettle being filled but their questions don't let up.

'Where was this?'

'What time did this happen?'

'I'm sorry, it's all very confused. I parked in the Grand Arcade because I needed to pop into Heffers. That was early evening, about seven o'clock. I wasn't there long. I planned to get some fuel, so I could have been on the way out towards the ring road.'

She wonders if she has been planning this for some time. A story of an accident, and a head injury, vague enough to withstand questioning.

'Did I hurt someone?' she asks in a small voice.

'Miss Lloyd, we need you to take a Breathalyser test.' The male constable has the equipment in his hand. 'If you decline to do so, you will be placed under arrest and escorted to the station where you will be obliged to take a blood test.'

'I don't mind. You can breathalyse me.'

The test is over soon. She passes easily and that is one disaster averted.

'Why did you leave the scene of the accident, Miss Lloyd? Why didn't you phone for assistance?'

'I don't have my phone,' she says. 'My handbag is gone.'

'Someone stole your handbag?'

'I can't remember when I last saw it. Do you mind if I find some paracetamol?'

As she is reaching into the cupboard the male constable receives a phone call and steps out into the hall.

'Your handbag's been found in a waste bin on Sidney Street,' he says when he comes back. 'There's no cash in your purse and if you had a mobile phone, it's missing, but your credit cards, your car keys and work ID all seem to be there.'

'Thank you,' she says.

'Miss Lloyd, do you need medical attention?' the female constable says.

She is stiff and sore, especially her hands and feet, but the last thing she wants is to end up in hospital again.

'No, I'm fine. I just need to get to bed. Can I collect my car in the morning, or does it need to be done now?'

'Your car was causing a hazard and has been towed to the city pound,' the man tells her. 'But we're actually more concerned to find out what happened to you between the time the accident took place, which we think was around seven thirty, and now. Where have you been, Miss Lloyd?'

She shakes her head. 'I'm not sure.'

'We had a report of a young woman in some distress on Hobson Street at eleven thirty. Would that have been you?'

'Do you own a white and pink lace dress, Miss Lloyd?'

'It's in the washing machine.'

The two officers exchange a glance and then the male says to her, 'Miss Lloyd, we'd like you to accompany us to the station.'

53

Joe

Two hours after returning home from his street patrol, Joe is in as deep a sleep as he manages these days, which isn't very. The phone wakes him at the first ring. He blinks at the screen lighting up the darkness. His mother is calling him at three thirty in the morning.

'We have Felicity Lloyd in our interview suite. I thought you'd want to know.'

Joe sits up in bed, not without checking the corners of the room to make sure no one is lurking in them.

'Is she under arrest? What has she done?'

'If you're coming, we can explain when you get here.'

Delilah meets him in the car park.

'How did you know she was my patient?' Joe asks as he and Delilah head into the building. 'How did you even connect her with me? Did she ask you to call me?'

'We're detectives.' A second later, Delilah's face softens. 'I remembered meeting her on your staircase. When I saw the footage tonight I put two and two together. The car accident gave us her name.'

She takes him into the open-plan office where most of her team work. At this hour, though, most of the team are at home. A solitary detective is chatting to a couple of uniforms, a man and a woman. After introductions, they gather around a desktop computer.

'Show him,' Delilah says.

Joe watches CCTV footage of Felicity, shoeless, wearing the white and pink dress of earlier, running down Sidney Street. The time in the corner of the screen says 22.16. He sees passers-by watch in astonishment, one or two trying to speak to her, but she runs on, wild-eyed and frantic.

'Her car was abandoned on Queen's Road,' Delilah says. 'Sometime between seven and eight o'clock. No one else involved, thank God, but it took a nasty bump when it hit a lamppost. She claims she swerved to avoid a cat and banged her head. Can't remember anything else.'

'She told us a dog at first,' the female uniform says.

'Animal of indeterminate species,' Delilah clarifies.

'This is the next piece,' the detective says, and Joe watches more footage, this time of Felicity slumped against a brick wall. The time is 23.28.

'What happened to her?' He leans closer. There is a dark stain on the front of her dress. Felicity looks as though she's been stabbed.

'We had reports of a young woman running around Cambridge covered in blood,' Delilah tells him. 'Miss Lloyd has some visible cuts and grazes but nothing that would cause that.'

'If it is blood,' the detective says. 'It's really not clear.'

'She's not injured?' Joe asks.

'She declined medical assistance and doesn't seem to be,' his mother tells him. 'She certainly wouldn't be up and walking around if she'd taken a wound to her stomach that would cause that amount of blood loss.'

'Is she still wearing the dress?' Joe asks.

'No, it's in her washing machine,' the female constable says.

'And we can't get it out without a search warrant,' says Delilah. 'Which at the moment, we don't have cause for. The only thing we can possibly charge her with is leaving the scene of an accident. And as no one else was involved, I doubt that will go very far.'

'So, she's free to go? I can take her home?'

The last time Joe saw that look on his mother's face, he'd been suspended from school for smuggling beer into class.

She says, 'Against my better judgement, Joe. That woman is trouble.'

Felicity is in jogging trousers and a sweatshirt, trainers on her feet. Her face is pale and all the make-up she wore earlier has been washed away. After apologising several times, she falls silent.

'Another fugue state?' he asks, as they head out of the city centre. It will not take long to reach her house.

When she answers she sounds exhausted. 'I think so. I can't remember everything. Bits of it, not everything.'

Her remembering even parts of what she did feels like progress, but Joe doesn't say this. They stop at a red light and its bright colour jogs his memory.

'Are you hurt?' he asks, remembering the dark stain on the front of her dress.

'A few cuts and bruises. Nothing serious.'

'Do you remember your appointment with me?' he asks.

'Yes. And afterwards I walked to Heffers. I had to collect . . .'

He glances over. 'What's up?'

In a small voice she says, 'I saw Freddie.'

'Who's Freddie?'

'He's my husband.'

It should be a thunderbolt. It isn't. Somehow, Joe isn't surprised. He says nothing more and drives her home. When they reach her house, he parks the car and gets out without asking her permission to come inside. Her handbag has been returned to her and she lets them both in via the back door.

'You're married?' he says, when they are seated at her kitchen island and the kettle is coming to the boil.

She nods.

'You're waiting for details, aren't you?' she says. 'You want to know how long I've been married, and what went wrong, and where he is now and why the sight of him would send me over the top into La-La Land. And most of all, you're waiting for me to explain why I didn't tell you.'

'You're telling me when you feel ready,' Joe says. 'And that's OK. I've said this before but it's worth repeating. You don't owe me anything.'

She won't look at him.

'I couldn't tell you before,' she says. 'I only found out when I saw a wedding photograph.'

Abruptly, she leaves the kitchen, returning a minute later with a black-and-white, framed photograph. Joe glances at the handsome groom, the lovely veiled bride. Yep, she's married. He puts it, face down, on the kitchen counter. He doesn't want to look at it again.

'Are you afraid of Freddie?' he asks.

She nods. 'Always,' she says. 'I'm always afraid.'

Joe gets up, to give her a moment, and makes tea, choosing a herbal blend because whilst he badly needs caffeine he thinks she should probably avoid it. In spite of the late hour he feels excitement tingling through him like electricity. He feels on the verge of something important.

'Tell me about Freddie,' he says, when he is once again sitting opposite her.

'I can't,' she says.

'That's OK,' he says. 'You have to be ready.'

'No, I mean I can't. I can't remember anything about him. I don't remember meeting him, I don't remember our wedding day, I can't remember where we lived, whether he's ever lived here, where we went on holiday, whether we wanted children.' She gasps. 'Oh God, I could have a child somewhere and not know anything about it.'

'Felicity.' He grabs both her hands. 'Look at me. Take it easy. Deep breaths.'

He gives her time.

'Why didn't you tell me this before?' he asks. 'When you saw the photograph, why didn't you say something then?'

She is very close to tears. 'Because it makes me sound nuts and I don't want to be nuts.'

'Do you remember anything about him?'

She nods. 'I think so, but it's all so vague and jumbled up.'

'What?'

In a small voice that he can barely hear, she says, 'I remember him hurting me.'

'Felicity, you've done nothing to be ashamed of. Can you tell me more about how?'

She shakes her head. 'Not really, because they're not proper memories. They're flashes, glimpses, all jumbled up. I can't really make sense of them, but in all these flashbacks he's hurting me.'

'How? How is he hurting you?'

'He burns me. And cuts me. I have so many scars, Joe. I tell people I got them working but I know that isn't true. Also, I think he kept me prisoner. I have these horrible dreams about being locked up in the dark. And, I think I've been raped. Many times.'

With a sense of so much falling into place, even if it is a dreadful place, Joe says, 'We need to go to the police. Tomorrow, if you prefer, but the police need to hear this.'

She stares at him, wide-eyed and fearful. 'And tell them what? There's no evidence that he's doing this, just my word against his and all I can offer is some vague feelings and flashbacks. Who will take me seriously?'

'Of course they'll take you seriously.'

She raises her voice and shouts at him. 'No, they'll think I'm mad. I can't be mad, Joe, I just can't.'

Joe takes a deep breath. 'Felicity, these amnesic periods you've been experiencing could be your way of coping with extremely stressful and frightening situations. If, even on a sub-conscious level, you're afraid of Freddie, it could explain why you've been having problems.'

She blinks away tears.

'Are there any other periods of your life that you can't remember?'

'There's a gap in my late teens. A couple of years, I think, when I can't remember anything much.'

'Will you come back to therapy?' he asks her. 'Your Tuesday slots are still open.'

Her eyes fall. 'OK.' She reaches out a hand to touch his. 'Joe, will you hypnotise me?'

'Of course. We can do it on—'

'No, I mean now.'

'Here?'

'I want to find out what I did tonight. I want to know if it was really Freddie I saw. I want to find out why I'm so afraid of him.'

Lying on the sofa, her head resting on cushions, Felicity falls into a hypnotic trance very quickly and easily. Joe pulls his mobile phone out of his pocket and switches it to silent, before activating the audio record app. He knows that his mother, at least, will applaud such a safeguard. Last, he finds a small notebook and pencil and opens it to a clean—

'Hello, Joe.'

Joe stops moving. It is a second, maybe more, before he has the nerve to turn his head to look at the woman on the sofa. Felicity lies still, her eyes closed, her lips slightly parted. She is breathing deeply. He gets to his feet and feels himself shaking.

That was not Felicity's voice. That was a child. There is a child in the room. He looks behind the sofa, even behind the chair. He finds no one. And yet . . .

I hear voices.

Heart racing, wishing he hadn't made the room quite so dark, Joe makes himself sit back down.

'How are you feeling, Felicity?' he asks.

The child replies, only this time he sees quite clearly that the child's voice is coming out of Felicity's mouth. He should be relieved. Not a ghost then. And yet . . .

'I'm not Felicity, silly,' the child says.

This is not just baby talk, this is the convincing voice of a young child. Joe feels a sweat break out between his shoulder blades.

'Who are you?' he asks.

'I'm Little Bitch.' Her voice is low, crestfallen, the voice of a child deeply ashamed and unhappy.

Joe checks his phone. He needs this to be recorded. 'Who calls you that?' he asks.

'Everyone. Not Mummy though.'

'What does Mummy call you?'

The child's voice flattens, losing all inflexion, as though reciting a learned script. 'Baby. Oh God, baby. I'm so sorry, baby.'

Joe swallows. 'How old are you?' he asks.

'Three and seven months. My birthday's in February.'

Felicity's date of birth is the ninth of February, but they are only five months past her birthday. On his pad Joe writes, *patient has regressed to a specific point in time.*

'Do you know where you live?' he asks.

She recites quickly. 'Twenty-two Clockhouse Road, Salisbury.'

Joe writes down the address and asks. 'Who lives there with you?'

A shudder runs through Felicity's body. 'Mummy,' she says. 'Only Mummy. Not the bad men. The bad men not s'posed to be here.'

Her face clenches as though in pain.

'What do the bad men do?' he asks.

In response, she whimpers and pushes herself into a sitting position. Her feet scuttle back until her legs are drawn up and she can wrap her arms around them. She presses herself into the back of the sofa as though trying to escape an imaginary foe. Her eyes are open now, big and scared, but they don't seem to focus on anything.

'Fel—' he stops himself. She does not want to be called Felicity. He cannot call her Little Bitch. 'Are you frightened?' he asks.

She nods. Every second or so, her eyes flick his way but don't settle.

'Are you frightened of me?'

Her eyes open wider, as though the thought has only just occurred to her.

'I won't hurt you,' he says. 'I'm Joe, your therapist. Please don't be afraid of me.'

She looks directly at him now and he has to suppress a shudder. The face is Felicity's, the eyes are not. 'Are you my friend?' she says.

'Yes, I'm your friend. What are you frightened of?'

'They hurt me. They hurt Mummy. I hear her screaming when they put me in the cupboard. And then they come and get me and

I scream, but they hit me and Mummy says, "So sorry, baby"'

'Where are you now?'

'In the cupboard.' Felicity's eyes are wide open, staring around the room, but Joe doesn't think she can see him. 'In the cupboard under the stairs. It's where they put me. They're coming now. I can hear them on the stairs. Eight, nine, ten, coming ready or not. No, no, Mummy, don't let them, please, make them stop.'

Felicity starts screaming. Moving fast, Joe leaves his chair and kneels by the sofa. He wraps his arms around her, holding her close. 'Felicity, I want you to come back out of your trance. You're perfectly safe and nothing can hurt you now.'

She fights him, but weakly, like a child.

'Come back, Felicity, it's over now.'

'He's opening the door. He's opening the door. No, no, no, Daddy, don't give me to the bad men.'

'Felicity, you're safe. You're in your house, with me, Joe, come back now.'

For several long seconds, as she continues to sob and shrink away from him, he thinks she will never come back, that he has sent her over the edge. Then, slowly, her sobbing subsides and stops. She slumps against him and he holds her for long moments. Outside, a milk truck trundles along the road.

'Are you back?' he says. 'Are you Felicity again?'

She eases herself away from him and he resumes his seat. She wipes a hand over her wet face.

'I remember what I just told you,' she says. 'But I don't remember any of it happening. It's as though I told you a story, something I made up.'

'Do you think you made it up?'

She shakes her head. 'I know it's true,' she says. 'Come with me.'

She gets to her feet and leads him out of the room. Back on

the ground floor, she pulls open the door to the under-stairs cupboard, the twin of the one she keeps padlocked in the basement, and stands back to let him see inside. He sees the pillow and the duvet. And a small pink teddy bear, shiny with age.

'Sometimes I wake in the night and I'm terrified,' she says to him. 'For no reason I can think of. When that happens, I come in here. I have to. It's the only way I can keep from going mad.'

54

Felicity

Felicity sleeps late. When she wakes, she feels like a premature chick, pulled too soon from its shell. The morning light seems to burn her skin as she makes coffee. The grazes on her hands have already scabbed over. In a few days, they'll be gone, she has always healed quickly. The wounds in her head, though? They are another matter entirely. Her head feels like a country she has never visited.

She knows, beyond any doubt, that everything she told Joe last night was true. Something dreadful happened to her once, to her and to her mother. For what feels like the first time, she wonders what really happened to her parents, and why she has no memories of them. Why her grandmother told her no stories, gave her no photographs.

And the warning voices in her head have been proven right after all. Her fears of a stalker, again revealed by Joe's hypnotherapy skills, are entirely justified. Freddie is not only real – she knew that of course, she knew it the second she saw the wedding photograph – is not only real but here, in Cambridge. He could knock on her door at any moment.

One problem at a time. She drinks coffee and orange juice and then goes down to her basement. She will have to call a glazier today to get the window fixed. First though, she can make it more secure. She has two strips of wood that she fastens across the empty frame, hammering them corner to corner with carpet tacks.

Window sorted, she empties the white dress and underwear from her washing machine. The stain on the front of her dress has faded to a dull brown but will never come out. She finds a plastic carrier bag and puts all three damp items in it.

When she is dressed, she arranges for a garage to collect her car from the pound. She tells them she wants to sell it and asks them to call her later with an offer. She will use cabs for the rest of her time in Cambridge.

She finds a glazier and then sets off on foot and picks up a bus in town. She gets off a stop early and throws the bag containing her dress and underwear into a bin before walking the rest of the way to her office. She has only a few days left at work and must start clearing out her personal possessions. Fortunately, there aren't many.

Her desk is as tidy as usual. She never leaves it without putting everything away and locking her cabinet. This morning, though, there is a yellow Post-it note facing her chair. It is dated the previous afternoon.

Man came by asking for you at 17.15. Wouldn't give his name. Lucy says he's been in before. Asked if you still live by the common. Thought you should know. Tall, blonde, nice looking.

Suddenly, her legs lose all strength and she is forced to pull out her chair and sit down. Freddie knows where she lives.

55

Joe

Joe knows, before he puts the phone down, that he has made a mistake. He can hear the voices of his mother and his supervisor, loud in his ear, telling him to call Felicity back right now, tell her he can't meet her that evening after all, that he is more than happy to see her again as a patient, if she makes an appointment in the usual way, but that dinner is inappropriate.

He goes into his bedroom to decide what to wear.

When he arrives at the restaurant by the river – her choice – she is already there and again her appearance surprises him. The cropped jeans she is wearing are spray tight and her vest top clings to her torso. She's brought a jacket, but for now it is hanging on the back of her chair. She's wearing make-up again, a lot of it, and brightly coloured costume jewellery. Her hair is pushed back from her face by a pair of huge designer sunglasses that sit on her head like a crown.

She's a very sick woman, he reminds himself. She needs a doctor, not a boyfriend. Oh, and she's married.

On the table is a bottle of Peroni and a bottle of pinot gris with two glasses. Judging by the level of wine in the bottle, she is on her second glass.

Seeing him she gets up and in high-heeled wedge sandals is almost his height. She leans in to kiss him on one cheek, to take hold of him lightly on his hip and upper arm, and he stiffens, wondering who might see them, even as her scent is stealing inside his head like a whispered proposition.

'How did you know I drink Peroni?' He takes his seat, still conscious of her touch on his hip, his arm, his cheek.

She pours the beer for him. 'Bottles in your recycling bin.'

He keeps his recycling bin in his kitchen, a room that Felicity has never seen.

'You put your rubbish out on Tuesday evening,' she says, correctly interpreting the puzzled look on his face. 'The day I have my appointments.'

That makes sense. Even so, he doesn't pick up his beer.

'Don't tell me you're driving.' She pouts. 'You live minutes away.'

'True enough.' Joe clinks glasses, sips his lager, and pushes his chair an inch back from the table.

'How are you feeling?' he asks.

She waves a hand as though to dismiss the subject. 'Fine,' she says. 'Never better.'

'Are you ready to order?' A waiter has appeared at their side.

'I quite fancy the rib eye,' Felicity says. 'Can you do a peppercorn sauce?'

'How would you like that cooked?' the waiter is scribbling notes in his book. Felicity catches Joe's eye and her cheeks turn pink.

'Kidding.' She grabs the menu, opening it again, flicking quickly through the pages. Her face is glowing. 'I'll have the gnocchi with field mushrooms.'

Joe orders a burger topped with crispy bacon and doesn't miss the flicker of annoyance on Felicity's face.

'Not that it isn't nice to see you,' he says, as the waiter is walking away, 'but we do have an appointment on Tuesday.'

'So why are you dressed for a date?' she rejoins.

He doesn't respond but is annoyed with himself for sending the wrong signals. Jeans and an old sweatshirt would have worked far better.

'That's what I wanted to talk to you about,' she says. 'I'm not coming back to therapy.'

He waits a second before replying. 'You're not?'

She shakes her head. 'I know what you're going to say. That was some serious shit I came out with last night, and I'm not denying that, but it's less than a month before I leave Cambridge and even you can't sort me out in that time.'

Again, Joe says nothing. He waits for her to fill the silence and doesn't have to wait long. She leans forward and lowers her voice, forcing him to move closer too.

'If I go back into therapy, it'll be like opening Pandora's box,' she tells him. 'Last night I found out that I was probably abused as a child, and that my father could have been part of that. Fuck knows what else I have in my closet just waiting for me to come digging.'

Still he doesn't respond, but he registers the uncharacteristic profanity.

'And I know how many metaphors I just mixed,' she says.

He allows himself a smile. 'You seem different,' he says.

'Different to what?'

'Different to how you normally are. There's an edge to you I haven't seen before.'

She reaches out and touches him lightly on the arm. 'I know how messed up I am,' she says. 'I think on some level I've known for a long time. After last night, I know there's probably a good reason for that, and weirdly, that helps. Thank you. You really have done me good.'

'Felicity, you have symptoms that I haven't even begun to properly explore, let alone diagnose. Think about what you told me last night. You can't sweep that under the carpet.'

She smiles. 'One day, maybe, I'll want to get to the bottom of it, find out what really happened when I was, what age did I say?'

'Three years and seven months,' he reminds her.

'And if I do, you're the one I'll come to. But for now, I can't do it. I can't cope with what I might find.'

The waiter arrives with cutlery and they wait for him to lay the table. As he is walking away Joe says, 'Felicity, has it occurred to you that all the problems you've been having recently, the fugue states, the memory losses at home, the voices, this sense you're being watched and followed, not to mention completely forgetting about the fact that you're married, they're all caused by hidden and traumatic memories starting to re-emerge. These symptoms won't go away. They'll get worse.'

She pushes her hair back away from her face. 'You can't know that for sure.'

'We didn't find out what happened to you last night. You said you saw your husband in town and that you ran away from him. I can't begin to count the number of questions that throws up.'

Her eyes drop.

'You nearly got into serious trouble with the police last night. They're still far from satisfied. They think you had blood on your dress. They're going to want to check it.'

She looks up then, and this time there is defiance in her eyes.

'You could have been hurt last night,' Joe says. 'You could have hurt someone else.'

Her eyes harden. In an instant, she has become a woman he would be wary of. 'I'm going to South Georgia,' she says. 'There is no one there who can hurt me. There is no one I can hurt.'

The waiter comes back with their food. He makes a big deal about offering them sauces, condiments, a twist of black pepper. At last they're alone again.

'You really think the new job is a good idea?' he asks her.

'I had a private medical examination and the results have been sent through to my employers.' She forks up some pasta and makes him wait while she eats it. 'My new GP has a copy and has seen no reason to question it. My notes haven't been sent to her yet, but even if they do arrive in the next few days, it won't be a problem. I'm no longer in therapy.'

She carries on eating. Joe has yet to pick up his knife and fork.

'I know you can cause me problems if you really put your mind to it,' she says. 'My question is, why would you?'

Confused and in need of a break, Joe allows her to change tack while they are eating, and the conversation veers away from therapy. Giving them both some breathing space, he tells her about his kids, about how Jake loves sport of all kinds and how diligent Ellie is at her lessons. He takes out his wallet and shows her photographs. He tells her what it was like growing up with a police officer mother and why he thinks his marriage went wrong.

In her turn, she tells him about the vast, white emptiness that is Antarctica, where the colours of the sky and the ocean take on a brilliance that the human brain can neither name nor describe, and about the heartbreaking beauty of the stars at night.

She is not the Felicity he has come to know and the unsettling edge is still there, floating like toxic weed beneath the surface, but she is fun and animated and there is a pleasure in her company. He wonders if perhaps this is the Felicity he would have known before her troubles began. As their coffee arrives, the streaks of gold on the horizon fade and the sky turns a deep turquoise. Joe catches a glimpse of a friendship that could have grown and become so much more, and he feels something that, were he to give way to it, could turn into a crippling sadness.

After the bill is paid he excuses himself to go to the bathroom and when he returns she is looking out towards the river, as though lost in thought.

'You ready, Felicity?' he asks her.

She doesn't respond, although he is almost close enough to touch. He takes a step closer.

'Felicity?'

Still nothing. He reaches out and touches her shoulder. She jumps like a burned cat and he steps back.

'Just me.' He holds both hands up in mock surrender, but the look on her face when she turned has unsettled him. For a second there, she really did look like someone else.

He walks her home because not to do so would feel rude and when she brushes her hand against his, twice, he does not move further from her. The scent of roses, stronger now that night has fallen, seems to follow them. It isn't far to Midsummer Common and it isn't particularly late when they arrive. The sky is still the indigo of a summer evening and they can hear shouts and laughter nearby. As they approach the row of cottages Joe has a sense of standing at a fork in the road.

'I should get back,' he says when she opens her front door.

She turns and faces him. 'I won't see you again. Ten more minutes? I want to ask you something.'

He knows that she has had all evening to ask him anything she wants, but he doesn't argue. The brandy bottle and glasses are ready on her kitchen island. He says nothing as she pours, nothing as she kicks off her shoes and climbs onto the stool facing him.

'What did you want to ask me?'

She glances down to the place on his abdomen where his scar is. 'Will you tell me what happened to you?'

'Why?'

'Because I think you're damaged,' she says. 'And yet you cope so well. I want to know how you do it.'

Since they've been inside her house, she has changed again, reverted back to the Felicity he feels more comfortable with, and this gives him enough reassurance. He lifts his glass and swirls the cognac around, brings it to his nose but still doesn't drink. He catches her watching him warily and wonders if she is playing him, again.

'There was a girl,' he says at last. 'She lived on the streets. I was never very sure how old she was, late teens at most. She looked young. She looked like someone who would always be the victim, someone easy to bully and pick on. She was tiny, and very thin. The sort of girl who wouldn't stand up to a strong breeze.'

He is drinking now. He takes a large sip, then another.

'How did you come across her?' Felicity asks.

'I think I mentioned that I work with the homeless,' he says. 'It's supposed to be therapy, but most of them either won't or can't commit to regular sessions. I'm just someone to talk to. Anyway, she approached me on the common one night and we talked. She told me about how her mother had remarried a man who was abusive. She'd left home, in fear of her life. To be honest, I don't know to this day whether that was true or not.'

Felicity lets the brandy moisten her lips and waits.

'Her name was Ezzy Sheeran,' he says. 'That part is true. Mum tracked her family down later. Her mother said she'd always been a difficult child. Her stepfather seemed like a decent bloke. As I say, who knows?'

Felicity does not take her eyes off him.

'She became fixated on me.' Joe is struggling to look at her now. 'She started turning up at the house, ringing the doorbell, expecting to be let in. She waited for me to finish my pro bono sessions at the church hall and followed me home. When I told her it had to stop, she became angry. Accused me of dumping her for another woman. It was make-believe. I'd only recently separated from my wife and I wasn't seeing anyone but she wouldn't listen to reason.'

Talking about Ezzy is always so hard. Sitting still suddenly feels impossible and he gets up. Once on his feet, he has no idea what to do so leans awkwardly against the worktop.

'She filed complaints against me with the police, claiming I'd forced her into having sex with me, which was complete non-sense.' He is no longer looking at Felicity. 'The police took her seriously, although they were fair to me for Mum's sake. Anyway, her stories didn't add up. She'd name dates when I could prove I was somewhere else. She claimed she'd been inside my flat, but she couldn't describe any of it.'

'This couldn't have helped you professionally,' Felicity says.

He shrugs. 'It happens. The profession has protocols and I'd followed them. It wasn't pleasant, either for me or for Mum, but I thought it would blow over.'

'I'm guessing it didn't.'

Leaning against the counter feels ridiculous. Joe sits down again.

'She started hanging around the family house. When I was married, we lived on that new development at Trumpington Meadows and Sarah and the kids are still there. At that point, it got serious. A woman on her own, two young kids in the house. And Ezzy lurking outside, doing stunts, trying to lure the kids out.'

'Stunts?'

'She was an exceptionally good roller-skater. Professional standard. I don't think I ever saw her walk around the city, she just used to speed around on – what's up?'

A shudder has gripped Felicity. 'Nothing,' she says. 'I must have left a window open. Go on.'

'Sarah called me one evening in April, seriously worried. Ezzy was skating up and down the drive, screaming abuse about me. I called Mum and headed round there myself.'

His glass is empty. She tops it up from the bottle.

'We had a confrontation in the street,' he says. 'I told her she had to leave my family alone, she told me I was a cheating bastard who would get what was coming to me.'

'Did your kids see this?'

'No, thank God. Sarah kept them at the back of the house. So, the police car pulled into the estate, Ezzy realised I'd shopped her and she came at me. She could move like lightning.'

Joe finds he can no longer sit down.

'I honestly didn't know what had hit me. I just remember lying on the road, hearing her wheels speeding away, and knowing I was in a whole heap of trouble.'

'Were you badly hurt?'

'I lost a lot of blood and went into shock. Luckily, the police were on hand and paramedics arrived very quickly. There was some damage to my small intestine that was fixed by surgery. Could have been worse.'

'What happened to Ezzy?'

'She vanished. A couple of weeks later, while I was still in hospital, some of her belongings were pulled out of the Cam. We assumed she'd drowned, whether accidentally or by taking her own life, we had no idea. Officially, she's missing, presumed dead.'

'But she might not be? Dead, I mean.'

'No confirmed sightings in nearly four months. She's either dead, or long gone.'

Joe's breathing has spiralled, as it always does when he thinks about Ezzy Sheeran. He feels the need for fresh air and is about to go to the back door when Felicity puts down her drink and gets down off her stool. He watches her take the three steps that will bring her close enough to touch. Slowly, as though approaching a nervous animal she reaches out and takes hold of his shirt.

'What are you doing?' His breathing is quickening again.

The buttons slip apart easily. 'Checking on your progress,' she says.

'Felicity.' He takes a step back, but she is holding on to his shirt. He can't easily get away. She opens the fabric and her eyes drop to his stomach. The scar she has revealed is ugly and obvious. Before he can stop her, she drops to her knees and presses her lips against it.

He gasps aloud.

She runs her lips along the ridge of the scar, tilting her head to reach its upper edge. He puts his hands on her shoulders to pull her back to her feet and finds there is no strength left in his arms.

'This is a really bad idea,' he says, and his voice has the undercurrent of a moan.

She stands, so that they are almost face to face. 'I am not your patient any more,' she reminds him.

He sees her lean in and knows she is about to kiss him. He doesn't give her chance. His hands grasp hold of her hair and he sees the snarl of triumph on her face. As his mouth finds hers, the dumbest thought occurs to him, and then he loses the ability to think. They kiss for long, long seconds, until he thinks that perhaps he has stopped breathing.

He breaks away and gasps for breath. She pulls his shirt from his shoulders. Her hair falls around his hands as he pulls her top over her head. He clasps her around the waist, they are staggering backwards towards the island. A glass falls to the floor and shatters. They ignore it.

A loud hammering sounds on her front door. They freeze and look at each other in shock.

'It's him,' she whimpers. 'He's here. He's found me.'

The banging sounds again. 'Open up, police!' calls a voice.

Joe bends to pick up his shirt. He pulls it on and hands Felicity her top. When they are both dressed again, a matter of only seconds, he steps to the kitchen door and looks down the hallway to the glass panel in the front door.

'It's my mother,' he says.

56

Joe

'Are you out of your mind?'

Joe closes the door of Delilah's car feeling as though he has gone back in time. He is twelve again and about to get the mother of all bollockings.

Delilah looks a mess. There are mascara smudges under her eyes and her skin is dry and grey. Her pink hair needs combing and he can see an inch of dark roots. She is wearing loose, pull-on trousers and a stained T-shirt.

'Seriously, have you lost your fucking mind?' she snaps at him. 'She is your patient.'

'Not any more.' Joe clips his seat belt and realises there are still two buttons of his shirt unfastened. He will not touch them in front of his mother. 'Seeing as how you're here, Mum, you might as well drive me home.' He glances up to the upper windows of Felicity's house. If she is watching him he can't see her.

His mother bangs both hands down on the steering wheel in temper. 'What the hell were you thinking? After Ezzy Sheeran? After Bella Barnes? Joe, you could be struck off.'

'Nothing happened.' As he speaks, he realises something major has happened. With Ezzy and Bella he, technically, stayed on the right side of professional conduct. With Felicity, he has crossed a line.

Delilah starts the engine and pulls away at speed. She drives quickly and recklessly through the emptying streets. No, he hasn't crossed a line, Felicity pulled him over it. And he let her. Remembering the random thought that sprang into his head as they kissed – *This isn't Felicity* – he realises how little he knows of her.

'Have you been following me?' he asks, when they turn into his street.

'No. But we are monitoring her. We picked her up on CCTV an hour ago and you were recognised. The team let me know as a favour.'

'And you thought you'd save me from myself?'

His anger is fading. His mother has probably done him a huge service. Had she arrived ten minutes sooner, his professional integrity might still be intact.

'She's leaving town,' he says.

'Good.'

Silence in the car.

'Soon?' Delilah says hopefully.

He shrugs. He doesn't know. Felicity has no plans to see him again. Her attempt at seduction had been entirely manipulative. Now, if he raises concerns about her mental health with her new GP, she will claim, with some truth, that the two of them have an intimate relationship. On top of the accusations he faced over the Ezzy Sheeran case, not to mention the suspicion that Bella Barnes, as well, got too close, it could end his career.

Three times now, he has allowed himself to be compromised by vulnerable and – might as well face it – attractive young women. His judgement has been seriously at fault.

Delilah pulls up outside his house and they sit in silence. Joe wishes he was twelve again, because when he was twelve there were no problems his mum couldn't fix.

'Thanks,' he says, in a small voice.

He feels her hand cover his.

'There's something wrong,' he says. 'More than her health problems. She's just admitted to being married and I think she's genuinely afraid of her husband.'

'Name?' Delilah has switched instantly to police mode.

'Frederick Lloyd, I assume. She calls him Freddie.'

Joe feels a pang of conscience as he speaks, and wonders if he is choosing to blame Freddie for Felicity's problems because it lessens his own failure to diagnose her properly.

'She told me she saw him in Heffers last night,' he continues. 'I think he's here, in the city. I think she's terrified of him for some reason she can't or won't admit to, and I think she's prepared to travel to the other side of the planet to get away from him.'

'Lots of women never report their abusive partners,' Delilah says. 'Even very smart ones.'

Joe knows this. He's met several before now.

'I'll make some enquiries,' she tells him. 'Now, get some rest. I'll wait till I see you in the window.'

He opens the passenger door and then bends low to say good night. 'When do I start looking after *you*?' he says.

57

Felicity

He's here.

Felicity starts awake to find her bedroom unusually dark. No light at all seems to be coming in from outside. She lies motionless, hot and damp between the bedsheets, her heart hammering. In the distance, she can hear a dog barking, and also the gentle roar of traffic. A subdued groan sounds from the hot-water system and music at a low volume is coming from one of the neighbouring houses. A minute goes by, and another. She tells herself that there is nothing to be afraid of.

Her skin prickles. Her beating heart will not listen to her. She eases herself up and turns her pillow. The reverse side is pleasantly cool and she pushes the duvet away from her shoulders. Her hair is damp against her neck and she finds that she is thirsty, as though she has drunk heavily. She pulls herself out of bed and switches on the light.

Nothing happens.

Bulbs blow all the time in old properties, she has been through several in recent months, a bedside lamp failing means nothing. Telling herself all this and more she steps carefully in what she thinks is the direction of the bedroom door. The room really is very dark.

The wall arrives sooner than expected. Her sense of direction has deserted her. Panic multiplies as she stumbles around, grasping for the main light switch. She finds it. Again, nothing. It doesn't work. The hall is as black as her bedroom. The tiny electronic lights that normally illuminate her house just enough for her to be able to walk around at night have vanished and from upstairs in the study she can hear the gentle beeping that tells her the laptop battery is nearly empty. She'd left it charging.

She is not going to think about the fuse box in the basement. One switch flicked and the house would lose all power. She is not going to think about the un-repaired window. This is a power cut. This is her house, not some nightmare world in which she is blind. She turns to where she thinks she will find the hall table, to where she is sure she will still find the soapstone bear, only because it doesn't hurt to be cautious.

Watch out. Watch out. Watch out.

Something springs at her from behind and she almost tumbles to the hall floor. Even as her mind screams that the threat cannot be real, a great weight is pulling her down. She staggers back and the two of them come up hard against a wall. Her scalp burns as her head is tugged backwards and metal gleams a few inches from her face. Thinking, *knife,* she twists, bucks, claws at anything she can reach.

He's got you. He's got you. Kill him now. This is your chance.

You're going to die, you're going to die.

Bitch! Bitch! Bitch!

Tear out his eyes. Pull his face apart.

Voices scream at her. Men, women, children. She has no idea which are in her head, and which are real. Some of them, she thinks, are her own. A hand wraps itself around her mouth and her hair is free. She slams her body backwards. A pained grunt sounds in her ear and she feels a second of freedom.

'Help!' She yells. 'Police!'

'Bitch, bitch, bitch. I'm going to kill you.'

She can feel breath against her face.

Fight him, come on, fight him. You've been waiting for this.

Two hands are on the knife now. Her own and another. It is tugged this way and that. It is inches from her throat. She is fighting someone with phenomenal strength. She screams again. She has neighbours on both sides. They can't hear this and do nothing.

'Shut up, bitch.'

They are speeding forward. She sees the faint outline of the front door's glass panel hurtling towards her. Her face is pressed against the glass. It is going to break. Someone is laughing. She kicks back and makes contact with bone, hears a cry of pain and then the pressure on her is released. She spins to face her assailant as the dark figure leaps on her again. Now she is on the floor. Her head bangs against the carpet of the stairs and tiny glints of light break up the darkness. Someone is kneeling on her chest and there are hands around her neck.

He's going to kill you. He was always going to kill you.

Thought you'd get away from him. You're a fool.

Die now. No one will miss you.

Something strikes the side of her head and her vision is filled with white light. She can't breathe. She grasps the hands around her throat, digs in her nails, tries to pull them away.

Someone is screaming and she doesn't think it is her. Something is banging, deafeningly loud, over and over again, and she wonders if it is her head, thudding against the stairs. She pictures the stone bear, smashing into her skull, breaking the bones like eggshell. Bang. Bang. Bang.

Everything goes away.

Her attacker becomes a uniformed police officer. He holds her wrists gently and says, 'Steady, steady, take it easy, Felicity.' Then he changes again, this time into a paramedic in a yellow vest, who puts a mask over her face.

The voices have become gentler, kinder.

'Stay with me, Felicity. Keep your eyes open.'

'You're safe now, Felicity. We've got you.'

She much prefers these voices to the last lot. One voice is most insistent that she stay with him. He repeats it over and over again, but she is so sleepy, she can't seem to keep her eyes open.

They will not let her sleep. The voices are ruthless beneath their gentle tones. They lean over her, patting the side of her face, lifting her hands, and saying her name. She can hear a siren. She has no idea how much time is passing. The lights get brighter. She is inside and surrounded by a rush of people. Still the voices sound in her ear.

Finally, when she can hear the city beginning to stir, she opens her eyes and sees that she is in a hospital room. Small and square, painted a dull matte white, she is surrounded by instruments that buzz and beep and the electronic dawn chorus has an oddly reassuring feel. She is alive, and for some time last night, she really didn't think she would be. Behind the window blinds, she has a sense of the darkness softening. It is nearly dawn, and Joe's mother is standing in the doorway of her room.

She lets the door close softly behind her. She is a large woman who, judging by the lines on her face and the puffiness of her skin, is fonder of alcohol than she should be. Her pink and blonde hair would be more suited to a teenager than a woman in her fifties and her trouser suit is a size too small. She looks nothing like Joe.

'Good morning, Miss Lloyd.' She pulls a chair away from the wall and sits beside Felicity's bed. She does not ask her how she is feeling, or whether she is up to answering a few questions. 'I'm

Detective Inspector Delilah Jones. Can you tell me when your basement window was broken?'

Detective Inspector Jones pulls a recording device from her bag and places it on the bedside cupboard. She switches it on without asking permission. 'We're thinking it wasn't last night.'

'It was Friday night.' Felicity's throat feels sore and she isn't sure until she hears words coming out of her mouth whether or not it will work. It does, but the effort hurts. 'At least, I found it on Friday night, it could have been earlier in the week and I didn't notice it. I couldn't get a glazier out before next week so I nailed some wood to the frame to make it safe.'

'Didn't work too well, did it? So, you've had two break-ins on two successive nights. Did you report the first one?'

Felicity shakes her head.

'I'm sorry, could you speak up for the tape?'

'Don't you need my permission to record me?'

'No, but you don't have to talk to me. Of course, if you refuse, I'll have to take this to the next level.'

Felicity doesn't need to ask what the next level is. The hospital, and her frail condition, will only protect her for so long.

'I didn't report the first break-in. Nothing was taken.'

'Even so, someone breaks a window to enter your house and you don't report it? Why ever not?'

'I don't know,' Felicity says. It is the truth. She doesn't know. So much of what she does she can make no sense of, even to herself.

Joe's mum is looking for something in her bag. When she straightens up, Felicity gasps. She is looking at a knife in a large plastic bag.

'Recognise this?' Joe's mum asks.

She can see faint brown specks on the blade that could be blood. 'Is it one of mine?' she asks.

'You tell me.'

'I have a set like that,' Felicity says. 'You can check easily. If there's one missing from the knife block, it's mine.'

The policewoman nods. 'We think it's yours,' she says. 'We'll need to keep it for a while.' The knife disappears back into the bag. 'What can you tell me about your assailant?'

'He was very strong,' she says. 'And fast. He kept coming at me. From every direction. I'm sorry, could you pass me some water?'

Breathing heavily, Joe's mum pours water from the jug on the bedside cabinet, spilling some of it. Felicity pushes herself up in the bed and holds out her hand.

'He?' DI Jones asks. She makes the handing over of water, the most simple of human courtesies, feel begrudged.

Swallowing hurts. 'I'm sorry?'

'You said "he". It was a male then?'

It has never occurred to Felicity that her attacker might not have been a man. She remembers the voices screaming in her ears. *Kill him, this is your chance.*

'I assumed so,' she says. 'He was very strong.'

'Can you describe him?'

'It was dark.'

'How tall?'

'He attacked me from behind. I didn't really see him.'

'Black, white, Asian?'

'It was too dark.'

'Was he masked?'

'Maybe. I'm not sure.'

'Did he speak to you? Did you hear his voice?'

Impossible to tell. She had heard so many voices.

'No. I didn't hear his voice.'

'The medical staff tell me you declined an intimate examination.'

'I wasn't raped.' There had been nothing sexual about the attack. It had been about maiming, killing, obliterating.

'There's a cut on your neck, some bruising on your head and around your neck,' DI Jones says. 'You had concussion. What do you think the motive was?'

'I don't know.'

'Do you have any enemies, Miss Lloyd?'

Does she? She feels as though she does, and yet none she can name. 'No,' she says.

'Was anyone behaving oddly when you were out last night?'

'I didn't go out last night. I was home all evening.' No sooner are the words out of her mouth than Felicity's heart starts to hammer in her chest. She tries to turn back the pages in her mind and sees them all blank. She has no memory of going out last night. And yet she has no idea what she did instead.

In the meantime, Delilah's eyes have become mean slits in her puffy face. 'You had dinner with my son at Galleria,' she says. 'You were both caught on camera on Jesus Lane. I collected him from your house myself.'

Felicity has no memory of meeting Joe. She is going to be sick. She looks around but she cannot get out of bed without unhooking herself from machines and drips.

DI Jones does not seem to notice her panic. 'My son tells me you have an estranged husband. He thinks you're afraid of him.'

Felicity gulps in air and says, 'Is he supposed to tell you that?'

The policewoman knows a threat when she hears one. She gets up from her chair. 'He also tells me you're leaving town,' she says, as she switches off the recording equipment. 'Have a good trip.'

58

Joe

Joe walks into the café expecting to meet his supervisor and sees his mother at a table by the window, tucking into smashed avocado on sourdough toast. She folds up her newspaper and lifts her bag from the other chair. For a moment, he is tempted to walk out.

'Seriously?' he says. 'This is verging on stalking.'

'Get over yourself,' Delilah snaps. 'I'll be gone in five minutes. I wanted to catch you before work. I won't get a moment to fart once I get in.'

'And people wonder why I'm a bit rough around the edges.'

Joe orders an Americano from the counter and sits down. 'What's up?' he says, although he knows this can only be about Felicity. He has spent twenty-four hours telling himself that he cannot visit her in hospital, that he can't even phone to check on her progress.

'Felicity Lloyd has discharged herself from hospital,' she begins.

Joe isn't surprised. 'Never a good idea,' he says.

'She wasn't that badly hurt.' Delilah slices into a tiny vine tomato. 'She's also contacted the station saying she doesn't want any further action taken in regard to her break-in. She thinks now that she was probably confused. She got up in the night, disorientated because all the lights were out and because she'd had a bit to drink the evening before – I guess you'd know something about

248

that – she fell down the stairs. She says she's sure now that she wasn't attacked and apologises for wasting our time.'

'Are you serious?'

Delilah drops her fork with a clang on the counter. 'Do I look like I'm playing for laughs?'

'Does it ring true to you?'

She resumes eating. 'It rings like complete bollocks. Even without two sets of fingerprints on the knife we found, and two distinct types of human blood. We've also found both sets of fingerprints in other places. One set occurs throughout the house, so probably Felicity's. The other in just a few places on the ground floor and around the basement window, so probably the intruder.'

'You say probably. You haven't checked?'

'If she's refusing to co-operate, this is going nowhere. I can't waste money getting forensics involved.'

Joe's coffee arrives. It's too hot to drink, but he warms his hands around the over-sized cup. His mother pushes her plate to one side.

'Joe, we see it all the time,' she says. 'Women will not testify against abusive husbands and partners. I feel for the lass. But I care more about you. I don't want you involved any more.'

'What if she's badly hurt next time? What if he kills her?'

His mother gives a long, drawn out sigh. She is about to re-spond when the doorbell chimes and Torquil bends his head to get in through the door.

'Delilah! How delightful.' He kisses her on both cheeks. 'Can I get anyone a top-up?'

Both Joe and his mother decline and his supervisor moves away towards the counter.

'Mum, there's something else I wanted to talk to you about,' Joe says. 'I'm worried about one of the rough sleepers.'

Delilah is gathering her things but he knows she is listening. She is always listening.

'Woman called Dora,' he goes on. 'Early sixties. White. Grey haired. Frail. Wears a blue hat and a green coat. No one's seen her for days. Not since Tuesday anyway.'

'They come and go.' Delilah is ready to leave now. 'You said yourself they're nervous about this Shane bloke, who must rise from a coffin when the sun goes down because I swear we can't find a frigging trace of him.'

'I know. But that doesn't make sense for Dora. She's lived here for years. I'm not sure she'd know how to go somewhere else. And she has a soft spot for me. I'm lucky if I can go three days without her popping up somewhere. And now she's vanished.'

Delilah's eyes narrow. 'You think something's happened to her?'

Joe doesn't want to think this, but still . . . 'It's not like her.'

'If you're going to make someone disappear, pick on the homeless,' Delilah says. 'No one looks out for them.'

'I know,' Joe says. 'Which is why we have to.'

'I love your mum,' Torquil says, as they watch Delilah stride down the street to her illegally parked car. 'But she always looks unhappy. Police officers need a settled private life, and so few of them have it.'

'She never got over Dad running off with one of my secondary-school teachers,' Joe says. 'Although she freely admits she was working every hour God sent. It's one of the reasons she's so protective of me now. She feels guilty about never being around when I was growing up.'

Joe changes the subject. He doesn't want to talk about his parents. 'So, how's this for a theory?' he says instead. 'Felicity's husband is hanging around town and he's dangerous. He's been stalking her for some time now. He's responsible for the break-ins at her house, for her cupboards being rearranged, for the abusive diary entries, for the TV being turned to channels she's never watched. She's seriously traumatised by all this. However, because of abuse she suffered as a child—'

'Which you have caught a mere glimpse of and cannot possibly verify.'

'Granted, but let's assume for now it happened. Because of abuse she suffered as a child, at the hands of someone she should have been able to trust, i.e. her own father, she's conditioned to think it's what she deserves. She tolerates her husband's abusive treatment because it feels normal.'

'It's a pattern we've both seen before.'

'Also, and here's the bit I'm struggling with, she's successfully wiping the encounters with her husband from her mind because she's terrified of him. These fugue states she's been experiencing – they mark times when she's encountered him and fled. After-wards, she makes herself forget, because it's too much to deal with.'

Torquil is looking doubtful. 'She's hearing voices. She's suffer-ing recurring episodes of amnesia. Felicity Lloyd's problems are in her head.'

'Some of them, I agree. But what if they're not all? What if she's really in danger?'

'She's an interesting case, I'll give you that. But not your case any more.'

'I can't just do nothing.'

'You're not going to like what I say next,' says Torquil.

Joe waits.

'Make your final report to her GP, then do nothing.'

59

Joe

The house where Felicity lived as a young child is a large Edward-
ian semi on a wide tree-lined street about a mile from Salisbury
city centre. Joe parks and stands for several minutes at the bottom
of the shared drive. He has no idea why he is here or what he
thinks he can achieve, and he is fighting off a sense of being in the
wrong place.

A voice inside him is telling him he shouldn't have left Cambridge. Even putting aside his anxiety about Felicity, who still
hasn't been in touch, Dora Hardwick didn't keep her appointment
the previous evening.

A car horn startles him and he jumps round to see a blue
Astra trying to enter the driveway. He raises a hand in apology
and steps to one side. The car draws level and the driver window
lowers.

'Help you?' The man behind the wheel is older than Joe, tall
and thin, wearing a tweed jacket and green tie.

'Sorry.' Joe has nothing prepared.

'You don't look like you're casing the joint, but we've had a
spate of break-ins recently and we're at the point of calling the
police first, asking questions later. If we're really worried, we ac-
tivate neighbourhood watch. There's a signal on the roof.'

Joe glances towards the roof of the house and can see nothing
but a satellite dish. When he looks back, the driver's face has the

pleased-with-himself look of someone who has cracked a good joke.

Joe takes his hospital ID from an inner pocket. 'My name's Joe Grant,' he says. 'A patient of mine lived in number twenty-two some years ago and frankly, I'm not sure why I'm here. Sorry to have bothered you.' He turns to walk back to his own car.

'How many years?' the man calls after him.

Joe hesitates.

'Twenty-five, by any chance?'

Joe says nothing.

'Come on up,' the car driver invites. 'I'm twiddling my thumbs right now and not about to turn down a chance to talk about the murder house.'

The car driver, whose name is Elwin Black, lives at number 24.

'The houses are twins,' he tells Joe, as they enter through a rear door. 'I can show you round, if you like. You'll get the idea of the layout. Coffee?'

'Thanks,' Joe says.

Black is an academic. His kitchen is piled high with books and files and papers. Maps and charts are pinned onto every available stretch of wall and Post-it notes are scattered across the room as though a paper machine has exploded. Joe steps closer to a series of photographs and starts back. The crime scenes depicted are lurid and explicit.

On the kitchen table is an old-fashioned manual typewriter. An ashtray overflows with cigarette stubs. There are sticky rings and two unwashed glass tumblers.

'I have three rooms in this house that I've tried to use as studies,' Black says. 'And this is the only place I can work.'

As his new friend pours water and ground coffee into a machine, Joe sees a long narrow garden beyond the window. The door to the rest of the house is open and Joe can see a hallway with black and white square tiles, a wide staircase and a wood-panelled, under-stairs cupboard.

'How long have you been here?' he asks, when the coffee arrives.

'Twelve years. Three different families have lived in number twenty-two in that time. No one ever stays long. Splash of bourbon in that?'

Joe declines. 'I can't talk about my patient,' he says. 'You do understand that, don't you?'

''Course.' Black invites him to sit and takes the stool opposite. 'What do you want to know?'

'Why do you call it the "murder house"?'

'Bloke went mad and killed his family. Cut his wife to pieces and then did the same thing to his little girl. Then he killed himself.'

Joe feels his breakfast churning in his stomach. He thinks he might, actually, be about to throw up on a stranger's kitchen floor.

'Actually,' he says. 'I will have a splash of bourbon. Thanks.'

'Thought you might.' Grinning, Black sloshes some amber liquid into Joe's cup. Joe drinks. The burning liquor has an instant, calming effect. 'That's quite a story,' Joe says, when the immediate threat of vomiting has passed. 'Is this common knowledge?'

'Absolutely. There are ghost tours of old Salisbury. Tourist things, and they usually include a visit here. Nice little earner for me.'

'Do you know the name of the family?'

'Lloyd. Struck a chord with me because my mother's maiden name was Lloyd. Her family came from the valleys.'

'And they all died? No survivors?'

Black shakes his head, and the tiny smile doesn't leave his face. 'Bodies all found in the under-stairs cupboard.'

★

It is pouring with rain when Joe arrives back in Cambridge and he is soaked to the skin by the time he reaches Torquil's boat. The cabin smells of the river and of fried onions.

'Well, that can't be right,' Torquil says, when Joe has finished his story. 'Felicity's still alive. Was there a sibling?'

'Who knows? To be honest, I suspect a combination of Chinese whispers, overactive imagination and love of an audience,' Joe says. 'The guy gets money from showing people around his house so it's in his interests to make it as lurid as possible. But there must be some truth in it. Felicity has a thing about under-stairs cupboards. And there was some major trauma involving her parents when she was about three years old, so the timing's right. She talked about "bad men" though, as in "Don't give me to the bad men, Daddy". In Felicity's subconscious, her father is an abuser.'

His supervisor looks thoughtful.

'And she definitely told me her parents are dead.'

'Maybe she witnessed her father killing her mother,' Torquil suggests. 'Maybe she hid in the under-stairs cupboard, which is how she survived.'

'It's possible.'

'If murder was committed, there'll be a record. Have you done a search?'

Joe shakes his head. 'Nothing on the internet, but it was over twenty years ago. Mum should be able to dig it all up, so to speak. She won't like it, but I can twist her arm.'

Torquil drops his eyes.

'What?' Joe says.

'I don't doubt you can find out exactly what went on twenty-five years ago, which will probably bear some resemblance, but not much, to the story you were told today. What I'm less sure about is what you'd gain.'

This takes Joe by surprise. 'How about the truth?'

'Felicity told you, in no uncertain terms, that she doesn't want to find out anything more about her past life,' Torquil says. 'She can't cope with it right now. And you cannot force a patient into therapy she isn't ready for. You're not going to like this, Joe, but—'

Joe gets to his feet. 'I know,' he agrees. 'Back away, stay away, she's not my problem any more.'

He has never seen his supervisor looking so worried. 'You won't, will you?' he says.

'No.'

At lunchtime the next day, Joe drives to the offices of the British Antarctic Survey on Cambridge's west campus. Two women are behind the reception desk, one staring at a computer screen, the other on her knees packing boxes.

'Hi,' Joe says, when the woman at the computer looks up. 'I was hoping to catch Felicity. Has she left for lunch yet?'

Turning up at her office will surprise her, maybe even embarrass her, but it still feels more professional than going to her house.

'Felicity isn't here.' The woman has a puzzled look on her face. 'Can anyone else help you?'

Joe forces a cheery smile. 'No, she's a mate. I hoped she might have time for some lunch.'

The receptionist frowns. 'Felicity doesn't work here any more.'

'Oh, she does work here.' The other woman has looked up from her box-packing. 'She just doesn't work *here*. She's on assignment.'

'She's finished already?' Joe says. 'I thought that was a couple of weeks away.'

'No, she finished on Friday,' the other woman says. 'We had a drinks party for her. I'm not sure if she's left the city yet. Do you know, Lucy?'

'I don't think she mentioned when she was flying out,' the woman called Lucy says. 'She talked about spending some time in South America though. You may catch her at home. We can't give out her address, but if you're a friend . . .'

'I know where she lives,' Joe says. 'Thanks.'

He has his hand on the door before he thinks of something.

'I've got some stuff of hers,' he says. 'If she's gone already, can you help me get in touch with her husband? I could pass it on to him.'

Both women look at him blankly.

'Her husband, Freddie?' he prompts.

The two women look at each other. 'Did you know Felicity was married?' the one called Lucy says.

The other shakes her head

'Sorry,' Lucy says. 'She never mentioned a husband.'

Joe is on the ground floor, ready to leave the building, when the other lift opens and a pair of heels clicks out.

'Wait a sec!'

He turns to see that Lucy has followed him down. Now that she is away from the reception desk he can see that she is heavily pregnant.

'I don't want you to think we're being unhelpful,' she says. 'You took us a bit by surprise. But I remembered when you'd gone, there was someone else asking after Felicity. He came in a couple of times. He never left his name, but I did press him once on what he wanted.' She puts her hand to her stomach and takes a deep breath. 'We get a lot of reps trying to get meetings with our scientists,' she goes on. 'Anyway, he said he was family. So, it could have been him, couldn't it? Tall guy? Blonde? Good looking? A bit older than she is?'

'Yes,' Joe says, thinking back to the wedding photograph. 'That sounds like Freddie.'

He waits for Lucy to turn back towards the lift. She doesn't.

'Thanks,' Joe says. Still she doesn't move.

'Is there something else?' Joe tries.

Lucy looks deeply uncomfortable. 'I probably shouldn't say this, but—'

'I'm worried about Felicity,' Joe says quickly. 'Looks like you are too.'

His words seem to give Lucy the permission she needs. 'She received letters,' she says. 'From prison. I see all the incoming mail, and obviously I don't open anything personal, but the postmark was obvious. HMP Durham.'

'How many?' Joe asks.

Lucy makes a thinking face. 'I can remember three,' she says. 'Could have been more.'

'Can you remember when they started?'

She nods. 'In March. I know that for a fact because she left the office the minute I gave it to her. I was a bit worried, I'd never seen her like that before, she looked – I don't know whether it was angry or scared but it was weird. Anyway, I watched her from the window and she opened the letter when she was standing near some daffodils. That's how I know it was March.'

Joe is thinking March. Felicity's problems began in March. That's when she experienced her first fugue state.

'Each time a letter came she changed,' Lucy says. 'It was a bit freaky to be honest. But what I'm trying to say is, maybe they were from her husband. Maybe her husband is in prison and that's why she never mentioned him.'

Joe nods.

'So this man who turned up here looking for her could also have been her husband, released from prison,' Lucy says. 'That would be pretty scary, wouldn't it?'

'It certainly would,' Joe agrees.

He drives to her house but he knows, even before he gets out of his car, that she has gone. He walks to the front door all the same and peers through into the hallway. The internal doors are all closed. At the back he lets himself into her courtyard. The back door is locked. The kitchen beyond looks spotless. He glances down and sees the basement window has been repaired with what looks like reinforced glass.

The lid on the recycling bin doesn't quite close. Joe wanders over and sees it is full of cardboard boxes, bubble wrap, the stuff people leave behind when they move house.

'She's gone.'

Joe starts round to see a man's face peering at him over the fence from the courtyard next door.

'Already?' Joe asks. 'I thought she had at least another week here.'

'Left the day before yesterday. Evening flight to Chile from Heathrow. I've to put the bins out on Wednesday.'

Knowing the neighbour is still watching him, and not caring, Joe lifts the dustbin lid on an impulse. On top of the bubble wrap and cardboard lies a slim white envelope. Pulling his handkerchief from his pocket as he's seen his mother do he wraps it over his hand and tips out the contents. Inside are four photographs of Felicity, taken at night or in the early evening, almost certainly without her knowledge.

They have been lying on an upturned photograph in a silver frame. Joe picks it up, still using the handkerchief and sees the black-and-white wedding picture. Felicity's face is hidden behind the gossamer mist of a bridal veil but the groom is shiningly hand-some, tall and fair as a Viking prince. The runaway bridesmaid is cute as a button. Joe takes both the envelope and the wedding photograph and leaves Felicity's property.

Part Three

CAMBRIDGE, ENGLAND

Seven Months Later

'Are the days of winter sunshine just as sad for you, too?'

Gustave Flaubert, *November*

60

Joe

Winters are rarely mild on the English Fens and this one is no exception. In January, snow falls early and often. Layer upon layer coats the city's roofs, piling high on gable ends and window ledges, until the rooms beyond take on a twilight cast, and even the college porters fear their ancient halls might not hold. From time to time, the old buildings groan, as though the burden is indeed too heavy, but the sound is only that of a thick wedge of snow breaking away and falling to the ground. Joe Grant walks the white streets of his city and thinks of tumbling icebergs, of silver-blue glaciers and biting blizzards, and wonders if his heart has frozen over.

Warmer days at the beginning of February turn the snow and ice into a rushing torrent of meltwater. The Cam overtops its banks and those who live close carry their valuables to upper floors. Towards the end of the month the snow returns, thicker and faster this time. Street signs, public benches and cycles are lost completely. Heraldic badges at the college gateways lose all distinction, and the great statue of Henry VIII doffs his hat, doublet and hose for a heavy-hooded mantle of white. Joe's hair and coat turn the colour of cobwebs as the snowflakes land and melt, land and melt.

The temperature drops again, and the willow trees along the riverbanks are claimed by frost. Tendrils of white lace droop into the water and the bridges turn silver. The water surface crinkles and its movement slows. The Cam is starting to freeze over. Snow slides down its banks and finds purchase on the ice. The Cam, too, is taken.

The council works hard to keep the main roads clear, but soiled, salt-strewn snow piles up at the roadside, and the Environment Agency worries about the already flooded groundwater system. Schools are closed more than they are open, the elderly keep to their homes, and the rough sleepers, those who can be found, are taken indoors, because when all is said and done, Cambridge is a kind city. Knowing his homeless are safe from the cold is a small comfort to Joe.

The weather turns once more, the snow melts and low-lying fields become shallow lakes. Swans glide proprietorially over the Backs and the water meadows. The Environment Agency opens all the floodgates but the run-off can't escape. Roads turn to rivers, cellars begin to stink and in an old drain not far from Peterhouse College, the body of Dora Hardwick is found at last.

Joe gets the call halfway through the morning and clears his afternoon appointments. He arrives at the hospital mortuary at three o'clock, when the sky outside is already darkening, and a minute or two before his mother. The pink hair of last summer has gone. Delilah is looking older and more tired, thinner but not healthier. The unsolved murder, possibly about to become two unsolved murders, has taken its toll. Since the start of the new year, she has been talking about retirement.

'Sorry,' she says to her son, when she has announced herself at reception and she and Joe are on their way to the place where the dead are stored. 'There wasn't anyone else.'

'How was she found?' There is no doubt in Joe's mind that he is about to identify Dora.

'Unusual flooding down at the Mill Pool off Silver Street,' his mother says, 'even allowing for how much snow we've had. The Environment Agency suspected a blocked storm drain and sent some equipment in to clear it. They pulled out Dora.'

'Do they know how long she'd been down there?'

His mother's face is grim. 'A while.'

In a brightly lit examination room they are met by a lab technician. Expecting to see a human form beneath a white sheet, Joe is puzzled by what lies on the central steel table.

'Clothes?'

'You don't need to see the body,' Delilah replies. 'There's very little of her left, and nothing recognizable. If you can identify the clothes, that will be enough.'

Ashamed of how relieved he feels, Joe steps closer. The green woollen duffle coat has not had chance to dry out but he knows it is Dora's. The toggle buttons are exactly as he remembers. The blue beret is Dora's, as are the Wellington boots. He is less sure about the dress but the blue sweatshirt carries a worn picture of Elsa, the heroine from *Frozen*.

'These are Dora's clothes,' he says.

'How sure are you?' his mother asks.

Joe looks sadly at the thick silver plait, the wry smile, the form-hugging blue dress of the Disney princess. 'One hundred per cent.'

'There was a wrapper from a packet of chocolate buttons in one pocket,' the lab technician tells him.

'Dora,' says Joe.

'There's also this.' The technician holds up a plastic evidence bag with a small slip of card inside. Joe takes the bag and sees one of his own visiting cards. On the reverse, he'd written, *8.20pm, Tuesday*.

'She liked to have appointment cards,' he says. 'I gave her one every time I saw her.'

'We found them in another pocket,' the lab assistant says. 'Wet through and stuck together. Looks like she kept them all.'

'This one gives us a good idea of when she died,' Delilah says. 'She obviously intended to keep that appointment with you.'

'She never missed,' Joe says.

His mum reaches out, as though to pat his shoulder, and thinks better of it. Her hand falls back to her side. 'So, if you can confirm when you last saw her, and what Tuesday that card refers to, we've got a window.'

Joe finds the calendar on his phone. 'Twenty-third of July,' he says. 'That's when I last saw her. That appointment is for the thirtieth, seven days later. Do you know how she died?'

'We're waiting for the results of the post-mortem,' Delilah says. 'But given the state of the body we might never know.'

'Could it have been an accident?' Joe asks. All the rough sleepers were running scared last summer. It isn't impossible that Dora saw the storm drain as a safe refuge for the night.

His mother and the lab technician exchange a glance.

'Not impossible,' Delilah says. 'The master of Peterhouse – a woman, go figure – tells us the drain leads into the old foundations. Peterhouse goes back to the iron age. There are cellars, dungeons for all I know. Someone desperate could have holed up down there.'

'What about her shopping trolley?' Joe asks. 'I never saw her without it.'

Dora might have taken refuge in a storm drain. She would never have left her trolley behind.

'We haven't found it yet,' Delilah says. 'But the foundations near the river have collapsed at some stage. We need to go slowly because the structure's so old. And archeologically significant.'

Joe wonders if his mother is keeping something from him. 'She could have got stuck,' he says.

Delilah pats his arm. 'You know what, lad. I kind of hope so.'

Snow is falling again as Joe leaves the hospital and the fog-yellow sky suggests there's more to come. He heads back into town and it takes longer than usual, because everyone slows down for the snow.

When he's finished for the day, he goes out for a walk, crossing the river at the same time as a crocodile of school boys clad in top hats, cloaks and purple and white scarves. The choristers are making their daily journey from the choir school to the chapel for evensong, and the snow is irresistible. They dart about, hurling snowballs at each other, at the master, into the river. One of them hits Joe on the neck and the boys flee, squealing.

As Joe heads for home, cold trickling under his collar, he thinks, as he so often does, of a land where the snow is almost constant. He has heard nothing from Felicity since she left for South Georgia. He'd hoped for, expected even, an email or two, letting him know she'd arrived safely, but nothing. He thinks perhaps he might rent *Frozen* this evening, open a bottle of red wine, and let himself cry.

Delilah phones him at six o'clock. 'This isn't public knowledge, so keep your mouth shut, but the poor old love didn't die of natural causes and it wasn't an accidental death.'

Joe really doesn't want to know. 'Go on,' he says, because he knows he must.

'Three wounds on her lower-left rib cage, compatible with knife marks. She was stabbed in the stomach, at least three times, by someone aiming upwards towards her heart.'

'Christ,' he says. Poor Dora. What a way to end a life gone wrong.

'And there was a rope round her neck.'

'What?'

'I didn't mention it before because we weren't sure whether it had killed her or not. Turns out it didn't, no damage to the neck bones consistent with hanging or extreme strangulation. We think whoever killed her tied the rope round her neck to drag her into the drain.'

Joe can sense his mother is in a hurry.

'I've got to run, love,' she goes on. 'I've got a press statement five minutes ago. I didn't want you hearing it on the news.'

Joe asks, 'Do you think whoever killed Dora killed Bella Barnes?'

'Two murders of rough sleepers within two months,' Delilah says. 'Both abdomen stab wounds. What are the chances of that being coincidence?'

As Delilah hangs up, Joe thinks of Ezzy Sheeran, a potential third murder victim. The brief flurry of possible sightings over the previous summer ended as quickly as it began, and the police have long since reverted to their missing-presumed-dead conclusion. He wonders if Ezzy, too, is under the city somewhere, waiting to be found.

Joe turns on the TV to catch his mother's press conference. There are no photographs of Dora, but Delilah has had an artist produce a drawing of a grey-haired old lady, small and thin, wearing a green coat, blue beret and wellingtons. She pulls along a battered old shopping trolley in a blue-and-red plaid pattern. He feels a moment of pride in his mother. She has got every detail right.

'Dora Hardwick was one of the most vulnerable members of our society,' Delilah tells the waiting journalists. 'We should have taken better care of her.'

Dora would have been tickled pink to see herself on the news.

★

Delilah turns up at his flat two hours later, her arms laden with Chinese takeaway.

'I've eaten,' he says.

'Good,' she snaps. 'I didn't get you anything. Pass me a plate.'

In spite of her grumpiness, and her usual appetite, she has brought far too much food for one, so they sit together at Joe's kitchen table and eat chicken chow mein, Singapore noodles, and sweet and sour pork.

'You need a hobby,' he tells her. 'Get you out of the house a bit, give you an interest. It's not too late to find a boyfriend.'

'Cheeky git.' She forks up noodles. 'And look who's talking.'

They eat in silence; Joe can't decide whether it is sad, or sweet, how much the two of them depend upon each other.

'Did you see me on telly?' she asks him.

'You looked great,' he lies. 'Any leads?' he adds, without much hope.

'We did the usual appeal for witnesses and information but after seven months?' Delilah shakes her head.

'Still no news on Shane?' Joe asks. The prime suspect in the murder of Bella Barnes has proven most adept at avoiding discovery. The darker nights of autumn and winter have only aided his powers of concealment.

'Gone,' Delilah confirms. 'If he was ever real in the first place. I tell you, love, my legacy is going to be the unsolved murder of two homeless women and a hunt for a phantom.'

When she's eaten, Delilah gets up. 'Got to get back in,' she tells him. 'See if anything's turned up.'

Joe walks his mother to her car and she is unusually silent. 'What's up?' he says, as he opens the driver door and wipes a dusting of snow from her windscreen.

She hovers, half in half out, of the car. 'Probably nothing,' she tells him. 'Probably coincidence.'

'What?'

'The two women who were killed, Bella and Dora? What did they have in common?'

Joe thinks he might laugh if he weren't so sad. 'Where do I start? Both rough sleepers. Both suffered physical and mental health problems. Both ridiculously unlucky, in life and death.'

'Yeah.' His mother gets into the car. 'And both very keen on you.'

Joe doesn't sleep much that night. He spends the hours after his mother has left combing the news channels on TV and the internet, looking for information on both murders. He checks his diary for last year to see what he was doing the night Bella was found dead and is worried, but not surprised, to find it was a Friday. He nearly always spends late Friday evenings out in the city, doing the rounds of all the rough sleepers. On that particular night, the seventh of June, he was still officially on sick leave but he's pretty certain he did go out that night.

All the time he searches and reads, he is conscious of his unease growing. He does not want to form the word *alibi*, even in his own mind.

He remembers the Friday night shortly after he last saw Dora, when he walked the streets checking on the homeless. He'd been afraid, as though sensing something very wrong was happening in the city, and he knows he won't be at all surprised if that turns out to be the night she died. He goes to bed at midnight and falls into a light doze, only to wake less than an hour later, convinced he has heard someone moving around in his flat. Sweating in spite of the chill he checks each room. Finding nothing doesn't reassure him.

The night seems to last forever. Finally, when the emerging sun casts a blood-red cloak over the pale and shivering city, he gives up trying to sleep. He makes coffee, sits at his window and waits. The call arrives shortly before nine in the morning. His mother is sending a car for him and he is wanted at the police station, immediately.

61

Joe

For once, Delilah isn't waiting in reception. Joe gives his name at the desk and a detective he doesn't know leads him to an interview room where a young woman is waiting. She introduces herself as a detective sergeant and he immediately forgets her name. She has dull brown hair tied back in a ponytail and wears a dark-blue suit with a white shirt. There is not a single feature, on her face, body or clothes, that strikes him as memorable.

Recording equipment is switched on and both detectives give their names for the tape. Both names strike Joe as being entirely bland and he makes no further attempt to remember them.

Over the sergeant's shoulder there is a large mirror. Joe looks into it and feels sure his mother is on the other side. He tries to remember what she has told him about how people behave in police interviews, what the right things to do are, and what will suggest his guilt. He wonders when, exactly, he started to apply the word *guilt* to himself.

The questions begin. He is asked about his relationship with Dora Hardwick, how long he knew her, how often he saw her, what they talked about, whether they'd had any falling out. He answers fully and frankly and knows that this is only the beginning. The two detectives take turns, and when he is certain they cannot possibly ask him anything more about Dora, they switch to Bella.

'And you're paid nothing for all this time you spend counselling homeless people?' the sergeant asks, when they've exhausted the Bella-related questions.

'You can't take money from people who don't have it,' Joe tells them.

At a nod from his sergeant, the constable switches on a wall-mounted screen.

'We were lucky in our TV appeal,' the sergeant says. 'A hardware shop on Fitzroy Street archives all its CCTV footage and they went back to the period shortly after the last known sighting of Dora Hardwick.'

The footage starts to play. Joe can read the date in the bottom right hand corner of the screen, but the constable confirms it for him all the same.

'This is Friday the twenty-sixth of July, eight thirty in the evening,' he says. 'Three days after your last appointment with her in the church hall.'

The scene is a Cambridge city street, not far from where Felicity lives. Joe watches three students walk along the pavement closest to the shop and a West Indian woman push a baby stroller in the opposite direction before Dora appears.

'That's Dora,' he confirms, and then finally they ask him the question that counts.

The sergeant says, 'Can you tell me where you were on the night of Friday the twenty-sixth of July?'

'I was out walking the streets,' Joe replies. 'Looking for the homeless.'

He is left alone. He realises, after several seconds, that he is sitting with his head in his hands.

He feels as though his whole life has been building up to this – the moment when everything falls apart – and yet he has no idea what he could have done differently. Ezzy? He'd just wanted to help her. Bella too. It is not entirely impossible, he realises, that he will be charged with murder. It will break his mum. And his kids. Sarah will have to take them out of the city.

The door opens. Expecting the forgettable sergeant and her unmemorable sidekick he is surprised to see Delilah clutching two steaming mugs. Another detective follows with a plate of custard creams and both take their seats. Delilah gives a heavy sigh and can't meet her son's eyes. Joe looks at the biscuits and thinks, as last meals go, this one sucks.

He waits to see if they have actually sent his mother to charge him. It seems beyond cruel, although he wouldn't put it past her to volunteer for the job, to prove she was entirely incorruptible.

'What happens now?' He wonders if this might be the moment when he accepts, once and for all, that his mum can't make everything right.

'We have a cup of tea,' she says. 'I put sugar in. I know you don't take it, but you look like you need it. Biscuit?'

She can't seem to look at him, but he does what he is told. The biscuit is stale and he takes a childish pleasure in putting it down on the table with only a bite missing.

'We tracked down Dora's shopping trolley,' Delilah says. 'We got a call first thing from a student who worked at the punt hire place on Silver Street last summer. He remembers finding one exactly like it in a punt early one morning. It was put in lost property and disposed of at the end of the season.'

'He checked the lost property log for us,' the other detective adds. 'It was found on the morning of Saturday the twenty-seventh of July, meaning it was left there sometime the previous night.'

'Probably thrown from Silver Street Bridge, intending to go into the water,' Delilah adds. 'Bad luck for the killer that it landed on a punt.'

'When you add it to the last sighting of Dora on Friday the twenty-sixth, it does suggest that was the night she was killed,' the other detective says.

Joe can't argue with any of that. And he is tired of pussyfooting around.

'Come on then.' He leans back in his chair, affecting a nonchalance he certainly doesn't feel. 'Let's get it over with.'

Delilah and her colleague share a puzzled look. 'Get what over with?' she says.

'Arrest me. Charge me. Whatever it is you want to do.'

'Why would we charge you?' his mother asks.

A split second later, the other detective asks, 'Do you want to confess to something?'

'No,' Joe insists. 'I thought you were going to charge me with Dora's murder.'

'God no.' His mother looks shocked. 'You were being interviewed as a witness, not a suspect, and obviously I couldn't be involved in that. Jesus save us, do you think I'd let you be interviewed under caution without a solicitor?'

The relief has hardly begun to wash over Joe when he realises there is more to come. He is not a suspect. That should be good news. Yet somehow—

'You haven't realised the significance of the date, have you?' his mother says, in an unusually gentle voice.

What date? Today's date?

'Friday twenty-sixth of July – the night Dora Hardwick was almost certainly murdered – is also the night Felicity Lloyd was seen running through the streets of Cambridge covered in blood,' the detective says.

'Bella Barnes was found dead close to midnight on Friday the seventh of June,' the other detective adds. 'That same evening, Dr Lloyd was admitted to hospital with numerous minor injuries and unable to account for her movements.'

'You're not a suspect, love,' his mother says. 'But she is.'

There is a knock on the door. 'Got the results back, Delilah.' A young uniformed copper pokes his head into the room. Delilah opens the file and takes several minutes to read what she finds inside.

'We ran Felicity's prints through the system,' she says, when she looks up. 'We had them from the time of the break-in at her house. When she claimed she'd been attacked and then withdrew her statement.'

'She was attacked,' Joe says. 'She refused to proceed because she was scared.'

'There was no reason to run them before now,' Delilah goes on. 'We couldn't investigate a break-in that might not have happened, but we kept them on file.'

'So you ran them. What did you find?'

'They match the ones found in your flat the night someone broke in.'

'That makes no sense,' Joe says after a moment. 'You told me someone called Shane broke into my flat.'

Delilah looks at her colleague. 'Show him,' she says.

The detective gets up, switches on the TV screen and presses several keys on his laptop. Joe watches as the screen springs to life, showing footage of the vehicular entrance to a car park. A male figure, wearing a black hooded sweatshirt walks at a side angle to the camera. He moves quickly, with the grace of the young. As he half turns, Joe can see the distinctive logo on the front of his hoody: a white circle around an offset triangle, surrounded by white lettering. There is a Nike tick logo on his right shoulder.

'The writing on the chest says "Golden State Warriors",' the detective says. 'It's an item of clothing only available in the United States or over the internet. Not commonly found in the UK.'

'This is the only video footage we have of Shane,' Delilah says. 'But he was spotted by a police car on the night of the ninth of July. He was pursued but got away, leaving a knife behind. The prints on that knife matched those found in your flat, remember?'

Joe remembers. He also thinks he has never seen his mother looking this unhappy.

'They're Felicity's prints, Joe,' she says. 'Felicity is Shane.'

Felicity's front door is broken open and Tyvek-clad crime scene officers enter first. Joe and Delilah sit in her car, watching.

'We don't know for sure Dora died that night,' Joe says.

Delilah doesn't respond.

'There was still Saturday, Sunday and Monday before she was due to see me on Tuesday,' he continues. 'Just because we've no trace of Dora on those days, doesn't mean she was dead.'

Still no reply.

'Shane is a bloke.' He tries a different tack. 'Felicity is not. Trust me on that one.'

'We assumed Shane was a male.' Delilah speaks softly. 'He's tall enough to be one. He wears men's clothes. No camera ever got a good picture of him and the people who saw him were out of their heads half the time. They assumed and we believed them.'

'Felicity has been in my flat,' he says. 'Of course her finger-prints would be there.'

'Has she been in your bedroom?' his mum asks. 'Has she ever climbed up your fire escape and slipped into your kitchen through a window?'

This time, it is Joe who has nothing to say.

'There have been no sightings of Shane since Felicity left Cam-bridge,' Delilah says.

'There were precious few before.'

'She left in a hurry. Even you said as much. She must have thought we were on to her. She ran, Joe.'

The head of the crime scene team is walking towards them. 'You can come in now,' he tells Delilah.

Joe and Delilah squeeze themselves into protective suits and enter Felicity's house.

'She didn't leave much behind,' the crime scene manager tells them. 'The whole place has been thoroughly cleaned.'

'Any sign of the white dress?' Delilah asks.

The crime scene manager shakes his head. 'We did find one thing,' he goes on. 'Downstairs.'

Delilah and Joe follow him into the basement. Beneath the stairs is a cupboard, the twin of the one immediately above in which Felicity spent her more difficult nights. The padlock has been forced apart.

'We had to break it open,' the crime scene manager tells them. 'Interesting collection of stuff inside.'

Delilah peers into the cupboard and then steps back to let Joe see.

Mainly, he sees clothes, but doesn't recognise any of them. Some of them are men's clothes, jeans and huge, baggy jackets. The dresses, though, are tight, short, made from shiny fabrics. He has never seen Felicity wearing any of them. There are sequined tops and tight Lycra leggings. High-heeled shoes. In one corner is a stack of DVDs. Horror and slasher films, judging by the titles on their spines. In the opposite corner is a similar stack of romantic comedies and Disney movies. He sees packs of cigarettes, bottles of whisky and the spectacles case he remembers from her living room, the one that she claimed not to own.

On the floor are two pairs of casual shoes, a pair of walking boots and some trainers. Delilah gets to her knees and examines the underside.

'Size nine,' she says.

'The ones in the wardrobe upstairs are sevens,' the crime scene manager tells her.

'Hello.' Delilah is feeling around the inside of a trainer. She pulls out a wad of newspaper from the toe.

On a top shelf several sweaters and sweatshirts are folded neatly. One of them is black.

'Bag,' Delilah instructs. 'Large one.'

With gloved hands, she lifts down the black garment and holds it by the shoulders. It falls open to reveal the logo of the Golden State Warriors.

62

Joe

Several hours later, Joe sits in the police meeting room wearing disposable gloves as he flicks through a wedding album found in a locked trunk in Felicity's loft. Also on the table is the silver-framed photograph he stole from her bin but hasn't examined properly before now. He doesn't look up when the door opens but knows from her perfume that his mother has joined him.

'This isn't Felicity's wedding.' He turns to the second picture in the album, that of the bride leaving home on her father's arm. The tall blonde-haired woman looks a lot like Felicity but the wedding car the pair are heading for is a black Mercedes from thirty years ago. The people watching in the street are wearing the fashions of the late 1980s. 'I think this is her mother.'

Delilah takes a seat beside him.

'She found this photograph not long before she left.' He holds up the silver-framed picture. 'It was the only real evidence I saw that she was married, that Freddie existed. Turns out it isn't even her wedding.'

'Are you sure?' Delilah asks. 'It's an odd thing to do, get your parents' wedding mixed up with your own.'

Joe holds the framed photograph next to a similar one in the album. 'Same dress, same groom, same guests, even the same bridesmaid.' Joe turns the pages to find a picture of the tiny bridesmaid offering a lucky horseshoe up to the bride. He points a gloved finger to the little girl. 'I think this is Felicity,' he says.

'So, what are you saying? That Freddie isn't real?'

Joe thinks back to his conversation with Felicity's work colleague, to the attack at her house, to her genuine terror.

'I have no idea who Freddie is,' he says. 'But I'm sure he's real.'

63

Joe

'I wish you'd let me drive.' Joe is breathing heavily as they slow down outside the residential home on the banks of the River Bourne. Ever since Delilah took a police driving course in her forties, he's been reluctant to get into a vehicle with her at the wheel. On the other hand, maybe the queasiness, the threatening headache, the shaking limbs, aren't entirely down to his mother's habit of fast acceleration and dramatic braking. He's been feeling unwell since Dora's body was found. Since Felicity became prime suspect, he's been tormented by visions of her, kneeling over the lifeless bodies of Dora, Bella, even Ezzy, with blood-stained hands and dead eyes. He doesn't think he's slept more than an hour or two in one stretch.

'If we need to park illegally,' Delilah pulls up on yellow lines, 'it's easier to do it in my car.' She opens her door and nearly knocks a cyclist off his bike.

The residential home for the elderly is new, made of red brick with large windows and high gables. It sits on carefully tended lawns with neat flower beds.

'We can't be long,' Delilah adds. 'I want to be there if they find anything under Peterhouse.'

The excavation of the collapsed drain where Dora was found is due to begin today.

'How did you find her?' Joe asks, as they walk towards the main door. 'Her' is an elderly former social worker called Margaret Jennings.

'Request to Salisbury social services,' Delilah replies. 'They found Felicity's case notes in the archives. Nobody still working there remembers it, but Mrs Jennings is still alive, compos mentis and willing to see us. We're not often this lucky.'

They are led to a room on the first floor. It might smell a little of urine, and a little more of disinfectant, but it is neat and bright and looks comfortable. The woman in the armchair is in her mid-eighties. She is tall, and robust still, but her hands shake with an uncontrollable tremor.

'You're here about Felicity Lloyd,' the old lady says when they are both seated. They have already been warned that she is rather deaf. She is certainly rather loud.

'We're worried about her,' Joe replies. 'We think she may be at risk.'

His mother snorts quietly.

'So, anything you can tell us would be very helpful.' Joe glares at Delilah.

'She was allocated to me in her mid-teens.' Mrs Jennings puts a hand to her chest and holds the other up in a give-me-a-moment gesture.

Delilah checks her phone.

'Her behaviour changed, almost overnight,' Mrs Jennings says when she has got her breath back. 'She went from being a normal, happy young girl' – another pause, another chance to recover – 'to someone who was, well, quite the opposite. Eventually she ran away. She missed a year of school.'

The old lady reaches a trembling hand towards a glass of water on the table by her side. 'She'd been living on the streets,' she adds. 'In London, we think, although she never told us much about it.'

Joe thinks back to his first session with Felicity. She'd mentioned a friend, who'd been homeless.

'Do you know what triggered the change?' Joe asks.

Mrs Jennings nods for several seconds. 'Her grandmother died, which would have been unsettling in itself. It left Felicity in the care of the local authority. The real problem though was that she got a letter from her father.'

Joe and Delilah exchange a look.

'Her father is dead,' Joe says. 'He killed himself when she was tiny.'

Mrs Jennings pulls a face. 'Did Felicity tell you that?'

'She says he died when she was young. A neighbour told me he'd killed himself and his wife.'

'Oh, that's just nonsense invented by the people who sell ghost tours in Salisbury. Felicity's mother was killed, and her father went after the men who did it. Killed all three of them in cold blood. He got life.'

Joe hears his mother breathe out a long, tired sigh as he thinks, *The men who did it? The 'bad men'?*

'So, he's not dead?'

'Who knows? It was a long time ago. He could have died in prison.'

Joe thinks back. Felicity definitely told him her father was dead.

'Felicity was taken completely by surprise,' Margaret Jennings says. 'Her grandmother had told her nothing about what happened when she was so young, about her mother's death, what her father did. I'm sure her father had written before and the grandmother kept the letters from her.'

'So, the news came as a shock?' Delilah asks. 'To Felicity, I mean?'

Mrs Jennings takes her time. 'She reacted badly,' she says eventually. 'Went off the rails. Started skipping school, hanging around with other troubled kids; under-age drinking, shoplifting, usual stuff.'

'We see it a lot.' Delilah has a sympathetic smile on her face. Joe isn't fooled. His mother's tapping foot is a sure sign of her impatience. And her phone has been quietly beeping away for several minutes.

'Felicity was terrified at the thought of seeing her father again,' Mrs Jennings says. 'She exhibited an unusual and completely irrational fear of him. He'd done a terrible thing, no one's saying he hadn't, but he hadn't hurt Felicity herself.'

He's opening the door. He's opening the door. No, no, no, Daddy, don't give me to the bad men.

Joe says, 'During hypnotherapy, Felicity regressed to being a very young child and she was frightened of someone she called "Daddy".'

'Memories from when we're very young are notoriously unreliable,' Mrs Jennings says. 'If she associated her father with her mother's killers, even on some deep level that she couldn't bring to mind, it would help to account for her terror of him.'

Delilah sighs. Joe deliberately turns his back on his mother. 'And her confusion could have led to her irrational and uncharacteristic behaviour. Were you able to reassure her at all?'

'I think so. We told her he wouldn't know her new address, that we wouldn't forward any more correspondence without her permission and that there was no possibility of him getting out for years. If ever.'

'Did it work?'

'Yes, it did. She settled down and got a place at Cambridge. She even started volunteering with the homeless. She was a bright girl. One of our success stories.'

Delilah doesn't look impressed. 'We need to get back. Thanks for your time, Mrs Jennings.'

★

'We're talking about when she was fifteen,' Delilah says when they are back in the car. 'It doesn't help us now.' She flicks through her phone messages.

'It establishes a pattern,' Joe says. 'When Felicity feels threatened, she acts out of character. She becomes someone else. Oh—'

Is it possible? He starts going through Felicity's symptoms in his head.

'Damn,' Delilah's expletive disrupts his train of thought.

'What's up?'

'The excavation at Silver Street has stopped. Some twat wittering on about the tomb of one of the founders.'

'What does that mean?'

She bangs a hand down on the steering wheel in frustration. 'It means we can't dig out the rest of the drain until the Indiana Jones squad have been through it. It could take weeks.'

Months, Joe thinks. 'You found Dora,' he says. 'That's the important thing.'

Delilah snorts as she scrolls through her messages. 'Oh, that's a bit more like it. 'Her face brightens. 'We've had a call from a businessman in Strasbourg. He was staying in the Hilton by Silver Street towards the end of July. His room overlooked the river and he thinks he saw the old dear the night she died.'

While his mother is reading the message in full, Joe thinks back to Felicity's symptoms. Fugue states. Amnesia. Hearing voices. The belief that she was being stalked. He remembers how she changed under hypnosis and again, when the two of them met in the restaurant. He remembers a phrase in her journal. *The others.*

Delilah looks up. 'He'll be back in the UK in a few days,' she says. 'We need to talk to him properly.'

He can't say anything yet. He needs to be sure. He needs to talk to Torquil.

Delilah puts her phone away. 'He also mentions seeing a young woman in a white dress.'

Joe wonders when the bad news will stop coming. Even so, if he's right . . .

'Mum, things are becoming a bit clearer,' he says. 'Felicity is a very damaged woman, but the damage is buried so deep even she doesn't know it's there most of the time. The important thing is, she can be cured.'

His mother starts the car. 'She's a killer, Joe. You can cure her in prison.'

64

Joe

Joe and his supervisor are the last to be shown into the meeting room at the police station. It is a large, low-ceilinged room, with windows running the length of one wall. Seven people are sitting around a table. The room smells of coffee but most of the cups he can see are empty. These people have been here for some time.

A man in uniform introduces himself as Assistant Chief Constable Elton Downey and runs through the introductions at speed. Delilah catches Joe's eye and gives him a tight-lipped smile that could either be meant to convey reassurance, or warn him to behave.

'To sum up where we are.' Downey remains standing after Joe and Torquil have taken their chairs. 'Dr Felicity Lloyd, currently living on the island of South Georgia, is our prime suspect in the murders of Dora Hardwick and Bella Barnes last summer. Our initial suspect was a person known as Shane. DI Jones, can you remind us why Shane was wanted in connection with the murders?'

Delilah taps her pen on the notebook in front of her, a sure sign that she is nervous.

'Bella Barnes was sleeping alone in the Grand Arcade car park on the night she was killed,' she says. 'Round about the estimated time of death, we have CCTV footage of a person leaving the car park, wearing a black hooded sweatshirt with a distinctive logo.

Other homeless people identified this individual as a man they knew as Shane. No one knew much about him, and efforts to track him down came to nothing, but he remained someone we very much wanted to speak to.'

'If I remember correctly, your experts confirmed that Shane was male,' Joe interrupts. 'He walked like a man, stood like a man, carried himself like a man.'

'He was believed at that time to be male, yes,' Delilah confirms. 'You yourself, Joe said the other rough sleepers were afraid of him. They thought him creepy, that he watched them while they were asleep. They believed him to have murdered Bella.'

Joe can remember saying exactly this to his mum.

'Time went by, and we couldn't find him,' Delilah goes on. 'Then, on the thirtieth of June, someone broke into my son's flat. Fingerprints on and around the fire escape suggested an intruder, but they didn't match any we had on the system. His identity remained a mystery. Joe installed extra security and nothing else happened.

'On the eleventh of July, a patrol car spotted someone answering Shane's description on New Park Street. They gave chase, but he got away. He had, though, left behind a knife. Fingerprints on the knife matched fingerprints found in Joe's flat. We knew beyond any doubt that Shane was the intruder.'

Around the table, people look at Joe as though expecting him to argue. He doesn't.

'The case went cold,' Delilah says. 'Then, a week ago, we found the body of Dora Hardwick, another homeless person, in a drain near Silver Street. From the last sighting of her alive, the finding of her belongings in the river, and from an appointment that she didn't keep, we assumed her most likely date of death was Friday the twenty-sixth of July. That same evening, Felicity Lloyd not only crashed her car and fled the scene of the accident, but was seen running around the streets of Cambridge, in some distress, and wearing a dress that appeared to be severely bloodstained.'

'You haven't actually found the dress, have you?' asks Torquil.

'She had plenty of time to get rid of it,' someone says.

'This coincidence enabled us to run fingerprints we had on file following an alleged break-in at Dr Lloyd's house,' Delilah continues. 'From that we were able to confirm that Felicity Lloyd's fingerprints and Shane's fingerprints are the same. She broke into Joe's flat. She is Shane.'

'I'd like the meeting to acknowledge that she is extremely convincing as a man,' Joe says.

Several puzzled faces turn his way.

'Duly acknowledged,' says Downey.

'This next bit is circumstantial,' Delilah says, 'but significant. Felicity Lloyd was admitted to hospital with minor injuries and claiming amnesia on the same night that Bella Barnes was found stabbed to death.'

She stops to take a breath, then hurries on.

'We had enough to apply for a warrant to search Felicity Lloyd's house.' Delilah has the air of someone wanting to get a difficult task over with. 'She'd cleaned it well, but there was enough DNA left to give us a further match to Shane. And significantly, we found the distinctive hoody that Shane was seen wearing.'

She holds up a photograph of the sweatshirt. 'That's it, sir,' she says. 'I'm done.'

'The isolated location of South Georgia presents us with some difficulties.' Downey takes over again. 'The nearest police force is on the Falkland Islands, some three to four days distant by boat, and even they aren't well resourced for apprehending and extraditing violent criminals. My plan is to put in a request to the RAF and the governor of the Falkland Islands for a joint police–RAF operation that arrests Lloyd on South Georgia and flies her home under military escort.'

'That would be the very worst thing you could do,' Joe says.

He feels the people around him knuckling down. They are ready for him. They have expected him to argue.

'The floor's yours, Dr Grant,' Downey tells him.

'Felicity Lloyd is seriously mentally ill,' Joe begins. 'She isn't responsible for her actions and she isn't fit to stand trial. If you have her arrested by the military, the consequences could be disastrous.'

'On what are you forming that judgment?' Downey asks.

Joe can sense Torquil, silent but supportive, by his side. 'Felicity came to see me in late June last year,' he begins. 'She was suffering from fugue states – periods of time when her recollection of events was entirely lost. She was unusually anxious and afraid, torn between the belief that someone was entering her house and rearranging her possessions, and believing she was doing it herself and then wiping it from her memory. She was a very confused and unhappy young woman.'

Faces stare back at him, impassive, but not hostile. One woman makes a note on her pad. They are being polite, possibly for his mother's sake.

'She also reported hearing voices, which led both me and Dr Bane to suspect schizophrenia as a possible diagnosis. Under hypnosis I discovered she believed she was being stalked. I think she was right to think that.'

'Stalked by who?' someone asks.

'A man called Freddie, whom she believed to be her husband. Towards the end of her therapy with me, Felicity was starting to open up about Freddie. She told me about serious abuse that she'd suffered at his hands. In any event, there can be no doubt that someone broke into her house shortly before she left and attacked her. If her neighbour hadn't heard the disturbance and called the police she could have been seriously hurt.'

'She claimed she'd been mistaken about that,' someone says.

'Someone went for her with a knife,' Joe says.

'I saw the lass the next morning,' Delilah adds. 'For what it's worth, I do believe she was attacked. And we found a lot of fingerprints in the house that we haven't been able to identify. Including on a knife that was lying on the kitchen floor.'

'But even if Dr Lloyd was being stalked by a man who may or may not have been her husband, it doesn't alter the fact that we can link her to Shane and the two murders,' Downey says. 'Or do you doubt that conclusion?'

Joe cannot doubt it. He has tried and failed.

'I think Felicity is suffering from a serious psychiatric condition,' he says. 'I'm furious with myself for not diagnosing it while she was still my patient. If I had, she could have been helped.'

'In Joe's defence, the condition he's talking about is extremely rare and very difficult to spot,' Torquil interrupts. 'I doubt anyone would have diagnosed it on the basis of what little evidence he had.'

'What condition?' the assistant chief constable asks.

'Dissociative Identity Disorder or DID,' Joe says. 'Previously known as Multiple Personality Disorder.'

Around the table, people are frowning, faces screwed in concentration or puzzlement.

'And what is it, exactly?' the assistant chief constable asks.

Joe glances at his supervisor. They have agreed that Torquil will take the technical questions.

'It's a rare and complex condition,' Torquil says. 'Case studies are few and far between and, to be perfectly candid, a lot of psychiatrists doubt its existence.'

'It's believed to be caused by severe trauma,' Joe steps in.

'Extreme physical, sexual or emotional abuse, nearly always in early childhood. We know that something very disturbing happened to Felicity when she was three years old, although I haven't managed to get to the bottom of it yet. What I do know is that her mother was killed and her father sentenced to life imprisonment.'

Joe sees his mother making a note.

'When she was in her teens, she got a letter from her father that, I think, triggered the onset of the Dissociative Identity Disorder,' he goes on. 'She ran away from home and lived on the streets for a while. We learned this from a former social worker. Felicity herself has no memory of it but her time on the streets could explain Shane's interest in the homeless.'

'She appears to have lived normally for quite some time,' Torquil says. 'She went to university and built a successful career. But Joe and I think something happened a few months before she left Cambridge – probably some reminder of what happened to her as a child – that triggered the onset of DID again.'

'People who have DID develop an ability to take themselves away from difficult situations,' Joe says. 'They step outside the room if you like. The body remains but the person inside goes to another place entirely. It's a coping mechanism.'

'And this is key,' Torquil says. 'Another personality steps in.'

Faces around the table register surprise, interest, doubt.

'The new personality, known as an alter, is more able to deal with the difficult situation,' Joe says. 'When things are reverting to normal, he or she leaves and the original personality, the host, resumes control. Significantly, the host has no knowledge of what has happened in the interim. It's disorientating and extremely frightening. I'm now sure that that's what was happening to Felicity while I was treating her.'

Encouraged by their attention, Joe talks them through the fugue states that Felicity experienced, and her memories, awoken under hypnosis, of what happened to her during one of them. 'She believed Freddie was stalking her,' he says. 'When she thought he was close, she became very afraid, and it triggered another personality to take over her body for several hours. When she came back to herself, she had no memory of it.'

'But she could recall under hypnosis?' someone questions.

'That shouldn't be surprising,' Joe says. 'Felicity was still in her body while all this was happening, so the memories were there, just buried quite deep.'

'It's a bit like someone else took over driving the car for a while,' Torquil adds. 'Felicity was still in the car, but in the back seat. She wasn't in control.'

'Maybe she was in the boot if she couldn't remember the journey,' someone quips.

'Twice, I saw Felicity change,' Joe says. 'The first was under hypnosis, when she became a child that she referred to as "Little Bitch". I'm guessing that was a regression to whatever abuse she suffered as a child. Her voice and her demeanour changed completely. It was very disturbing to witness.'

'Curiously, the child called Little Bitch exhibited extreme fear of her father,' Torquil adds. 'Again, a reference to her childhood trauma.'

'The other time was the last occasion I saw her,' Joe says. 'She rang to invite me out to dinner, something she'd never done before. She behaved very differently. She was flirtatious, much more rough and ready in her manner. She almost ordered a steak and then remembered she was vegetarian. I called her Felicity once and she didn't acknowledge me. I think now that I was actually having dinner with one of her alters.'

'Hold on, I'm confused.' One of the detectives speaks up. 'Does Felicity know that she has this condition?'

Joe and his supervisor share a look.

'I don't believe so,' Joe says. 'The fugue states were totally bewildering to her. I also think her symptoms have only emerged very recently. If they'd been occurring for any length of time, she and we would know about it. I think something happened, last summer, to trigger their onset.'

'Something pretty worrying,' his supervisor adds. 'Possibly connected with her husband.'

'No, hold on.' The same detective interrupts. 'Felicity doesn't know about the others, about Little Bitch and whoever else she turns into, is that right?'

'That's my belief,' Joe confirms.

'But they know about her? They must do, or how else could one of them pretend to be her? This woman you had dinner with didn't say, no actually, my name is, I don't know, Kimberly?'

'No, she was definitely pretending to be Felicity.'

'Why would she do that?'

Delilah has her eyes fixed on the tabletop.

'She was trying to draw me into an intimate relationship,' Joe says. 'She knew that if she and I were involved, my credibility would be seriously undermined. I wouldn't be able to stop her taking up a new job she desperately wanted.'

'With this condition, the alters typically know more than the host,' Torquil says. 'All of them will know of Felicity's existence, they will know that they share a body with her. Some of them might know each of the alters who comes and goes. Others might only be aware of one or two.'

'So, to cut to the chase,' Downey says, 'are you saying that the person we believed to be called Shane is one of Felicity's – what did you call them – others?'

'Alters,' Joe replies. 'Although "others" is also used by the various personalities to describe their cohabitees. And yes, I'm sure that Shane is one of her alters.'

'Nearly always with these cases, at least one of the alters will be much more streetwise and aggressive than the host,' Torquil says. 'From what Joe has told me, Felicity is rather a gentle personality, somewhat lacking in self-confidence and a little shy. I think Shane is the personality that goes into battle when Felicity is afraid. Shane takes care of her.'

'Shane's a man,' someone says. 'How can she turn into a man?'

'The alters can appear to be very different to the host,' Torquil says. 'They believe themselves to be different ages, sexes, races and act accordingly. They can have different levels of sight or hearing. One alter can be a very fast runner. Another might believe he can't possibly drive. One might speak a foreign language. I know this sounds far-fetched but there is so much about this condition we don't yet understand.'

'Remember how convinced you were that Shane was a man,' Joe says. 'He fooled the experts you brought in. When she's Shane, she completely believes she's a young man with that name.'

'None of this changes the fact that whoever she believed she was at the time, Felicity murdered Dora Hardwick and Bella Barnes,' Downey says.

'Not necessarily,' Joe argues. 'We know Felicity and Shane are the same person, but we don't know that Shane killed Dora and Bella. Shane stood in my bedroom while I was asleep, with a knife that could have slit my throat. He didn't touch me.'

'Joe, there's something you need to know,' Delilah says.

'What?'

'We found blood on Dora's coat that isn't hers. It is Felicity's. There is no doubt that she and Dora had a close encounter the night Dora died. She may not know it, love, but she is a killer.'

'And a very dangerous woman indeed,' Downey adds.

'She's only dangerous when she's Shane,' Torquil says. 'When she's Felicity, she probably wouldn't harm a fly.'

'So, what is it you want from us?' Downey says.

'You can't send a team of strange police officers and soldiers to arrest Felicity,' Joe says. 'She won't have a clue what's going on and it will terrify her. She'll almost certainly become Shane—'

'Or someone even worse,' Torquil interrupts.

'And someone will get hurt. Probably her.'

'What's the alternative?' Downey asks.

'Send someone she knows and trusts,' Joe says. 'Send my mother. And me.'

Part Four

SOUTH GEORGIA

Present Day

'I seemed to vow to myself that someday I would go
to the region of ice and snow.'

Ernest Shackleton

65

Joe

The windows of the harbour master's office look out towards emerald hills tumbling into an azure blue ocean. Joe can see a waterfall like a silver ribbon, slicing a snow-tipped summit in half, and the rusting carcass of a wrecked steam ship stranded in the bay. On the northern horizon, a berg lies like a fallen mountain and the air above it is alive with seabirds.

The eardrum-splitting cacophony of noise has softened since he, Delilah and Superintendent Skye McNair have come indoors, but even through the reinforced glass Joe can hear the bird screams and the grunting of seals. All the while, the wind uses the building and its surrounds as musical instruments: whistling, singing, moaning. Every few minutes, the structure trembles as a stronger gust hits it.

South Georgia is incredible. In spite of everything, Joe feels a moment of joy that he's been able to share it – albeit briefly – with Felicity. And yet, darker clouds are rolling in from the west, as though to remind him that nothing good can come from this visit. He'll see her again, and his mother will arrest her for murder.

The pre-fab exterior of King Edward Point's administrative centre hasn't prepared him for the scale of the technology on the inside. The harbour master's desk, close to one of two huge windows, holds four large computer screens, each showing satellite images of different points on the islands. A further monitor on another desk shows a constantly updating weather report, and a screen hanging from the ceiling displays the visiting ship's itinerary. Noticeboards hold tide tables, work schedules, equipment requisitions.

The man who introduced himself as Nigel and who revels in the combined titles of harbour master, fisheries officer, post master and tourism manager is making coffee. As he adds milk and sugar, he chats to Superintendent McNair about events on the Falkland Islands. Joe is only half listening. Sick with nerves himself, he is anxious about his mother. Delilah, at his side, is slumped in a chair. The seasickness that has plagued her since they left Stanley isn't letting a detail like solid land get in its way.

'How did Rob Duncan's hip operation work out?' Nigel is asking. 'They were flying him out when I left.'

Skye pulls a face. 'He was seen on horseback last week. Rachel went nuts.' She glances over at Joe. 'Oldest resident of the Falkland Islands. Drives us all to distraction.' Turning back to Nigel she says, 'Oh, and did you hear Jennie Taggert's youngest qualified for—'

Joe sees his own impatience mirrored on his mother's face but she has already made it clear that McNair is in charge of the operation to find and apprehend Felicity. So far away from the UK, they will need her co-operation, and that of the officials here. Even so, he lifts his eyebrows in a silent question. Delilah shrugs, as though the effort of anything more is beyond her. Outside the black clouds are low in the sky, almost touching the sea.

He spots a photograph of Felicity pinned to a noticeboard. Taken from above it shows her scaling a wall of ice. Below the safety helmet, her face is strained with effort and yet she is smiling for the camera. A few feet below her is a man of about her own age. He too is smiling. It takes several seconds for Joe to realise why the picture depresses him. He's never seen her looking happy before.

Behind them, the external door opens. Papers dance in the air and the window blinds rattle against the glass. Nigel says, 'Ah, here she is!'

Heart pounding, Joe turns to see a woman in her forties, stout and plain.

'Dr Susan Brindle,' Nigel introduces the newcomer. 'Sue, you know Skye, of course. And this is Detective Inspector Jones from England, and her colleague, Dr Grant.'

'Joe.' He holds his hand out. 'Is Felicity on her way?'

'Susan is the station chief here,' Nigel explains. 'All the BAS staff report to her. Sue, Detective Inspector Jones and Dr Grant would like to see Felicity.'

'May I ask why?' Brindle is hovering in the doorway, as though entering the room properly might commit her in some way.

'I'm afraid that's confidential,' Joe replies before Delilah can speak.

'Is she expecting you?' Brindle asks.

'This is a police matter,' Delilah says. 'Please have Miss Lloyd brought here immediately.'

There follows a moment of stalemate, which the harbour master breaks by handing round mugs of coffee. 'She said something this morning about a boyfriend,' he tells them. 'She's been very keen on the visiting cruise ships the last couple of weeks. Pouring over the passenger manifests.' He holds coffee out to Joe. 'Is it you she was expecting?'

'She didn't mention a boyfriend to me.' Susan Brindle still hasn't entered the room. 'We usually know if staff are expecting family or friends. They have to book leave.'

Delilah puts her mug down untouched. 'My son is not Felicity Lloyd's boyfriend. I have a warrant for—'

'OK, thank you, Delilah.' Skye McNair speaks up. 'I'll take it from here.'

To Susan Brindle she says, 'These people have travelled a long way to see Dr Lloyd and there is no reason I can think of why she shouldn't be brought here immediately.'

'I can,' says the harbour master. 'She left an hour ago.'

'Left to go where?' Delilah demands.

'Do I have your permission to request Ralph join us?' Nigel asks Skye. 'I think you'll find he was the last person to see her.'

Frowning, Skye nods and the harbour master makes a quick phone call. 'Ralph's our head boatman,' he explains. 'He's on his way up.'

'Is Felicity in trouble?' Brindle asks.

'Oh, I'm sure it's nothing like that,' Nigel says. 'Probably just bad news for the lass. Although obviously I hope not.' He looks, expectantly, at Delilah and Joe. 'Your son, you say? Didn't realise the two of you were related. Is Felicity family?'

Delilah purses her lips. Joe gives a tiny shake of his head. The door opens again and a middle-aged man in outdoor clothing brings with him the smell of the ocean, engine oil and guano.

'Ralph Chapman, who runs our boatyard,' Nigel makes the introductions. Ralph nods to Skye and asks about her family. Joe puts a hand on his mother's arm.

'We're looking for Felicity Lloyd,' Skye explains, as soon as she can interrupt. 'Can you help?'

'Why?' Ralph asks.

'For the love of God!' Delilah gets to her feet. 'I have a warrant to take her into custody and I am this close to arresting the lot of you for obstruction of justice.'

Skye opens her mouth.

'No,' snaps Delilah. 'With respect, Superintendent, this is a

British protectorate, subject to the laws of the United Kingdom and their precious Felicity is wanted for murder.'

'Mum, sit down, you're not well,' Joe says, and to his surprise, Delilah does what she's told. Keeping half an eye on her, because he doesn't like the way her breathing has escalated, he addresses the room. 'I'm Felicity's doctor, or at least I was when she lived in Cambridge and I'm worried for her safety. Please tell us where you think she is.'

'Several miles up the coast by now.' Ralph speaks as though the words are being dragged from him.

'Where's she going?'

'Bird Island.' Ralph frowns at one of the computer screens. 'She's due back towards the end of the week.'

Delilah says, 'We have to go after her.'

'I'm afraid we do,' Skye tells Nigel. 'Can you organise a boat for us?'

'I don't recommend anyone else setting out for Bird today.' Ralph is leaning over one of the monitors now. 'The weather's taken a turn. I've been trying to get Flick on the radio, persuade her to turn around. And I can't seem to find her on radar.'

The harbour master joins him at the monitor.

'Is she alone?' Joe asks.

'I think she took Jack with her,' Ralph says. 'At least I hope she did. I didn't see them leave though.'

'She's not with Jack,' Brindle says. 'I saw him a while back, when that other chap was here.'

Skye looks up. 'What other chap?'

'I'll try her now.' Nigel turns to the radio.

'Can I see her room?' Joe asks.

'Why?' asks Brindle.

His mother gets to her feet and holds up her warrant card. 'What part of wanted in connection with murder do you people not understand? Now, show my son to Miss Lloyd's room – take me while you're at it – and answer Superintendent McNair's question. What other chap?'

Felicity's room is small and feels even smaller when Joe, his mother, Susan Brindle and Skye are squeezed inside it. The neatness is familiar, as is the white dressing gown hanging on the back of the door, but the photograph by the bed is new; a shot of Felicity standing amidst towering columns of ice. Again, she looks happy.

'And you didn't ask his name?' Skye is saying.

'He was very cagey.' The station chief sounds defensive. 'And he scarpered pretty quickly.'

The window looks inland. A short stretch of green meadow dotted with red flowers gives way to a massive slope of rock and scree, its peak shrouded in mist.

'What exactly is it you're looking for?' Brindle asks.

'What's going on?'

Joe glances back to see a man of about his own age, an inch or so shorter, but of a stockier build, with fair hair and bright blue eyes.

'Jack, these people are looking for Felicity,' Brindle says.

The newcomer's blue eyes linger on Joe. 'Popular woman this morning.'

'Can you help?' Brindle asks him.

'Why?' The man called Jack speaks directly to Joe. 'Why do you need to see her?'

'They're police,' the station chief tells him, in a hushed voice.

Jack's face clouds over. 'Is that other bloke with you?'

'Very good question,' Skye mutters.

'Close the door, please, I need to work in peace,' Delilah says. 'Superintendent, can you keep these people outside?'

'Have you authority to be here?' Jack takes a step into the room.

'Is this where she was going?' Joe has spotted the chart on the desk, a circle drawn around Bird Island. He glances over the Post-it notes, the weather forecasts, the journey times, the shopping lists.

'Outside,' Delilah points to the corridor.

'They're saying Felicity's killed someone,' Brindle says.

Jack sneers. 'Bullshit.'

'We didn't say that,' Joe says. 'We said "wanted in connection with murder". Now, if you want to help, answer some questions. Is there a locked cupboard in this room? Or a locker somewhere that she had access to? Anywhere she could keep stuff she didn't want anyone else to see?'

Two mystified and hostile faces look back at him.

'Felicity adopts orphan penguins in breeding season,' Jack says. 'She wouldn't hurt a fly.'

'That's a point,' Susan Brindle says. 'Where are they?'

'My room,' Jack tells her. 'Making a hell of a racket.'

'Does she have a private locker?' Delilah almost yells.

'She has a locker in the boot room,' Jack says. 'She gave me the key to it this morning. No dead bodies that I could see. Just climbing gear, some diving equipment and a packet of butterscotch.'

It doesn't take long to search Felicity's room and other than clear evidence that she's left for Bird Island, they find nothing that can help. They return to the harbour master's office as he's finishing a telephone call. By this time, raindrops are splashing against the windows.

Ralph, the boat man, is at the radio. 'King Edward Point to Felicity, come in, Felicity.' He shakes his head. 'I can't understand why the tracker on the RIB isn't working. She wouldn't have disabled it.'

'All the visitors are going back to the ship,' Nigel announces. 'There's a squall heading down off the mountain.'

Delilah says, 'So she could be anywhere?'

Nigel says, 'I got through to the station on Bird. They'll be in touch the minute they hear from her.'

Delilah says, 'We need to go after her.'

Ralph shakes his head without taking his eyes of the weather report. 'Not a good idea. It'll be a rough trip. And you don't look like you've recovered from your last session on a boat.'

'You're going to leave a woman out on her own in a storm?' Delilah demands.

Ralph leans around Delilah to speak to Jack. 'I thought you were going with her.'

As Joe tells himself not to read too much into the worried expressions he can see around him, the phone rings. Distracted by the sound of his mother arguing with the boat man, Joe tries to hear what is being said to the harbour master. At last, after writing several notes on a desk pad, Nigel holds up a hand for silence.

'That was the ship,' he announces. 'Like we haven't got enough problems. One of the passengers is missing. The crew are organising a search party.'

Joe feels a deadweight settling on his chest. 'What's his name?' he asks.

Nigel checks his notes. 'Bloke called Lloyd. Freddie Lloyd.'

66

Joe

A party of five – Joe, Delilah, Skye, Jack and Ralph – set off from King Edward Point in the pouring rain and even before they leave the sheltered waters of the bay, Delilah is throwing up. When they turn north-west into heavy seas, Joe knows that he's made a mistake allowing her to come along. The launch is travelling directly into oncoming waves and every few seconds the boat climbs a turquoise wall of water before slamming down the other side.

Skye, who seems unaffected by the sea state, is at the chart table speaking to the captain of the ship via radio and using the satellite phone to contact her office on the Falkland Islands.

'Lloyd was last seen heading west out of Grytviken,' she tells Joe.

'How did we miss him?' Delilah groans from her supine position on the cabin seat. 'How could he be on our boat and we not know it?'

Joe too is starting to feel uncomfortable. The cabin is hot and smells of diesel fuel, whilst the rain and spray have turned the windows opaque. It is a little like being trapped inside a washing machine.

'You were in your cabin for most of the trip over, Delilah,' Skye says. 'As were a lot of people, to be honest. He might never have appeared in the communal parts of the ship.'

'I should have checked the passenger list,' Delilah mumbles.

'We were never sure there was a Freddie,' Joe says. 'And we had no idea what he looked like.'

'Well, he won't walk to Bird Island,' Skye says. 'It's sixty miles of mountains and glaciers, and he'd have to swim the last bit. If that's where he's heading, he's on a suicide mission.'

'Long way to come to commit suicide.' Joe groans as the launch takes a sudden dive down a steep wave.

'Joe, you don't look good either,' Skye says. 'Go up and get some air.'

Hating to leave his mother, knowing Skye is right, Joe pulls up the hood of his coat and climbs into the cockpit. Ralph is at the helm in a heavy oilskin coat and Jack is sheltering in the lee of the cabin wall.

'How long to Bird Island?' Joe takes the opposite seat.

'Five hours in good conditions.' Jack is holding binoculars to his eyes. 'These are not good conditions.'

It is a little after one o'clock in the afternoon.

'Ralph's keeping us close to land,' Jack says. 'He's trying to avoid the bigger seas. We'll have a more comfortable trip, but it will take longer.'

Joe looks down into the cabin. His mother isn't moving.

'We're keeping an eye out for Felicity's RIB,' Ralph shouts. 'She may have decided to sit the storm out.'

Joe turns to face land. The mountains are almost black in the storm, broken by streaks of white where the glaciers meet the sea. He switches seats, sitting next to Jack on the starboard side.

'So, who's this Freddie bloke?' Jack asks, without lowering his binoculars.

'According to Felicity, he's her husband.'

The binoculars drop. 'She's married?'

Joe takes a mean pleasure in saying, 'Guess there's a lot you don't know about Felicity.'

'I know she's not a murderer.'

Joe says nothing.

'Seriously?' Jack breaks the silence first. 'You really think she killed someone?'

'There's evidence.'

Jack shakes his head. 'I can't see it.' He lifts the binoculars again, as though the subject is closed.

'She has a condition,' Joe says, after a moment. 'She may not have known what she was doing. I think she needs help. And a hospital, not a prison.' He lets his eyes travel back towards the cabin. 'Not everyone agrees with me.'

'What sort of condition?'

'I shouldn't discuss her. She was my patient.'

Jack turns to face him and once again Joe is struck by how blue his eyes are. 'I've seen Felicity every day for nine months,' Jack says. 'Her compulsion to tidy everything is verging on obsessive. She may have a mild form of OCD. Other than that, nothing. She's completely normal.'

'It's possible being here helped her.' Joe pushes down the surge of jealousy that this man has seen Felicity at her best. 'I think fear of her husband triggered her symptoms back in Cambridge. On the other side of the planet she felt safe.'

'Until you brought him.'

There is no answer to that, so Joe resumes looking for Felicity's RIB. The land is cloaked in a grey mist and he can barely make out the reddish-brown outlines of buildings. Something that looks like a tower, and a shipwreck close to shore.

'Sorry,' Jack says. 'That was uncalled for.'

'We don't have to worry about Freddie yet,' Joe says. 'From what Skye tells me, he won't get anywhere near her. What's that place?'

'Husvik,' Jack says. 'Another old whaling station. Bit like

Grytviken, but not safe for visitors. We'll pass another in a while, at Stromness. Then Prince Olav a bit further up.'

The cabin door opens and Skye appears. 'You're wanted,' she tells Joe.

Down in the cabin, Delilah has managed to sit upright. 'Tell him,' she says.

'We've had some more news from the ship,' Skye tells Joe. 'Freddie Lloyd saw the ship's doctor just before we arrived. He's recently been released from prison.'

67

Joe

The storm is at its height by the time they reach their destination – a single storey, green-painted building nestling in the foot of low hills. After Ralph and Jack have tied up the launch, Joe and Skye help Delilah onto a salt-encrusted jetty and then across a beach of kelp-covered rocks. The six-hour trip has taken its toll. Even Ralph and Skye are pale and Delilah is on the verge of collapse.

The news awaiting them is not good.

'She's not here? How can she not be here?' Skye demands of the married couple who run the station.

'We are expecting her,' Jan explains as her husband Frank organises hot drinks. 'Just not necessarily today.'

'So where the hell is she?'

'Mum, take it easy,' Joe warns, even as he is thinking about accidents at sea, Felicity's boat overcome by waves.

'There you go, love.' Ralph hands Delilah a steaming mug. 'Use your mouth for drinking not talking until you're a bit more yourself.'

'Fuck off,' Delilah tells him, but she clutches the mug with shaking hands as a flurry of raindrops, possibly spray, hits the window. The sea seems dangerously close. 'Where else could she have gone?'

'Camping out would be stupid,' Ralph says. 'She's not stupid.'

'Husvik,' Jack says. 'There's an old manager's villa there. It's the only place apart from Bird Island and KEP where she could hang out safely, especially in a storm.'

'Husvik?' Delilah gasps. 'You're not serious?'

'No sign of the RIB,' Ralph tells him. 'I watched the entire coastline on the way up.'

'That's miles back, isn't it?' Delilah's colour is returning rapidly. 'Someone get me a map.'

'She hid it,' Joe says.

'Why would she do that?'

'She doesn't want to be found. She's hiding.'

'From us?' Jack asks.

'From Freddie. She's terrified of Freddie.'

He remembers her trembling even as she mentioned Freddie's name, her whispered memories of what she suffered at his hands. And the break-in at her house, when someone – probably Freddie – nearly killed her, and not a single one of them took it seriously.

'Could he walk to Husvik?' Skye asks.

'Ten miles or so,' Ralph tells her.

'He'd have to cross three glaciers not to mention climbing several mountains,' Jack says. 'Unlikely. Not impossible.'

'Can we go back?' Delilah asks Ralph.

He laughs. 'You're a game old bird, I'll give you that. But no one is going anywhere until this storm dies down.'

Joe thinks of Freddie, relentlessly tracking Felicity down, of her hiding up somewhere in fear of her life, while they are miles away.

'Can we get a helicopter out here?' he asks. 'Skye, you must be able to organise that. From the RAF base on the Falklands?'

Skye looks miserable. 'It can't be done, Joe. South Georgia is too far for a helicopter to travel.'

'We get around by sea, or we don't get around,' Ralph adds.

'So, what do we do?' Delilah asks.

Ralph looks outside as another burst of rain, or spray, hits the windows. 'We wait.'

And pray, Joe thinks.

68

Freddie

Freddie comes round to a sense of being immobile. A weight on his chest is making it hard to breathe and he can feel a warm trickle running into the crease of his neck. There is pain at the back of his skull and his ears are ringing from the sound of gun-fire. He thinks a sheet of corrugated iron has fallen on top of him. For several seconds he doesn't move, trying to make sense out of what has happened.

And then, in a flash, it comes back. He's been shot. A woman who looks and sounds nothing like Felicity, and yet so plainly was her all the same, has just shot him. Bamber, she called herself, and she might be standing over him now waiting to finish the job.

He lies still, hearing his own breathing. In all these months of planning this visit, preparing for the first confrontation, it has never occurred to him to be afraid of Felicity. Now, he realises, he has no idea who she is any more, and he is hopelessly unprepared.

Outside the store the wind is screaming and the building shakes violently. The whole lot might come down any second and it is the thought of being crushed to death that gives him courage to move.

The sheet of iron is corroded, not heavy, and can be pushed to one side. Upright again, he sees his torch, still lit, a few yards away. He risks crawling to it and shines it around the store. The woman in the doorway – Felicity – is gone. He struggles to his feet and knows that Felicity's shot has missed. He couldn't possibly be standing upright, feeling more or less OK, if he'd been hit.

She's left the gun behind. He can see it, caught in the torch beam, immediately inside the doorway. He snatches it up, checks the safety catch and tucks it into his pocket. Breathing more easily, he gives himself a minute to take stock, to come up with another plan. He will not look for her again, not in the dark. He'll find her boat and disable it, then go back to the manager's villa and wait until morning.

Outside, the wind hits him again, and debris comes scurrying up the street like a pack of attack dogs. Sidestepping the bigger pieces, he sets off towards the water's edge.

He finds the RIB behind a pile of rubble a little way up from the slipway. He is debating how best to disable it when he spots a light on the outskirts of the settlement. He raises his binoculars but the surrounding hills are too dark for him to see anything much. Definitely a light though, weaving in and out of the tussock grass.

Freddie thinks back to the maps and charts he studied on the journey. She isn't going back to Grytviken, but in the opposite direction entirely. Felicity is heading towards the glacier.

69

Felicity

Felicity ignores the pain in her wounded leg and keeps going. Terror is stealing her breath and she has to stop every few minutes to gulp in more air. She leaves the tussock grass behind and starts climbing the scree slope towards the vast expanse of white that she knows is ahead. After a while her neck and shoulders begin to ache from constantly looking back for signs of pursuit. She sees nothing but forces herself on. He will never be able to track her on the glacier. No one knows ice the way she does. If she can make it to the upper ice sheet she'll be safe. She'll spend the night in an ice cave that the team use as a base when they're working up there. It will be cold, but she'll live.

She remembers hands around her throat, the gleam of a blade in the moonlight. She has no idea why Freddie should want to kill her but there was no mistaking the intent of the person who attacked her that night.

Bitch, bitch, bitch. I'm going to kill you.

For the first time, she wonders if she's been a fool to leave the safety of the base behind. Her friends, Jack, Nigel, Ralph, wouldn't let anyone hurt her. But how can she explain a husband she has never mentioned, a marriage she has no memory of, and the knowledge of dreadful, shameful abuse that she will never be able to prove?

The terrain grows steeper and her footsteps noisier as each

step sends loose shale scurrying down the slope. Once, she looks back and sees a torch beam near the water's edge, a long way below. The voice she hears next, though, is as clear as if someone walked beside her.

He's not dead then?

Felicity stops walking and remembers. There was a shot, a sound so loud that even the chaos of the wind seemed to die down in shock. She remembers the building shaking, parts of it falling, she remembers turning and running. Did he shoot her? Shoot her and miss?

No. She looks down and sees her own right hand raised, clutching the torch, as though holding a gun, and she remembers seeing the gun in her own hand. She remembers firing and dropping it in horror at what seemed exactly the same moment. She remembers Freddie crying out and then falling. She shot him.

How is that possible? She doesn't own a gun. She has never even fired a gun.

Felicity's chest tightens and suddenly her head is full of voices, each of them clamouring to be heard. They tell her to flee up the glacier, to turn around and head for Grytviken, that she is a killer, that she is useless, that she's always been useless, that she deserves everything she gets and more. So much is being shouted at her, each voice contradicting the last.

She starts to run and realises she is heading the wrong way, back down to Husvik. Stopping again, she struggles to get her breath. She has a vision of her skull bones, pulsating outwards, being stretched to the point where they might shatter, because the contents of her head has become a virulent, violent mob.

Bewildered, fighting back sobs, she sets off again, up this time, pushing her body to climb higher, move faster. If she slows down for even a moment, she'll have to ask herself what the hell is happening. She pushes on, as the great towers and peaks of the glacier emerge from the darkness and she closes her ears to the rancour in her head. She's reached the snowline when a single voice sings up, louder and clearer than the others.

He'll come after us, you know that, don't you? He'll never give up.

Felicity stops walking. She knows that voice. She's heard it before.

'Who are you?' She speaks quietly, knowing her voice doesn't need to carry. The conversation she is having is entirely in her own head. The voices have always been her own. A gust of icy wind blows down from the glacier, lifting her hair and cooling her hot scalp. She has a sense of having reached a fork in the road. The noise in her head abates a little, and with the settling quiet comes a sense of – more.

She is bigger than she knows. She is more.

'Who are you?' she repeats and this time she wants the answer.

I'm Bamber, says one of her other selves. *Hello, Felicity.*

Felicity takes courage and says, 'Are you me?'

Oh no. The denial is instant and immediate. A second later the tone becomes more considered. *But you might say so.*

The voice is her, but not her? It makes no sense. What the hell is happening to her? 'Stop it,' Felicity says. 'Go away.'

She sets off again, faster, but this time, she isn't entirely sure who she is running from.

70

Joe

'Christ, does nobody in this place sleep?'

It is nearly one o'clock in the morning when Jack enters the common room of the Bird Island research station, where Ralph and Joe have been sharing the last few inches of a bottle of scotch. The station can sleep ten, mainly in two dorm rooms, and they've all been provided with beds. Neither Joe nor Ralph have been to bed yet.

'My mother,' Joe replies, 'went out like a light at ten.'

'Seasickness does that to you.' Ralph tops up both their drinks. 'She ate well though. Glasses in the cupboard, Jack.'

Earlier, they'd had a surprisingly good dinner of reindeer steak with a salad of dandelion leaves and tussock roots. Jan had even baked her own bread. The station is warm, given the storm blowing outside, and Joe is surprised at how comfortable he's been made. He still doesn't feel like sleeping though.

'Takes a lot to put Mum off her food,' he says.

'So, is there a dad in the picture?' Ralph asks.

Jack is hiding a smile as he joins them.

'They divorced when I was fifteen,' Joe replies. 'He lives in Wales with his second family.'

'Any news?' Jack asks.

'Storm's clearing,' Ralph tells him. 'Should be OK to head out by four. It'll take us three hours if we borrow Jen and Frank's

RIB. I'm not taking your mum though, Joe. Not at that speed. I'll collect her later, when she's had time to recover.'

Joe isn't arguing. 'She needs to talk to her office anyway.' He turns to Jack. 'We had a message from the ship a half-hour ago. Cambridge CID have been trying to get in touch with her.'

'Any news on the missing passenger?' Jack asks.

'They called off the search at midnight,' Joe says. 'They think he must have gone onto the glacier. They're bracing themselves to find his body in the morning.'

All three men drink in silence for several minutes.

'He can't have reached Felicity,' Jack says. 'He can't have crossed three glaciers.'

'You wouldn't think so,' Ralph agrees

'Nigel will send a boat to Husvik in the morning,' Ralph says. 'It'll be touch and go who gets there first. Them or us.'

'Nobody should approach Felicity,' Joe says. 'We need to warn the other group. Make sure she's OK and then stay away from her until we get there.'

'Oh, come on,' Jack scoffs. 'Felicity isn't dangerous.'

Joe thinks for a second. He is going to have to take these people into his confidence or they'll never take him seriously.

'No, she isn't,' he says. 'But she isn't always Felicity.'

71

Freddie

By the time he reaches the snow line, Freddie has no idea whether he is still on Felicity's trail or not. Over the last hour he has caught glimpses of her light, but there are no paths to follow and more than once he has had to stumble sideways across fields of scree to get back on track. He has found, though, that the closer he gets to the glacier, the better he can see. The great expanse of white is acting like a mirror, reflecting back and increasing the light from the moon and stars.

When he sees the hut, a small black rectangle against the white, his heart leaps but before he is close he knows that he won't find her inside it. It is padlocked shut with a combination lock. He tries her birthday and her mother's birthday but neither works. There will be equipment in this hut – crampons, walking sticks, even skis – that she has had access to and that he will have to manage without. He kicks the door in frustration and carries on. Unsurprisingly, it's grown colder as he's neared the ice and the wind has picked up.

The snow beneath his feet hardens and the bedrock becomes ice. Walking without bespoke footwear is almost impossible. Occasional drifts of snow give him some purchase, but the sheets of solid ice are treacherous. Every few steps he slides a little way back. He stumbles often and the ground is sharp as broken glass. Before long there are several cuts on his hands.

As he's neared the glacier the moaning of the wind has taken on an almost human tone and there are times, with a particularly strong gust, when the human voice sounds close to insane. From somewhere in the distance he hears a roar like that of a great animal and a thundering crash. He falls, hurting himself again. When he is upright once more, he carries on with an increasing anxiety, knowing that time he didn't lose his footing. The ice beneath him moved.

An instinctive, primitive fear grips him; this is a wild and dangerous place.

A hundred yards higher up and the smooth surface of the ice has become ruptured and cracked. He stops for a second and wonders how he can possibly go on. The slope ahead of him, that would be punishingly steep were it smooth and stable rock, is like a turbulent sea that has frozen solid. The ice rears and drops all around him, forming tunnels and crevices and holes that might be bottomless. It soars above his head in majestic columns and cuts across his path with peaks as sharp as knives. He knows that on glaciers, flimsy bridges of snow can conceal drops of forty feet or more. Worse, he knows that glaciers move, especially at the end of the summer. Meltwater erodes the massive structures, weakening the glue that holds them together. As long as he is up here, he is in constant danger of avalanche, of crevices opening beneath him, of being crushed beneath giant boulders. The glacier is a deathtrap.

His foot slides again and he tumbles several feet before landing hard against a low ridge of ice. He lies, winded, on the verge of giving up, and has a moment of luck. There are six indentations in the crusty covering of snow on top of the ice. She is wearing crampons. And she has left a trail.

72

Felicity

Felicity is moving dangerously fast up the glacier but after two hours she has to rest. She is hotter than she should be, even given how quickly she's been moving, and the wound on her thigh is throbbing. She finds a smooth patch of ice to sit on and pulls her pack from her shoulders. Sipping water and nibbling chocolate, she knows she has to keep moving. The storm is dying away but if another comes up, she cannot be on the glacier without shelter. A strong gust will send her skidding over a cliff or into a deep fissure. Worse, she suspects a bigger movement of the ice is imminent. As she's climbed, she's felt tremors, heard the regular thunder of falling snow and ice, even the sonorous groaning of shifting ice plates. She knows she has some distance to go before she reaches the ice sheet and the hidden cave. This is not a good place to linger.

The physical exertion has helped, though, and her head is more like itself again. She can no longer sense a host of trapped creatures scrabbling to get out. They are still there, but they are behaving. They are a little like children, or pets, waiting to see what the woman in charge will do. The sense of authority makes her feel calmer. Ready to take a risk.

'Bamber,' she says. 'Are you there?'

The voice snaps back. *Always.*

She shouldn't have asked. It is too horrible, this sense of a parasite inside her. Felicity shuts her eyes tight, and clamps her hands over her ears, but there is no shutting out a voice that comes from her own head.

'Who are you,' she says, 'if you're not me?'

Silence.

Felicity tries again. 'Is it, I don't know, a Jekyll-and-Hyde thing?'

A subdued giggle.

How can part of her be laughing, when there is nothing remotely funny about the situation? How can she have no control over her own feelings?

'Do you hate me?' she asks, remembering the journal she found at home in Cambridge. 'Are we enemies?'

Another fast response. *No. I look after you.*

From somewhere nearby comes a crashing that echoes around the mountain. A huge piece of ice has fallen from one of the upper peaks.

He's coming. We have to go. Now.

Felicity feels an urgent compulsion to get up and run, as though hands are on her shoulders, tugging her upwards. She resists, but it isn't easy.

'Who are you afraid of?' Felicity asks.

Freddie, replies Bamber. *Freddie, Freddie, Freddie. Come on, we have to go.*

There is no mistaking the fear in Bamber's voice, a fear reflected inside Felicity. Still she stays where she is. 'Can you remember Freddie?' she asks. 'The things he did, why we're so afraid of him? Because I can't.'

Yes, of course I remember Freddie. He hurts us. He puts us in the cupboard. He attacked us in Cambridge. He tried to kill us.

It is too frustrating. Felicity wants to bang her head against the ice, to release the memories that have to be in there somewhere. How can Bamber know all this and she not?

'Did he rape me? Us, I mean.'

Yes, yes, yes. At least, I think so.

'What do you mean, you think so?'

I can't remember. Long time ago. Ask one of the others.

'Others?' Felicity feels physically sick. 'There are others?' Even as she says the words, she knows it is true. They are with her now, watching, waiting for their moment to step in. A memory strikes her, a phrase in a journal entry. *The others tell me . . .*

Beneath her, the ice shudders. She has to move.

'Did you write the journal?' she asks.

No, that was – someone else. I told you, I don't hate you. I look after you.

'Who? Who else? Who hates me?'

Bamber is silent.

Another sound from the glacier, but not tumbling ice this time. She hears a muffled cry and the sound of something heavy sliding down the ice. Freddie has almost caught up.

Come on, come on.

This time Felicity can't resist Bamber's panic. She gets to her feet and sets off again.

73

Freddie

Freddie has heard Felicity speaking. Her voice has drifted down to him on the wind. Knowing her to be close, he picks up his pace, takes risks he is neither fit enough nor properly equipped to take safely. He falls and slides back nearly ten feet. By the time he has retraced his steps he is tiring fast but the blackness of the sky in the east is softening.

His head is bleeding. He doesn't think he's losing much blood, but there is a smear of crimson on the ice where he fell. He gathers a handful of clean snow and holds it to his wound to numb the pain. Then he sets off again.

Momentarily distracted by a flock of birds flying towards the ocean he looks up, but in the darkness, can only make out their linear shapes, the beating of strong wings. There is something about the birds' flight, though, that suggests panic. They are fleeing a place they can sense is no longer safe.

Around him, the ice is closing in. Columns stand like armed ranks and small cliffs rise up on either side. Pushing down his disquiet, he follows Felicity's trail into a long V-shaped crevice. The walls soar above him, reaching fifteen feet or more and the floor is only inches wide. His boots, encrusted with snow, can barely move through it.

He isn't claustrophobic. Few people can spend years in prison and have a fear of small spaces, but as he makes his way through the fissure, that gets narrower as it climbs, he finds his heartbeat accelerating. If these walls move even a few inches, he will be crushed. His torch beam spots a mark of red on the fissure wall. He touches it to find it damp. Blood. Felicity, too, is injured.

He pushes through the fissure for ten yards, and then it veers to the right. Turning the corner he sees the trap that Felicity has led him into. Ahead the crevice becomes too narrow for him to carry on. She has squeezed through but for him this is a dead end and if he has to go all the way back he might lose her completely. He turns, and a thick lump of ice, heavier and more deadly than many rocks, narrowly misses breaking open his skull.

74

Felicity

Again, hisses Bamber in her ear. *Another one. Kill him.*

Above the fissure where Freddie is trapped, Felicity is surrounded by blocks of ice. It would be the easiest thing in the world to do what Bamber is asking. She lifts a block high and steps to the edge of the crevice.

Drop it. Now.

Freddie is several feet below her, looking up. Even in the strange, half-twilight coming off the ice, he is impossibly handsome. The lines of his face are long and straight and in perfect proportion. The glimpses of hair not covered by the thick woollen cap are more grey than blond but his brows are still perfectly shaped, his lips full. The habitual sternness of expression is there, of course, given the circumstances, but she remembers how it disappears when he smiles. It is a face she once loved, completely and utterly.

She could crush that face, smash it to a pulp. She is standing directly above him. All she has to do is let go.

'Don't move,' she orders.

He's got the gun, Bamber says. *I dropped it.*

A picture flashes before Felicity's eyes. A shop in South America, handing over money for a gun. She has no idea whether the memory is hers, or Bamber's, or whether perhaps the two are starting to merge.

'Are you OK?' he asks. 'I've seen blood. Are you hurt?'

'Why are you here?'

Don't talk to him. Don't listen to him. Throw it. Just throw it.

He calls up to her. 'I only want to talk to you. I came here to explain.'

He ruined your life.

This feels so true that Felicity is compelled to repeat it. 'You ruined my life,' she shouts down.

'I know,' he says. 'What I did was unspeakable.'

See, he admits it. Kill him. Do it now.

The ice she is holding is growing too heavy. She must either throw it or put it down.

'There hasn't been a day when I haven't regretted it,' he says. 'I should have been there for you. I should never have left you. You were the only thing that really mattered, and I lost sight of that.'

This is making no sense.

Don't listen to him.

'What does he mean, he left me? Do you remember that?'

The face below her turns puzzled. 'What did you say? Felicity, I didn't catch that.'

Yes. I mean no. He hurt us. He raped us. He locked us in the cupboard, you remember that, don't you?

She thinks she does. Except—

He broke into our house in Cambridge. He tried to kill us. Have you forgotten that?

She hasn't forgotten that.

He's come to finish the job. He'll never stop. You have to end it.

Felicity lowers the ice to the ground. Bamber may be a killer. She is not.

'It ends now,' she calls down. 'Today. This minute. I want you out of my life, once and for all.'

It won't work. He'll trick you.

She spots then, for the first time, that there is blood on Freddie's head. He is hurt.

'I should never have married you,' she shouts down. 'I've no idea why I did, but it ends now. We get divorced, if we're not already, and then there'll be some sort of restraining order that you agree to. I'm not going to run away again and you're never going to hurt me again.'

'Felicity?' It is impossible to read the expression that has taken hold of his face.

'That's what's going to happen. We're going back to King Edward Point, you're getting on board that ship, you'll agree to a divorce and we'll never see each other again. Agree to that now, or I'm leaving you up here.'

'Felicity.' He is shaking his head, and finally she recognises that look. He is bewildered. He leans back against the ice wall, as though exhausted. 'I'm not your husband,' he says. 'I'm your father.'

75

Joe

Joe is dozing on a sofa when the door opens.

'This came through for your mother.' Frank, the BAS scientist, holds out several sheets of paper. 'I didn't like to wake her up but it looks important.'

Rubbing his eyes, Joe takes a print-out of an email from one of Delilah's colleagues in the Cambridge police station. Before leaving England, she'd asked her team to do some digging into the twenty-five-year-old Salisbury murder. Joe scans the covering note and turns to the attachment to see the front page of the Salisbury Gazette dated Saturday 20 May 1994.

Mother Killed in Horror House. Husband Suspected.

A nationwide hunt is underway for the chief suspect in the murder of a young Salisbury mother. Wilfred Lloyd is believed to be on the run after killing his wife, Faye, and subjecting both her and their three-year-old daughter, Felicity, to a sustained period of torture and abuse.

The body of Faye Lloyd was found by local police on Friday night, after neighbours reported a disturbance at 22 Clockhouse Road. The couple's little girl was found, injured and dehydrated, in a cupboard, where it is feared she may have spent some days. She is currently in the care of social services.

People are warned not to approach Lloyd, but to report any sightings to the police.

Joe needs a moment to take it in. Felicity's father was Wilfred Lloyd. Freddie Lloyd. The man who has followed her to South Georgia, the man who, according to what he's just read, she has every reason to fear, isn't her husband, but her father.

The story was still front page news on the following Monday.

Wilfred Lloyd is still at large nearly forty-eight hours after he is believed to have killed his wife Faye in a vicious attack at their home in Clock-house Road, Salisbury. Sightings in Andover, Basingstoke and London have proved inconclusive and police believe he may be attempting to leave the country.

Police have refused to confirm that luggage and travel papers found in the Lloyd family house indicate that Lloyd arrived back in the country from where he was working in Brazil on Friday afternoon. A source who declined to be named, though, told the Gazette *that the findings threw doubt on the previous belief that Lloyd had subjected his wife and daughter to a prolonged period of abuse, before murdering his wife.*

'He'd only just got back,' neighbour Mrs Singer told the Gazette*. 'He couldn't have hurt his wife and kiddy.'*

The couple's daughter, three-year-old Felicity, is recovering in hospital. It is believed her maternal grandmother is travelling to Salisbury from North Wales to take care of her granddaughter.

The story was covered again in both the Tuesday and Wednesday editions of the papers, slipping to the inside page and then to page four, as no further news emerged. Then, on the Thursday, it was back on the front page.

In a grim twist to the Lloyd murder investigation, Wilfred Lloyd handed himself into police custody at Basingstoke Police Station in the early hours of this morning and was immediately arrested. Police spokesman,

Detective Chief Superintendent Allan Edwards would neither confirm nor deny that Lloyd's arrest is linked to the discovery, yesterday, of the remains of three men in a house in the Shepherd's Hill district of the town.

Once again, the story went quiet. The paper carried picture-stories of friends and neighbours leaving flowers and gifts for the dead woman and her daughter, and there was a small piece that was mainly speculation on the part of neighbours and friends, most of whom believed the young couple to be very happy and devoted to their daughter. Finally, on 29 May, an update.

In a statement given today at 2 p.m. this afternoon, Detective Chief Superintendent Edwards told waiting reporters that Wilfred Lloyd has been charged with three counts of murder, of Thomas Lee, 35, Ron Lovell, 29 and Jake Ellery, 34. All three men were known to have carried out work on the Lloyds' property in recent months. Edwards went on to confirm that Lloyd would not now be facing charges for the murder of his wife, or for the abuse of his daughter. The police are not seeking anyone else in connection with those crimes.

The next day, a very brief piece.

Wilfred Lloyd pleaded guilty yesterday at Salisbury Magistrates Court to three charges of murder. The magistrate referred the case to the Crown Court and remanded Lloyd in custody. The trial is expected in the summer.

The door opens again and Jack appears. Without speaking, Joe hands over the articles before turning back to the email from Delilah's detective sergeant. The detective wrote:

Faye Lloyd hired three men to help her clear the garden before the summer. If she'd known that two of them had convictions for sex offences and the third for GBH she probably wouldn't have. They realised she and the little girl were alone in the house and decided to move in.

They kept her as a sex slave, subjecting her to abuse and torture, for three days before her husband arrived back on extended leave. He got in, arms full of souvenirs, looking forward to a marital reunion, to find his wife dead in the bedroom. Felicity had been locked in the under-stairs cupboard for God knows how long.

'Did these blokes hurt Felicity too?' Jack asks, when he's caught up.

Joe nods. 'Medical evidence suggested she'd been raped and beaten too. The public were hugely sympathetic to Lloyd, but he'd deliberately hunted down his wife's killers and murdered them in cold blood. And showed no remorse. The judge had no choice but to send him down. He got a whole life tariff.'

All colour seems to have drained from Jack's face. 'Does Felicity know any of this?'

'She was three years old. People retain very few memories from being so young. She did recall some of it under hypnosis one time but it was very confused.'

'How so?'

'She remembered her mother screaming and being locked in the cupboard. And she talked about the bad men coming to get her out of the cupboard and hurting her.'

Jack is looking through the newspaper reports again. 'According to this, her father found her.'

'Found her and then fled, never to reappear in her life. So, her terrified, toddler brain confused him with the bad men. All

Felicity's fears of a man she knew as Freddie stem from inaccurate recollections of when she was three years old.'

'So, she has no reason to be afraid of Freddie?'

Joe drops his head into his hands. 'No. He's the one in danger.'

76

Freddie

'Felicity? Felicity? Are you still there?'

She has backed away from the fissure edge. For several seconds there is no response, and then Freddie hears her voice, low and unhappy.

'Bamber?' she says. 'What's he talking about?'

'Felicity,' he shouts up. 'Lissy, why on Earth do you think I'm your husband? Are you married? I suppose you could be, and you might have married someone who reminds you of me, people do that, but how could you even remember me after so much time? Felicity, please come back. Please talk to me.'

There is movement above, loose snow falls, then she reappears. Thank God, she's put the lump of ice down. Instead she holds her flashlight and shines it directly onto his face.

'Stop trying to trick me,' she says. 'You're Freddie.'

The light half blinds him. 'Yes, Freddie is my name. Wilfred, actually, but your mother always called me Freddie and you did too when you were tiny. You said Freddie, not Daddy. Do you remember anything about back then?'

She mutters something.

'What? What did you say? Is there someone up there with you?'

'I have a wedding ring,' she tells him.

'Is it this one?' He fumbles inside his jacket until he finds the ring he stole from her room the previous morning. The torch beam shifts to focus on it. 'This is your mother's ring. See the *F & F* on the inside? Freddie and Faye. You've got a silver lily on a chain too. That was your mother's. I bought it for her when we were students. She kept it in a porcelain box with violets on the lid.'

Seeing the look on her face, he is glad the gun is in his pocket now.

'Felicity, what's going on? How can you not know who I am?'

'There is a wedding dress in my loft,' she tells him.

He nods his head, ignoring the thump of pain. 'White lace, with long sleeves and a sweetheart neckline? I'll bet you've never tried it on, have you? It won't fit. You're three inches taller than your mother was, and a size bigger. You take after me, Lissy, although your face is a lot like hers.'

The face above him, so like that of the woman he once loved more than his own life, seems to change. Her eyes open wider, her eyebrows lift, and her lips purse. 'Seven, eight, nine, ten,' she says, in the voice of a young child. 'Coming ready or not.'

'What?' Afraid, suddenly, Freddie backs away, retracing his steps. He remembers the gun in his pocket and knows it can't help him. He will not aim a loaded gun at his daughter.

She speaks again, and her voice is normal this time. 'If you're my father, why do I not know you? Why can't I remember you?'

Freddie takes a deep breath. He'd known this would be hard. 'I've been away, Lissy,' he says. 'Do you remember anything about what happened when you were tiny?'

Again, the child's voice. 'Eight, nine, ten, coming ready or not.' Then, Felicity's own voice again. 'You attacked me in my house. You tried to strangle me.'

He shakes his head. 'No, I did not. I came to your house once. It was June last year. I knocked on your door. I shouldn't have done that. I shouldn't have taken you by surprise. You ran away.

Lissy, you must remember that. You ran across the common. I went after you but I lost you. After that, I didn't see you again until that time in the bookshop.'

'You broke into my house.' She is shouting at him now. 'You broke a window. You put a knife to my throat.'

He keeps moving backwards. 'I've no idea what you're talking about.'

'You locked me in the cupboard. You gave me to the bad men. They raped me and they killed Mummy.'

'Absolutely not. I would never hurt you.'

'Liar!'

She screams down at him. And then she bends and picks up a block of ice. It is huge, over a foot in length, and narrowing to an evil spike. He turns, tries to run. His foot catches in the narrow V of the fissure and the ice block comes thundering down.

77

Felicity

Felicity runs, and the voices drive her on.

So, you're not married. It makes no difference, he still wants to hurt you.

He hurt you when you were a baby. It was his fault, everything that happened.

He should have been there. He should have saved you.

Run, run, run!

She flees through snow that is getting deeper as she climbs, and she knows she is running from herself, as much as from the father who, her whole life, has been the hidden monster in her nightmares. She runs, and finally, her memories start to emerge.

The men who'd worked in the garden, who'd played with her and given her chocolate, turning into bad men, coming into the house and locking the doors, holding her down while they pinned Mummy onto the kitchen floor and did horrible things to her.

Stop your screaming. Shut the little bitch up.

She reaches a snowfall, the result of a recent avalanche and can go no further this way. She heads west, knowing that to leave the familiar route is foolish, but compelled to keep going.

You've killed him. That block of ice split his head in two. You're a killer now.

He deserved it. He would have killed you. It was you or him.

She has no idea of the time, but the night sky has turned the deep mauve of mourning. The clouds are low and heavy but above them she can see the lighter hues of an impending dawn. A streak of gold, the width of a human hair, appears on the horizon and, in the distance, the mountain tops are becoming visible.

Has she really just killed her father?

Distracted, she misses her footing and drops the flashlight. Before she can grab hold of it again, it rolls away down a snow slope that is the same purple colour as the sky. She doesn't chase it. Soon she will have no need of a torch. She pushes herself to her feet and goes on. The slope becomes steeper. She isn't entirely sure where she is any more. She looks around for a familiar peak, a landmark of some kind, but it is too dark and the mountain tops are unfamiliar from this angle. Her muscles are burning and each breath comes out as a sob. Still the memories keep coming. The dam has broken now and there is no holding back the flood.

The men put her in the cupboard under the stairs. She's hungry and terrified of the dark, but the games they play with her when they take her out are even worse. They take her clothes away and when she soils herself, because she is only three years old, and can't hold on, especially when she is so frightened, they slap her. They pin her down and climb on top of her and the pain is beyond anything she could have imagined. This pain will kill her. She hears Mummy sobbing and screams for Daddy, but Daddy doesn't come and she's in the cupboard again and she can't decide whether she is afraid of the cupboard because of the dark and the rat she can hear scrabbling around, or whether the cupboard is the only place she will ever feel safe again.

It goes on, for days and days, until she thinks it will never stop, that the only sound she will hear for the rest of her life is that of Mummy sobbing and screaming, and then Mummy stops screaming, and she doesn't sob any more, and the three-year-old Felicity knows that this is far worse. And still they keep coming.

Seven, eight, nine, ten, coming ready or not, and the footsteps get closer and the door opens.

She is staggering over the snow now, exhausted, hardly knowing which way she is going. There is no point in running anyway, she realises, not if she's killed him. She thinks about the blue lake. It will kill her in minutes. All she will have to do is jump in and start swimming. It will claim her before she can even think about trying to get out.

Another memory pushes aside thoughts of suicide. Footsteps, approaching the cupboard. The tiny naked Felicity huddles as far from the door as she can get. They're not saying the words this time. This is a new game.

'Faye?' A voice calls, hesitant and nervous, a voice that knows something has gone horribly wrong. 'Felicity?'

Daddy's voice. Daddy at last.

The door opens and it is Daddy, it is. He lets out a strangled cry. He bends down and lifts his daughter out.

Felicity sees a peak she recognises. She is only a short climb from the ice sheet. The sky in the north-east is growing lighter now and the world around her is losing the dark chill of night. In less than an hour the sun will be up. She turns and sees, fifty yards below her, the man whom she has tried to kill twice.

'Daddy!' she calls, a second before the ledge she is standing on gives way. She feels a moment of sickening weightlessness and then plummets into the icy heart of the world.

78

Joe

Joe is putting the phone down when he hears footsteps. He looks around and Delilah appears. She has slept in her clothes, her hair is like straw and the dark shadows under her eyes could be bruises, but she has lost the ghastly colour of the previous evening.

'Skye's on her way,' she says. 'I don't know how that woman can look so chipper after what we've been through. I'm not sure she's human.'

'How are you feeling?' Joe asks.

Delilah looks around as though not entirely sure where she is. 'Like I died in the night.' Her eyes linger on Jack in the kitchen area. 'Tea please. White, no sugar.' She turns back to her son. 'I've read the stuff the team sent over. Frank says you took a phone call a while ago.'

Late the previous day, Delilah's colleagues in Cambridge had got through to the *Snow Queen* in Grytviken harbour. During the night, the captain relayed the message to Bird Island. Joe doesn't bother with the details. 'You might need to sit down,' he tells her.

'I need to sit down anyway. This room is moving, isn't it, it's not just me?'

Jack hands Delilah a mug. She takes it with shaking hands and lowers herself into an armchair.

'They need you to call them back,' Joe tells his mother. 'But they wanted you to know right away that they've traced Freddie Lloyd's movements since he left prison.'

Tea spills onto Delilah's hand. 'Hit me,' she says.

'Morning all,' Skye, fully kitted up, enters the room. 'Tea, lovely. Anyone seen Ralph?'

Joe joins his mother in the seating area. 'He was given temporary release from Durham prison on the tenth of June last year, but he broke the terms and left the north-east to travel to Cambridge. We can assume he was looking for his daughter. He also wrote to her several times before his release.'

Delilah thinks for a moment. 'Eleventh of June is the date Felicity was admitted to hospital after her mysterious adventure on Midsummer Common.'

Eleventh of June is also the night Bella Barnes was murdered. Neither of them say it, but Joe is pretty sure both are thinking it.

'Exactly,' he agrees. 'And her problems stemmed from then or shortly before. I think Freddie's appearance after so long triggered her mental health problems and led to the other personalities emerging. Just as they did when she was a teenager, after he wrote to her from prison.'

'So, this stalker she talked about, it was him? Freddie, her dad?'

Joe has spent much of the night thinking about this. 'Impossible. After he broke the terms of his temporary release, he was sent back to prison until his final release on the twenty-fifth of July. The day before she saw him in Heffers.'

'So, he wasn't stalking her in Cambridge?'

'Couldn't have been. The stalker was a figment of her imagination, as she herself argued, but one that arose from her real fear of the man who'd come back into her life.'

As he speaks, Joe remembers the photographs he found in Felicity's bin. Weren't they actual physical evidence of a stalker? But Freddie couldn't have taken them.

'So, what's he been doing the past nine months?' Delilah asks, before he has a chance to speak.

'Living in Nottingham, working with a small building firm,' he tells her. 'Getting the money together to fund his trip out here.'

The outside door opens and a gust of wind blows inside, bringing Ralph with it. 'Well, you can get back to bed, missus,' he says to Delilah. 'I'm taking you nowhere.'

'You're not bloody well leaving me here.'

'Take a wildlife walk. I'll pick you up in the launch when we're done.'

Delilah pulls herself upright.

'He's right, Mum,' Joe jumps in. 'The RIB will go at twice the speed of the launch and be twice as rough.'

'Three times,' Ralph adds. 'It planes across those wave tops. Bounce, bounce.'

Delilah glares.

'And your office want to talk to you,' Joe reminds her. 'It could be important.'

'No phone on the RIB.' Ralph turns back to the kitchen area. 'Don't go near the seals. They bite.'

Jack comes to join them. 'That stuff you said last night, Joe,' he begins, 'about how what happened to Flick when she was a baby led to her personality fracturing? How many personalities are we talking about?'

'I can't say,' Joe replies. 'There's a documented case in America in the early twentieth century of a woman with sixteen different personalities.'

'Sixteen? You're kidding?' Jack says.

'There are reports of even more than that. Numbers reaching twenty, even thirty.'

'Christ.'

'We only really know of one with Felicity, don't we?' Delilah says. 'I'm talking about Shane now.'

Joe sighs. He's already broken so much of Felicity's confidence, it hardly matters now. In any case, if they are to take her back to Grytviken safely, he'll need the others on side.

'We have proof that a young bloke, going by the name of Shane, who is wanted by the police in Cambridge, is actually Felicity.' He holds up a hand to quell the outburst he can see is coming from Jack. 'Mate, you've got to take our word on this.'

'It's very worrying,' Skye says.

'One feature of her disorder is that at least one of the personalities takes on an aggressive, confrontational role,' Joe explains. 'I think Shane emerges when Felicity is afraid and he copes by being violent. It's terribly sad. Without the early trauma, she'd have been a normal, rather gentle young woman. The woman you've seen here.'

'So, just Shane?' Jack asks. 'Not fifteen or sixteen, or thirty?'

'Another emerged under hypnosis one time,' Joe says. 'A child who was very afraid of her father. And one night she was very different with me. I think I was dealing with another then, but I never learned who it was. A woman, I think. Yeah, definitely a woman.'

'She denied having seen you that night,' Delilah tells him. 'I thought she was lying, but maybe she genuinely didn't remember.'

'If she has no memory of what she does when another personality takes over, how can she be held responsible?' Jack asks.

'She killed two homeless women,' Delilah says. 'And I don't care who she thought she was at the time. I know you're both sweet on her, but you have to accept that. She has to be brought in before she hurts anyone else.'

79

Freddie

He thinks he is gaining on her. A couple of times, he has caught a glimpse of dark clothing, vanishing around an ice column. He has seen several drops of blood on the snow.

The night is departing fast. For some time now, he's been able to see his own shadow running ahead of him on snow that is losing its deep-plum colour. Another shadow appears in the snow, alarmingly close, but it is only a bird directly above him. Huge and silent, its feathers are turned gold by a sun that he still can't quite see.

Freddie makes his way around a boulder of ice and there she is. About twenty yards higher up the slope, standing as still as the columns and peaks around her. She turns and sees him.

'Daddy!' she calls and then the earth shudders and she is gone.

80

Felicity

One second Felicity is falling, the next all breath is knocked from her body and she is trapped in a freezing, white cloud. Avalanche, she thinks. She hears the sound of running water and it makes no sense. Pain runs through her arm and shoulder as she realises she has no idea which way is up.

We're going to die, we're going to die.

At last, this is it. It's over.

Stop it!

This last is her own voice. She isn't speaking out loud, she would choke on snow, but she can hear it dominating the others in her head. *We're not going to die,* she tells her panicking alters.

The voices die down as she realises that she can breathe. And that she is no longer falling.

See, she tells the others. *We're not dead yet.*

They aren't convinced. They are clamouring at the edges of her brain, fretting and snapping at each other, at her, fighting to get control.

Felicity tells herself to focus. She tries to move and the weight of her own body gives her a sense of direction. Slowly, knowing how volatile the glacier can be, she pushes herself upwards and her head breaks free. She blinks snow out of her eyes and thinks it might have been better if the fall had killed her.

The ground around her, still out of reach of any dawn light, is a tortured mass of ice boulders and snow piles. In every direction, sheer walls of ice rise up like the cruellest prison imaginable. She has fallen into a circular shaft that is a common feature of glaciers. This one is unusually short, or she would have been killed for sure, and the dawn sky is, at a guess, twenty feet above her.

Where are we, where are we?

It is like having a pack of wolves in her head. 'It's a moulin,' she says. 'You find them a lot on glaciers. They're part of the drainage system.'

Get us out, get us out, get us out.

A pack of wolves, and she must be its leader.

The walls of the shaft are pitted and rough and were she able-bodied she might stand a chance of climbing. She is certain, though, that her right arm is broken. Worse she is sitting in a fast-running stream of glacial meltwater.

That should not be possible.

Getting up, she turns a slow circle and sees that the base of the moulin is dissected by a tunnel. For a moment, she forgets her predicament. She has heard of these tunnels, seen photographs taken on glaciers around the world, but this is the first time she has come across one.

What is it? Where are we?

'Be quiet.'

The moulin tunnel is huge. A car could be driven through it. A frisson of excitement and dread runs through her. She is in the glacier's drainage system.

'Felicity!'

This voice is real. She looks up to see Freddie peering down at her. 'Are you hurt?' he calls.

'That edge might not be stable,' she shouts back.

'I know. I can feel the ground moving. What's going on? Is it an earthquake?'

She thinks about the huge expanse of blue water, just a little further up the glacier.

'Can you climb out?' Freddie shouts.

'My arm's broken.'

'I'm coming down.'

'No!'

That will not help. She cannot climb with or without his assistance. 'Can you go back to the equipment hut? You'll find rope in it, and a pulley system.'

'It's locked.'

'Twenty-four-ten,' she tells him. 'That's the combination.'

'I'll be as quick as I can.'

He vanishes.

81

Joe

The RIB flies back towards Husvik. Bundled up against the wind, the three passengers cling to the hand grips as Ralph planes the craft over the waves. They reach the coast of the mainland while it is still dark and cross Right Whale Bay as the sun is coming up. In the Bay of Isles, when Ralph has to cut the speed to steer around a cluster of rocks in the water, a school of dolphins keeps pace with them until they reach the eastern headland.

The derelict whaling station of Prince Olav Harbour is gleaming copper red in the morning sun as Joe's phone vibrates in his pocket. He pulls it out to see his mother is calling but when he presses *answer* he can't hear a thing. A few minutes later, a text comes in.

Call me. Urgent.

Ralph cuts the engine and Joe tries again. No luck.

'There's a radio at Husvik,' Jack tells him.

'We should press on,' Joe says.

Ralph fires up the engine again.

82

Freddie

Freddie tugs off his backpack and starts to run down the glacier. It will take him an hour to get to the equipment hut and back and he has left his daughter in a stream of freezing water. An hour in such conditions will see the onset of hypothermia. Her voice, as she called up to him, was already shaky, possibly with shock, but more likely indicating that shivering has set in. Within the next hour, her pulse will weaken, her breathing turn rapid and shallow, and she'll start to feel drowsy. She'll become confused, clumsy, possibly make stupid decisions. The pain from her broken arm won't help. If she loses consciousness, he'll never get her out.

He runs on, knowing there is no danger of him forgetting the combination number that will unlock the hut. Twenty-four-ten. The twenty-fourth of October. His birthday.

83

Felicity

When Freddie goes, the voices start up again, telling Felicity to give up, that it's hopeless, that the water level is rising, and that she might as well lie down in the freezing stream and have done with it. Some of them sound terrified, others gleeful. Somewhere, in the back of her mind, she can hear laughter. Other voices urge her to keep going.

Walk up the tunnel, look at the size of it, it's huge, it must lead some-where. We can get out that way.

'Stop it, all of you.'

Like chastened children, the voices hush.

'Glaciers are my thing,' she tells them. 'I'm in charge.'

Knowing she has to keep out of the water, she spots a boulder of ice and heads towards it. She finds that by edging her way around the shaft's wall, she can keep her feet out of the wet. When she reaches the ice block, she climbs onto it and pulls off her backpack.

She has barely managed two bites of chocolate before the world around her trembles and a fresh fall of snow flutters down the shaft. Above her, the dawn sky is the palest shade of blue and she wonders at the irony of the man she has feared for so long being the one person who might save her.

As the sun gets higher, light creeps down the moulin until she can see it properly. About twenty metres in diameter it is an almost perfect circle; white, of course, but gleaming silver in the light and streaked throughout with flashes of blue.

The tunnel, too, is as huge as she first thought. A great deal of water has travelled this way very quickly to carve out both the tunnel and the moulin.

The water's getting higher.

This is Bamber's voice, but Felicity too has noticed that the milky blue stream of meltwater running through the base of the moulin has swollen even in the brief time that she has been here.

The world quivers again, unleashing a blizzard of snow. She looks at the ice blocks around her, most of them already partly submerged, and knows that if a boulder falls from the top, she will be crushed.

'This is how the lake drains,' she says. 'Meltwater around the glacier accumulates over the summer and the ice starts to break apart. The plug at the bottom of the lake gets dislodged and the water empties through this drainage system. I've solved it.'

I'm really happy for you, Bamber grumbles. *Tell me something, is this about to happen now?*

Felicity doesn't reply, but Bamber can see as well as she that the water level is rising. The plug probably hasn't broken yet, or the stream would be a torrent, but it can't last much longer.

84

Joe

Stromness Bay is calm after the heavy swell of open sea. Through water as clear as glass, Joe can see kelp swaying like underwater forests in a gentle breeze. Shadows dart here and there, too fast for him to make out what is swimming below. A powerful smell of guano hits the back of his throat as Ralph steers them through the seals and penguins to the slipway at Husvik. They haul the RIB out of reach of the tide and then both Ralph and Jack arm themselves with boat hooks to fend off aggressive seals.

'Stick to the path and take care,' Jack tells them. 'In fact, stay in single file behind me. This place isn't safe.'

They head inland, watched by a thousand pairs of eyes. They pass a penguin colony amid the grass. The birds are small, a little over two feet in height, with black heads, shoulders and backs and white breasts. They have bright-yellow feathers above each scarlet red eye. Their beaks are orange and hooked.

'Macaroni penguins,' Ralph tells them. 'They'll be gone in a couple of weeks. The young are almost ready to go out to sea.'

'Mum would have loved this,' Joe says.

'I'll stop off with her on the way back,' Ralph promises. 'Can't have the lovely Delilah going home without a proper look at the place.'

They steer their way through the derelict buildings of the whaling station and then Jack opens the BAS facility and leads them inside. He makes immediately for the radio in the office while the others look around.

'No sign of her,' Ralph says, unnecessarily, when they've searched the building.

'Would she have stayed in one of the other buildings?' Joe asks.

'Not if she's half a brain,' Jack replies. 'They're riddled with asbestos and completely unstable. I reached base, by the way. There's another RIB about an hour away.'

'Any news on Freddie?' Joe asks.

Jack shakes his head. 'They haven't found him.'

Skye says. 'Where would she go from here?'

'The glacier,' Jack says, after a moment's thought. 'There's a cave where we keep stuff. And an equipment hut on the way. She could get everything she needed in there.'

Joe looks at him carefully. 'Is there something you're not telling us?'

Jack seems to be thinking for a moment. Then, 'Nigel mentioned something else on the radio,' he says. 'It may be nothing, but . . .'

They wait.

'We've been monitoring a glacial lake for some weeks.' He glances, uncomfortably, at Ralph. 'We put some equipment in it a couple of days ago to monitor the water levels.'

'Starting to drop?' Ralph asks.

Grim-faced, Jack lets his head fall and rise.

'What does that mean?' asks Skye.

'It means the glacier will be very unstable,' Jack tells her. 'Not a good place to be.'

For a moment, no one speaks.

'You need to contact your mum,' Ralph tells Joe. 'I'll show you.'

'Skye and I will set off,' Jack says. 'We'll wait at the equipment hut.'

It takes Joe no time at all to reach his mother on Bird Island. The signal isn't great, but his mum has been using radios her whole adult life.

'I'm going to tell you in snippets, Joe. I need you to confirm you understand or request that I repeat. No unnecessary chat.'

'We got here safely, thanks for asking,' Ralph mutters.

'Understood,' Joe says into the transmitter.

'The business man from Strasbourg, you know the witness from the night Dora was murdered? He's arrived and was interviewed first thing this morning. You'll recall that the UK is two hours ahead of us.'

'Understood.' Joe looks at his watch. Half past nine in the UK.

'His hotel room on the night in question was on the third floor, directly overlooking the river and an area of public open space. He claims he saw a young woman with long blonde hair wearing a white dress.'

Joe glances up at Ralph and sees him mouth the word, *Felicity*.

'He's quite specific about the time, and even wrote it down. It was twenty-three-ten hours. Are you getting all this, Joe?'

'I am. Carry on.'

'He saw Felicity being attacked by another person. I repeat, Felicity was attacked. He saw the two of them fighting for several seconds and while he can't be sure about this, he though the other person had a knife. He—'

'Was this Dora?' Joe asks.

'Don't interrupt me, Joe. He tried to call down but the window only opened a couple of inches. Health and safety regs. While he was wondering what to do, a third person appeared, this one answering the description of Dora Hardwick. Dora appeared to be trying to intervene. At this point, our witness decided to run outside, but by the time he got there, all three of them had vanished. He saw what he thought might be the woman in the white dress some distance away and ran after her but he lost track. When he got back to the place where he'd seen the fight, there was no sign of anyone. Are you still with me? Over.'

'I am. Did he report it? And do we have any idea who the third person was?'

'He didn't report it. He just assumed it was a quarrel that had been settled. And his description of the third party is vague. Young, possibly white, dressed in dark casual clothes and wearing a backpack, but could have been male or female. Joe, would it be in character for Dora to intervene in a fight? Over.'

'Yes.' Joe can feel the back of his throat stinging. 'She was fearless.'

'The key thing is that Felicity does not seem to have been the aggressor. And she was seen running away. She couldn't have put Dora's body in the drain. Why the hell she didn't tell us this and save us all some time—'

'She couldn't,' Joe says. 'She wasn't Felicity. She was one of the alters. She would have no memory of it.'

'Felicity didn't kill anyone?' Ralph asks. 'Let me talk to her.' He grabs the transmitter. 'Delilah, love, are you saying Felicity didn't kill this old dear? Over.'

'I'm saying the situation is becoming more complicated. Now, put my son back on.'

Joe takes the transmitter back. 'We need to find out who this other person is,' he says. 'Could it have been Freddie?'

'We know he was in Cambridge that night, but the description doesn't fit. According to our witness, the aggressor was five-four or five-five at most and a very slim build. And he or she moved like a young person. Felicity's dad is said to be well over six foot.'

'So who the hell—'

'Hold that thought, because there's more. The team are at Peterhouse College now. They finally got permission to excavate the drain. They've cleared the way into the old cellars and found evidence that someone was living in them.'

'Living in the cellars?'

'Sleeping bag, blankets, remains of food packaging. Someone was definitely bedding down in there, crawling in and out through the drain.'

'Dora?' Joe says. He can't see it. She was too old, too frail.

There is a frustrating crackle of static and then his mother says, 'Not necessarily. They've found another body.'

85

Freddie

Freddie is on the point of heading back up the glacier when he spots the RIB coming into harbour at Husvik. He lifts his binoculars and sees the three men and one woman. He is tempted to go down, attract their attention, wait for them. Five people will have a much better chance of rescuing Felicity than he will alone, but he cannot leave her for any longer than he has to.

He goes back into the equipment hut and looks around. There, on a shelf at head height, is a canvas bag of small flags, no doubt used to mark positions on the ice. There is a hammer in the bag too. He slings it over his shoulder and leaves the hut door open before starting to climb again. The daylight makes it easier this time, and he can follow his own footsteps in the snow for most of the way. Twenty yards up, he hammers a yellow flag into the ice and carries on. Another twenty yards, and he leaves another flag, a red one this time. Each time he stops, he looks down towards Husvik but the team from King Edward Point have gone inside the manager's villa.

The glacier shifts again before he is halfway back but this time he is ready for it. He has fastened crampons onto his boots and carries twin walking poles. He plants his feet and waits for the shaking to subside. A little further up he spots his backpack on the ground and picks up his pace. He is almost there.

'Felicity, I'm back. I've got rope. Not much longer now.'

There is no answer. He carries on, drops his equipment and falls flat so that he can look over the edge of the moulin. He sees boulders of ice, gleaming silver, white and blue. He sees heaps of snow. He sees the milky turquoise stream of meltwater, so much wider and faster than when he left an hour ago, but no sign of his daughter.

And then he spots something, a fragment of black cloth. She is still there, twenty feet below him, curled into a ball and almost covered in snow. She doesn't move. Struck with fear that she has frozen to death, he yells down.

'Felicity!'

86

Felicity

Even as the walls of the moulin have taken on a soft gold sheen with the rising sun, the cold has become a living thing in Felicity's mind. It has seeped out of the ice and stretched its long, thin fingers towards her. It has laughed and chattered at her as it raced past in the ever-growing stream of meltwater. It has tickled and kissed and teased her in the flurries of snow. Most of all, it has pressed up into her bones from the boulder she is sitting on. Last time she tried to shift her position, she had to prise the seat of her trousers away. She hasn't moved since.

For the first half-hour, she tried to eat but after a while even the chocolate became so cold and hard that biting it made things worse. She cannot bear to drink because the thought of putting cold liquid inside her fills her with dread. She thinks she might freeze from the inside out, that her throat will fill with ice. For a while her wet feet burned but it is some time since she has felt them.

The voices, that were so loud in their panic at first have fallen silent. She's sensed them slipping away. Even Bamber hasn't spoken for some time. At last, Felicity is alone.

She wraps her arms around her body and lets her head fall. She feels a deep sense of peace and knows that to fall asleep will be very easy. Somewhere, at the back of her head, one of the voices whispers that this is the very worst thing that she can do.

'Shush,' Felicity mumbles, and closes her eyes.

'Felicity! Felicity, wake up. I'm back. I need to get you out of there. Felicity, wake the fuck up.'

The voice penetrates her dreams and she knows that somewhere in the world that she gladly left behind, someone wants to pull her back. She can't though. Her eyelids are frozen shut and she really, really needs to sleep. These voices have to stop telling her what to do. Only she decides what she is going to do and right now she needs to sleep.

'Felicity! For God's sake, you have to wake up. You're sitting in freezing water.'

The voice is right. The cold around her legs is different. It has become cold that moves. It's wetter. She feels herself stirring but, oh no, it's too hard. Better to stay down here, where it's peaceful. Better to drift away completely. She feels a sense of rightness. This is how it is supposed to be. She is a woman of ice. Truly now. Forever.

'Felicity, I'm coming down. Hold on.'

These voices will not leave her alone. She can hear hammering. The sound is rough, grating on her ears. How can she sleep with this racket? And now she becomes aware of the sound of running water. It is musical and pleasant but maybe a bit too loud. Irritation grows as she realises the lovely calm sleepiness is drifting away. She might, actually, be waking up.

The hammering stops, but a second later she hears a loud clatter and feels the ice tremble as something heavy lands close by. Then there is a sliding sound, followed by several loud bumps. Something is pulling at her. There are hands on her shoulders, then under her arms and she is being lifted. Gloved hands are wiping the snow from her face and her cheeks are being slapped.

'Felicity, wake up. Come on, wake up, we have to get you out of here.'

She knows that voice. Freddie is here. She is afraid of Freddie, isn't she? And yet leaning against him, feeling the warmth of his body, even through the thick clothing, is nice. Even nicer than the cold sleepiness he has dragged her from.

'Arm hurts,' she says.

'I know, and I'm sorry, but I have to get this harness on you. I have to pull you out. Felicity, listen to me, there are other people coming. They'll be here in an hour, maybe less, but I don't think you can wait. You need to be out of the wet.'

The pain in her arm brings her out of her stupor. She opens her eyes and sees Freddie by her side. They are up to their thighs in water and he is tugging a climbing harness over her shoulders. Behind him, she can see a double rope hanging down over the side of the moulin.

'How will you get out?' she says.

'Shush. I need to bring your arm through here. Steady now.'

She cries but he is ruthless and she can hear the harness being clipped together at her chest.

'Ok, let's get you to the rope. Just a few feet. Come on, I've got you.'

The world around them shakes again, a bigger tremor than any they have felt so far and a thundering sound fills their ears. For a second, she can't place it. Then she does. It is the sound of a great quantity of water falling.

'It's too late,' she says.

The ice is trembling. The river they are standing in rises rapidly now, reaching their waists.

'Shit,' Freddie says.

Felicity follows her father's gaze to see a wall of blue water hurtling towards them down the tunnel. The plug at the lake has broken at last, the water is draining and a hundred thousand cubic metres are heading their way.

'Come on.' Freddie reaches up for the pulley that will fasten her to the rope and give her a chance of getting out, but she squirms in his arms and with her left hand, clips the front of her harness on to his life jacket.

'What the fuck?'

He brushes her hand aside, and tries to undo what she's just done, but the wall of water hits them and sweeps them both away.

87

Joe

Joe and Ralph catch up with the other two at a small equipment hut at the foot of the Konig Glacier.

'They've been here,' Skye tells them. 'It looked like the hut had been ransacked when we arrived.'

'Not Felicity's doing,' Jack adds. 'She's incapable of leaving a cupboard untidy.'

'She may not have been herself,' Joe tells him. Not allowing himself to hope, he is keeping the information from his mother at bay. But another body in the drain with Dora? A third person spotted that night, someone small and thin and unusually aggressive?

'We normally land in the next bay along, Fortuna Bay, when we're working here.' Jack hands crampons to Joe and Ralph. 'It's a shorter walk. Here, you'll need poles, the ice is very unstable. Everyone ready?'

'What's that?' Joe has spotted a yellow flag in the ice.

'Good question,' Jack replies. 'There are more higher up.'

'Jack went up a short way while we were waiting,' Skye explains, as she and Joe follow the other two up onto the ice. 'There's a trail of flags going up the glacier. And he thinks he saw tracks. Two sets of footsteps. One much bigger than the other.'

'Freddie,' says Joe. 'He's followed her up.'

They begin to climb, Joe at the rear. Ahead, he hears Ralph

telling Jack and Skye what they've recently learned from Delilah. Behind them, the sun is rising higher and the glacier comes alive with sound that is almost musical. Melting water drips into blue pools and snow particles in the air glint like diamonds.

'She's definitely heading for the ice sheet,' Jack calls back. 'Can we step it up a bit?'

The climb already feels punishingly steep, and Joe has barely slept the previous night, but he forces his feet to move faster. They pass a red flag, and an orange one.

'So, what does it mean,' Skye asks, when Ralph has finished. 'Is she not this Shane after all?'

'Oh, she's Shane all right, there's no doubt about that,' Joe calls up. 'But Shane may not have killed anyone.'

So where did Bella Barnes fit in? If Dora's death was a result of being in the wrong place at the wrong time, what happened to Bella? A different killer or the same? And who have his mother's team found in the cellars beneath Peterhouse College? He has no answers, and so he stops asking questions.

They continue up. The ice turns into a landscape that belongs on another, frozen, world. Around him, Joe sees abstract sculptures that could have been carved from human hands, so perfect are they in form and structure.

'What was that?' Skye turns pale when the second tremor halts them all in their tracks.

'The ice sheets are moving.' Jack is stony-faced. 'Come on.'

They carry on. When both Skye and Ralph have fallen behind and Joe isn't sure he can go much further, he hears a cry from Jack. The man actually steps up his pace.

'This isn't Felicity's.' When Joe catches up Jack is holding a rucksack. 'Can you see up there?' He is pointing to several feet higher up the slope.

'Rope?'

Pegs have been hammered into the ice and two lines of rope disappear into the ground. Scattered around is more equipment, and the bag of flags that they've been following.

'Stay there!' Jack yells down to Skye and Ralph. 'Don't move. Stay still and wait.'

'What's going on?' Joe is suddenly very afraid.

'The ice is very unstable. Stay exactly behind me and move slowly.'

Joe does what he is told, following the other man the short distance to where the rope has been hammered into the ice. Before they reach it, the sound of the running water has become almost deafening, all the more unnerving because no water can be seen. Joe spots the moulin a few yards before he reaches it and without being told, follows Jack's example when the other man drops to all fours. Side by side, they crawl to the edge of the shaft.

Twenty feet below they see Freddie and Felicity standing face to face, as though embracing. Then a torrent of water sweeps into the moulin and washes them away.

For several seconds, both men stare down at the rushing water. Then Joe leaps to his feet.

'Pull them up!' He throws himself towards the rope.

Jack is still staring down as Joe starts to pull. The rope comes up too quickly, too easily. There is no weight attached to it at all.

'The water's not rising,' Jack says. 'It's flowing out again somewhere. They've been swept under the glacier.'

Joe closes his eyes in horror.

Jack jumps to his feet. 'Can you run?' he says.

'What?'

'You look fit, you've kept up with me. Can you run?'

Joe stares at him for a second. The idea seems madness but doing nothing feels infinitely worse. 'I can run.'

'Come on then. Stay behind me. Take care but we have to go fast.'

Jack sets off running, back down the track, slowing only to shout a few words to Ralph and Skye and then he and Joe are racing back to Husvik.

88

Joe

Joe falls into the bottom of the boat as the engine roars and Jack takes it up to what feels like its top speed. For several minutes Joe lies still, getting his breath back.

When he can breathe again, he struggles against the force of the wind to get upright. Jack at the helm is looking out towards the horizon. Behind him, the buildings of Husvik have shrunk and the tiny figures of Skye and Ralph are pushing another RIB, Felicity's, through the shallows to follow them.

'Where are we going?' Joe shouts.

'Round the headland,' Jack yells back. 'Fortuna Bay. Explain when we get there.'

The engine roars in response to Jack pushing forward on the throttle control, they go faster and Joe pulls himself round to face the bow.

When they clear the first headland, Jack turns north. Joe lies flat against the side of the RIB and wonders how there can possibly be a point to what they are doing. Felicity and her father have drowned, their bodies trapped beneath the glacier. This frantic chase around the coast is futile.

It is impossible to argue, though, at the speed they are travelling. Joe feels the craft turn back towards land and lifts his eyes as Jack slows and then cuts the engine. In neutral gear, the RIB bounces on the rising sea.

Fortuna Bay is a long, thin cove flanked by black mountains and the hundred-metre-high white cliff of the glacier. Joe opens his mouth to ask what the hell they are doing and Jack hands him binoculars.

'There's a chance, a very slim one mind you, that we'll find them here.'

'How is that possible?' Joe asks, even as he is scanning the water. Fortuna Bay is alive with bobbing seal heads and feeding birds.

'See that ice cliff?' Jack doesn't take his eyes off the water. 'That's the mouth of the glacier. It calves into this bay and meltwater enters the ocean here.'

Joe thinks back. 'The water we saw, that swept them away, it's coming here?'

'Almost certainly.'

'But the tunnel would have to be incredibly wide, wouldn't it? For two adult humans to be swept all the way through.'

Jack's face is grim. 'It would. And, from what I saw, it is. We don't know that it continues to be, all the way to the bay, but from the speed the water was moving, and the fact the moulin wasn't filling up, there's a chance.'

The radio crackles and then Ralph's voice can be heard. 'Jack, where do you want us?'

The second RIB, with Skye and Ralph on board, has turned around the headland.

'Am I right in thinking the tide's coming in?' Jack asks over the radio.

'High tide at eleven thirty this morning,' Ralph replies.

'Stay a hundred feet to my starboard side and follow us in.' Jack takes the engine out of neutral and eases the RIB forward. 'They'd have reached this bay before we got here,' he tells Joe. 'The force of the current would have swept them some way out, but the tide will bring them back in.'

Joe looks around at the vast expanse of water and a sound like thunder shakes the bay. A massive piece of ice falls from the cliff as a circular wall of sea water rises up around it.

'That can't be good,' Joe says.

A few seconds later, the wash reaches them and both men grip the RIB's rope handles. A hundred feet to starboard, Joe sees Ralph's RIB being tossed up high.

'That's not an iceberg,' Jack says. 'It's what we call a bergy bit. If an iceberg calves, we'll know about it.'

'Will it hit us?' Joe asks. The bergy bit, the size of a house, seems to be heading directly for them.

'Not if we keep an eye on it.'

'Joe, your mum's on the radio.' Ralph's voice crackles over the airways. 'Channel nine.'

Joe does not want to talk to Delilah. Not now. He wants to look for Felicity and keep an eye on that menacing wall of white.

'She says it's urgent,' Ralph adds.

With freezing fingers, Jack switches to channel nine.

'Go ahead, love,' they hear Ralph say, followed by Delilah asking for Joe.

'I can hear you, Mum, go ahead,' Joe says.

'The other body has been recovered from the Peterhouse College cellar.' Delilah's voice is broken up and difficult to make out. 'We haven't officially confirmed identity but it fits the description given by our Strasbourg businessman. Small, thin, probably young. And female we think. We have reason to believe this is our killer's body, and that her coming and going in the old foundations caused them to collapse. She was trapped and starved to death.'

What Delilah says next is lost amid static. Ralph asks her to repeat herself. Joe doesn't need her to. He knows now who has been trapped in the Peterhouse foundations along with Dora's dead body all these months. He knows who killed Dora, who tried to kill Felicity too.

'Our deceased had a few personal possessions in the cellar with her,' Delilah says, when they can hear her again. 'We found ID. I can't confirm it over the airwaves Joe, but we also found a pair of roller skates.'

Joe tells himself he cannot close his eyes, he has to look for Felicity. It's all that matters now, finding Felicity.

'I won't keep you, love,' Joe's mother says. 'Good luck.'

The radio falls silent and once again they can hear the cacophony of bird cries and the banging of water against the vessel's sides.

Ezzy Sheeran, the roller-skating fiend, not dead after all. Ezzy who attacked Felicity in the city centre that night, only to be foiled by an old lady with the heart of a lion. Ezzy, who killed Dora in a fit of rage and then dragged her dead body into the drain before becoming trapped herself. Ezzy, who probably killed Bella Barnes as well, because like Felicity, she was young and pretty and got too close to Joe.

Felicity is not a murderer, and they have found out too late.

The radio crackles again. 'Skye thinks she heard a whistle,' Ralph's voice emerges. 'I'm cutting my engine.'

Jack does the same. They listen, but the air is full of noise. Shrieks, cries, whistles, the keening of the wind along the glacier. Skye cannot have heard a human-made sound amidst this din.

'See anything?' Jack asks.

'What looks like an orange ping pong ball.' Joe is on the point of despair. 'Actually more than one. Probably some weird species of sea weed.'

'Where?' The RIB rocks dangerously as Jack stands up.

Joe points. Jack adjusts the focus of his binoculars then picks up the radio.

'We've spotted Flick's marker balls,' he tells his colleagues. 'I'm heading over. Follow slowly.'

'Those balls were in the blue lake,' he tells Joe as he turns the RIB. 'Flick left them the day before yesterday. They've come the same way she and Freddie did.'

Joe understands little of this, but he keeps his eyes peeled on the tiny specks of orange. When he can see them with the naked eye, he puts the binoculars down and starts scanning the ocean surface. Seal heads, birds bouncing on the waves, even fish leaping. It is impossible, in a sea churning with life, to spot anything—

'Jack, slow down,' Joe says. 'There's something over there. Fifty yards. Two o'clock.'

Both men fix their attention on the point Joe is indicating. Several of the orange balls are floating together, rising and falling on the waves.

'Do you see something red?' Joe asks.

Jack shakes his head. 'Flick wears black on the ice. He looked to be in khaki.'

'Freddie was wearing a red life jacket,' Joe reminds him. 'I saw it before they got swept away. It will have inflated, won't it, when the water hit them?'

The RIB gets closer. A whistle sounds. They see the twin red stripes of the life preserver and the bare head of the man in the water. There is another head, a blonde one, leaning on his chest.

They know that Freddie is alive before they reach him. He manages to raise one hand to wave. The other is wrapped around his daughter who lies, as though sleeping, against him. The two of them are fastened together at the chest and Freddie's hands are too cold to unclip them. His face is the colour of a corpse and he cannot speak. Felicity doesn't move.

Joe grits his teeth together to stop himself screaming something hysterical and totally unhelpful.

Ralph's RIB pulls up alongside and both he and Jack rope the two crafts together. Joe watches, feeling helpless, but knowing the worst thing he can do is get in the way, as Jack pulls off his coat, sweater and boots and jumps into the water. Within seconds, Felicity is unclipped from Freddie's life jacket and lifted into the RIB with Ralph and Skye. She slumps, lifeless, in the bottom of the boat and Skye leans over her.

'Flick, can you hear me?' Ralph is calling. 'We've got you, you're safe now.'

Joe can't see a thing. His view is completely blocked by Ralph and Skye.

'Come on, love, come on,' Skye is saying.

'Joe, we need a hand.'

Jack's voice is failing. Joe turns back to pull Freddie into his RIB. The water is so cold it burns Joe's hands but eventually Jack is back on board too.

'Thermal blankets in the stern locker,' Ralph shouts over, and Joe realises that, for the time being, he is in charge of his RIB. 'Skye, can you do CPR?'

CPR means she's not breathing. They can't find a heartbeat.

Joe finds the blankets. In only a few minutes he can see that Jack will be fine. Already, he is sitting upright and pulling his boots back on. Freddie he is less sure about, but the man is conscious and even managing to speak the odd word. Felicity, though . . .

In the other RIB, she is as pale as the ice that nearly claimed her for its own and her hair lies like weeds around her face. Skye, still pumping her chest and blowing into her mouth, looks on the verge of tears.

'I'll take ov—' Joe begins, but doesn't finish. A sound like that of an angry dragon fills the bay and all around them, sea birds flee in panic.

'We need to get out of here.' His eyes gleaming, Ralph fires up his RIB's engine. 'Hold tight everyone.'

The two boats, still rafted together, move back towards open sea.

Joe and Jack turn to follow Ralph's terrified stare. The mouth of the glacier is crumbling before their eyes. An avalanche of snow slides down its sheer face, turning the bay into a churning white mass.

'It's calving,' Jack says.

They are little more than two hundred yards from shore and the mountain of ice that they can see breaking away. The mouth of the glacier has splintered, and a great white wall, a hundred meters high, is moving towards them. The glacier it left behind seems to be disintegrating. Boulders of ice fall into the water, until the whole bay is a thick white soup.

'It's going,' Jack calls. 'Everyone, hold on!'

The ice mountain leans towards them, gravity winning the battle with momentum, and the sea begins to churn. The new iceberg topples, finds its new, horizontal gravity, and a wall of turquoise water, thirty metres high, surges towards them.

Ralph spins them around, so that Joe's RIB swings and threatens to tip. He fires up the engine and finally they are moving out of the bay at a decent pace but the tsunami is snapping at their heels. They can feel the chill of the iceberg like the cold breath of a ghost and then they are being swept up high and fast, they are riding the freezing wave like surfers, Ralph woops, but whether with terror or elation Joe has no idea and then finally, the waters calm, they pass the head of the bay and are safe.

Joe turns to make sure everyone is still on board the two RIBs. They are. And Felicity's eyes are open.

89

Joe

And so the story ends, as it began, in the frozen land of the far south. The autumn snows have arrived early this year and already the land around Grytviken is the pure white of an artist's canvas, seconds before he lifts his brush. In the harbour, the *Snow Queen* is back from its trip to the South Sandwich Isles and the Antarctic. The captain has agreed to an unscheduled stop on South Georgia but is eager now to weigh anchor and sail north to calmer seas and warmer winds. He is impatient for the return of his last four passengers. Had two of them not been senior police officers, he might be making more of a fuss. As it is, he contents himself with sending irritated radio messages to Nigel in the harbour master's office.

Nigel, in his turn, has been relaying them to the BAS launch waiting at the jetty, but Ralph has the volume turned down. He is talking quietly to Delilah who sits, in the seat of honour beside him, with the look of a woman on her way to the gallows. Delilah will never make a sailor and yet she has shown a surprising willingness over the last few days to be ferried up and down the coastline to see the wildlife. It is possible that this will not be her only visit to South Georgia.

Their conversation is interrupted as Freddie and Skye reach the launch. Skye stumbles at the last minute, and almost goes into the water, but Freddie catches her. Completely recovered from his ordeal, he has declared a newfound interest in cold-water swimming, is trying to persuade Jack to teach him to scuba dive and is determined to take part in this year's midwinter swim at Surf Bay on the Falkland Islands. He will spend the winter in Stanley and the supply ship that visits South Georgia every six weeks will give him plenty of opportunities to get to know his daughter again. They have twenty-five years to catch up on. Seeing his last two passengers emerge from the base, Ralph gets up to release the lines.

Joe and Felicity walk slowly down to the jetty.

'Did Mum speak to you this morning?' he asks.

Felicity's right arm is in plaster, but like her father, she has recovered quickly from her immersion in the icy waters of Fortuna Bay and the station doctor has seen no reason to send her away from South Georgia.

'She told me that Ezzy's fingerprints match those found in my house the night I was attacked,' Felicity says. 'It was Ezzy who tried to kill me. First by the river, when that old lady saved me, and then the following night, at home.'

Joe says nothing but in his head he is running through the likely progress of events that night. Felicity in a confused and vulnerable fugue state being attacked by Ezzy. Dora intervening and taking the knife that was meant for the younger woman. Ezzy hiding Dora's body in the drain, never imagining that, little more than a day later, it would become her tomb too.

'And she said you found those photographs of me in my bin,' Felicity goes on. 'Ezzy's prints were on those as well. She'd been watching me for a while before I left. I think she drew some eyes on my window one time. She was trying to scare me away, get me to leave you alone. I guess it worked.'

'You don't remember coming across her and Dora by the river?' Joe ignores the rise of guilt at the knowledge that he nearly got Felicity killed. And probably was indirectly responsible for Bella's death. He will have plenty of time on the trip home to come to terms with it. 'Was that one of the – you know, the others?'

Felicity bites on her bottom lip. 'Bamber thinks it was Shane, but she isn't sure. She says he won't talk about it, that it's really shaken him up.'

Joe waits, knowing there is more to come.

'Bamber says Shane was – born, came into being – I don't really know the words, when I was living on the streets in my late teens. He became obsessed with the homeless, with watching over them.'

She glances sideways at him. 'I know it's nuts,' she says. 'I hear myself and think, how can this be happening to me. How can all this be going on in my head and I have no idea?'

'Just acknowledging that it's happening is progress,' Joe says. 'Even if it doesn't feel that way right now.'

Felicity stops walking. 'If it had been me, I wouldn't have run,' she says. 'I wouldn't have left Dora to face Ezzy by herself. I know I wouldn't. I feel so—'

Joe puts a hand on her shoulder. 'It's not your fault,' he says. 'Whoever you were at the time, you're not to blame for what Ezzy did.'

And neither am I, Joe thinks to himself, and wonders if there might come a time when he believes it.

'Thank you for coming all this way,' Felicity says.

'To arrest you?'

'To save me.'

Joe feels like a fraud. 'Freddie kept you alive in the water. Jack knew where to find you. I did nothing, really.'

They are both silent for a moment and then, 'I really don't like leaving you alone here,' he says.

'I'm going to give you a minute to appreciate the irony of that,' Felicity replies.

Joe laughs, although it is the last thing he feels like doing.

'I'm better here,' she says. 'The others are quieter here. It's as though they know this is my place, I have to lead the pack.'

Joe has no arguments left. There are no criminal charges left for Felicity to answer. Neither he nor anyone else can force her to seek treatment before she is ready. And she may never be ready.

'Do you have any sense,' he asks, 'of how many others there are? I mean we know about Shane, obviously, the one who looks after you, but—'

Felicity shakes her head. 'No, Bamber looks after me. She's the street fighter. Shane is very troubled. He only hurts himself.'

'If you know that, you've come a long way already.'

'Bamber knows most of the others. She's told me about the little girl, who's always so afraid, and about a woman who's quite old, who hates me. She sounds a bit like my grandmother.'

'Did Granny write the diary?' Joe asks.

'Bamber thinks so.' Felicity blushes and for a second can't meet his eyes. 'She and I talk to each other. I know, of course, that what's really going on is I'm letting myself remember, but it's easier to do it this way.'

'Whatever works.'

'I think the others emerge when I need them. When Freddie started writing to me from prison, I freaked out. On some level, I was terrified of him.'

'This was in March last year.' Joe has already worked this out for himself. Freddie's reappearances in Felicity's life, in her late teens, and a year ago, triggered her mental health problems.

Felicity nods. 'I couldn't cope alone. So I fractured.'

'Fractured suggests you're broken,' Joe says. 'You're not.'

'Split?' says Felicity. 'Is that a better word?'

He smiles. 'Splits can be healed.'

They set off again and the jetty rocks beneath their feet. Joe turns on impulse back to the administrative buildings and sees the cold blue eyes of Jack watching them from Nigel's office. There are more reasons than one why he doesn't want to leave her here. But time is no more forgiving than the tide and they have reached the boat.

'My contract ends in fifteen months,' Felicity says. 'I'm coming back to England then.'

'I'll be waiting,' Joe tells her.

She steps forward and kisses him softly on the lips. He counts three, four seconds, then she pulls away. 'Safe trip,' she tells him, as Ralph starts the engine.

'I met Bamber,' Joe says. 'The last night you were in Cambridge. She kissed me too.'

Felicity steps back to let him board the launch. She is smiling and Joe realises that it is the first time, except in photographs, that he has seen her happy.

'Well,' she says, 'that bitch and I have some talking to do.'

Acknowledgements

My sincere love and thanks to the following:

Anna Valentine and her colleagues at Trapeze and Orion for their faith in me and my books, and their tireless efforts on my behalf; Phoebe Morgan, a great editor, whom it was a pleasure to get to know; Sam Eades and Rose, for regularly brightening my day with their Instagram posts.

Anne Marie Doulton, my agent, who is extraordinary; and the Buckmans, who are pretty great too.

My family, even the annoying ones.